D1106684

COLETTE

Stories

This limited edition
is published by
The Franklin Library
exclusively for subscribers to

THE COLLECTED STORIES OF
THE WORLD'S GREATEST WRITERS

SIDONIE GABRIELLE COLETTE

by Chris Duke

SIDONIE GABRIELLE

COLETTE

Stories

Illustrated by David McCall Johnston

A LIMITED EDITION

THE FRANKLIN LIBRARY
Franklin Center, Pennsylvania

1977

Chéri: Paris, A. Fayard, 1920; English translation first published 1930. *La Fin de Chéri*: Paris, E. Flammarion, 1926; English translation first published 1933. *Julie de Carnheilhan*: Paris, A. Fayard, 1941. *Gigi*: Lausanne, La Guilde du Livre, 1944. English translations from the Fleuron edition oeuvres completes de Colette de l'Academie Goncourt, 1949, first published in a uniform edition in England by Martin Secker & Warburg Limited in 1951 (*Chéri* and *The Last of Chéri*), 1952 (*Julie de Carnheilhan*), and 1953 (*Gigi*). This edition published by arrangement with Martin Secker & Warburg Limited and Farrar, Straus & Giroux, Inc. Printed in the United States of America.

Contents

COLETTE

Stories

GIGI

Translated by Roger Senhouse

"DON'T FORGET you are going to Aunt Alicia's. Do you hear me, Gilberte? Come here and let me do your curls. Gilberte, do you hear me?"

"Couldn't I go there without having my hair curled, Grandmamma?"

"I should think not," said Madame Alvarez, quietly. She took an old pair of curling irons, with prongs ending in little round metal knobs, and put them to heat over the blue flame of a spirit lamp while she prepared the tissue papers.

"Grandmamma, couldn't you crimp my hair in waves down the side of my head for a change?"

"Out of the question. Ringlets at the very ends — that's as far as a girl of your age can possibly go. Now sit down on the footstool."

To do so, Gilberte folded up under her the heron-like legs of a girl of fifteen. Below her tartan skirt, she revealed ribbed cotton stockings to just above the knees, unconscious of the perfect oval shape of her kneecaps. Slender calf and high arched instep — Madame Alvarez never let her eyes run over these fine points without regretting that her granddaughter had not studied dancing professionally. At the moment, she was thinking only of the girl's hair. She had corkscrewed the ends and fixed them in tissue paper, and was now compressing the ash-blond ringlets between the heated knobs. With patient, soft-fingered skill, she gathered up the full magnificent weight of finely kept hair into sleek ripples which fell to just below Gilberte's shoulders. The girl sat quite still. The smell of the heated tongs, and the whiff of vanilla in the curling papers, made her feel drowsy. Besides, Gilberte knew that resistance would be useless. She hardly ever tried to elude the authority exercised by her family.

"Is Mamma singing *Frasquita* today?"

"Yes. And this evening in *Si j'étais Roi.* I have told you before, when you're sitting on a low seat you must keep your knees close to each other, and lean both of them together, either to the right or to the left, for the sake of decorum."

"But, Grandmamma, I've got on my drawers and my petticoat."

"Drawers are one thing, decorum is another," said Madame Alvarez. "Everything depends on the attitude."

"Yes, I know. Aunt Alicia has told me often enough," Gilberte murmured from under her tent of hair.

"I do not require the help of my sister," said Madame Alvarez testily, "to instruct you in the elements of propriety. On that subject, thank goodness, I know rather more than she does."

"Supposing you let me stay here with you today, Grandmamma, couldn't I go and see Aunt Alicia next Sunday?"

"What next!" said Madame Alvarez haughtily. "Have you any other *purposal* to make to me?"

"Yes, I have," said Gilberte. "Have my skirts made a little longer, so I don't have to fold myself up in a Z every time I sit down. You see, Grandmamma, with my skirts too short, I have to keep thinking of my you-know-what."

"Silence! Aren't you ashamed to call it your you-know-what?"

"I don't mind calling it by any other name, only . . ."

Madame Alvarez blew out the spirit lamp, looked at the reflection of her heavy Spanish face in the looking glass above the mantelpiece, and then laid down the law.

"There is no other name."

A skeptical look passed across the girl's eyes. Beneath the

cockleshells of fair hair they showed a lovely dark blue, the color of glistening slate. Gilberte unfolded with a bound.

"But, Grandmamma, all the same, do look! If only my skirts were just that much longer! Or if a small frill could be added!"

"That *would* be nice for your mother, to be seen with a great gawk looking at least eighteen! In her profession! Where are your brains!"

"In my head," said Gilberte. "Since I hardly ever go out with Mamma, what would it matter?"

She pulled down her skirt, which had rucked up toward her slim waist, and asked, "Can I go in my everyday coat? It's quite good enough."

"That wouldn't show that it's Sunday! Put on your serge coat and blue sailor hat. When will you learn what's what?"

When on her feet, Gilberte was as tall as her grandmother. Madame Alvarez had taken the name of a Spanish lover now dead, and accordingly had acquired a creamy complexion, an ample bust, and hair lustrous with brilliantine. She used too white a powder, her heavy cheeks had begun to draw down her lower eyelids a little, and so eventually she took to calling herself Inez. Her family pursued their fixed orbit around her. Her unmarried daughter Andrée, forsaken by Gilberte's father, now preferred the sober life of a second-lead singer in a State-controlled theater to the fitful opulence of a life of gallantry. Aunt Alicia — none of her admirers, it seemed, had ever mentioned marriage — lived alone, on an income she pretended was modest. The family had a high opinion of Alicia's judgment, and of her jewels.

Madame Alvarez looked her granddaughter up and down, from the felt sailor hat trimmed with a quill to the ready-made cavalier shoes.

"Can't you ever manage to keep your legs together? When you stand like that, the Seine could flow between them. You haven't the shadow of a stomach, and yet you somehow contrive to stick it out. And don't forget your gloves, I beg of you."

Gilberte's every posture was still governed by the unconcern of childish innocence. At times she looked like Robin Hood, at others like a carved angel, or again like a boy in skirts; but she seldom resembled a nearly grown-up girl. "How can you expect to be put into long skirts, when you haven't the sense of a child of eight?" Madame Alvarez asked. And Andrée sighed, "I find Gilberte so discouraging." To which Gilberte answered quietly, "If you didn't find *me* discouraging, then you'd find something else." For she was sweet and gentle, resigned to a stay-at-home life and seeing few people outside the family. As for her features, no one could yet predict the final mold. A large mouth, which showed beautiful strong white teeth when she laughed, no chin to speak of, and, between high cheekbones, a nose — "Heavens, where did she get that button?" whispered her mother under her breath. "If you can't answer that question, my girl, who can?" retorted Madame Alvarez. Whereupon Andrée, who had become prudish too late in life and disgruntled too soon, relapsed into silence, automatically stroking her sensitive larynx. "Gigi is just a bundle of raw material," Aunt Alicia affirmed, "it may turn out very well — and, just as easily, all wrong."

"Grandmamma, there's the bell! I'll open the door on my way out. Grandmamma," Gigi shouted from the passage, "It's Uncle Gaston!"

She came back into the room with a tall, youngish-looking man, her arm linked through his, chattering to him with the childish pomposity of a schoolgirl out of class.

"What a pity it is, Tonton, that I've got to desert you so soon! Grandmamma wishes me to pay a call on Aunt Alicia. Which motorcar are you using today? Did you come in the new four-seater de Dion-Bouton with the collapsible hood? I hear it can be driven simply with one hand! Goodness, Tonton, those are smart gloves, and no mistake! So you've had a row with Liane, Tonton?"

"Gilberte," scolded Madame Alvarez, "what business of yours can that be?"

"But, Grandmamma, everybody knows about it. The whole story was in the *Gil Blas.* It began: *A secret bitterness is seeping into the sweet product of the sugarbeet. . . .* At school all the girls were asking me about it, for of course they know I know you. And I can tell you, Tonton, there's not a soul at school who takes Liane's side! They all agree that she's behaved disgracefully!"

"Gilberte!" repeated Madame Alvarez, "Say good-bye to Monsieur Lachaille, and run along!"

"Leave her alone, poor child," Gaston Lachaille sighed. "She, at any rate, intends no harm. And it's perfectly true that all's over between Liane and me. You're off to Aunt Alicia's, Gigi? Take my motorcar and send it back for me."

Gilberte gave a little cry, a jump of joy, and hugged Lachaille.

"Thank you, Tonton! Just think of Aunt Alicia's face! The concierge's eyes will be popping from her head!"

Off she went, with the chatter of a young filly not yet shod.

"You spoil her, Gaston," said Madame Alvarez.

But in this she was not altogether speaking the truth. Gaston Lachaille did not know how to "spoil" anyone — even himself. His luxuries were cut and dried: motorcars, a dreary mansion on the Parc Monceau, Liane's monthly allowance and birthday jewels, champagne and baccarat at Deauville in the summer, at Monte Carlo in the winter. From time to time he would drop a fat check into some charity fund, or finance a new daily paper, or buy a yacht only to resell it almost at once to some Central European monarch: yet from none of this did he get any fun. He would say, as he looked at himself in the glass, "That's the face of a man who is branded." Because of his rather long nose and large dark eyes he was regarded on all sides as easy game. His commercial instinct and rich man's caution stood him in good stead, however; no one had succeeded in robbing him of his pearl studs, of his massive gold or silver cigarette cases encrusted with precious stones, of his dark sable-lined topcoat.

From the window he watched his motorcar start up. That year, fashionable automobiles were being built with a slightly higher body and a rather wider top, to accommodate the exaggerated hats affected by Caroline Otero, Liane de Pougy, and other conspicuous figures of 1899: and, in consequence, they would sway gently at every turn of the wheel.

"Mamita," said Gaston Lachaille, "you wouldn't make me a cup of camomile?"

"Two rather than one," answered Madame Alvarez. "Sit down, my poor Gaston."

From the depths of a dilapidated armchair she removed some crumpled illustrated papers, a stocking waiting to be darned, and a box of liquorice candies known as *agents de change*. The jilted man settled down into the chair luxuriously, while his hostess put out the tray and two cups.

"Why does the camomile they brew at home always smell of faded chrysanthemums?" sighed Gaston.

"It's simply a matter of taking pains. You may not believe it, Gaston, but I often pick my best camomile flowers in Paris, growing on waste ground, insignificant little flowers you would hardly notice. But they have a taste that is *unesteemable.* My goodness, what beautiful cloth your suit is made of! That deep-woven stripe is as smart as can be. Just the sort of material your father liked! But, I must confess, he would never have carried it so elegantly."

Never more than once during the course of a conversation did Madame Alvarez evoke the memory of an elder Lachaille, whom she claimed to have known intimately. From her former relationship, real or invented, she drew no advantage other than the close relationship of Gaston Lachaille, and the pleasure to be derived from watching a rich man enjoying the comforts of the poor when he made himself at home in her old armchair. Under their gas-blackened ceiling, these three feminine creatures never asked him for pearls, chinchillas, or solitaire diamonds, and they knew how to converse with tact and due solemnity on scandalous topics traditional and recondite. From the age of twelve, Gigi had known that Madame Otero's string of large black pearls were "dipped," that is to say, artificially tinted, while the three strings of her matchlessly graded pearl necklace were worth "a king's ransom"; that Madame de Pougy's seven rows lacked "life"; that Eugénie Fougère's famous diamond bolero was quite worthless; and that no self-respecting woman gadded about, like Madame Antokolski, in a coupé upholstered in mauve satin. She had obediently broken her friendship with a school friend, Lydia Poret, after the girl had shown her a solitaire, set as a ring, presented by the Baron Ephraim.

"A solitaire!" Madame Alvarez had exclaimed. "For a girl of fifteen! Her mother must be mad!"

"But, Grandmamma," pleaded Gigi, "it's not Lydia's fault if the Baron gave it to her!"

"Silence! I'm not blaming the Baron. The Baron knows what is expected of him. But plain common sense should have told the mother to put the ring in a safe at the bank, while waiting."

"While waiting for what, Grandmamma?"

"To see how things turn out."

"Why not in her jewel case?"

"Because one never knows. Especially as the Baron is the sort of man who might change his mind. If, on the other hand, he has declared himself openly, Madame Poret has only to withdraw her daughter from her studies. Until the matter has been properly cleared up, you will oblige me by not walking home with that little Poret. Who ever heard of such a thing!"

"But supposing she marries, Grandmamma?"

"Marries? Marries whom, pray?"

"Why, the Baron!"

Madame Alvarez and her daughter exchanged glances of stupefaction. "I find the child so discouraging," Andrée had murmured. "She comes from another planet."

"My poor Gaston," said Madame Alvarez, "is it really true, then, that you have broken with her? In some way, it may be the best thing for you; but in others, I'm sure you must find it most upsetting. Whom can one trust, I ask you!"

Poor Gaston listened while he drank the scalding camomile.

The taste of it gave him as much comfort as the sight of the plaster rose on the ceiling, still black from the hanging lamp now "converted to electricity," still faithfully retaining its shade — a vast frilly bell of palest green. Half the contents of a workbasket lay strewn over the dining room table, from which Gilberte had forgotten to remove her copybook. Above the upright piano hung an enlarged photograph of Gilberte at eight months, as a pendant to a portrait in oils of Andrée, dressed for her part in *Si j'étais Roi.* The perfectly inoffensive untidiness, the ray of spring sunshine coming through the point-lace curtains, the warmth given out by a little stove kept at a low heat — all these homely things were like so many soothing potions to the nerves of a jilted and lonely millionaire.

"Are you positively in torment, my poor Gaston?"

"To be exact, I'm not in torment. I'm just very upset, as you say."

"I have no wish to appear inquisitive," said Madame Alvarez, "but how did it all happen? I've read the papers, of course; but can one believe what they say?"

Lachaille tugged at his small waxed mustache, and ran his fingers over his thick, cropped hair.

"Oh, much the same as on previous occasions. She waited for the birthday present, then off she trotted. And, into the bargain, she must needs go and bury herself in such a wretched little hole in Normandy — so stupid of her! Any fool could have discovered that there were only two rooms at the inn, one occupied by Liane, the other by Sandomir, a skating instructor from the *Palais de Glace.*"

"He's Polaire's teatime waltzing partner, isn't he? Oh, women don't know where to draw the line nowadays! And just after her birthday, too! Oh! it's so tactless! What could be more unladylike!"

Madame Alvarez stirred the teaspoon round and round in her cup, her little finger in the air. When she lowered her gaze, her lids did not quite cover her protuberant eyeballs, and her resemblance to George Sand became marked.

"I'd given her a rope," said Gaston Lachaille. "What you

might call a rope — thirty-seven pearls. The middle one as big as the ball of my thumb."

He held out his white, beautifully manicured thumb, to which Madame Alvarez accorded the admiration due to a middle pearl.

"You certainly know how to do things in style," she said. "You came out of it extremely well, Gaston."

"I came out of it with a pair of horns, certainly."

Madame Alvarez did not seem to have heard him.

"If I were you, Gaston, I should try to get your own back on her. I should take up with some society lady."

"That's a nice pill to offer me," said Lachaille, who was absentmindedly helping himself to the *agents de change.*

"Yes, indeed, I might even say that sometimes the cure may prove worse than the disease," Madame Alvarez continued, tactfully agreeing with him. "Out of the frying pan into the fire." After which she respected Gaston Lachaille's silence.

The muffled sounds of a piano penetrated through the ceiling. Without a word, the visitor held out his empty cup, and Madame Alvarez refilled it.

"Is the family all right? What news of Aunt Alicia?"

"Oh, my sister, you know, is always the same. She's smart enough to keep herself to herself. She says she would rather live in a splendid past than an ugly present. Her King of Spain, her Milan of Serbia, her Khedive, her rajahs by the half-dozen — or so she would have you believe! She is very considerate to Gigi. She finds her a trifle backward for her age, as indeed she is, and puts her through her paces. Last week, for instance, she taught her how to eat *homard à l'Américaine* in faultless style."

"Whatever for?"

"Alicia says it will be extremely useful. The three great difficulties in a girl's education, she maintains, are *homard à l'Américaine,* a boiled egg, and asparagus. Bad table manners, she says, have broken up many a happy home."

"That can happen," said Lachaille dreamily.

"Oh, Alicia is no fool! And it's just what Gigi requires—

she is so greedy! If only her brain worked as well as her jaws! But she might well be a child of ten! And what breathtaking scheme have you got for the Battle of Flowers? Are you going to dazzle us again this year?"

"O Lord no!" groaned Gaston. "I shall take advantage of my misfortune, and save on the red roses."

Madame Alvarez wrung her hands.

"Oh, Gaston, you mustn't do that! If you're not there, the procession will look like a funeral!"

"I don't care what it looks like," said Gaston gloomily.

"You're never going to leave the prize banner to people like Valérie Cheniaguine? Oh, Gaston, we can't allow that!"

"You will have to. Valérie can very well afford it."

"Especially since she does it on the cheap. Gaston, do you know where she went for the ten thousand bunches thrown last year? She had three women tying them up for two days and two nights, and the flowers were bought in the flower market! In the market! Only the four wheels, and the coachman's whip, and the harness trappings bore the label of Lachaume."

"That's a dodge to remember!" said Lachaille, cheering up. "Good Lord! I've finished the liquorice!"

The tap-tap of Gilberte's marching footsteps could be heard crossing the outer room.

"Back already!" said Madame Alvarez. "What's the meaning of this?"

"The meaning," said the girl, "is that Aunt Alicia wasn't in good form. But I've been out in Tonton's 'tuf-tuf.' "

Her lips parted in a bright smile.

"You know, Tonton, all the time I was in your automobile, I put on a martyred expression — like this — as if I was bored to death with every luxury under the sun. I had the time of my life."

She sent her hat flying across the room, and her hair fell tumbling over her forehead and cheeks. She perched herself on a rather high stool, and tucked her knees up under her chin.

"Well, Tonton? You look as if you were dying of boredom.

What about a game of piquet? It's Sunday, and Mamma doesn't come back between the two performances. Who's been eating all my liquorice? Oh, Tonton, you can't get away with that! The least you can do is to send me some more to make up for it."

"Gilberte, your manners!" scolded Madame Alvarez. "Your knees! Gaston hasn't the time to bother about your liquorice. Pull down your skirts. Gaston, would you like me to send her to her room?"

Young Lachaille, with one eye on the dirty pack of cards in Gilberte's hand, was longing simultaneously to give way to tears, to confide his sorrows, to go to sleep in the old armchair, and to play piquet.

"Let the child stay! In this room I can relax. It's restful. Gigi, I'll play you for twenty pounds of sugar."

"Your sugar's not very tempting. I much prefer sweets."

"It's the same thing. And sugar is better for you than sweets."

"You only say that because you make it."

"Gilberte, you forget yourself!"

A smile enlivened the mournful eyes of Gaston Lachaille.

"Let her say what she likes, Mamita. And if I lose, Gigi, what would you like? A pair of silk stockings?"

The corners of Gilberte's big childish mouth fell.

"Silk stockings make my legs itch. I would rather. . . ."

She raised the snub-nosed face of an angel toward the ceiling, put her head on one side, and tossed her curls from one cheek to the other.

"I would rather have an *eau-de-nil* Persephone corset, with rococo roses embroidered on the garters. No, I'd rather have a music case."

"Are you studying music now?"

"No, but my older friends at school carry their copybooks in music cases, because it makes them look like students at the Conservatoire."

"Gilberte, you are making too free!" said Madame Alvarez.

"You shall have your case, and your liquorice. Cut, Gigi."

The next moment, the heir of Lachaille-Sugar was deep in the game. His prominent nose, large enough to appear false, and his slightly negroid eyes did not in the least intimidate his opponent. With her elbows on the table, her shoulders on a level with her ears, and her blue eyes and red cheeks at their most vivid, she looked like a tipsy page. They both played passionately, almost in silence, exchanging occasional insults under their breath. *"You spindly spider! you sorrel run to seed!"* Lachaille muttered. *"You old crow's beak!"* the girl countered. The March twilight deepened over the narrow street.

"Please don't think I want you to go, Gaston," said Madame Alvarez, "but it's half-past seven. Will you excuse me while I just see about our dinner?"

"Half-past seven!" cried Lachaille, "and I'm supposed to be dining at Larue with de Dion, Feydeau, and one of the Barthous! This must be the last hand, Gigi."

"Why one of the Barthous?" asked Gilberte. "Are there several of them?"

"Two. One handsome and the other less so. The best known is the least handsome."

"That's not fair," said Gilberte. "And Feydeau, who's he?"

Lachaille plopped down his cards in amazement.

"Well, I declare! She doesn't know who Feydeau is! Don't you ever go to a play?"

"Hardly ever, Tonton."

"Don't you like the theater?"

"I'm not mad about it. And Grandmamma and Aunt Alicia both say that going to plays prevents one from thinking about the serious side of life. Don't tell Grandmamma I told you."

She lifted the weight of her hair away from her ears, and let it fall forward again. "Phew!" she sighed. "This mane does make me hot!"

"And what do they mean by the serious side of life?"

"Oh, I don't know it all off by heart, Uncle Gaston. And, what's more, they don't always agree about it. Grandmamma says: 'Don't read novels, they only depress you. Don't put on powder, it ruins the complexion. Don't wear stays, they spoil the figure. Don't dawdle and gaze at shop windows when you're by yourself. Don't get to know the families of your school friends, especially not the fathers who wait at the gates to fetch their daughters home from school.' "

She spoke very rapidly, panting between words like a child who has been running.

"And on top of that, Aunt Alicia goes off on another tack! I've reached the age when I can wear stays, and I should take lessons in dancing and deportment, and I should be aware of what's going on, and know the meaning of 'caret,' and not be taken in by the clothes that actresses wear. 'It's quite simple,' she tells me, 'of all the dresses you see on the stage, nineteen out of twenty would look ridiculous in the paddock.' In fact, my head is fit to split with it all! What will you be eating at Larue this evening, Tonton?"

"How should I know! *Filets de sole aux moules,* for a change. And of course, saddle of lamb with truffles. Do get on with the game, Gigi! I've got a point of five."

"That won't get you anywhere. I've got all the cards in the pack. Here, at home, we're having the warmed up remains of the *cassoulet.* I'm very fond of *cassoulet.*"

"A plain dish of *cassoulet* with bacon rind," said Inez Alvarez modestly, as she came in. "Goose was exorbitant this week."

"I'll have one sent to you from Bon-Abri," said Gaston.

"Thank you very much, Gaston. Gigi, help Monsieur Lachaille on with his overcoat. Fetch him his hat and stick!"

When Lachaille had gone, rather sulky after a regretful sniff at the warmed up *cassoulet,* Madame Alvarez turned to her granddaughter.

"Will you please inform me, Gilberte, why it was you returned so early from Aunt Alicia's? I didn't ask you in front of Gaston. Family matters must never be discussed in front of a third person, remember that!"

"There's no mystery about it, Grandmamma. Aunt Alicia

was wearing her little lace cap to show me she had a headache. She said to me, 'I'm not very well.' I said to her, 'Oh! Then I mustn't tire you out, I'll go home again.' She said to me, 'Sit down and rest for five minutes.' 'Oh!' I said to her, 'I'm not tired. I drove here.' 'You drove here!' she said to me, raising her hands like this. As you may imagine, I had kept the motorcar waiting a few minutes, to show Aunt Alicia. 'Yes,' I said to her, 'The four-seater de-Dion-Bouton-with-the-collapsible-hood, which Tonton lent me while he was paying a call on us. He has had a rumpus with Liane.' 'Who do you think you're talking to?' she says to me, 'I've not yet got one foot in the grave! I'm still kept informed about public events when they're important. I know that he has had a rumpus with that great lamppost of a woman. Well, you'd better run along home, and not bother about a poor ill old creature like me.' She waved to me from the window as I got into the motorcar."

Madame Alvarez pursed her lips.

"A poor ill old creature! She has never suffered so much as a cold in her life! I like that! What . . ."

"Grandmamma, do you think he'll remember my liquorice and the music case?"

Madame Alvarez slowly lifted her heavy eyes toward the ceiling.

"Perhaps, my child, perhaps."

"But, as he lost, he owes them to me, doesn't he?"

"Yes, yes, he owes them to you. Perhaps you'll get them after all. Slip on your pinafore, and set the table. Put away your cards."

"Yes, Grandmamma. Grandmamma, what did he tell you about Madame Liane? Is it true she ran out on him with Sandomir and the rope of pearls?"

"In the first place, one doesn't say 'ran out on' anyone. In the second, come here and let me tighten your ribbon, so that your curls won't get soaked in the soup. And finally, the sayings and doings of a person who has broken the rules of etiquette are not for your ears. These happen to be Gaston's private affairs."

"But, Grandmamma, they are no longer private, since everyone's talking about them, and the whole thing came out in *Gil Blas.*"

"Silence! All you need to know is that the conduct of Madame Liane d'Exelmans has been the reverse of sensible. The ham for your mother is between two plates: you will put it in the larder."

Gilberte was asleep when her mother — Andrée Alvar, in small type on the Opéra-Comique playbills — returned home. Madame Alvarez, the elder, seated at a game of patience, inquired from force of habit whether she was not too tired. Following polite family custom, Andrée reproached her mother for having waited up, and Madame Alvarez made her ritual reply.

"I shouldn't sleep in peace unless I knew you were in. There is some ham, and a little bowl of warm *cassoulet.* And some stewed prunes. The beer is on the windowsill."

"The child is in bed?"

"Of course."

Andrée Alvar made a solid meal — pessimists have good appetites. She still looked pretty in theatrical makeup. Without it, the rims of her eyes were pink and her lips colorless. For this reason, Aunt Alicia declared, Andrée never met with the admiration in real life that she gained on the stage.

"Did you sing well, my child?"

"Yes, I sang well. But where does it get me? All the applause goes to Tiphaine, as you may well imagine. Oh dear, oh dear, I really don't think I can bear to go on with this sort of life."

"It was your own choice. But you would bear it much better," said Madame Alvarez sententiously, "if you had someone! It's your loneliness that gets on your nerves, and you take such black views. You're behaving contrary to nature."

"Oh, Mother, don't start that all over again, I'm tired enough as it is. What news is there?"

"None. Everyone's talking of Gaston's break with Liane."

"Yes, they certainly are! Even in the green room at the Opéra-Comique, which can hardly be called up-to-date."

"It's an event of worldwide interest," said Madame Alvarez.

"Is there talk of who's in the running?"

"I should think not! It's far too recent. He is in full mourning, so to speak. Can you believe it, at a quarter to eight he was sitting exactly where you are now, playing a game of piquet with Gigi? He says he has no wish to attend the Battle of Flowers."

"Not really!"

"Yes. If he doesn't go, it will cause a great deal of talk. I advised him to think twice before taking such a decision."

"They were saying at the *Théâtre* that a certain music-hall artiste might stand a chance," said Andrée. "The one billed as the Cobra at the Olympia. It seems she does an acrobatic turn, and is brought on in a basket hardly big enough for a fox terrier, and from this she uncurls like a snake."

Madame Alvarez protruded her heavy lower lip in contempt.

"What an idea! Gaston Lachaille has not sunk to that level! A music-hall performer! Do him the justice to admit that, as befits a bachelor of his standing, he has always confined himself to the great ladies of the profession."

"A fine pack of bitches!" murmured Andrée.

"Be more careful how you express yourself, my child. Calling people and things by their names has never done anyone any good. Gaston's mistresses have all had an air about them. A liaison with a great professional lady is the only suitable way for him to wait for a great marriage, always supposing that some day he does marry. Whatever may happen, we're in the front row when anything fresh turns up. Gaston has such confidence in me! I wish you had seen him asking me for camomile! A boy, a regular boy! Indeed, he is only thirty-three. And all that wealth weighs so heavily on his shoulders."

Andrée's pink eyelids blinked ironically.

"Pity him, Mother, if you like. I'm not complaining, but all the time we've known Gaston, he has never given you anything except his confidence."

"He owes us nothing. And thanks to him we've always had sugar for our jams, and, from time to time, for my *curaçao;* and birds from his farm, and odds and ends for the child."

"If you're satisfied with that!"

Madame Alvarez held high her majestic head.

"Perfectly satisfied. And even if I was not, what difference would it make?"

"In fact, as far as we're concerned, Gaston Lachaille, rich as he is, behaves as if he wasn't rich at all. Supposing we were in real straits! Would he come to our rescue, do you suppose?"

Madame Alvarez placed her hand on her heart.

"I'm convinced that he would," she said. And after a pause, she added, "But I would rather not have to ask him."

Andrée picked up the *Journal* again, in which there was a photograph of Liane the ex-mistress. "When you take a good look at her, she's not so extraordinary."

"You're wrong," retorted Madame Alvarez, "she is extraordinary. Otherwise she would not be so famous. Successes and celebrity are not a matter of luck. You talk like those scatterbrains who say, 'Seven rows of pearls would look every bit as well on me as on Madame de Pougy. She certainly cuts a dash — but so could I.' Such nonsense makes me laugh. Take what's left of the camomile to bathe your eyes."

"Thank you, Mother. Did the child go to Aunt Alicia's?"

"She did indeed, and in Gaston's motorcar, what's more! He lent it to her. It can go forty miles an hour, I believe! She was in seventh heaven."

"Poor lamb, I wonder what she'll make of her life. She's quite capable of ending up as a mannequin or a saleswoman. She's so backward. At her age, I — "

There was no indulgence in the glance Madame Alvarez gave her daughter.

"Don't boast too much about what you were doing when you were her age. If I remember rightly, at her age you were snapping your fingers at Monsieur Mennesson and all his flour mills, though he was perfectly ready to make you your fortune. Instead, you must needs bolt with a wretched music master."

Andrée Alvar kissed her mother's lustrous plaits.

"My darling mother, don't curse me at this hour, I'm so sleepy. Goodnight, Mother. I've a rehearsal tomorrow at a quarter to one. I'll eat at the dairy during the entr'acte; don't bother about me."

She yawned and walked in the dark through the little room where her daughter was asleep. All she could see of Gilberte in the obscurity was a bush of hair and the Russian braid of her nightdress. She locked herself into the exiguous bathroom and, late though it was, lit the gas under a kettle. Madame Alvarez had instilled into her progeny, among other virtues, a respect for certain rites. One of her maxims was, "You can, at a pinch, leave the face till the morning, when traveling or pressed for time. For a woman, attention to the lower parts is the first law of self-respect."

The last to go to bed, Madame Alvarez was the first to rise, and allowed the daily cleaning woman no hand in preparing the breakfast coffee. She slept in the dining–sitting room, on a divan–bed, and, at the stroke of half-past seven, she opened the door to the papers, the quart of milk, and the daily maid—who was carrying the others. By eight o'clock she had taken out her curling pins, and her beautiful coils of hair were dressed and smooth. At ten minutes to nine, Gilberte left for school, clean and tidy, her hair well-brushed. At ten o'clock Madame Alvarez was "thinking about" the midday meal, that is, she got into her mackintosh, slipped her arm through the handle of her shopping net, and set off to market.

Today, as on all other days, she made sure that her granddaughter would not be late; she placed the coffeepot and the jug of milk piping hot on the table, and unfolded the newspaper while waiting for her. Gilberte came in fresh as a flower, smelling of lavender water, with some vestiges of sleep still clinging to her. A cry from Madame Alvarez made her fully wide awake.

"Call your mother, Gigi! Liane d'Exelmans has committed suicide."

The child replied with a long drawn-out "Oooh!" and asked, "Is she dead?"

"Of course not. She knows what she's about."

"How did she do it, Grandmamma? A revolver?"

Madame Alvarez looked pityingly at her granddaughter.

"The idea! Laudanum, as usual. *'Doctors Morèze and Pelledoux, who have never left the heartbroken beauty's bedside, cannot yet answer for her life, but their diagnosis is reassuring . . .'* My own diagnosis is that if Madame d'Exelmans goes on playing that game, she'll end by ruining her stomach."

"The last time she killed herself, Grandmamma, was for the sake of Prince Georgevitch, wasn't it?"

"Where are your brains, my darling? It was for Count Berthou de Sauveterre."

"Oh, so it was. And what will Tonton do now, do you think?"

A dreamy look passed across the huge eyes of Madame Alvarez.

"It's a toss-up, my child. We shall know everything in good time, even if he starts by refusing to give an interview to anybody. You must always start by refusing to give an interview to anybody. Then later you can fill the front page. Tell the concierge, by the way, to get us the evening papers. Have you had enough to eat? Did you have your second cup of milk, and your two pieces of bread and butter? Put on your gloves before you go out. Don't dawdle on the way. I'm going to call your mother. What a story! Andrée, are you asleep? Oh, so you're out of bed! Andrée, Liane has committed suicide!"

"That's a nice change," muttered Andrée. "She has only the one idea in her head, that woman, but she sticks to it."

"You've not taken out your curlers yet, Andrée?"

"And have my hair go limp in the middle of rehearsal? No thank you!"

Madame Alvarez ran her eyes over her daughter, from the spiky tips of her curlers to the felt slippers. "It's plain that there's no man here for you to bother about, my child! A man in the house soon cures a woman of traipsing about in dressing gown and slippers. What an excitement, this suicide! Unsuccessful, of course."

Andrée's pallid lips parted in a contemptuous smile: "It's getting too boring — the way she takes laudanum as if it were castor oil!"

"Anyhow, who cares about her? It's the Lachaille heir who matters. This is the first time such a thing has happened to him. He's already had — let me see. He's had Gentiane, who stole his private papers; then that foreigner, who tried to force him into marriage, but Liane is his first suicide. In such circumstances, a man so much in the public eye has to be extremely careful about what line he takes."

"Hm! He'll be bursting with pride, you may be sure."

"And with good reason, too," said Madame Alvarez. "We shall be seeing great things before very long. I wonder what Alicia will have to say about the situation."

"She'll do her best to make a mountain of a molehill."

"Alicia is no angel. But I must confess that she is long-sighted. And that without ever leaving her room!"

"She's no need to, since she has the telephone. Mother, won't you have one put in here?"

"It's expensive," said Madame Alvarez, thoughtfully. "We only just manage to make both ends meet, as it is. The telephone is of real use only to important businessmen, or to women who have something to hide. Now, if you were to change your mode of life — and I'm only putting it forward as a supposition — and if Gigi were to start on a life of her own, I should be the first to say, 'We'll have the telephone put in.' But we haven't reached that point yet, unfortunately."

She allowed herself a single sigh, pulled on her rubber gloves, and coolly set about her household chores. Thanks to her care, the modest flat was growing old without too many signs of deterioration. She retained, from her past life, the honorable habits of women who have lost their honor, and these she taught to her daughter and her daughter's daughter.

Sheets never stayed on the beds longer than ten days, and the combination char- and washerwoman told everyone that the chemises and drawers of the ladies of Madame Alvarez' household were changed more often than she could count, and so were the table napkins. At any moment, at the cry of "Gigi, take off your shoes!" Gilberte had to remove shoes and stockings, exhibit white feet to the closest inspection, and announce the least suspicion of a corn.

During the week following Madame d'Exelmans' suicide, Lachaille's reactions were somewhat incoherent. He engaged the stars of the National Musical Academy to dance at a midnight fête held at his own house, and, wishing to give a supper party at the Pré-Catalan, he arranged for that restaurant to open a fortnight earlier than was their custom. The clowns, Footit *et* Chocolat, did a turn: Rita del Erido caracoled on horseback between the supper tables, wearing a divided skirt of white lace flounces, a white hat on her black hair with white ostrich feathers frothing round the relentless beauty of her face. Indeed, Paris mistakenly proclaimed, such was her beauty, that Gaston Lachaille was hoisting her astride a throne of sugar. Twenty-four hours later, Paris was undeceived. For in the false prophecies it had published, *Gil Blas* nearly lost the subsidy it received from Gaston Lachaille. A specialized weekly, *Paris en amour,* provided another red herring, under the headline: "Young Yankee millionairess makes no secret of weakness for French sugar."

Madame Alvarez' ample bust shook with incredulous laughter when she read the daily papers: she had received her information from none other than Gaston Lachaille in person. Twice in ten days, he had found time to drop in for a cup of camomile, to sink into the depths of the now sagging conch-shaped armchair, and there forget his business worries and his dislike of being unattached. He even brought Gigi an absurd Russian leather music case with a silver-gilt clasp, and twenty boxes of liquorice. Madame Alvarez was given a *pâté de foie gras* and six bottles of champagne, and of these bounties Tonton Lachaille partook by inviting himself to dinner. Throughout the meal, Gilberte regaled them rather tipsily with tittle-tattle about her school, and later won Gaston's gold pencil at piquet. He lost with good grace, recovered his spirits, laughed, and, pointing to the child, said to Madame Alvarez, "There's my best pal!" Madame Alvarez' Spanish eyes moved with slow watchfulness from Gigi's reddened cheeks and white teeth to Lachaille, who was pulling her hair by the fistful. "You little devil, you had the fourth king up your sleeve all the time!"

It was at this moment that Andrée, coming back from the Opéra-Comique, looked at Gigi's disheveled head rolling against Lachaille's sleeve, and saw the tears of excited laughter in her lovely slate-blue eyes. She said nothing, and accepted a glass of champagne, then another, and yet another. After her third glass, Gaston Lachaille was threatened with the Bell Song from *Lakmé,* at which point Andrée's mother led her away to bed.

The following day, no one spoke of this family party except Gilberte, who exclaimed, "Never, never in all my life, have I laughed so much! And the pencil is real gold!" Her unreserved chatter met with a strange silence, or rather with "Now then, Gigi, try to be a little more serious!" thrown out almost absentmindedly.

After that, Gaston Lachaille let a fortnight go by without giving a sign of life, and the Alvarez family gathered its information from the papers only.

"Did you see, Andrée? In the gossip column it says that Monsieur Gaston Lachaille has left for Monte Carlo. *'The reason for this seems to be of a sentimental nature — a secret that we respect.'* What next!"

"Would you believe it, Grandmamma, Lydia Poret was saying at the dancing class that Liane traveled on the same train as Tonton, but in another compartment! Grandmamma, do you think it can be true?"

Madame Alvarez shrugged her shoulders.

"If it was true, how on earth would those Porets know?

Have they become friends with Monsieur Lachaille all of a sudden?"

"No, but Lydia Poret heard the story in her aunt's dressing room at the Comédie Française."

Madame Alvarez exchanged looks with her daughter.

"In her dressing room! That explains everything!" she exclaimed, for she held the theatrical profession in contempt, although Andrée worked so hard. When Madame Emilienne d'Alençon had decided to present performing rabbits, and Madame de Pougy — shyer on the stage than any young girl — had amused herself by miming the part of Columbine in spangled black tulle, Madame Alvarez had stigmatized them both in a single phrase, "What! have they sunk to that?"

"Grandmamma, tell me, Grandmamma, do you know him, this Prince Radziwill?" Gilberte went on again.

"What's come over the child today? Has she been bitten by a flea? Which Prince Radziwill, to begin with? There's more than one."

"I don't know," said Gigi. "The one who's getting married. Among the list of presents, it says here, *'are three writing sets in malachite.'* What is malachite?"

"Oh, you're being tiresome, child. If he's getting married, he's no longer interesting."

"But if Tonton got married, wouldn't he be interesting either?"

"It all depends. It would be interesting if he were to marry his mistress. When Prince Cheniaguine married Valérie d'Aigreville, it was obvious that the life she had led him for the past fifteen years was all he wanted; scenes, plates flung across the room, and reconciliations in the middle of the restaurant Durand, Place de la Madeleine. Clearly, she was a woman who knew how to make herself valued. But all that is too complicated for you, my poor Gigi."

"And do you think it's to marry Liane that they've gone away together?"

Madame Alvarez pressed her forehead against the windowpane, and seemed to be consulting the spring sunshine, which bestowed upon the street a sunny side and one with shade.

"No," she said, "not if I know anything about anything. I must have a word with Alicia. Gigi, come with me as far as her house; you can leave me there and find your way back along the quais. It will give you some fresh air, since, it would seem, one must have fresh air nowadays. I have never been in the habit of taking the air more than twice a year, myself, at Cabourg and at Monte Carlo. And I am none the worse for that."

That evening Madame Alvarez came in so late that the family dined off tepid soup, cold meat, and some cakes sent round by Aunt Alicia. To Gilberte's "Well, what did she have to say?" she presented an icy front, and answered in clarion tones.

"She says that she is going to teach you how to eat ortolans."

"Lovely!" cried Gilberte. "And what did she say about the summer frock she promised me?"

"She said she would see. And that there's no reason why you should be displeased with the result."

"Oh!" said Gilberte, gloomily.

"She also wants you to go to luncheon with her on Thursday, sharp at twelve."

"With you, too, Grandmamma?"

Madame Alvarez looked at the willowy slip of a girl facing her across the table, at her high, rosy cheekbones beneath eyes as blue as an evening sky, at her strong even teeth biting a fresh-colored but slightly chapped lip, and at the primitive splendor of her ash-gold hair.

"No," she said at last. "Without me."

Gilberte got up and wound an arm about her grandmother's neck.

"The way you said that, Grandmamma, surely doesn't mean that you're going to send me to live with Aunt Alicia? I don't want to leave here, Grandmamma!"

Madame Alvarez cleared her throat, gave a little cough, and smiled.

"Goodness gracious! what a foolish creature you are! Leave here! Why, my poor Gigi, I'm not scolding you, but you've not reached the first stage toward leaving."

For a bellpull, Aunt Alicia had hung from her front door a length of bead-embroidered braid on a background of twining green vine leaves and purple grapes. The door itself, varnished and revarnished till it glistened, shone with the glow of a dark brown caramel. From the very threshold, where she was admitted by a "manservant," Gilberte enjoyed in her undiscriminating way an atmosphere of discreet luxury. The carpet, spread with Persian rugs, seemed to lend her wings. After hearing Madame Alvarez pronounce her sister's Louis XV little drawing room to be "boredom itself," Gilberte echoed her words by saying: "Aunt Alicia's drawing room is very pretty, but it's boredom itself!" reserving her admiration for the dining room, furnished in pale, almost golden, lemon wood dating from the Directoire, quite plain but for the grain of a wood as transparent as wax. "I shall buy myself a set like that one day," Gigi had once said in all innocence.

"In the Faubourg Antoine, I dare say," Aunt Alicia had answered teasingly, with a smile of her cupid's bow mouth and a flash of small teeth.

She was seventy years old. Her fastidious taste was everywhere apparent: in her silver-gray bedroom with its red Chinese vases, in her narrow white bathroom as warm as a hothouse, and in her robust health, concealed by a pretense of delicacy. The men of her generation, when trying to describe Alicia de Saint-Efflam, fumbled for words and could only exclaim, "Ah, my deah fellow!" or "Nothing could give you the faintest idea . . ." Those who had known her intimately produced photographs which younger men found ordinary enough. "Was she really so lovely? You wouldn't think so from her photographs!" Looking at portraits of her, old admirers would pause for an instant, recollecting the turn of a wrist like a swan's neck, the tiny ear, the profile revealing a delicious kinship between the heart-shaped mouth and the wide-cut eyelids with their long lashes.

Gilberte kissed the pretty old lady, who was wearing a peak of black Chantilly lace on her white hair, and, on her slightly dumpy figure, a tea gown of shot taffeta.

"You have one of your headaches, Aunt Alicia?"

"I'm not sure yet," replied Aunt Alicia, "it depends on the luncheon. Come quickly, the eggs are ready! Take off your coat! What on earth is that dress?"

"One of Mamma's, altered to fit me. Are they difficult eggs today?"

"Not at all. *Oeufs brouillés aux croutons.* The ortolans are not difficult, either. And you shall have chocolate cream. So shall I."

With her young voice, a touch of pink on her amiable wrinkles, and lace on her white hair, Aunt Alicia was the perfect stage marquise. Gilberte had the greatest reverence for her aunt. In sitting down to table in her presence, she would pull her skirt up behind, join her knees, hold her elbows close to her sides, straighten her shoulder blades, and to all appearances become the perfect young lady. She would remember what she had been taught, break her bread quickly, eat with her mouth shut, and take care, when cutting her meat, not to let her forefinger reach the blade of her knife.

Today her hair, severely tied back in a heavy knot at the nape of her neck, disclosed the fresh line of her forehead and ears, and a very powerful throat, rising from the rather ill-cut opening of her altered dress. This was a dingy blue, the bodice pleated about a let-in piece, and to cheer up this patchwork, three rows of mohair braid had been sewn round the hem of the skirt, and three times three rows of mohair braid round the sleeves, between the wrist and the elbow.

Aunt Alicia, sitting opposite her niece and examining her through fine dark eyes, could find no fault.

"How old are you?" she asked suddenly.

"The same as I was the other day, Aunt. Fifteen and a half. Aunt, what do you really think of this business of Tonton Gaston?"

"Why? Does it interest you?"

"Of course, Aunt. It worries me. If Tonton takes up with another lady, he won't come and play piquet with us any more or drink camomile tea—at least not for some time. That would be a shame."

"That's one way of looking at it, certainly."

Aunt Alicia examined her niece critically, through narrowed eyelids.

"Do you work hard, in class? Who are your friends? Ortolans should be cut in two, with one quick stroke of the knife, and no grating of the blade on the plate. Bite up each half. The bones don't matter. Go on eating while you answer my question, but don't talk with your mouth full. You must manage it. If I can, you can. What friends have you made?"

"None, Aunt. Grandmamma won't even let me have tea with the families of my school friends."

"She is quite right. Apart from that, there is no one who follows you, no little clerk hanging round your skirts? No schoolboy? No older man? I warn you, I shall know at once if you lie to me."

Gilberte gazed at the bright face of the imperious old lady who was questioning her so sharply.

"Why, no, Aunt, no one. Has somebody been telling you tales about me? I am always on my own. And why does Grandmamma stop me from accepting invitations?"

"She is right, for once. You would only be invited by ordinary people, that is to say, useless people."

"And what about us? Aren't we ordinary people ourselves?"

"No."

"What makes these ordinary people inferior to us?"

"They have weak heads and dissolute bodies. Besides, they are married. But I don't think you understand."

"Yes, Aunt, I understand that we don't marry."

"Marriage is not forbidden to us. Instead of marrying 'at once,' it sometimes happens that we marry 'at last.' "

"But does that prevent me from seeing girls of my own age?"

"Yes. Are you bored at home? Well, be a little bored. It's not a bad thing. Boredom helps one to make decisions. What is the matter? Tears? The tears of a silly child who is backward for her age. Have another ortolan."

Aunt Alicia, with three glittering fingers, grasped the stem of her glass and raised it in a toast.

"To you and me, Gigi! You shall have an Egyptian cigarette with your coffee. On condition that you do not wet the end of your cigarette, and that you don't spit out specks of tobacco—going *ptu, ptu.* I shall also give you a note to the *première vendeuse* at Béchoff-David, an old friend of mine who was not a success. Your wardrobe is going to be changed. Nothing venture, nothing gain."

The dark blue eyes gleamed. Gilberte stammered with joy.

"Aunt! Aunt! I'm going . . . to Bé—"

"—choff-David. But I thought you weren't interested in clothes?"

Gilberte blushed.

"Aunt, I'm not interested in homemade clothes."

"I sympathize with you. Can it be that you have taste? When you think of looking your best, how do you see yourself dressed?"

"Oh, but I know just what would suit me, Aunt! I've seen—"

"Explain yourself without gestures. The moment you gesticulate you look common."

"I've seen a dress . . . oh, a dress created for Madame Lucy Gérard! Hundreds of tiny ruffles of pearl-gray silk muslin from top to bottom. And then a dress of lavender-blue cloth cut out on a black velvet foundation, the cutout design making a sort of peacock's tail on the train."

The small hand with its precious stones flashed through the air.

"Enough! Enough! I see your fancy is to be dressed like a leading *comédienne* at the Théâtre Français—and don't take that as a compliment! Come and pour out the coffee. And without jerking up the lip of the coffeepot to prevent the drop from falling. I'd rather have a footbath in my saucer than see you juggling like a waiter in a café."

The next hour passed very quickly for Gilberte: Aunt Alicia had unlocked a casket of jewels to use for a lesson that dazzled her.

"What is that, Gigi?"

"A marquise diamond."

"We say, a marquise-shaped brilliant. And that?"

"A topaz."

Aunt Alicia threw up her hands and the sunlight, glancing off her rings, set off a myriad scintillations.

"A topaz! I have suffered many humiliations, but this surpasses them all. A topaz among my jewels! Why not an aquamarine or a chrysolite? It's a yellow diamond, little goose, and you won't often see its like. And this?"

Gilberte half opened her mouth, as if in a dream.

"Oh! That's an emerald. Oh, how beautiful it is!"

Aunt Alicia slipped the large square-cut emerald on one of her thin fingers and was lost in silence.

"Do you see," she said in a hushed voice, "that almost-blue flame darting about in the depths of the green light? Only the most beautiful emeralds contain that miracle of elusive blue."

"Who gave it to you, Aunt?" Gilberte dared to ask.

"A king," said Aunt Alicia simply.

"A great king?"

"No. A little one. Great kings do not give very fine stones."

"Why not?"

For a fleeting moment, Aunt Alicia proffered a glimpse of her tiny white teeth.

"If you want my opinion, it's because they don't want to. Between ourselves, the little ones don't either."

"Then who does give great big stones?"

"Who? The shy. The proud, too. And the bounders, because they think that to give a monster jewel is a sign of good breeding. Sometimes a woman does, to humiliate a man. Never wear second-rate jewels, wait till the really good ones come to you."

"And if they don't?"

"Well, then it can't be helped. Rather than a wretched little diamond full of flaws, wear a simple, plainly inexpensive ring. In that case you can say, 'It's a memento. I never part with it, day or night.' Don't ever wear artistic jewelry, it wrecks a woman's reputation."

"What is an artistic jewel?"

"It all depends. A mermaid in gold with eyes of chrysoprase. An Egyptian scarab. A large engraved amethyst. A not very heavy bracelet said to have been chased by a master hand. A lyre or star, mounted as a brooch. A studded tortoise. In a word, all of them, frightful. Never wear baroque pearls, not even as hatpins. Beware, above all things, of family jewels!"

"But Grandmamma has a beautiful cameo, set as a medallion."

"There are no beautiful cameos," said Alicia, with a toss of the head. "There are precious stones and pearls. There are white, yellow, blue, blue-white, or pink diamonds. We won't speak of black diamonds, they're not worth mentioning. Then there are rubies—when you can be sure of them; sapphires, when they come from Kashmir; emeralds, provided they have no fatal flaw, or are not too light in color, or have a yellowish tint."

"Aunt, I'm very fond of opals, too."

"I am very sorry, but you are not to wear them. I won't allow it."

Dumbfounded, Gilberte remained for a moment open-mouthed.

"Oh! Do you too, Aunt, really believe that they bring bad luck?"

"Why in the world not? You silly little creature," Alicia went bubbling on, "you must pretend to believe in such things. Believe in opals, believe—let's see, what can I suggest—in turquoises that die, in the evil eye . . ."

"But," said Gigi, haltingly, "those are . . . are superstitions!"

"Of course they are, child. They also go by the name of weaknesses. A pretty little collection of weaknesses, and a terror of spiders, are indispensable stock-in-trade with men."

"Why, Aunt?"

The old lady closed the casket, and kept Gilberte kneeling before her.

"Because nine men out of ten are superstitious, nineteen out of twenty believe in the evil eye, and ninety-eight out of a hundred are afraid of spiders. They forgive us—oh! for many things, but not for the absence in us of their own failings," she said. "What makes you sigh?"

"I shall never remember all that!"

"The important thing is not for *you* to remember, but for me to know it."

"Aunt, what is a writing set in . . . in malachite?"

"Always a calamity. But where on earth did you pick up such terms?"

"From the list of presents at grand weddings, Aunt, printed in the papers."

"Nice reading! But, at least you can gather from it what kind of presents you should never give, or accept."

While speaking, she began to touch here and there the young face on a level with her own, with the sharp pointed nail of her index finger. She lifted one slightly chapped lip, inspected the spotless enamel of the teeth.

"A fine jaw, my girl! With such teeth, I should have gobbled up Paris, and the rest of the world into the bargain. As it was, I had a good bite out of it. What's this you've got here? A small pimple? You shouldn't have a small pimple near your nose. And this? You've pinched a blackhead. You've no business to have such things, or to pinch them. I'll give you some of my astringent lotion. You musn't eat anything from the pork butchers' except cooked ham. You don't put on powder?"

"Grandmamma won't let me."

"I should hope not. You go you-know-where regularly? Let me smell your breath. Not that it means anything at this hour, you've just had luncheon."

She laid her hands on Gigi's shoulders.

"Pay attention to what I'm going to say. You have it in your power to please. You have an impossible little nose, a non-descript mouth, cheeks rather like the wife of a moujik—"

"Oh, Aunt!" sighed Gilberte.

"But, with your eyes and eyelashes, your teeth, and your hair, you can get away with it, if you're not a perfect fool. As for the rest—"

She cupped her hands like conch shells over Gigi's bosom and smiled.

"A promise, but a pretty promise, neatly molded. Don't eat too many almonds, they add weight to the breasts. Ah! remind me to teach you how to choose cigars."

Gilberte opened her eyes so wide that the tips of her lashes touched her eyebrows.

"Why?"

She received a little tap on the cheek.

"Because—because I do nothing without good reason. If I take you in hand at all, I must do it thoroughly. Once a woman understands the tastes of a man, cigars included, and once a man knows what pleases a woman, they may be said to be well matched."

"And then they fight," concluded Gigi with a knowing air.

"What do you mean, they fight?"

The old lady looked at Gigi in consternation.

"Ah!" she added, "You certainly never invented the triple mirror! Come, you little psychologist! Let me give you a note for Madame Henriette at Béchoff."

While her aunt was writing at a miniature rose-pink escritoire, Gilberte breathed in the scent of the fastidiously furnished room. Without wanting them for herself, she examined the objects she knew so well but hardly appreciated: Cupid, the Archer, pointing to the hours on the mantelpiece;

two rather daring pictures; a bed like the basin of a fountain and its chinchilla coverlet; a rosary of small seed pearls and the New Testament on the bedside table; two red Chinese vases fitted as lamps—a happy note against the gray of the walls.

"Run along, my little one. I shall send for you again quite soon. Don't forget to ask Victor for the cake you're to take home. Gently, don't disarrange my hair! And remember, I shall have my eye on you as you leave the house. Woe betide you if you march like a guardsman, or drag your feet behind you!"

The month of May fetched Gaston Lachaille back to Paris, and brought to Gilberte two well-cut dresses and a lightweight coat—"a sack coat like Cléo de Mérode's" she called it—as well as hats and boots and shoes. To these she added, on her own account, a few curls over the forehead, which cheapened her appearance. She paraded in front of Gaston in a blue and white dress reaching almost to the ground. "A full seven and a half yards round, Tonton, my skirt measures!" She was more than proud of her slender waist, held in by a grosgrain sash with a silver buckle; but she tried every dodge to free her lovely strong neck from its whalebone collar of "imitation Venetian point" which matched the tucks of the bodice. The full sleeves and wide flounced skirt of blue and white striped silk rustled deliciously, and Gilberte delighted in picking at the sleeves, to puff them out just below the shoulder.

"You remind me of a performing monkey," Lachaille said to her. "I liked you much better in your old tartan dress. In that uncomfortable collar you look just like a hen with a full crop. Take a peep at yourself!"

Feeling a little ruffled, Gilberte turned round to face the looking glass. She had a lump in one of her cheeks caused by a large caramel, out of a box sent all the way from Nice at Gaston's order.

"I've heard a good deal about you, Tonton," she retorted, "but I've never heard it said that you had any taste in clothes."

He stared, almost choking, at this newly fledged young woman, then turned to Madame Alvarez.

"Charming manners you've taught her! I congratulate you!"

Whereupon he left the house without drinking his camomile tea, and Madame Alvarez wrung her hands.

"Look what you've done to us now, my poor Gigi!"

"I know," said Gigi, "but then why does he fly at me? He must know by now, I should think, that I can give as good as I get!"

Her grandmother shook her by the arm.

"But think what you've done, you wretched child! Good heavens! when will you learn to think? You've mortally offended the man, as likely as not. Just when we are doing our utmost to—"

"To do what, Grandmamma?"

"Why! to do everything, to make an elegant young lady of you, to show you off to advantage."

"For whose benefit, Grandmamma? You must admit that one doesn't have to turn oneself inside out for an old friend like Tonton!"

But Madame Alvarez admitted nothing; not even to her astonishment, when, the following day, Gaston Lachaille arrived in the best of spirits, wearing a light-colored suit.

"Put on your hat, Gigi! I'm taking you out to tea."

"Where?" cried Gigi.

"To the *Réservoirs,* at Versailles!"

"Hurrah! Hurrah! Hurrah!" chanted Gilberte.

She turned toward the kitchen.

"Grandmamma, I'm having tea at the *Réservoirs,* with Tonton!"

Madame Alvarez appeared, and without stopping to untie the flowered satinette apron across her stomach, interposed her soft hand between Gilberte's arm and that of Gaston Lachaille.

"No, Gaston," she said simply.

"What do you mean, 'No'?"

"Oh! Grandmamma!" wailed Gigi.

Madame Alvarez seemed not to hear her.

"Go to your room a minute, Gigi. I should like to talk to Monsieur Lachaille in private."

She watched Gilberte leave the room and close the door behind her; then, returning to Gaston, she met his dark, rather brutal stare without flinching.

"What is the meaning of all this, Mamita? Ever since yesterday, I find quite a change here. What's going on?"

"I shall be glad if you will sit down, Gaston, I'm tired," said Madame Alvarez. "Oh, my poor legs!"

She sighed, waited for a response that did not come, and then untied her apron, under which she was wearing a black dress with a large cameo pinned upon it. She motioned her guest to a high-backed chair, keeping the armchair for herself. Then she sat down heavily, smoothed her graying black coils, and folded her hands on her lap. The unhurried movement of her large dark lambent eyes, and the ease with which she remained motionless, were sure signs of her self-control.

"Gaston, you cannot doubt my friendship for you!" Lachaille emitted a short, businesslike laugh, and tugged at his mustache. "My friendship and my gratitude. Nevertheless, I must never forget that I have a soul entrusted to my care. Andrée, as you know, has neither the time nor the inclination to look after the girl. Our Gilberte has not got the gumption to make her own way in the world, like so many. She is just a child."

"Of sixteen," said Lachaille.

"Of nearly sixteen," consented Madame Alvarez. "For years you have been giving her sweets and playthings. She swears by Tonton, and by him alone. And now you want to take her out to tea, in your automobile, to the *Réservoirs!*"

Madame Alvarez placed a hand on her heart.

"Upon my soul and conscience, Gaston, if there were only you and me, I should say to you, 'Take Gilberte anywhere you like, I entrust her to you blindly.' But there are always the others. The eyes of the world are on you. To be seen tête-à-tête with you, is, for a woman—"

Gaston Lachaille lost patience.

"All right, all right, I understand. You want me to believe that once she is seen having tea with me, Gilberte is compromised! A slip of a girl, a flapper, a chit whom no one knows, whom no one notices!"

"Let us say, rather," interrupted Madame Alvarez gently, "that she will be labeled. No matter where you put in an appearance, Gaston, your presence is remarked upon. A young girl who goes out alone with you is no longer an ordinary girl, or even—to put it bluntly—a respectable girl. Now our little Gilberte must not, above all things, cease to be an ordinary young girl, at least not by that method. So far as it concerns you, it will simply end in one more story to be added to the long list already in existence but, personally, when I read of it in *Gil Blas,* I shall not be amused."

Gaston Lachaille rose, paced from the table to the door, then from the door to the window, before replying.

"Very good, Mamita, I have no wish to vex you. I shan't argue," he said coldly. "Keep your precious child."

He turned round again to face Madame Alvarez, his chin held high.

"I can't help wondering, as a matter of interest, whom you are keeping her for! A clerk earning a hundred a year, who'll marry her and give her four children in three years?"

"I know the duty of a mother better than that," said Madame Alvarez composedly. "I shall do my best to entrust Gigi only to the care of a man capable of saying, 'I take charge of her and answer for her future.' May I have the pleasure of brewing you some camomile tea, Gaston?"

"No, thank you. I'm late already."

"Would you like Gigi to come and say good-bye?"

"Don't bother, I'll see her another time. I can't say when, I'm sure. I'm very much taken up these days."

"Never mind, Gaston, don't worry about her. Have a good time, Gaston."

Once alone, Madame Alvarez mopped her forehead, and went to open the door of Gilberte's room.

"You were listening at the door, Gigi!"

"No, Grandmamma."

"Yes, you had your ear to the keyhole. You must never listen at keyholes. You don't hear properly and so you get things all wrong. Monsieur Lachaille has gone."

"So I can see," said Gilberte.

"Now you must rub the new potatoes in a cloth. I'll sauté them when I come in."

"Are you going out, Grandmamma?"

"I'm going round to see Alicia."

"Again?"

"Is it your place to object?" said Madame Alvarez severely. "You had better bathe your eyes in cold water, since you have been silly enough to cry."

"Grandmamma!"

"What?"

"What difference could it make to you, if you'd let me go out with Tonton Gaston in my new dress?"

"Silence! If you can't understand anything about anything, at least let those who are capable of using their reason do so for you. And put on my rubber gloves before you touch the potatoes!"

Throughout the whole of the following week, silence reigned over the Alvarez household, except for a surprise visit, one day, from Aunt Alicia. She arrived in a hired brougham, all black lace and dull silk with a rose at her shoulder, and carried on an anxious conversation, strictly between themselves, with her younger sister. As she was leaving, she bestowed only a moment's attention on Gilberte, pecked at her cheek with a fleeting kiss, and was gone.

"What did she want?" Gilberte asked Madame Alvarez.

"Oh, nothing . . . the address of the heart specialist who treated Madame Buffetery."

Gilberte reflected for a moment.

"It was a long one," she said.

"What was long?"

"The address of the heart specialist. Grandmamma, I should like a *cachet*. I have a headache."

"But you had one yesterday. A headache doesn't last forty-eight hours!"

"Presumably my headaches are different from other people's," said Gilberte, offended.

She was losing some of her sweetness, and, on her return from school, would make some such remark as "My teacher has it in for me!" or complain of not being able to sleep. She was gradually slipping into a state of idleness, which her grandmother noticed, but did nothing to overcome.

One day Gigi was busy applying liquid chalk to her white canvas button boots, when Gaston Lachaille put in an appearance without ringing the bell. His hair was too long, his complexion suntanned, and he was wearing a broad-check summer suit. He stopped short in front of Gilberte, who was perched high on a kitchen stool, her left hand shod with a boot.

"Oh! Grandmamma left the key in the door, that's just like her!"

As Gaston Lachaille looked at her without saying a word, she began to blush, put down the boot on the table and pulled her skirt down over her knees.

"So, Tonton, you slip in like a burglar! I believe you're thinner. Aren't you fed properly by that famous chef of yours who used to be with the Prince of Wales? Being thinner makes your eyes look larger, and at the same time makes your nose longer, and—"

"I have something to say to your grandmother," interrupted Gaston Lachaille. "Run into your room, Gigi."

For a moment she remained openmouthed, then she jumped off her stool. The strong column of her neck, like an archangel's, swelled with anger as she advanced on Lachaille.

"Run into your room! Run into your room! And suppose I said the same to you? Who do you think you are here, ordering me to run into my room? All right, I'm going to my room! And I can tell you one thing; so long as you're in the house, I shan't come out of it!"

She slammed the door behind her, and there was a dramatic click of the bolt.

"Gaston," breathed Madame Alvarez, "I shall insist on the child apologizing, yes, I shall insist; if necessary, I'll . . ."

Gaston was not listening to her, and stood staring at the closed door.

"Now, Mamita," said he, "let us talk briefly and to the point."

"Let us go over it all once again," said Aunt Alicia. "To begin with, you are quite sure he said, 'She shall be spoiled, more than—' "

"Than any woman before her!"

"Yes, but that's the sort of vague phrase that every man comes out with. I like things cut and dried."

"Just what they were, Alicia, for he said that he would guarantee Gigi against every imaginable mishap, even against himself, by an insurance policy; and that he regarded himself more or less as her godfather."

"Yes, hmm. . . . Not bad, not bad. But vague, vague as ever."

She was still in bed, her white hair arranged in curls against the pink pillow. She was absentmindedly tying and untying the ribbon of her nightdress. Madame Alvarez, pale and wan under her morning hat as the moon behind passing clouds, was leaning cross-armed against the bedside.

"And he added, 'I don't wish to rush anything. Above all, I am Gigi's best pal. I shall give her all the time she wants to get used to me.' There were tears in his eyes. And he also said, 'After all, she won't have to deal with a savage.' A gentleman, in fact. A perfect gentleman."

"Yes, yes. Rather a vague gentleman. And the child, have you spoken frankly to her?"

"As was my duty, Alicia. This is no time for us to be treating her like a child from whom the cakes have to be hidden. Yes, I spoke frankly. I referred to Gaston as a miracle, as a god, as—"

"Tut, tut, tut," criticized Alicia, "I should have stressed the difficulties rather: the cards to be played, the fury of all those ladies, the conquest represented by so conspicuous a man."

Madame Alvarez wrung her hands.

"The difficulties! The cards to be played! Do you imagine she's like you? Don't you know her at all? She's very far from calculating, she's—"

"Thank you."

"I mean she has no ambition. I was even struck by the fact that she did not react either one way or the other. No cries of joy, no tears of emotion! All I got from her was, 'Oh, yes! Oh, it's very considerate of him.' Then, only at the every end, did she lay down, as her conditions—"

"Conditions, indeed!" murmured Alicia.

"—that she would answer Monsieur Lachaille's proposals herself, and discuss the matter alone with him. In other words, it was her business, and hers only."

"Let us be prepared for the worst! You've brought a nitwit into the world. She will ask for the moon and, if I know him, she won't get it. He is coming at four o'clock?"

"Yes."

"Hasn't he sent anything? No flowers? No little present?"

"Nothing. Do you think that's a bad sign?"

"No. It's what one would expect. See that the child is nicely dressed. How is she looking?"

"Not too well, today. Poor little lamb—"

"Come, come!" said Alicia heartlessly. "You'll have time for tears another day—when she's succeeded in ruining the whole affair."

"You've eaten scarcely anything, Gigi."

"I wasn't too hungry, Grandmamma. May I have a little more coffee?"

"Of course."

"And a drop of Combier?"

"Why, yes. There's nothing in the world better than Combier for settling the stomach."

Through the open window rose the noise and heat from the street below. Gigi let the tip of her tongue lick round the bottom of her liqueur glass.

"If Aunt Alicia could see you, Gigi!" said Madame Alvarez lightheartedly.

Gigi's only reply was a disillusioned little smile. Her old plaid dress was too tight across the breast, and under the table she stretched out her long legs well beyond the limits of her skirt.

"What can Mamma be rehearsing today that's kept her from coming back to eat with us, Grandmamma? Do you think there really is a rehearsal going on at her Opéra-Comique?"

"She said so, didn't she?"

"Personally, I don't think she wanted to eat here."

"What makes you think that?"

Without taking her eyes off the sunny window, Gigi simply shrugged her shoulders.

"Oh, nothing, Grandmamma."

When she had drained the last drop of her Combier, she rose and began to clear the table.

"Leave all that, Gigi, I'll do it."

"Why, Grandmamma? I do it as a rule."

She looked Madame Alvarez straight in the face, with an expression the old lady could not meet.

"We began our meal late, it's almost three o'clock and you're not dressed yet; do pull yourself together, Gigi."

"It's never before taken me a whole hour to change my clothes."

"Won't you need my help? Are you satisfied your hair's all right?"

"It will do, Grandmamma. When the doorbell rings, don't bother, I'll go and open it."

On the stroke of four, Gaston Lachaille rang three times. A

childish, wistful face looked out from the bedroom door, listening. After three more impatient rings, Gilberte advanced as far as the middle of the hall. She still had on her old plaid dress and cotton stockings. She rubbed her cheeks with both fists, then ran to open the door.

"Good afternoon, Uncle Gaston."

"Didn't you want to let me in, you bad girl?"

They bumped shoulders in passing through the door, said "Oh, sorry!" a little too self-consciously, then laughed awkwardly.

"Please sit down, Tonton. D'you know, I didn't have time to change. Not like you! That navy blue serge couldn't look better!"

"You don't know what you're talking about! It's tweed."

"Of course. How silly of me!"

She sat down facing him, pulled her skirt over her knees, and they stared at each other. Gilberte's tomboy assurance deserted her; a strange woebegone look made her blue eyes seem twice their natural size.

"What's the matter with you, Gigi?" asked Lachaille softly. "Tell me something! Do you know why I'm here?"

She assented with an exaggerated nod.

"Do you want to, or don't you?" he asked, lowering his voice.

She pushed a curl behind her ear, and swallowed bravely.

"I don't want to."

Lachaille twirled the tips of his mustache between two fingers, and for a moment looked away from a pair of darkened blue eyes, a pink cheek with a single freckle, curved lashes, a mouth unaware of its power, a heavy mass of ash-gold hair, and a neck as straight as a column, strong, hardly feminine, all of a piece, innocent of jewelry.

"I don't want what you want," Gilberte began again. "You said to Grandmamma . . ."

He put out his hand to stop her. His mouth was slightly twisted to one side, as if he had the toothache.

"I know what I said to your grandmother. It's not worth

repeating. Just tell me what it is you don't want. You can then tell me what you do want. I shall give it to you."

"You mean that?" cried Gilberte.

He nodded, letting his shoulders droop, as if tired out. She watched, with surprise, these signs of exhaustion and torment.

"Tonton, you told Grandmamma you wanted to make me my fortune."

"A very fine one," said Lachaille firmly.

"It will be fine if I like it," said Gilberte, no less firmly. "They've drummed into my ears that I am backward for my age, but all the same I know the meaning of words. 'Make me my fortune,' that means I should go away from here with you, and that I should sleep in your bed."

"Gigi, I beg of you!"

She stopped, because of the strong note of appeal in his voice.

"But, Tonton, why should I mind speaking of it to you? You didn't mind speaking of it to Grandmamma. Neither did Grandmamma mind speaking of it to me. Grandmamma wanted me to see nothing but the bright side. But I know more than she told me. I know very well that if you make me my fortune, then I must have my photograph in the papers, go to the Battle of Flowers and to the races at Deauville. When we quarrel, *Gil Blas* and *Paris en amour* will tell the whole story. When you throw me over once and for all, as you did Gentiane des Cevennes when you'd had enough of her—"

"What! You've heard about that? They've bothered you with all those old stories?"

She gave a solemn little nod.

"Grandmamma and Aunt Alicia. They've taught me that you're world famous. I know too that Maryse Chuquet stole your letters, and you brought an action against her. I know that Countess Pariewsky was angry with you, because you didn't want to marry a *divorcée,* and she tried to shoot you. I know what all the world knows."

Lachaille put his hand on Gilberte's knee.

"Those are not the things we have to talk about together, Gigi. All that's in the past. All that's over and done with."

"Of course, Tonton, until it begins again. It's not your fault if you're world famous. But I haven't got a world-famous sort of nature. So it won't do for me."

In pulling at the hem of her skirt, she caused Lachaille's hand to slip off her knee.

"Aunt Alicia and Grandmamma are on your side. But as it concerns me a little, after all, I think you must allow me to say a word on the subject. And my word is, that it won't do for me."

She got up and walked about the room. Gaston Lachaille's silence seemed to embarrass her. She punctuated her wanderings with, "After all, it's true, I suppose! No, it really won't do!"

"I should like to know," said Gaston at last, "whether you're not just trying to hide from me the fact that you dislike me. If you dislike me, you had better say so at once."

"Oh no, Tonton, I don't dislike you at all! I'm always delighted to see you! I'll prove it by making a suggestion in my turn. You could go on coming here as usual, even more often. No one would see any harm in it, since you're a friend of the family. You could go on bringing me liquorice, champagne on my birthdays, and on Sunday we should have an extra special game of piquet. Wouldn't that be a pleasant little life? A life without all this business of sleeping in your bed and everybody knowing about it, losing strings of pearls, being photographed all the time and having to be so careful."

She was absentmindedly twisting a strand of hair round her nose, and pulled it so tight that she snuffled and the tip of her nose turned purple.

"A very pretty little life, as you say," interrupted Gaston Lachaille. "You're forgetting one thing only, Gigi, and that is, I'm in love with you."

"Oh!" she cried, "you never told me that."

"Well," he owned uneasily, "I'm telling you now."

She remained standing before him, silent and breathing

fast. There was no concealing her embarrassment; the rise and fall of her bosom under the tight bodice, the hectic flush high on her cheeks, and the quivering of her close-pressed lips—albeit ready to open again and taste of life.

"That's quite another thing!" she cried at last. "But then you are a terrible man! You're in love with me, and you want to drag me into a life where I'll have nothing but worries, where everyone gossips about everyone else, where the papers print nasty stories. You're in love with me, and you don't care a fig if you let me in for all sorts of horrible adventures, ending in separations, quarrels, Sandomirs, revolvers, and lau . . . and laudanum."

She burst into violent sobs, which made as much noise as a fit of coughing. Gaston put his arms round her to bend her toward him like a branch, but she escaped and took refuge between the wall and the piano.

"But listen, Gigi! Listen to me!"

"Never! I never want to see you again! I should never have believed it of you. You're not in love with me, you're a wicked man! Go away from here!"

She shut him out from sight by rubbing her eyes with closed fists. Gaston had moved over to her and was trying to discover some place on her well-guarded face where he could kiss her. But his lips found only the point of a small chin wet with tears. At the sound of sobbing, Madame Alvarez had hurried in. Pale and circumspect, she had stopped in hesitation at the door to the kitchen.

"Good gracious, Gaston!" she said. "What on earth's the matter with her?"

"The matter!" said Lachaille. "The matter is that she doesn't want to."

"She doesn't want to!" repeated Madame Alvarez. "What do you mean, she doesn't want to?"

"No, she doesn't want to. I speak plainly enough, don't I?"

"No. I don't want to," whimpered Gigi.

Madame Alvarez looked at her granddaughter in a sort of terror.

"Gigi! It's enough to drive one raving mad! But I told you, Gigi. Gaston, as God is my witness, I told her—"

"You have told her too much!" cried Lachaille.

He turned his face toward the child, looking just a poor, sad, lovesick creature, but all he saw of her was a slim back shaken by sobs and a disheveled head of hair.

"Oh!" he exclaimed hoarsely, "I've had enough of this!" and he went out, banging the door.

The next day, at three o'clock, Aunt Alicia, summoned by *pneumatique,* stepped out from her hired brougham. She climbed the stairs up to the Alvarez' floor—pretending to the shortness of breath proper to someone with a weak heart—and noiselessly pushed open the door which her sister had left on the latch.

"Where's the child?"

"In her room. Do you want to see her?"

"There's plenty of time. How is she?"

"Very calm."

Alicia shook two angry little fists.

"Very calm! She has pulled the roof down about our heads, and she is very calm! These young people of today!"

Once again she raised her spotted veil and withered her sister with a single glance.

"And you, standing there, what do you propose doing?"

With a face like a crumpled rose, she sternly confronted the large pallid face of her sister, whose retort was mild in the extreme.

"What do I propose doing? How do you mean? I can't, after all, tie the child up!" Her burdened shoulders rose on a long sigh. "I surely have not deserved such children as these!"

"While you stand there wringing your hands, Lachaille has rushed away from here and in such a state that he may do something idiotic!"

"And even without his straw hat," said Madame Alvarez. "He got into his motor bareheaded! The whole street might have seen him!"

"If I were to be told that by this time he's already become

engaged, or is busy making it up with Liane, it would not surprise me in the least!"

"It is a moment fraught with destiny," said Madame Alvarez lugubriously.

"And afterward, how did you speak to that little brat?"

Madame Alvarez pursed her lips.

"Gigi may be a bit scatterbrained in certain things and backward for her age, but she's not what you say. A young girl who has held the attention of Monsieur Lachaille is not a little brat."

A furious shrug of the shoulders sent Alicia's black lace quivering.

"All right, all right! With all due respect, then, how did you handle your precious princess?"

"I talked sense to her. I spoke to her of the family. I tried to make her understand that we sink or swim together. I enumerated all the things she could do for herself and for us."

"And what about nonsense? Did you talk nonsense to her? Didn't you talk to her of love, travel, moonlight, Italy? You must know how to harp on every string. Didn't you tell her that on the other side of the world the sea is phosphorescent, that there are hummingbirds in all the flowers, and that you make love under gardenias in full bloom beside a moonlit fountain?"

Madame Alvarez looked at her spirited elder sister with sadness in her eyes.

"I couldn't tell her all that, Alicia, because I know nothing about it. I've never been further afield than Cabourg and Monte Carlo."

"Aren't you capable of inventing it?"

"No, Alicia."

Both fell silent. Alicia, with a gesture, made up her mind.

"Call the chit in to me. We shall see."

When Gilberte came in, Aunt Alicia had resumed all the airs and graces of a frivolous old lady and was smelling the tea rose pinned near her chin.

"Good afternoon, my little Gigi."

"Good afternoon, Aunt Alicia."

"What is this Inez has been telling me? You have an admirer? And *what* an admirer! For your first attempt, it's a masterstroke!"

Gilberte acquiesced with a guarded, resigned little smile. She offered to Alicia's darting curiosity a fresh young face, to which the violet-blue shadow on her eyelids and the high color of her mouth gave an almost artificial effect. For coolness' sake, she had dragged back the hair off her temples with the help of two combs, and this drew up the corners of her eyes.

"And it seems you have been playing the naughty girl, and tried your claws on Monsieur Lachaille! Bravo, my brave little girl!"

Gilberte raised incredulous eyes to her aunt.

"Yes, indeed! Bravo! It will only make him all the happier when you are nice to him again."

"But I am nice to him, Aunt. Only, I don't want to, that's all."

"Yes, yes, we know. You've sent him packing to his sugar refinery, that's perfect. But don't send him to the Devil, he's quite capable of going. The fact is, you don't love him."

Gilberte gave a little childish shrug.

"Yes, Aunt, I'm very fond of him."

"Just what I said, you don't love him. Mind you, there's no harm in that, it leaves you free to act as you please. Ah, if you'd been head over heels in love with him, then I should have been a little anxious. Lachaille is a fine figure of a man. Well built — you've only to look at the photographs of him taken at Deauville in bathing costume. He's famous for that. Yes, I should feel sorry for you, my poor Gigi. To start by having a passionate love affair — to go away all by your two selves to the other side of the world, forgetting everything in the arms of the man who adores you, listening to the song of love in an eternal spring — surely things of that sort must touch your heart! What does all that say to you?"

"It says to me that when the eternal spring is over Monsieur Lachaille will go off with another lady. Or else that the lady — me if you like — will leave Monsieur Lachaille, and Monsieur Lachaille will hurry off to blab the whole story. And then the lady, still me if you like, will have nothing else to do but get into another gentleman's bed. I don't want that. I'm not changeable by nature, indeed I'm not."

She crossed her arms over her breasts and shivered slightly.

"Grandmamma, may I have a *cachet faivre*? I want to go to bed, I feel cold."

"You great goose!" burst out Aunt Alicia, "a silly little milliner's shop is all you deserve! Be off, go and marry a bank clerk!"

"If you wish it, Aunt. But I want to go to bed."

Madame Alvarez put her hand on Gigi's forehead.

"Don't you feel well?"

"I'm all right, Grandmamma. Only I'm sad."

She leaned her head on Madame Alvarez' shoulder, and, for the first time in her life, closed her eyes pathetically like a grown woman. The two sisters exchanged glances.

"You must know, my Gigi," said Madame Alvarez, "that we won't torment you to that extent. If you say you really don't want to — "

"A failure is a failure," said Alicia caustically. "We can't go on discussing it forever."

"You'll never be able to say you didn't have good advice and the very best at that," said Madame Alvarez.

"I know, Grandmamma, but I'm sad, all the same."

"Why?"

A tear trickled over Gilberte's downy cheek without wetting it, but she did not answer. A brisk peel of the doorbell made her jump where she stood.

"Oh, it must be him," she said. "It is him! Grandmamma, I don't want to see him! Hide me, Grandmamma!"

At the low, passionate tone of her voice, Aunt Alicia raised an attentive head, and pricked an expert ear. Then she ran to open the door and came back a moment later. Gaston Lachaille, haggard, his eyes bloodshot, followed close behind her.

"Good afternoon, Mamita. Good afternoon, Gigi!" he said airily. "Please don't move, I've come to retrieve my straw hat."

None of the three women replied, and his assurance left him.

"Well, you might at least say a word to me, even if it's only How-d'you-do?"

Gilberte took a step toward him.

"No," she said, "You've not come to retrieve your straw hat. You have another one in your hand. And you would never bother about a hat. You've come to make me more miserable than ever."

"Really!" burst out Madame Alvarez. "This is more than I can stomach. How can you, Gigi! Here is a man who, out of the goodness of his generous heart — "

"If you please, Grandmamma, just a moment, and I shall have finished."

Instinctively she straightened her dress, adjusted the buckle of her sash, and marched up to Gaston.

"I've been thinking, Gaston. In fact, I've been thinking a great deal — "

He interrupted her, to stop her saying what he was afraid to hear.

"I swear to you, my darling — "

"No, don't swear to me. I've been thinking I would rather be miserable with you than without you. So . . ."

She tried twice to go on.

"So. . . . There you are. How d'you do, Gaston, how d'you do?"

She offered him her cheek, in her usual way. He held her, a little longer than usual, until he felt her relax, and become calm and gentle in his arms. Madame Alvarez seemed about to hurry forward, but Alicia's impatient little hand restrained her.

"Leave well alone. Don't meddle anymore. Can't you see she is far beyond us?"

She pointed to Gigi, who was resting a trusting head and

the rich abundance of her hair on Lachaille's shoulder.

The happy man turned to Madame Alvarez.

"Mamita," he said, "will you do me the honor, the favor, give me the infinite joy of bestowing on me the hand . . ."

JULIE DE CARNEILHAN

Translated by Patrick Leigh Fermor

MME. DE CARNEILHAN turned off the gas, leaving the earthenware saucepan on the stove. Beside the stove she laid out the Empire teacup, the Swedish spoon and the rye bread folded in a rough silk Turkish napkin. The smell of hot chocolate made her yawn with hunger, for she had not eaten much for luncheon — a cold pork cutlet, a slice of bread and butter, half a pound of red currants and a cup of excellent coffee. During the meal she had worked away at a triangular cushion, cut out of an old pair of faded gray corduroy riding breeches. A fine-linked steel chain, which had once belonged, so Julie de Carneilhan said, to a monkey (though according to her brother the monkey had belonged to the chain), was to be sewn on one side of the cushion in the shape of a C, or possibly a J. "C would be easier to sew, but J is more decorative: it'll look terrific," she said to herself.

She put the lid on the steaming saucepan, mopped the kitchen slab with a cloth, and then filled the milk can with water and shut the dustbin. Feeling that she had lived up to her principles as the perfect housewife, she went into the studio. In front of a looking glass in the hall, she put on a certain expression, a sort of contraction of the nostrils, to which she was specially attached. It accentuated, she maintained, the "wild animal" side of her character.

Thinking that she heard voices on the stairs, Julie hurriedly put on her hat and a light overcoat the color of her ash-blond hair, which she wore cut short and curled *à la Caracalla.* She threw down a pair of not quite clean gloves, and picked them up again — "Good enough to go to the pictures in" — then switched off two of the four lights, and sat down to wait in the best armchair. "This is the last time," she thought as she glanced round the studio, "that I'll ever do up a room in red and blue. The color positively eats up the light, and costs the earth in electricity!"

One of the walls was red, one gray, and the other two were blue. The furniture was an odd mixture of style, the effect slightly too colonial, perhaps, but not unpleasing. The room was encumbered with a twelve-sided bronze tray table from Indochina, an armchair of South African oxhide, bits of tooled leather from Fez, and basketwork which had originally been plaited round English tobacco tins by the natives of the Gold Coast. The rest of the furniture was good eighteenth-century work, but it remained on its legs only because Mme. de Carneilhan's strong, deft hands were clever with gluepot and pegs, and could even, when necessary, slide thin metal rods inside old bamboo and the broken chair legs.

She waited ten minutes. Her patience came from fundamental humility. Her training and a superficial pride made her sit upright in her chair.

The studio gained depth from a long, unframed looking glass. She looked with pleasure at the reflection of her well-set neck, at her bust which stubbornly retained its shape and firmness. A sheaf of dog whips and riding switches, valued as collector's pieces because they came from the Caucasus or Siberia, hung down in coils over the looking glass.

Julie de Carneilhan resumed work on the cushion, boldly marking out the lines of the letter. And then suddenly she lost heart. "It's no good," she thought; "it would be hideous."

After ten minutes of waiting, Julie's proud and charming nose and her small, well-defined mouth began to twitch nervously, and two large tears sparkled in the corners of her blue eyes. Her spirits revived at the sound of the bell, and she ran to the door.

"This is a fine time to come! It's no good trying to get round me, I loathe people who . . ."

She drew back and her voice changed.

"Oh, it's you."

"Yes, it's me. May I come in?"

"Have I ever kept you out?"

"Oh, once or twice — perhaps three times. Are you going out?"

"Yes. I'm waiting for some friends, that is, and they're disgustingly late."

"It's wretched weather, you know."

Léon de Carneilhan pulled off his gloves and rubbed his hands together. They were tanned by his open-air life and polished by everyday contact with bridles. As he passed the looking glass he contracted his nostrils like his sister, and, with his fair graying hair and blue eyes, this underlined the resemblance between them.

"What are you up to with those old breeches of mine?"

"Making a cushion. Do you mind?"

"It's too late to mind, seeing you've already cut them up."

His presence exuded an atmosphere of absentminded distrust, and Julie scrutinized him with a similar look of suspicion. They lighted their cigarettes with the same match.

"Do you mind if I leave you?" Julie said. "I'm going to the pictures."

"I'm afraid I've come at an awkward time," Carneilhan said. Her only answer was a vague shrug. He then turned on his sister. Judging horseflesh had given his eyes a keen look, and her eyes, though softened by her makeup, wore an identical expression.

"Your husband is very ill."

"You don't say so!" said Julie in tones of mock horror. "Poor old Becker!"

"No, not Becker. Your second, Espivant."

For a moment she remained motionless, her mouth half open.

"How do you mean, Espivant?" she asked in a hesitant

voice. "He was out and about yesterday, talking of a question he intended to ask in the *Chambre.* I heard that from one of the barmen at Maxim's who used to be my butler. What's wrong with him?"

"He suddenly collapsed, flat on his face, and had to be carried home."

"What about his wife? What's she got to say about it?"

"Nobody knows. It only happened at three this afternoon."

"She's probably letting down her long tresses and beseeching a last kiss while counting her rows of pearls with the other hand." They both gave a short laugh and continued smoking in silence. Julie blew the smoke out through her narrow and faultless nostrils.

"Do you think he'll die?"

Léon struck his bony knees with his hand. "How should I know? You might as well ask me to whom he'll leave the money that Marianne brought him in the marriage settlement."

"I bet it was the only way of getting him to make up his mind," said Julie with a grin.

"You may laugh, my dear. But think of Marianne's money and her looks! Herbert might well be tempted by less than that."

"Might be? He was," Julie said.

"You're too modest."

She lifted her smooth arrogant nose. "I'm not talking about me! I mean Galatée des Conches, and that idiot Beatrix."

Léon wagged his head with an experienced air. He was a fair-haired, fierce, and aging man, who had had great success with women.

"Beatrix is not bad, not bad at all."

"Do you know, I'm rather bored by the whole business," said Julie shortly.

She put on her gloves, and, straightening her little hat of plaited felt, made it quite clear that she wished to see the last of her visitor.

"Tell me, Julie," Léon went on reflectively, "has Herbert been feeling friendly to you these last months?"

"Friendly? Yes. As with all the women he drops. He's always one move behind in his friendliness."

"Much more so with you than with the others. Didn't he pay your debts when he remarried?"

"What nonsense. I only had about twenty-two thousand francs' worth. One can't run up debts any more. Everything's cash nowadays."

"Supposing he leaves you a token of his friendship, a really solid one, when he dies!"

Julie's blue eyes assumed an expression of childish credulity.

"No? Do you really think he might die?"

"Of course I don't! I only said supposing when he died, he left you . . ."

Julie had stopped listening. She was running through her furniture in her mind, banishing her Colonial freaks and her Louis XIV relics, planning a change of house, a bathroom in yellow and black. She was not really grasping, only improvident and rather careless.

"Listen, my dear, I'm going out, as my young friends haven't put in an appearance. I'm going to the pictures."

"Do you really think you should? The news of Herbert's illness is already in the later edition of the evening papers. *'The physicians have so far issued no statement as to the gravity of the sudden illness which at five o'clock overcame the Comte d'Espivant, right-wing Deputy. . . .'* "

"What about it? Am I expected to put on mourning in advance for a man who was unfaithful to me for eight years and has been married again for another three?"

"It makes no difference. You were the wife people talked about. You can bet that everyone tonight has forgotten Marianne and is asking how Julie de Carneilhan is taking it."

"Do you really think so? You may be right."

Flattered by the thought, she smiled and brushed back a

pretty little lock of hair that half covered her ear. But at the sound of a footfall on the stairs and loud laughter she at once became nervous and flustered.

"Do you hear that? They were supposed to pick me up at a quarter past eight. It's turned nine, and there they are kicking up a row on the stairs. Aren't people awful nowadays? What a crew!"

"Who are they?"

Julie shrugged her shoulders.

"Nobody. Some young friends of mine."

"Our sort of age?"

She gave him a long, challenging look.

"My dear, would you expect them to be!"

"Well for Heaven's sake, drop them for this evening."

She blushed, and tears came to her eyes.

"No, no, I won't! Why should I remain all alone when everybody else is having fun? There is a very good film at the Marboeuf and the program changes tomorrow."

She protested as though she were struggling against some violent danger, and flogged the arm of her chair with her gloves. Her brother contemplated her with a kind of bad-tempered patience. He was used to dealing with mares that were far more intractable.

"Listen to me. Don't behave like an idiot. It's only for this evening, and who knows if Herbert . . ."

'But I don't *care* about Herbert. I don't see why I should in any way concern myself each time he catches a chill! I forbid you to mention it in front of my friends."

"What do you bet they don't already know? There goes the bell. Shall I let them in?"

"No, no. I'll go."

She ran to the door like a little girl. Léon de Carneilhan, pricking his ears, could hear only his sister's voice.

"Ah! So there you are, only an hour late! Come on in; we can't stand talking here."

Two women and a young man came in without a word.

"My brother, the Comte de Carneilhan, Madame Encelade,

Mademoiselle Lucie Albert, Monsieur Vatard, my brother, the Comte de Carneilhan. No, don't sit down. What have you got to say for yourselves?"

M. Vatard and Mme. Encelade tacitly delegated the spokesmanship to Mlle. Lucie Albert, who seemed the shyest of the three, her eyes were so enormous.

"We weren't going to come. I said we ought to telephone. . . . We read in the papers that . . . that the Count was ill. . . ."

Julie, unwillingly admitting defeat, shot a glance at her brother, and the three newcomers did the same. In answer to these deferential glances, Léon de Carneilhan put on the expression that his sister called "the mask of a fox that has betrayed its king by hunting with humans." But Julie gave up the struggle.

"My dears, it can't be helped," she declared. "Herbert and I got ourselves talked about far too much for his illness not to draw a certain amount of attention to me. So . . ."

"I understand," said Coco Vatard.

"You're not the only one who understands," said Mme. Encelade tartly. "Lucie and I understand too."

"I'll give you a ring tomorrow."

"Is there anything I can do to help?" asked Lucie Albert.

"Nothing, darling. You're an angel. Let's all meet again soon, dears. I'll see you out."

From the studio Carneilhan could hear the four of them laughing and talking in low voices. One of the three women called Coco Vatard a crackpot, and then the door closed.

Her brother displayed no surprise when Julie returned. He knew of old the sudden weaknesses of this beautiful creature: she flouted public opinion, emerged cool and serene from conjugal disasters, and put up with the makeshift existence of a woman living without money or help, but was unable to miss a treat, to which she'd been looking forward, without crying a little and bowing her shoulders and suddenly looking her age.

"My poor Julie, won't you ever change?"

She sat upright. Her eyes were wet but furious.

"I'm not 'your poor Julie' for a start! You stick to selling old hacks and young pigs and leave me alone!"

"Shall I take you out to dinner somewhere?"

"No!"

"Have you got anything in the flat?"

"I've got some chocolate. . . ."

"To eat?"

"What a horrid thought! No; to drink. I was going to have it when I came home. You know, young people are quite capable of dropping you at your door after the pictures without so much as giving you a drink. They're like that. There are some plums, and three eggs . . . yes, and some tinned tunny and a lettuce."

"Any whiskey?"

"Of course. That's one thing I've always got."

"It's started raining. Would you like me to go?"

She caught at her brother with a gesture of alarm.

"No; please don't!"

"Well, let's try and soften the shock we've had! I'll lend you a hand. How do you want the eggs?"

"Don't care."

"I'll do you a tunny omelet. Put the chocolate on the stove for afterward."

Gaily, as though armed against the worst by a frivolity that closely resembled courage (and which frequently promoted it), they forgot everything except getting their meal ready. They set about it with the skill and competitiveness of overgrown Boy Scouts. Léon de Carneilhan discovered the remains of some crème d'Isigny, and poured it into the salad. He tied a red-striped towel round his waist under his coat, and Julie took off her dress and put on a dressing gown. They escaped all trace of absurdity by the deftness of their movements, their long and unself-conscious practice in handling humble everyday objects. While Léon was beating the eggs for the omelet, Julie laid the card table with two blue and two red plates, a handsome decanter and a rather ugly jug, and, then, putting a small pot of bright blue lobelias between the places, cried, "That looks grand!"

The gusto with which they ate had its roots in their indestructible appetites and digestions. In their friendship they were like two of a litter that can never play together without leaving traces of tooth and claw, wounding each other in the most sensitive places. Neither of them complained about their frugal supper; they rose nourished, but without having eaten their fill. The plates were replaced by ashtrays and cards. Relaxed at last, Julie answered all her brother's questions with a good grace. A rainy draft from the window stirred her ringlets; and from her brother's "traitor-fox" look, she perceived that the arrogant carriage of her head, her blue eyes, so prompt to sparkle with tears, and the radiance of her downy complexion and her hair, made her still the beautiful Julie de Carneilhan. Julie de Carneilhan, as people, in spite of a couple of marriages and divorces, still called her.

Léon had taken off his coat. He never wore a waistcoat and he felt stifled the moment he was confined in a room. The body under the shirt was lean and hard—all table corners, Julie called it—a body almost numb to feeling and pitilessly ill-treated by its owner.

"How are the ducks going, Léon?"

"Badly. If only I hadn't got those wretched little pigs on my hands! I've sent one of the brood mares back to Père Carneilhan. Henrietta, the bay."

"Sent it back? By train?"

"No fear. By road. Gayant rode her."

"Lucky chap! I'd have loved to have ridden her there for you."

"You're too busy," said Carneilhan, not without irony. "It took him twelve days. He and the mare slept in the fields, a blanket apiece. She stuffed herself with all the oats she came across on the way! They'd have been in the soup if anybody'd caught them. Gayant's fodder was bread and cheese and garlic. She was so fat when they arrived that Père Carneilhan thought she was in foal, and Gayant had to disillusion him."

"When was all this?"

"In June."

Without more words, they both fell into a daydream of

roads in June running through the green oat fields. Thinking of the lulling gait of the mare, the cool freshness between four and eight o'clock in the morning, the little rhythmical creak of the saddle and the first red streak of sunlight over the squat towers of Carneilhan, Julie felt her eyes growing moist once again. She flung a quick malevolent glance at her brother.

"It's very odd, when you're in shirt-sleeves, you look like a cavalry lieutenant who's taken to the bottle."

"Thanks."

"Don't mention it, dear."

"I mean thanks for 'lieutenant.' Who on earth's that chap you call Coco Vatard?"

"Nothing. Just somebody with a motorcar."

"A flame?"

"No."

"What about the girl, the one you called an angel? Is she your fancy?"

"Heavens no," sighed Julie. "I'm absolutely heart-whole. I think my life's heading for a big change. She's a very interesting little thing; a pianist and cashier in a nightclub, and today's her night off."

"It's none of my business, Julie, but what exactly would you do if you had any money?"

"Oh, thousands of idiotic things," said Julie haughtily. "Why?"

"Well, this Herbert affair. I can't help thinking about it, that's all."

She put her hand on her brother's arm, and he looked at it as though taken unawares by the fraternal gesture.

"It's not worth worrying about. That flighty line of his took us all in. If he dies, he dies. No one will see the color of any money that he has."

"You're talking like a fortune-teller."

Julie's eyes lit up.

"Oh, my dear, I know one! It's priceless. She tells your fortune in melted candlewax! She told me, all in one sitting, that another war would break out, that I should have a sensational meeting and that Marianne would die of cancer."

"Marianne? How did you know she was talking about Marianne?"

The blood flowed into Julie's cheeks. She was splendid in attack, but inclined to lose her head when she was on the defensive.

"Why, I understood perfectly well from her description. It's the kind of thing you feel."

"How did you know she was talking about Marianne?" repeated Léon. "Tell me, or I'll tickle you up and down your spine!"

"Pax! I'll tell you, I promise!" Julie cried in haste. "Well, it was Toni. . . ."

"Toni? Marianne's son?"

"Yes. I asked him, my dear—we're on the best of terms—I asked him to pinch one of his mother's silk stockings, when she took them off before going to bed. You see, the candle woman has to have something worn by the person concerned."

"And did he bring it?"

Julie nodded.

"What a queer family," said Carneilhan. "It's all rather comic," he went on lightly. "It's getting late, and I must be on my way, old girl. It's an hour past midnight."

"How small . . ." said Julie.

"How do you mean, small?"

"Only that people always talk about 'the small hours.' Ha! ha ha!"

She burst out laughing, and he realized that she was slightly tipsy. But she managed to walk steadily as far as the window.

"There's still a taxi on the rank. Shall I whistle for it?"

"Don't bother. I'll walk back. It's not raining."

She did not insist. Her brother often walked back to Saint Cloud, crossing the Bois de Boulogne with a tireless stride. One night, at the approach of an ugly-looking customer, he had jumped straight into a thicket with a leap of such length and swiftness that the stranger, frightened out of his wits, had taken to his heels. He loved the hours of the night as day began to break, always got home before six, and his horses started to whinny expectantly while he was still a long way off.

He shook Julie's hand in a vague manner and made off toward the thing he cared for most in the world: the shrill whinny of his faithful mares, and the friendly language of their great affectionate lips close to their master's expert ear.

"It must be Friday," thought Mme. de Carneilhan, still half asleep. "I can smell fish."

There was a large general grocer's shop at the corner of the street. When Julie had taken the lease of the "studio with every modern comfort" she had sacrificed smartness to convenience, a bargain she never ceased regretting, especially on fish days, cabbage days, and melon days.

The presence of the daily cleaning woman washing up in the kitchen–bathroom indicated that it was only about half-past nine, so Julie went to sleep again; but not without twinges of guilt dating from her earliest childhood, when she had been used to sharp little cuts with a riding crop from her father's stern but equitable hand. In those days Julie and Léon, barefoot and in silence, used to fight in front of the door (which opened ineluctably at seven in winter and six in summer) to avoid being beaten the first. Well warmed up and still tingling, they put on their sole-worn shoes without an atom of rancor, and threw themselves upon the backs of their ponies and galloped to catch up with the Comte de Carneilhan. Their father would be mounted on a Breton nag with a back like a basket, or on a bag of bones as high as a church, or even on a saddled cow. She was a light-colored animal, as fair as himself, oat-fed and fiery-eyed, and she cocked up her tail when she took the jumps with her teats swinging to and fro like bell clappers. He used to ride her just to demonstrate what he could get out of anything with hooves and flat teeth, and to draw attention to himself at the horse fairs and important market days in Périgord.

On such days he lent Julie and Léon the pick of his stable. Having set out from Carneilhan on horseback, the children often had to trudge home with their saddles on their shoulders or get a lift in a peasant's cart, their smart appearance and good seats having helped to sell the ponies on the spot. For a time they would remain obdurate and embittered, shedding secret tears for the little horse they had loved. But, as they grew up, they developed a taste for these frequent changes of mount. And when, at the age of seventeen, Julie de Carneilhan married a rich man from Holland called Julius Becker, she was not particularly worried. "I'll change him," she thought vaguely to herself, "next market day."

As other people dream longingly of university degrees or legal briefs, Julie would often dream that she was on horseback. Mme. Encelade, who was given to interpreting dreams, declared: "That means that you ought to go to bed with somebody."

"No it doesn't," Julie insisted. "It simply means that I want to be on horseback."

And she would plan to borrow her brother's mare, Hirondelle. But the next morning she would wake up late, and fall into a brown study. Léon, what's more, refused to lend her Hirondelle, and suggested Tullia—a quiet, uninteresting, sure-footed animal, compact of all the virtues of a nursery governess. Julie was on her dignity at once.

"My dear boy, you don't expect me to appear in the Bois on a dappled mare?"

The water, as it gurgled into the bath in the kitchen next to the studio, set the narrow partition shaking musically. "Ten o'clock!" Julie got out of bed and pulled her pajama belt tight. Feeling well and sprightly, with a clean taste on her tongue and throat, she remembered that she had been drinking the night before. Spirits treated her mercifully, as they did Père Carneilhan. They cleared her complexion and her brain. She could boast without lying that never a drop of syrupy liqueur had been allowed to pass the barrier of her mouth. Her teeth were healthy and unevenly set, the two middle incisors being on the large side and the two others smaller and slanting slightly backward.

"I'm going to dip my teeth in a glass of water," she would say in the morning, and then go and drink a tumblerful at the kitchen tap. This family catch phrase, she was in the habit of telling her friends, had cost her the affections of a good-looking lieutenant she had hardly got to work on; failing to catch the joke, he had assumed that she wore a set of false teeth.

She stopped in front of the looking glass and screwed up her nose. Sleep had put all her ringlets out of curl: they stood out stiffly all over her head like bits of straw.

"I look as though I'd been sleeping in the stables," she observed to herself. She stopped again to telephone, and listened motionlessly to the prolonged ringing tone at the other end. "Hello? Hello? . . . Really, what a bore this is! What? M. Vatard has gone out? Already? Good, thank you." Grimacing scornfully, she pulled a stray slipper toward her with her big toe. "Oh dear, oh dear, that boy and his beastly factory . . ." and made for the part of the kitchen curtained off by a waterproof hanging fitted to a rod, and known as the bathroom.

An electric stove with two rings was fitted to the top of a cupboard beside the bath. When the cleaning woman was out, Mme. de Carneilhan could have her bath and keep an eye on her breakfast at the same time. She had retained, from a childhood steeped in assured if penurious family pride, a profound lack of bashfulness and a total disregard for the presence of servants. "Stir up the water for me, Peyre," she used to shout to the kitchen gardener at Carneilhan when she was thirteen, fourteen, fifteen years old. The man would then beat the surface of the fishpond by the spring, for Julie could not bear the sinuous, invisible creatures that haunted its depths. Then she would shout: "Turn round and look the other way!" and throwing off her dress, slip into the water—

it was warm on top, but ice-cold lower down—swim round a bit and then get out, as oblivious of the man who beat the water for her as she was of her own beauty.

"Good morning to you, Madame du Sabrier," she called to her daily woman in tones of mock ceremony as she pulled off her crumpled pajamas.

Before getting into the bath, she did some deep breathing exercises and a few knee bends like a dancer. Disapproving of naked beauty, Mme. Sabrier turned the other way.

"Are you having lunch in, Madame? What would you like to eat?"

"I'd like—let me see—cream cheese and skate in black butter. The black and white together would look particularly smart."

She laughed under a helmet of lather. When she was in her bath, Julie soaped herself all over, including her head, like a man.

Mme. Sabrier heaved a deep sigh.

"It's not fair. There's no justice in the world," she said. "You were up drinking last night, weren't you? I saw the glasses. And there you are, spry as a goldfish. And I've never drunk a drop, and here am I all doubled up. And you are forty-four, too. . . . It's not fair. . . ."

"I don't want to seem inquisitive, but I'd like to know the name of the pig who told you how old I was?"

Mme. Sabrier smiled at last.

"Well now! I've got my little ways and means, Madame. It was the chauffeur who brought a letter for you one day. A chauffeur from the left bank of the river."

"So that's how they behave on the left bank? They'll catch it when I get at them. Give me my dressing gown."

"Now don't you go making wet footmarks all over my clean floor, please. He told me he got it from your first husband."

"It's Herbert's chauffeur," thought Julie as she went out. She stopped at the doorway—she made "good exits" through force of habit—and said "My second, Madame Sabrier. My second husband. And not the last either!"

"It's not fair," sighed Mme. Sabrier. "Here are your newspapers."

"Dead? Or not? If he's dead, it'll be on the front page." Clutching the papers in her wet hand, she went and sat on her bed. "Nobody on the front page. He must be just ill on page two: What did I say? *'We are happy to announce that the sudden illness of the Comte d'Espivant appears to offer no cause for alarm.'* " "There," Julie cried out loud, "I was sure of it! I could have gone to the pictures after all! The dirty dog! And Professors Hattoutant and Giscard at his bedside, if you please! Marianne must be getting worried about her source of . . ."

She threw the paper aside and opened the only cupboard in the studio, which she had lined with looking glass as a makeup cabinet and fitted with electric light. She was clever with her fingers and impulsively attacked any job in hand; but she soon grew bored and her unfinished handiwork would remain as a series of little monuments to her skill and her inconstancy.

"A chauffeur from the left bank," she thought. "That must have been my old Beaupied bringing a letter from Toni. It's Toni's fault. . . . What a nuisance boys of that age are! He decided he wanted to see me, and who does he send with the letter? His stepfather's chauffeur! Herbert has a mania for keeping on his chauffeurs till they fall to bits. He thinks that what was 'aristocratic' where coachmen were concerned now applies to mechanics."

She brushed her wet hair back till it lay flat against her scalp. Taken unawares like this, with nothing on her face and plunged in disgruntled thoughts, Julie resembled her brother in certain characteristics—a wild look, with narrowing temples and the chin and jawbone fining down into a muzzle. But everything was redeemed by her nose and a rosy coloring that could stand up to anything. She dabbed a patch of face cream on her delicious nose, and spread it on with her forefinger. She made herself up with skill, plucked a couple of hairs from her upper lip, curled her hair with lively twists of the hand. "I'll walk in the Bois for a bit," she said to herself. "I won't put on my lizard-skin shoes, or they won't last out the year."

She ran to answer the telephone, cursing jubilantly to herself. She did this whenever her restless indolence and overencumbered solitude were forced into action.

"Hello? Is that you, Coco? Does that mean that it's past twelve and you've got away from the office? Oh! What rotten luck. . . . I wanted to go for a tremendous walk. What? No, I wanted to go today. Tomorrow's not the same thing at all. What? Herbert? He's better, of course. All he cares about is being a nuisance to other people. All right, tonight then, but I loathe having to wait for anything I enjoy. What? My dear boy, who on earth do you think you're talking to? See you this evening." She put the receiver back and broke into a little urchin-like smile that put years on her all at once. She quickly resumed her serious expression and became once more a tempestuous and masterful blond. In five minutes' time she was dressed in a white tailored shirt, a skirt with a pattern of black and white birds' feet, and a black jacket that flouted every current fashion. Her slightly overdone trimness betrayed the fact that Julie de Carneilhan was approaching the age when women decide to sacrifice their faces to their figures.

"I ought to have a purple carnation. Ten francs . . . no joke at the moment." She rummaged among her handkerchiefs and found a small one of mauve crepe which she twisted into the shape of a flower. She snipped at it deftly with her scissors and then frilled it out in her buttonhole. "Marvelous!" Then her face clouded over with the same alacrity. "What an idiot I am! The handkerchief cost a whole *louis*." She always reckoned in louis out of smartness and what she called "good form." A cloud drifted across the sky and chased away all desire to go for a walk. "Shall I ring up Lucie? Or find out when the sales begin at Hermès? Or . . ."

She trembled at the sound of the telephone, which started to ring just as she was stretching out her hand for the receiver.

Like many creatures leading an unprotected life, she regarded the telephone as her only source of help.

"Hello! Yes, speaking. What? I can't hear. Would you say it again? Who did you say was speaking?" The tone of her voice altered and her shoulders fell into a slight stoop.

"Is . . . is that you, Herbert? Yes, of course, I read it in the papers like everybody else. So it wasn't anything serious?" She saw herself across the room in the looking glass and sat up straight. "Frightening us all like that! What? Well, *us* means the whole of Paris, my dear, half of France, and a good hunk of abroad."

She laughed, listened for a moment and then stopped laughing.

"Where are you telephoning from? What? Come there, to your house? Oh, nothing. I was going to have luncheon alone. No, nobody. No, of course I'm not saying no, but . . . what about Marianne? All right. Yes. But it's nothing. Don't be absurd. Yes; I'll keep an eye out of the window."

Julie replaced the receiver slowly. She put on a black straw hat that reminded her of her early childhood, and opened the door into the kitchen.

"Madame Sabrier," she said, in an uncertain voice. Then she was suddenly on the alert with her nostrils wide.

"What's that awful stink of fish?"

"Why, it's the skate, Madame. Madame told me. White cheese and black butter."

"But it's frightful. You didn't really think . . ."

The corners of her mouth sank, and she said, in piteous tones: "I only thought I was saying something funny. You can eat your wretched skate. But leave me the cream cheese. I'll buy . . . well, we'll see. . . ."

She sank back into uncertainty, fiddling idly with some oddments on the chimneypiece, and then she went to lean on the windowsill, with one foot resting on top of the other. When a long black motor drew up among the delivery tricycles outside the grocers', Julie pulled herself together and ran downstairs like a girl, feeling all the exhilaration of her firm, slim legs, her light breasts and her freedom from a single ounce of extra flesh.

"Why, of course, it's Beaupied. How are you, Beaupied? You never change a bit."

"Madame la Comtesse flatters me."

"No, Beaupied, really. You're always the same, specially since I can't turn my back on you for five minutes without your telling my charwoman that I'm forty-four!"

"Me? Oh! I can promise your Ladyship . . ."

"Anyway, I'm not forty-four, Beaupied. I'm forty-five. Drive home, would you."

"Er—home," repeated the gray-haired chauffeur. "Which . . . ?"

"Yours," said Mme. de Carneilhan kindly. "Ours, I mean the same one, in the Rue Saint-Sabas."

Once the door was shut, she brought the stern and critical eye of the impecunious to bear on the car. "A real bounder's turnout! They bought it at a motor show. It must have been left over by a Maharajah. Herbert always did have a tendency to buy motor hearses. And all upholstered in pearl gray! Why not mauve satin? And a chauffeur rigged up in summer livery. I suppose one can't have everything—millions and taste as well. . . ." Her critical sense was equally hard upon the cutout flower in her buttonhole. She took it off and threw it out of the window as they drove into the flower-planted courtyard.

Julie had not foreseen the evocative power of the surroundings which she herself had once chosen and loved. Her pulse was thumping in her eardrums, and before shaking her head to the chauffeur when he asked if her ladyship would like to be driven back later, she raised her eyes to the first floor. Her second husband, drawn to the window by the sound of the motorcar, was leaning out and shouting "Two o'clock sharp!" to Beaupied.

"Two o'clock sharp," she repeated to herself, "and the car used to hang about till four! Unless, of course, Herbert slunk off in a taxi to see some wretched girlfriend." She ascended the little flight of steps and went through the door of the hall almost without being aware of it, guided unerringly by the memory of her foot on the stone stairs, her hand on the doorknob. The moment she crossed the threshold, a heavy atmosphere of feminine scent pulled her together. "Marianne's scent . . . too much of it, too much money, too many diamonds, too much hair. . . ." An unexpected irritation sharpened her faculties. On the first floor she thought she caught, through a half-open door, the thread of a brilliant glance, an intake of breath; and the door closed. Her room! A footman paced along in front of her. She expected him to open the door of the study next to Espivant's room, but he asked her to wait in a little room that she could not remember. She could hear Espivant's voice somewhere behind the thin walls, and for a moment she lost all sense of time. The present became meaningless, as if lost in the heart of a dream, yet she was aware that she was dreaming. The footman came back and she followed him.

"Where on earth does Herbert sleep?" she wondered, counting the closed doors. "My room . . . the linen cupboard . . . his room . . . the room we used to call the nursery . . ." She stopped dead all at once with a gesture of despair. "I forgot to change my old shoes!" She almost turned right about and took to her heels. Her calm was restored by a second's consideration. "After all, what does it matter? Well I never, he's gone and settled in the nursery. How very odd!" Her guide vanished and Julie made a fine entrance with her charming nose in the air, her eyes feigning short sight, her small mouth half open in an agreeable but unaffectionate smile, and her gaze focused straight ahead at the level of her eyes. But Herbert's voice rose from a little bed much lower down.

"So I'm reduced to sending for you? It never occurred to you to come and ask how I was?"

His voice was young and cheerful and pitched in a key that Julie was still unable to hear without anger and pain. She lowered her eyes and saw Herbert in bed. She took him in at a glance. "Oh!" she said to herself. "He's done for." The smell of ether, well-known to Julie from many a disreputable haunt, suddenly assumed a terrible significance. It gave her the cue for her words and behavior.

"Herbert," she said, a little too fulsomely. "What's this new stunt of yours, and all this publicity in the papers? And are those pale gray silk pajamas for my benefit? What sort of opinion do you expect me to carry away of a man who interviews me in pale gray silk?"

The hand that Herbert stretched out to her seemed to have thickened. It waved her into a little armchair close to the bed.

"Would you like to smoke?" he said. "You can."

"What about you?"

"Not this morning, my dear. I don't even want to."

She was unable to single out any definite sign of deterioration in Espivant's face. He was "switching on the charm" for her, as he did for everybody, from pure force of habit. But a mysterious process seemed imperceptibly to have puffed up all that had been hollow the day before, and conversely, to have scooped out the convexities of the slim brown Gascon mask. Julie had long realized that his handsome face was merely, under its masculine brow, a collection of slightly effeminate features. But the fire in the light brown eyes, the mouth retaining all its youthful delicacy and the deliberately unfashionable mustache, there they all were before her eyes again, and once again she bit the edge of her tongue to punish herself for still being hurt by them.

"Have you had luncheon yet, Youlka? Do have something with me! Just to please me!"

" 'Just to please me' . . . D, E flat, E natural, A flat. Same phrase on the same notes," thought Julie.

"But . . ." she began, turning toward the door.

"I'm having my tiny luncheon all alone. Marianne, who was up all night—there was not the slightest need for it—is having a rest."

"Just anything, then. Some fruit. . . . It's my day for fruit."

"Lovely. Darling, I'm going to ring. Nobody will disturb us

once they've brought the food. I'll tell you all about my tiresome attack, if you'd like to hear it. But perhaps it would be a bore. Youlka, does being here mean anything to you?"

Julie understood, from the caressing tone of his voice, that he still enjoyed hurting her.

"No," she said coldly.

In came a male nurse, in white, followed by a secretary with a handful of telegrams. Espivant began speaking before the latter could get a word out.

"No, no, Cousteix. Nothing for the moment. You just see to them all, there's a good chap. After all, I *am* ill!" he said with a laugh. "I'll have a look at my letters this evening. Perhaps . . . !"

He propped himself on his fists to hoist himself into a sitting position. The effort lasted only a moment, but his mouth gaped strangely open, and Julie perceived genuine anxiety rather than mere officiousness in the haste with which the nurse ran to help him.

"What a ridiculously narrow bed," Julie reproached him. "It's only about eighty centimeters wide, like a housemaid's!"

The nurse glanced at her approvingly as he left the room. "Sh!" whispered Espivant. "It's all part of my plan! It's my self-defense bed!"

They were still laughing with spiteful complicity when two tables laden with fruit were wheeled in. Julie found it all faultless: late cherries, rose-colored peaches, thin-skinned Marseilles figs, cloudy hothouse grapes that had been carefully protected from the wasps. Iced water and champagne trembled in thick cut-glass jugs, chiseled with a pattern of nailheads. Julie's nostrils opened wide to the fumes of the coffee and the smell of the yellow rose standing next to a pot of fresh cream. She carefully concealed the pleasure she derived from all this luxury.

"Who asked for this ham, Herbert? Nobody wants it."

Espivant made a careless gesture.

"Marianne, I expect. Anything else you want?"

"No, thanks. So Marianne knew that I . . . ?"

"What are you worrying about? Please don't tire me!"

A ray of sunshine fell across the gleaming silver. Herbert chose the best of the peaches, still adorned with its living green leaf, and let it rest in the palm of his hand.

"How lovely it is . . ." he sighed. "Take this one. Do you still drink your coffee while you're eating fruit?"

This reminder of their old life together caught Julie unawares. She flushed, and steadied herself by drinking a glass of champagne.

"How pretty the table looks," she said. "Cherries too! Let me play with all this for a bit; don't you worry about me. Is there some medicine or other you ought to take?"

Espivant, who had cut one of the peaches, left it on his plate. He took a handful of cherries and held them up to the full light.

"Look, they're so clear you can almost see the stones inside! What have I ever had of my own after all? All I'll have to say good-bye to amounts to just about this."

He dropped the cherries and waved toward the little sunlit table. His gesture did not exclude the tall fair-haired woman sitting slantwise in her chair, facing the light, and feeling as happy as a wasp in the sun. She wiped her lips, wrinkling her brows as she did so.

"Good-bye? How do you mean?"

Espivant leaned toward her. As he emerged from the shadow, the strange almost vegetable color of his face became at once apparent, the greenish white of his forehead and temples and of the skin round his mouth. Round his brown eyes were dark circles; so many women, too many women, had painted them there and loved them.

"It's all up with me, Youlka," he said with affected lightness. "No, do let me talk about it! Pour out the coffee. Yes, yes, I'm allowed coffee. Aren't you surprised to see so few doctors 'at my bedside,' as they say? No? What a brute you are; you never notice anything! You don't even notice what a man looks like unless you've got him face to face. And, when I use the expression 'face to face,' it's only because I respect the precincts of a dwelling that matrimony has doubly sanctified."

He laughed, and made Julie laugh too. This she did with constraint at first; then she gave way to a helpless fit of laughing as easily as she might have burst into tears.

"Suppose she heard us . . . " she said.

"Who? Marianne? She's bound to, a bit."

"You behave like a cad to her, Herbert."

"No, I lie to her. I . . . I was a cad to you because I used to tell you the truth."

Her nostrils stiffened as she tore open a fig with her teeth.

"You've got to admit I paid you back in the same coin."

"Only because I wrung your neck until you owned up."

He threw her one of those deep and slanting glances that he had employed when he was still her unfaithful and jealous husband. He even stuck his fist on his hip. Some divine intervention had stripped him forever of the most effectual elements of his attractiveness, and all the violence aroused in Julie by these accents of a bygone day melted in pity. "Poor man . . . " And since, through lack of vocation or from habit, she was prone to confuse pity with boredom, she felt herself practically a prisoner between the bedridden Herbert, the elaborate silver, and the various knickknacks that were calling her. She longed for her street full of shops and for Coco Vatard and Lucie Albert with all their youth and naive intentness on their work and amusements. She looked about her and began to criticize the furniture.

"Herbert, are you really attached to that chintz? Has nobody ever told you that the pink-and-black chintz suited you about as well as a rope of pearls would a bulldog? Haven't you got any real friends?"

"Very few."

"And what on earth are you doing, all tucked up here in the nursery? Is it an attempt to make yourself seem younger? That's *too* much."

Espivant, leaning on the pillow, was drinking his coffee.

"Shove the table to one side, would you?" he asked her without answering her question. "Put your coffee on top of mine, and bring the cigarettes over. I want to talk to you."

Julie obeyed quickly lest he should catch sight of her old shoes and went on pulling the furniture to pieces in order to distract his attention.

"Lovely lemon wood. But surely a bit chichi for a man's room?"

The secretary came back holding a telephone with a long trailing wire. "It's the President of the Republic asking for news."

"How well all those spirals of telephone wire suit you, Cousteix! You look like a vine. This is my friend Cousteix, who is kind enough to be my secretary: the Comtesse de Carneilhan. Thank the President, Cousteix. Say I'm ill. Not very ill. Just fairly ill—anything you like. Oh, and while you're there, Cousteix———Julie, will you excuse me a moment?"

"It's very odd," Julie was thinking, "Herbert has never been able to talk naturally to a secretary or an inferior. The authority of the Espivants is just about as recent as their title. Saint-Simon saw them moving in, and Viel-Castel made fun of them. And now, there's Herbert bitching about in the hopes of putting his secretary into an estasy."

She cried "Oh!" and leapt forward. For, the moment the door was closed behind Cousteix, Espivant fell back with his eyes shut. Julie found a bottle, opened it, damped a napkin with sal volatile, and fanned Herbert's nostrils so vigorously that his fainting fit lasted less than sixty seconds.

"Don't call anyone; it's nothing," Herbert said in a clear voice. "I'm getting used to it. Any coffee left? Do give me some. You were so quick. I didn't have time to lose consciousness. Thank you."

He sat up without any help and breathed deeply. The whole of his greenish face was smiling.

"It's queer, you know, the feeling of well-being, of optimism, that accompanies each of these, what shall I call them—little deaths. Would you like some brandy, Youlka? I've got some here that dates from—oh, from Pepin the Short."

He was slightly out of breath and overcome by a sudden gloom. She could not take her eyes off his pale face and deep eye sockets.

"Thanks, I won't. I drank too much last night."

"Ah? Who with? Where? Was it fun? Go on, tell!"

He leant forward and the blood returned to his cheeks. Julie recognized his mode of speech, his veiled eyes, the wild hope of widening the range of his senses, and began to hate him again.

"No, it was nothing. I sat up drinking whiskey with Léon, that's all. Pure hygiene! Do you want to talk to me, or shall I let you rest? I can always come back."

"Yes, but perhaps I shan't always be able to. Do stay! Even if it bores you. You're so easily bored."

He smiled at her without a trace of goodwill, but went on holding her hand. "We know each other too well," thought Julie. "We're still quite capable of playing dirty tricks on each other, but we can no longer deceive each other." She shook her head in token of denial, sat down opposite Espivant and poured cream into a second cup of coffee. A young male voice shouted a few words in the courtyard below.

"It's Toni," Espivant explained.

Julie lowered her eyes to conceal a smile. "If you really think I need you," she thought, "to tell me that it's Toni . . . "

"My darling pet," Herbert began, "we were saying that I was going to die. You can't always be there to intervene. . . . Oh, I remember one day, when you'd got a saucepan of milk on the stove, the telephone began ringing, the milk was rising and you dealt with the telephone and the milk at the same time, turning off the gas with your elbow without letting go of the saucepan or the receiver. You were superb. We were poor then."

"I still am," she thought to herself and hid her feet under the chair. But, as Espivant grew less pale and vague and more animated, she felt strangely happy and proud that he owed his present well-being to her.

"How's Becker, by the way?"

"All right. He's in Amsterdam."

"Does he still give you an allowance? How much?"

Julie blushed, and did not answer. She was hesitating between the truth and a lie, and finally voted for the truth.

"Four thousand a month."

"Not what you'd call royal."

"Why should it be royal? He's only a baron, and then only if you don't look too close."

"Including rent?"

"Yes."

"He hasn't canceled the insurance in his own favor?"

"No."

Espivant gazed at her with what she always called his "small look"; pointed, expert, and pressed tight between his eyelids. She knew that his attention had alighted at last on her slightly faded black jacket and her white shirt, spotless, but so often laundered. His eyes came to rest on her feet. "That's done it. He's seen them." She heaved a breath of deliverance, ate the last of the cherries, and slowly powdered her nose. Her bag was almost new.

"You never told me," Espivant coldly reproached her.

"It's against all my principles," she answered in the same tone. He made his voice still harder.

"Of course, your way of life has got nothing to do with me."

"No, nothing at all."

She lowered her forehead, arming herself against whatever blows were coming; but Espivant remained calm. "He's sparing himself, not me," thought Julie.

"Idiot," he said gently, "let's talk. I've announced my impending dissolution to you three times, and all you do is talk about furniture and interior decoration because you don't like this sexless room. Give me a cigarette. You haven't grasped the fact that I 'happen' to sleep here at least three times a week: 'No, no, don't change a thing in this ugly room, my darling, you know I only want your—our—room. But I've got to work late this evening, and I'm feeling tired and ugly.' "

He imitated himself talking to his second wife, and Julie could not help admiring so much languor and amorous authoritativeness. "He's a past master in treachery," she thought.

"Do you call her *vous* like that?"

"Not always. She likes contrasts. So you see, that's how I'm able to wriggle out of it."

"Wriggle out of it?" Julie repeated thoughtfully.

"Well," Herbert said crossly, "you don't need a translation, do you?"

"Oh, no . . . only I say it in a different way. Go on, though. I'd never have thought that Marianne was so——It's true she's only thirty-five: the age when a woman doesn't know that, once out of twice, she ought to say 'No' to a man of . . . our age. A respectable spouse will finish off a man of fifty twice as quickly as a clever tart who knows better than to wear out her own property."

"Here, I'm not fifty!"

"I know. Not for another six months. I was talking in general terms."

She gazed at Espivant with a look that derived nearly all its kindness from the blue makeup round her eyes. "Perhaps," she thought, "he will never be fifty."

"Well," she resumed, "you've got a wife who stands no nonsense. Go on."

He absentmindedly crushed out his half-smoked cigarette.

"Go on? There's nothing more to say. You've just told my entire story . . . and my wife's."

"Rich wives are expensive."

"So are beautiful ones. Oh, I realize now what an idiot I was! I've tried all sorts of things, gadgets, pills."

"Like the Duc de Morny?"

"Like the Duc de Morny. We'll not come to much good copying the Napoleonic nobility."

"We? How does he mean 'we'?"—malicious gaiety

suddenly overcame her at the thought—"Once 'we' no longer means Herbert and Julie. He's surely not lumping together the Carneilhans and the Espivants?" She was careful to conceal the pride that bound her to the name of her family, to its ragged antiquity and to the remains of the massive-walled castle, half manor and half farmhouse, which, for the last nine hundred years, had never been called anything but Carneilhan.

"Don't be rude to the Second Empire," she said. "I'm having my boudoir all quilted and buttoned like the Comtesse de Teba's. But, seriously, Herbert, why don't you just go away? Surely you've had enough of this house and its dismal little box hedges? Go away. Take your pale gray pajamas . . . and your dowry."

"Ah! My dowry!"

He gazed dreamily at the chintz-covered ceiling and seemed on the point of a decison.

"How they talked about the 'dowry' that fixed my election! Five millions? Four millions? How much, Julie?"

"Some people said five. Some two."

She wanted to please and insult him at the same time. She stroked his lip and his small musketeer's mustache.

"Five or two, you were cheap at the price."

He caught her hand, the hand so skillful at every task it touched, and kissed it vaguely as she withdrew it.

"Did you hear that? There have been at least four rings at the door since you arrived. I bet Marianne's been entertaining in my place and that she's already promised since this morning to build a bridge, a school, a washhouse, and an orphanage."

"And will she really do it?"

"They'll bring her the estimates, and she'll have them looked into. All that takes time."

He sat up and undid the button of the pale gray pajamas at his thick neck.

"She pays for things; she doesn't give. Do you get the idea, Youlka?"

"American style?"

"I don't know. I haven't married any American so far. My dowry! She's put 'all her worldly goods' at my disposal. You see the difference?"

"Of course I do. You've been had."

They went on smoking in silence. Espivant, from tiredness and perhaps from chronic flirtatiousness, lowered his dark eyelids. Julie listened to light feminine footsteps in the corridor. "Perhaps that's her. I've been here over an hour," she thought. "Is that all he wanted to tell me?"

"Actually, why *did* you marry her?"

Herbert opened his eyes again and looked at her like a reproachful schoolmaster.

"My dear child, what a question! Four months to run an election campaign, a widowed beauty paying me her *devoirs,* a . . . an extremely embarrassed financial situation. That was my position."

"Nobody quite knows what's going on, even in a very dicky financial situation. But a marriage like yours makes everything as clear as daylight."

"Yes, but supposing I'd only been Marianne's lover, just think of the massed howling going up from my old friends and political enemies. *'Where does the money come from?'* "

"Nobody asks where the money comes from once the candidate's elected."

Espivant sat up laughing.

"You seem to know a lot all at once! Who told you all this?"

"You did. I'm just dishing up what you told me about Puylamare's candidature."

Herbert gave her an attentive look from between his lashes, and she met it without embarrassment.

"It seems you're always destined to fill me with admiration, Youlka."

"Yes; like a racehorse that starts winning the moment it's been sold. You're simply a child with a mustache. You thought you'd be rich because Marianne was; that's your excuse. You were desperately in need of a lot of useless odds and ends, you wanted motorcars like the Argyropoulos; you wanted to throw Venetian parties like the Fauchier-Magnans; you even wanted a more beautiful wife than anyone else."

She was talking airily, knitting round her eyes the network of wrinkles blurred by her gray-blue makeup. Herbert let her run on, greedy for flattery and insult. He made a gesture of protest, and the sunlight on his bloated white hand for an instant robbed Julie of speech.

"I wanted," Herbert went on plaintively, "I wanted a sheaf of Corneille's unpublished manuscripts enough to fill a great book . . . and then I wanted a château. Oh! how I wanted a château!"

He jerked himself into a sitting position with the agility of a healthy young man.

"Just imagine it, Julie. It was called Maucombe. The whole castle lies reflected in a magnificent lake. It looks as if it doesn't take itself quite seriously, as if it felt almost too fifteenth-century with all those corner towers and pinnacles and gateways and gothic arches! And the looking glass it is built in the middle of! I wanted things I'd been dreaming of for so long!"

He looked at Julie and went on. ". . . That we'd been dreaming of for so long!"

She smiled at him generously.

"Oh, I'm quicker than you at forgetting what I want. I do think Marianne might have . . ."

The swollen white hand reappeared in the sunbeam, and made a gesture of indecision. "I'd have given it him, in the old days, if I'd been Marianne," she went on thinking. "He's never more irresistible than when he wants something for entirely selfish reasons!"

"So you didn't get your fairy-tale Robida castle in the end? Why not?"

"Oh, it's most involved. It meant draining a swamp that had formed because they'd allowed the dikes to go to pot. Too dear; not a healthy enough region. Too isolated. People like that have got two passwords that crop up the whole time—'too much,' and 'not enough.' "

"Who have?"

Espivant looked for a moment like a man who is being spied on. "I really don't know, to tell you the truth. You don't tumble bang into the *middle* of a fortune like Marianne's; you fall *alongside* it, somewhere in the neighborhood. You arrive there. . . . I'm not boring you, Julie?"

"Don't be silly."

"Well, you arrive there like a chap who has been forced by a motor accident to spend half a day with a strange family that live by the roadside, and whose new hosts will keep on repeating, 'This is Uncle Reveillaud, and that lady is my sister-in-law, Charlotte's aunt, and that tall boy over there is George, who is going to Saint-Cyr next term.' As if the poor wretch could remember any of it after five minutes!"

He was interrupted by a fit of coughing.

"Herbert, you're tiring yourself. Shall I give you something to drink?"

He made a gesture of refusal.

"I'm not coughing from my throat, but from my heart. Never mind. Marianne's fortune is a . . . a huge foreign body, something fearful, enormous and secretive, talking every known language and always having something wrong with it, just as I might feel sick or you'd have a pain in the back."

"I *beg* your pardon, I never have a pain in the back," said Julie proudly.

"Yes, yes, we all know it's made of solid steel!" Espivant said, raising his shoulders. "Unlike the mineral resources of Marianne. Whenever you want . . . well, I don't know."

"The moon?" Julie suggested.

"Let's say the moon—you suddenly discover that copper has got chlorosis that year, weevils have got at the diamonds, and the swallows have gobbled up all the groundnuts from the trees."

Julie burst into one of her real laughs, with tears in her eyes and her mouth wide open. She thought she heard a rustle outside the door, and laughed a bit louder, while Espivant dropped his voice.

"Reams and reams of paper, portfolios, calculating machines, arcticly cold offices in impossible parts of the town, hideous malformed little brats carting piles of documents about, and lawyers better dressed than I am, who say: 'The Comte d'Espivant is no concern of ours. Our business is direct with the lady, called Anfredi Marianne-Hélène, widow of Hortiz Ludovic-Ramon. . . .' That's Marianne's fortune for you, that and lots of other things; but it's not what you would call 'money.' It's a board of directors. It's a labyrinth. At last, at the end of a corridor, you bump up against a tiny old man called Saillard, who is racked with asthma, and whose name is always just mentioned like that. Just Saillard. Marianne's always going to see Saillard, or coming back from seeing Saillard. She *often* comes back with a face as long as your arm, saying, 'It's no good. Saillard was against it!' "

"Against what?"

"Against immobilizing four millions for the purchase of a country estate, against advancing eighteen hundred thousand francs to buy a ravishing little Fragonard, an extraordinary bargain. Saillard would like to point out to Madame la Comtesse d'Espivant that her diamonds were reset in the modern fashion at the time of her marriage, and besides there is that new set of emeralds which was recently acquired. That, as guardian of her son, who is still a minor, Hortiz Antoine-René, she is obliged to . . . Oh! I'm fed up with it all!" cried Espivant, stretching his arms. "It's a funny thing, when I open my arms wide, there's a place here where . . ."

He pricked his ears toward the garden. "Oh, I know who that is. Professor Giscard. Oh dear, I can't just put him off like an office boy. Julie, you must come again. We've only had time to talk nonsense. Tell me, would you like to? Would it amuse you in the slightest to come again?"

"Of course, I'm quite ready to."

"Quite ready to! You'd catch it, you condescending bitch, if only I were better!"

Julie thought he was making a sort of heavy joke, but she was astounded to see that he was heading for one of those sharp, unpredictable outbursts that used to rock their conjugal household, and reach a resounding climax that died away only in the dust and ashes of broken plates. "Oh really," she thought, "he's too tiresome. . . ." But she hastened to laugh as though she were still afraid of him, and promised to come again.

"You know, a bus brings me straight to your door. I'd prefer it to Beaupied. The back of his neck wobbles and it looks beastly if you're sitting behind him. Your servants' hall always looks like an almshouse for old-age pensioners. And that motor! Do you think I like bowling about in an archbishop's car all done up in pearl gray? And you might tell the Countess—I mean the second of the name—that in Paris, in a motorcar like that, one doesn't dress up one's chauffeur in white linen."

"If you don't go, you'll have to tell her yourself," Espivant interrupted, "because she'll be coming upstairs with Giscard. Off you go, my darling. I'll give you a ring. God, what a lovely figure you've got! Indestructible monster!"

He looked at her enviously and then turned away to fix his eyes on the door through which could come help and condemnation.

On the landing Julie realized that she had lost some of the self-assurance which, two hours earlier, had lightened her step and predisposed her for adventure. All the closed doors along the gallery, which she had slyly scrutinized on the way up, now seemed suspicious. Downstairs she manhandled the old iron latch that had been swinging on the glass-paneled door since Louis XV's day, and almost sprained her ankle on the gravel. "Ah," she sighed when she was on the pavement at last, "that's better. I'm sure Marianne watched me leaving. She was watching me from all those doorways. She hoped I'd break my leg in the garden. And, with all that fuss, what did I have for lunch? I don't feel an ounce heavier! A peach, some cherries, a few figs. And, I must say, wonderful coffee."

Cheered by having turned her back on what she most abhorred, a sickbed, she breathed in the brief Parisian summer. The yellow rosebud pinned to her lapel was beginning to droop. "One of Marianne's roses." Far from wishing to throw it away, she pressed it tight in her hand like plundered treasure. Two or three times her thoughts returned, almost gluttonously, to the two hours she had just spent in the forbidden zone. But she wisely postponed analyzing them. She would pull everything to pieces when she got home. The men who passed her ran their eyes from the ash-blond nape of her neck down to her shabby shoes, and she stopped a moment in front of all the shoeshops. "It'll be time to start thinking about gloves next," she sighed. And she sought sanctuary from temptation inside a bus.

She felt a spasm of affection, as though she were just returning after a long absence, at the sight of the quavering little lift and the ramshackle staircase with its peeling plaster. On a sudden impulse she changed the position of several bits of furniture in the studio. Then, plugging in the electric iron, she spread a cloth over the kitchen table, and set to work. A black marocain crepe dress, that had been overworked for both evening and afternoon wear, was attacked with the iron and diluted ammonia. Water mixed with glycerine was dabbed onto elbows and hips that were threatening to turn shiny. A navy-blue tailor-made, whose four little pockets were covered with dull blue and red sequins, received the same careful treatment, and Julie was busy soaping a blouse, two pairs of camiknickers, and some silk stockings when she was disturbed by three rings on the bell. She kept her overall on while she answered the door and brought her visitor back into the kitchen.

"What's the time, Coco? I wasn't expecting you yet!"

"Five o'clock."

"Already!"

"You might say 'at last.' "

"I was busy, as you see. The day seems to have flown."

"Lucky you!"

"Me?"

She surveyed the young man with cheerful derision. How odd that anyone should call her "lucky."

"You can wait in the studio, if you like."

"May I stay here?"

"You won't be in my way. Sit down on Madame Sabrier's stool. I'll only be another ten minutes."

She went on with her work, rolled her washing up in a damp towel, ironed the pleats of a skirt, changed her shoes, and stitched up a hem. Coco Vatard followed her every movement since his arrival. Julie had devoted a slightly insulting attention to her various tasks, spreading cream on the heels of her shoes and plying the velvet polishing rag with rapid strokes of her forearm.

"Is it fun watching?" she asked him.

His light-colored eyes remained fixed upon her. "Yes," he said in an earnest voice. "Nobody works like you. If only my dyers at the factory worked like that! You've such a deft and easy knack of doing things. I could watch you forever."

"Wouldn't you care to help me? Or for me to have a rest?"

Sitting on the edge of the bathtub, she unfastened her overall and whisked it off with an aggressive gesture. She splashed cold water on her downy arms, on her shoulders and throat, barely distinguishable in color from her hair. Her one concession to modesty was to tie a little Tyrolean scarf round her neck. Only under her chin could she detect the least sign of flabbiness.

"No," Coco said after a moment's reflection. "I haven't got your knack of doing things so well. And why should you want to rest? You're always bored when you're not busy."

"That's not true!" she exclaimed.

Anger could bring tears to her eyes as promptly as laughter. But Coco showed no feeling other than admiration. He lifted the edge of his jacket and punctiliously pulled up the knees of his trousers. He was so near to being impeccably dressed that Julie hoped that she might actually make him so by putting a finishing touch to the knot of his tie. But she gave up the attempt almost at once, and drew back as he was about to take her into his arms.

"How good you smell," he said, with a sincerity which never deserted him. "You smell of under the arms and polish. Won't you be kind to me today?"

She gave him a distant look, her head tilted to one side. "He really is rather nice," she thought, "in spite of his Sunday-best look on every day of the week. A decent young industrialist with big childish eyes and a turned-up nose. But as for . . ."

She sighed, and said, "I'm hungry."

"Hungry? Why on earth?"

She dilated her nostrils and raised her chin.

"Because, my dear boy, I had no time for luncheon. The Comte d'Espivant sent his car for me, and I sat by his bed for three or four hours, perhaps longer."

"Is he better?" asked Coco carelessly.

"No. Worse."

As she wanted to dine out and go to the cinema afterward, she added, in a businesslike way, "Professor Giscard is pessimistic, that's to say, but there is no immediate danger."

"And what does his wife think of your going to see your — her husband?"

"Nothing. She wasn't present at our meeting."

"Ah," said Coco reflectively, before he finally made up his mind. "It's disgusting!"

"What's disgusting?"

"Calling on each other like that. It's disgusting of him to have sent for you, disgusting of you to have gone, and disgusting of the other woman to have stood for it."

Julie did not react, and went on soaping her hands under the kitchen tap, looking at Coco's reflection in the small looking glass over the sink. "A lot he knows about it," she thought. "A first-rate executive in the cleaning and dyeing industry, no doubt, and treats himself to a mild binge at regular intervals. I bet he's got a faded photograph of his father in his wallet, dressed as a private. He's a nice boy."

"You poor wretch," she said out loud. "What do you suppose you and I have got in common?"

"What?"

"I suppose that we both want to go out. Where are we going to dine? Are you meeting Lucie Albert? But not old Encelade, I presume?"

"No," Coco said. "Neither. You gave me no marching orders. Will it bore you if there's just the two of us?"

She smoothed out the three little vertical lines that the slightest vexation incised between her eyebrows.

"Of course not. But make me swallow something before dinner, or I'll eat one of your cheeks off."

Julie gently touched with her painted lips the clean-shaven cheek he proffered.

She was still in bed at ten o'clock next morning. She listened through her sleep to the familiar sounds of activity in the kitchen. When Mme. Sabrier half opened the studio door, Julie allowed her no time for her usual grievances.

"A glass of cold water, and some cocoa made with water, not milk. No breakfast or luncheon. No electric cleaner. See to my shoes and my tailor-made suit, and then off you go. I'm asleep. No letters? See you tomorrow, Madame Sabrier. Don't brush the sequins on the little pockets; they might come off."

She rolled over like a gundog and lay with her forehead against the wall. But she was unable to slip back into the pleasant, slumbrous condition that usually followed her brief and tumultuous nights of imbibing mixed drinks. "It's the fault of the champagne," she thought. "Anyway, to be good at all, champagne must be marvelous. Nowadays, nightclubs are all supplied with a standard champagne that tastes metallic. Give me brandy every time, with or without water, or a decent whiskey that leaves you with a clean tongue." The smell of cold tobacco smoke still lingered in her hair. "My mouth and nose feel positively poisonous this morning. What on earth's the matter with me?"

A glass of cold water swept away the morning fog.

"Of course!" she cried aloud, "I had a row with Coco Vatard!"

She got back into bed and carefully pulled up the single sheet; it was worn, but made of linen and large enough to double over and tuck into her narrow divan bed. Gazing at the ceiling, she went back over the course of her evening. Shadow Number One had been the *tête-à-tête* dinner in the outskirts of Paris. When they left, in spite of Coco's misgivings, she had sat at the steering wheel. "Do be careful," he begged her. "It's Papa's car; mine's being relined. If Papa saw you taking corners like that!"

"We ought to have brought Papa along too," she had said at length. "You'd have been happier then."

Her harmless little remark transformed Coco. He became mute and pompous and unready to accept any joke against his family. In other circumstances, the restaurant and the dinner would have met with Julie's approval. The dusk was darkening into night, the lights were reflected in the diminutive lake, the soft damp air carried the smell of geraniums, and there was music which set her humming. But all this was too much for Coco.

"Why is it all so sad, Julie?"

She surveyed him with what remained of her benevolence, still humming softly to avoid having to say: "It's so sad, because you're the wrong person to be here with me. And nothing here is really meant for you. You're not made for drinking or for dining with a woman who doesn't love you, somebody who comes from far away and remains there even when you hold her to your heart. You're really cut out for family dinners at home, for having a night out on Saturdays, for pretending to have outstripped your father when you are barely able to follow in his tracks or even to respect him as he deserves. It makes me sad to be here, too. But then I've been here often enough with other men, so it's not so serious in my case. I share out the sadness between Becker and Espivant and Puylamare, and others you've never heard of. Or perhaps you have, and it makes no difference. Once, for instance, I had dinner at that table down there with my first husband. I was called Baroness Becker then. At another table sat a lieutenant in uniform, with a civilian. I couldn't take my eyes off the lieutenant. It's a funny thing, nowadays one no longer sees those really fair-haired lieutenants. This one got up all of a sudden, came straight over to our table, apologized, and then stated his name, adding, 'Your humble cousin, Madame!' Then up he climbed into a genealogical tree, reeling off strings of names and marriages and kinships. Becker kept nodding his head and saying, 'Of course . . . yes, yes, I see. . . . Quite right. It's true there is quite a family likeness between my wife and you.' And there wasn't a shred of truth in it, except the lieutenant's spun-gold hair and certain other qualities, very authentic ones, that he revealed later. But I can't tell that sort of story to someone like you. You're only sitting beside me because we went home together after supper — two? three months ago? — I've forgotten. I must say, we both had a wonderful time. But why should we begin all over again? You're like one of those old-fashioned French girls, who say 'Mama, I'm engaged to be married, a gentleman kissed me in the garden!' Yes, that's the way, order some more champagne. Two hundred and sixty francs are my entire fortune at the moment, and there are still several days till Becker's check turns up. After all, I can't soak you for anything, my-poor-boy-who-is-not-yet-rich! I've never liked taking money from men. Treat the Comtesse de Carneilhan to food and drink. She's not really a Countess, anyway, but only, this evening, disgustingly Carneilhan, and a bad lot like all of them!"

But she knew that with her flat dark-blue felt hat tilted over one eye, and her yellow rose-petal skin toning with her hair, both the time of night and the lighting were becoming to her.

Others dining there had recognized her, and Coco found her ravishing. It was just about then that her young companion had tried to snatch her hand and kiss it under the table, and she had slapped his face. As bad luck would have it, this gesture, applied to Coco's flat compact cheek, was as clear and resounding as a stage smack, and everyone who did not see it heard it.

They laughed, and Coco had the sense to do the same. So Julie, wrinkling up her nose "like a wild animal," was the only one to be cross, and she had trouble in recovering her temper.

"Going on to the Bal Tabarin was my idea. The drive back. Oh yes! He didn't want me to drive Papa's car. He wanted us to pull up by the side of the road in the Bois des Fausses-Reposes and make love. A regular picnic! A charming idea, really, and I can't think why I put a stop to it. Just my luck, I'm hungry again!"

Getting out of bed, she hunted through the food locker, which did its best to look like a frigidaire, and found a triangle of white cheese left over from the day before. Sprinkling a slice of bread with salt and pepper, most of her optimism returned to her as she munched away. But she always dreaded, during these difficult last days of the month, her punctual and ineluctable yearnings for food. Spurned and postponed by endless cigarettes on an empty stomach, these yearnings came back again to torment her digestion. Julie had broken herself in to every kind of diet and could cope with anything except hunger. "Too early for oysters, but there are all sorts of little things I could swallow piping hot. I could do myself proud on ten francs, on the terrace of the little café. With a glass of muscadot to wash it down!" As she ate her bread and cheese, she sniffed the warm, damp noonday. "If only we could have two more months of this weather, two months without having to think about a warm coat!"

Without looking at the time, she went and smoked her first cigarette on her bed. All the details of the night before came back to her, from the gloomy dinner to the floor show at the Tabarin, and the encounter with Beatrix de la Roche-Tannoy. She was an ex-society woman turned cabaret singer. "Third star on the posters of the Ba-Ta-Clan! Poor Beatrix imagines a scandal in high life remains exciting forever! We all went to see her when she first appeared on the stage at the Casino.

But it didn't take long to see that the big la Roche-Tannoy nose, under all those paste tiaras and ostrich feathers, was even more tiresome than in ordinary life. So we all forgot about it."

Julie was still bored, despite the castles of naked flesh piled up on the stage and dance floor of the Tabarin, so she made room for her friend. She was on the plump side and dressed in a little conical medieval headdress covered with sequins. Julie introduced Coco Vatard.

"Coco, order some more champagne for Madame de la Roche-Tannoy."

"Here we go," said Coco with a sort of polite familiarity.

"Are you alone, Beatrix?"

"Yes. I came on business. I've got to see Sandrini after the show. He wants to sign me up for the winter Revue."

"Are you . . . happy about it?"

"Delighted. Goodness, if only I'd known, I'd have dropped that gang of stuck-up idiots ten years sooner!"

"You didn't lose much time as it was," said Julie with a certain ferocity.

"And what about you? How is your father keeping?"

"My dear, he's amazing. He's still training a few colts at Carneilhan."

"No, really?" said Coco. "I say, I never knew you had a father."

Julie looked at him without saying a word, and then exchanged smiles with Beatrix.

"You never told me you had a father. Why didn't you tell me?"

"Haven't had time," Julie said.

With a pointed laugh, she made clear to Beatrix the recent date and the unimportance of her relationship with Coco Vatard. Beatrix, amused, buried her big nose in her big glass.

"And how's your mother?" Julie asked her.

"Married again, my dear, just to spite me. At seventy-one!"

"Well, I must say!" said Coco Vatard. "That's going it."

"Coco," Julie said, "pour out some champagne for Madame de la Roche-Tannoy. But what did Volodia say about her marrying again?"

"Volodia? He wanted to commit suicide. Just imagine, he'd been officially engaged to my mother for thirty years!"

"Good God!" said Coco Vatard. "Do you mean to say he wanted to commit suicide because of the old ha —— I mean, because of a person of seventy-one? I must be dreaming!"

Neither of the two women appeared to have heard. Julie pushed the plate of little sandwiches to one side and put her elbows on the table so that she could lean closer to Beatrix, who followed her lead.

"Do you still see your sister Castelbeluze?" Julie asked.

Beatrix sat up straight and opened her fur coat, revealing breasts pressed tightly together by her low-cut dress.

"Her? Most certainly I don't! She took sides the moment I changed my way of living, and stirred up my whole family against me." The huge, historical nose was lowered confidentially. "But, I must say, my brother-in-law behaved very well. He didn't chime in with the rest of the pack. He gets nicer the more you know him," Beatrix whispered. "And talking of that, do tell me how things are between you and Espivant?"

"Much the same! We dote on each other as long as we're not married. I spent at least three hours with him today! So you see."

"At his house?"

"At his house, of course. He's still laid up."

"But, Julie! What about his wife all this time?"

"Marianne? Nothing to do with me, darling. She was minding her own business, I expect."

Beatrix's close-set eyes and long nose registered such utter if belated astonishment that Julie, relishing its full flavor, blushed and then laughed exultantly. "She'll repeat that to the whole of Christendom!" she thought.

"Is it true that Espivant is going to die?"

"Of course it isn't! His pulse is violently irregular; that's all due to the strain of parliamentary life, and so on. . . ."

"You told me," interrupted Coco, "that the Comte d'Espivant was in a really bad way."

"Your lighter, Coco. Thanks."

"I asked you," Madame de la Roche-Tannoy went on, "because Espivant, after all, has got no relations."

"Don't I know it, my dear! None at all."

A prolonged glance, fanned into flame by the champagne, passed between them. No alcoholic languor, however, loosened the fiber of these two steady drinkers or made their intimacy less cautious.

"Of course, you know the rumor that has been going round for the last few days? About Espivant's divorce?"

"I know something even more interesting," Julie answered smoothly. "Not an immediate divorce, perhaps, but a separation. It seems that Marianne is suffering from some very serious illness."

Beatrix whinnied with laughter.

"A serious illness is a promise people very seldom keep."

"Pure gossip," Julie said.

"If you aren't certain," said Coco, "why do you talk about it? What business is it of yours?"

Julie pushed the young man's glass and ashtray to one side, and leaning forward, covered half of the little table with her bust. Her sleeves were once again beside Beatrix's bare arms and bracelets. They both gave way to the need, which they would have denied hotly if they had had nothing to drink, of stealing back, like burglars, into the world they had abandoned with such pointless ostentation. Their conversation became an exchange of scandals and mendacious confidences, of slanders and boasts which they only half believed. Dates were quoted and, above all, names usually qualified by outrageous epithets. A *rinforzando* of the orchestra wrenched them back from this passionate preoccupation.

"My dear," cried Beatrix, "it's the end. The Apotheosis of Woman! Where's your young friend got to?"

"Powdering his nose, I suppose."

"Will you excuse me if I leave you now? I don't want to miss

Sandrini. Do let's meet soon."

"Darling, do let's."

Julie, left alone, watched the lights going out one by one while the crowd thronged toward the exit, stirring up, as they went, a nimbus of hanging dust. She made a sign to the barman, and he came up to her table.

"The gentleman apologized for not being able to wait. Everything is paid for."

"Splendid," said Julie.

She went down as far as the church of Saint-Augustin on foot. The cool night air played about her coatless shoulders, her face, whose warm colors were lost in the gloaming. She felt acutely aware of her solitude all of a sudden, and at once lost the sense of well-being she had felt after hours in the open air, the good dinner and the abundance of wine. "Ah, why isn't that young idiot here?" As it was long past midnight, she climbed into a *fiacre* to save money, bewailing, in a confused fashion, the lot of the old broken-down cab horse, Espivant's inconsequent greed, and the taciturn mood of the cabby who refused, as they drove from the eighth to the sixteenth *arrondissement,* to tell his life story to Julie de Carneilhan.

Once she was out of her bath and had made up her face, she planned to lie down for an hour on her newly made bed; but she was summoned by the ring of the telephone. She ran into the studio stark naked, with muttered objurations and an assumed bad temper that changed tone as soon as she heard the voice of Lucie Albert.

"Is that you, my pet? Did you have a nice evening? Oh, of course, it was Saturday. It's no use, I'll never get used to Saturday."

In the looking glass opposite, a tall, naked woman was watching her. From her feet to her small head with its golden-beige hair she was the color of a yellow tea rose, with the rather spare, flat belly of a barren woman, a pretty navel placed high at her middle and breasts that had lost none of their fineness, except in her own severely critical eyes. "Just a shade more like jellyfish than apples cut in half these days," was her verdict. Reiterated squeaks of "Hello! Hello!" were calling her, and she realized that she was not listening.

"Yes, my pet, we were cut off. What? Oh! A procession of Beauty Queens! Yes, yes, it would be great fun, the prizewinners are always so wonderfully inadequate, aren't they? What, tea thrown in? What a Saturnalia! I said, 'What a Saturnalia!' No, 'Saturnalia.' . . . It doesn't matter, darling. All right, I'll meet you here about four."

She remained standing there naked, with her hand on the telephone, overcome with gloom at the thought of the emptiness of the day ahead, though it was no different from most of her days. "It's Beatrix's fault. That great nose of hers brings me bad luck. To be quite fair, it's also because it's the eighth of the month. From the eighth to the fifteenth, my morale varies with the state of my finances." She struck a few becoming attitudes with her feet together and her arms above her head, and then stopped because the need for food was gnawing the pit of her stomach. "How I loathe eating alone, but I suppose I'd better resign myself to doing so till the Becker check turns up!"

The telephone sounded once more and for a moment she stood in nervous immobility, thinking that Espivant might be calling her. But it was only Coco Vatard, for whose benefit she quite pointlessly raised her eyebrows, dilated her nostrils, and rested a hand on her hip. She spoke to him in the second person plural.

"What? You're phenomenally ignorant of how to behave, my dear boy. Angry? Me? But you're merely grotesque! What did you say? You needn't bother about me. Besides, Beatrix had her car and very kindly drove me home."

Far away, in an echoing atmosphere where Julie could hear a typewriter at work and the slower rhythm of some kind of motor, Coco was obstinately and sincerely attempting to explain. "You don't understand. Do let me speak, Julie. No, I didn't mean to play you a dirty trick, but I had Papa's car, and

I saw that it was past one o'clock, and the cleaners turn up at home at five and always tackle the cars first. I get up at six-thirty on Sundays and weekdays alike, and I said to myself, 'Those two with their interminable mutterings have dropped me flat as if I wasn't there, and then supposing I strike lucky and Julie is kind to me, I know I'll be out till half-past five in the morning. I'll cut my losses and go home, at least I'll have a full working day and no rows with Papa.' Julie, no, do listen. Julie, I'll come and collect you. We'll have lunch in the Bois. Listen, Julie. I was only doing everything for the best."

All of a sudden Mme. de Carneilhan renounced her dignity and the pompous *vous,* and burst out laughing as she sized herself up in the looking glass.

"Come here now, you idiot! Didn't I take you in beautifully? See you in a moment."

She looked fiercely at the telephone, believing she hated the person to whom, without appearing to, she had just surrendered. From Becker to Coco Vatard, how many men had she given in to on a tone of command?

She had to answer the telephone yet a third time, and listen to a grating, constricted voice that she did not recognize at first.

"Oh!" she said. "It's you, Toni? Have you got a sore throat? Good morning. I didn't recognize your voice. Is everybody well?"

"You went to the Rue Saint-Sabas."

"Yes. I even heard you talking in the garden."

"You went to the Rue Saint-Sabas," the voice grated. "You went and saw your — my stepfather. I don't want you to go and see that man. I forbid you to see him. Yes, that's it. I forbid you. No, it's *not* because of my mother. I don't want you to see him again, nor him to see you. Yes, I forbid you."

Julie put the receiver gently back on its hook without listening further. She heard another ring, and a second explosion of the broken voice punctuated by tears. "As for that one," she thought, "he's the most difficult of the lot."

She dressed with automatic deftness, putting on her black-and-white dress. "Don't talk to me about boys in their 'teens,'" she thought. "What business is it of his? Young boys are a real pest. It's lucky I don't like them. A kiss on the forehead and a couple of dabs of my scent behind his ears, and he thinks he's my lover, if you please! All the same, I've a feeling he may turn out to be most tiresome. I might get rid of him by seeing Espivant only very rarely." She knew, as she looked at her reflection, that she would do nothing so reasonable.

A moment later, she was completely taken up with Coco's arrival, and with the only too well known pleasure she derived from the presence of a man. "A tree in the desert," she thought, looking at Coco. However, she listened to Coco's version of the night before with an expression of supreme mockery.

"You see, Julie . . ." As he spoke he bumped into the twelve-sided table and almost upset the pot of lobelias. ". . . I've got my dignity as well, Julie."

To punish him for the word she tweaked the ends of his bow tie, rucked up his hair and pulled him about in all directions, like a sharp-toothed bitch that pretends to play so that she can bite. He only just managed to laugh, and tried to protect himself. "Julie, it's my new suit! I hate anyone touching my tie!" She kissed him absentmindedly, and at the touch of her strong, cold, painted lips, he stopped speaking in devout expectancy. But Julie rewarded him no further and led the way downstairs.

They both took trouble to be pleasant while they ate their luncheon. In front of some worried-looking businessmen and a few young women destined for a cinema career and a Deputy who greeted her a shade too familiarly, Julie posed as a woman indifferent to her reputation, calling Coco *tu* in a loud voice. Coco automatically slipped into the part of an adored young man. He plunged his honest gray eyes into Julie's, where they struck shallow bottom on a spangled, cold and unconfiding blue sand.

"Who was the chap you said 'Hello' to, Julie, over there in the corner?"

"A Deputy called Puylamare."

"Do you know him well?"

"Enough not to want to know him better."

"So you don't mind him seeing us together?"

"My dear infant, please get it into your head that I don't care a damn. Not only Puylamare, I mean, but everybody."

"How nice you are!"

But, even as he spoke he did not seem sure that she was so nice after all. Near the muddy little lake a swarm of starlings, about a hundred strong, settled among the branches where the leaves were already turning to gold. They were plump and heavy, and their whistling sounded like a winter wind.

"What are you doing today, Julie?"

"It all depends. What is today?"

"Don't you ever know what day it is, Julie?"

"Yes, whenever the fifteenth turns out to be a Saturday or Sunday."

"Why?"

"Because then I can't get my . . . my allowance till Monday."

"Julie," he said kindly, "it's the ninth today. You wouldn't be needing any money, would you?"

Julie turned to him in surprise.

"It's usually women," she thought, "who make these offers so diffidently." She said "No" with her head, preferring not to speak. "I should only say something silly," she pondered, "or rather I couldn't help saying 'Yes,' that I've got to pay Madame Sabrier for the week, that I've only got two hundred and forty francs left, that . . . yes, that I do need some money."

Leaning on the table, she kept brushing Coco's hand with a rose she had been given by the *maître d'hôtel.* She felt a faint wave of friendship toward the hand with its thumb deformed by an accident with some piece of machinery: the manicurist did not always succeed in removing a line of vivid green round the edge of the nail, the acid stain of some color test.

"Once," she said, "I tried to dye a blouse by myself. Oh, my dear, for a month I could never take my gloves off, except at home."

"Of course you couldn't manage it; you're only a beginner," said Coco. "Julie, please be kind and tell me—wouldn't you like a little money?"

She shook her head once more. "If I start talking about it I'll let myself go, and admit I'm gnawed all of a sudden by a longing for all kinds of things I need; I'd say I'd like some stockings, gloves, a fur coat, two new tailor-mades, scent by the liter, and cakes of soap by the dozen. I haven't been like this for ages. What's got into me? If I don't hold myself back, if this blessed innocent gives me some of his salary and then thinks I'm in his debt, life will again be hell."

She shook herself, smiled, and began powdering her nose.

"You're an angel. Send me a little bottle of *Fairyland.* And take me home. I've got to change my suit. I've got a date with Lucie. We're going to have a great time at the procession of Beauty Queens in the banqueting hall of *Le Journal.*"

"What about me?" Coco begged.

Julie put on her faraway look, and glanced at Coco between her darkened lashes.

"If you'd like to . . . if you're free."

"Free as air. But only till half-past seven. We've got a dinner tonight for the anniversary of my parents' wedding."

"Really? You haven't talked about them for ages. Come on, then; it's three o'clock! It's absurd, sitting on at a table as though we were at a wedding breakfast. Just look at Puylamare on the job! He arrived long before us, and there he is still, drinking *Franciscaine.* He's not fifty yet, and he looks old enough to be my grandfather!"

As they crossed the room, she vaguely acknowledged an inquisitive and familiar greeting from the Deputy, who looked Coco up and down.

They drove back to Paris the long way round, and Coco's gray eyes made it clear to Julie how much he longed for her to be "kind" to him. With a glance and a dilation of the nostrils, she promised she would, and he began driving the car like a taximan at the outset of his career.

Feeling relaxed and faintly perturbed and at the mercy of a melancholy she forbade herself to explore, Julie laughed at the speed of his driving and the rash way he took the corners. "He's not a clumsy lover by any means," she thought. "He's full of instinct and warmth. I am too. We've got lots of time before Lucie comes to pick me up. I won't take the cover off the divan. I've only got one sheet on the bed, and it's a turned one with a seam down the middle. We'll carry on just as if we were on the grass."

In the hall Julie saw that Coco Vatard's face had turned into the very picture of carnal desire—foolish-featured, and lilac-colored, as if bruised, under the eyes. She had to push him aside and say, "Wait, wait a minute," in a low voice, feeling an access of indulgence for this healthy and uncomplicated young male in all the confusion of his impatience.

But, before the elevator began to move, the *concierge* ran up and pushed an envelope through the bars.

"A chauffeur brought this for you."

"When?" shouted Julie, sailing up into the air.

"Just a moment ago!" squeaked the concierge. "No message!"

In spite of the half-darkness, Julie recognized Espivant's writing—sharp, incisive writing which often cut into the paper. Coco Vatard's hand pressed hers softly.

"Do leave me alone, you!" she said crossly.

He recoiled as far as the narrow elevator would allow.

"Why 'me'?" he asked in an offended voice.

"Really, Coco, you might at least behave in the elevator."

When they were in her flat, she left him standing while she read the letter. He walked up and down the studio, and, of course, banged into the twelve-sided table, to which he said "Sorry." When he saw Julie folding the letter up, he risked a question.

"Nothing nasty?"

"No, no," said Julie quickly. Then she added, more slowly, "Only it's rather a bore. I shan't be able to go with Lucie to the

Beauty Queens at five. . . . Quick. Go and open the door. That's Lucie ringing. She's early for once."

Coco Vatard came back, followed by Lucie.

"Julie can't come with us to the Beauty Queens at five," he repeated in a gloomy voice.

"Why?" asked Lucie Albert.

At the slightest provocation she would open her anxious eyes wide: eyes which a year before had taken the first prize as "the largest in Paris." But everybody had forgotten that by now, although she would still unveil those vast orbs—beyond the bounds of decency or tact—till they seemed the size of a mare's; swamped by dark irises and equally devoid of intelligence.

"You might at least say good afternoon, Julie!"

"Good afternoon, my angel. You look very pretty today," Julie added without thinking.

"But why can't you come? Why did you tell me you could come, then? What shall I do if you don't come?"

"She's awful," thought Julie. "When she opens her eyes like that, it makes my head ache. And that little purple hat!" She turned to Coco, as though in search of help.

"Coco can tell you that a letter I've just received has upset all my plans for the afternoon, can't you, Coco?"

"Yes," said Coco impassively. "Julie's not coming with us because she wants to go and see Monsieur d'Espivant."

"How do you mean? Nobody said anything about Monsieur d'Espivant that I know."

"That's got nothing to do with it. I say you want to go and see him. And that this is rotten for us. And also that you're wrong to go. If you want my advice, you oughtn't to."

"What on earth is he talking about? Advising me not to go . . . He offers me his good advice. It's grotesque, it's . . ." She had grown so red in the face that the down on her cheeks and close to her ears veiled her skin like silver gauze.

"That's quite right," said Lucie Albert. "You oughtn't to go. Anyway, what did the Count say in his letter? Probably lies. Just think, after the way he treated you!"

"Oh, she knows all right," said Coco Vatard.

"And we'd have a lovely time at *Le Journal.* Maurice de Waleffe told me he'd put us in the very best places and that he'd keep some chocolate for us, whatever happens. Because you know how people carry on when the refreshments are free, the chocolate's always the first to go."

Coco frowned.

"No need to bother about free refreshments if I'm coming with you."

Julie emerged painfully from her silence, lifted her nose in the air and adopted her thin head voice.

"When you've quite finished, may I say something? I'm not compelled to account for my actions to either of you. But I admit it is a question of Monsieur d'Espivant's health, which is in a bad enough condition . . ."

"To have you on toast," said Coco.

"What exactly does that mean?"

He became very young and contrite: "Oh! Nothing, Julie. You know, you hurt my feelings, and then I get spiteful. Julie, anybody else in my place. . . ."

She calmed down, smiled at his gray eyes and turned-up nose, and thought, vaguely, "I'd have done much better to let him have a few moments of fun and, incidentally, enjoyed myself too in the bargain. It's too late now. Also, they're bound to be right, he and that little idiot. Probably all lies." Four strokes chimed from the clock of the neighboring school. Julie picked Coco's gloves up from the table and Lucie's bag and tossed them over to their owners.

"Off you go. Quick."

"Oh!" Lucie was outraged.

"And supposing I don't come back?" ventured Coco in a challenging tone.

Julie gazed at him from a long way off.

"You're a good boy," she said.

She went up to him and diplomatically stroked his clear cheek.

"And very good-looking . . . very. Lucie, my love, do excuse me."

She pushed them both out and shot the bolt in order to feel more definitely separated from them, free to remain standing with her arms hanging at her sides and listen to their footsteps dying away down the staircase. She dressed herself with her usual speed and efficiency, and, when she was ready, wondered why she was going. "Probably lies, as Lucie says, nothing but lies."

She had lived a great deal among lies, before plumping for a small life of her own, a sincere and restricted life from which all pretense, even in matters sensual, was banished. How many crazy decisions and allegiances to successive aspects of the truth! Had she not, one day when her costume for a fancy dress had demanded short hair, cut off the great chestnut mane that fell below her waist when she let it down? "I could have hired a wig," she thought. "I might also, at a pinch, have passed the rest of my life with Becker, or with Espivant. If it comes to that, I could also have gone on stirring puddings in an old saucepan at Carneilhan. The things one might have done are, in fact, the things one could not do. Lies? After all, why not?" She had not always taken sides against the fascination of destroying truth and confidence. "The man who wrote this knew what he was about!"

When she had found a seat in the bus, she unfolded the letter, thinking she might have read it too hastily. But she remembered the most important words: "Please come," that is to say, and "darling Youlka."

Julie was not particularly surprised to find Herbert d'Espivant up and dressed and in his study. "But why, oh why," she thought, "that maroon-colored velvet jacket?" No trace remained of the exhilarated mood in which she had stepped onto the bus, with the letter crackling in her bag like a new banknote. She felt absentminded, aware of her surroundings, sharply critical and rather coarse-grained, and she had the bad taste to go and lean, for a moment, on the open windowsill.

"Did I introduce my friend Cousteix?"

"Of course," she said, and she stretched out her hand with

the gracious gesture of a hostess, to a young man slightly aged by a beard. "Model secretary for a pretentious politician. Young tutor for an adolescent prince. Herbert always knew how to choose his secretaries." Cousteix vanished like a shadow and Herbert took Julie by the elbow and led her into the sunlight by the window.

"What if they see us from the garden?" she said. "You're not interesting any more, now you're well on the road to recovery."

"I thought," Herbert said, "you were only interested in men in full possession of their powers. No, I'm not well yet. But I almost look it, don't I?"

He confronted the daylight, and she observed his clean-shaven cheek, his short hair, the mustache skillfully clipped and trimmed. "It's a disaster," thought Julie and her eyes grew moist, not with pity, but with regret for the past, for this faithless musketeer of hers, with his delicate beauty and his faintly martial pose. Espivant's smile died away. He became hard, businesslike and preoccupied once more.

"Sit down. Get it into your head that I'm lonely here. Lonely as I suppose everybody is. Are you? You wouldn't tell me. I'm absolutely alone, living beside a woman who's in love with me, and ill now that I'm faced with a political life I started too late. Anyway, there's going to be a war."

"A war?" said Julie.

"Does that surprise you? You read the papers, don't you?"

"The illustrated ones, now and then. But I only looked surprised because a fortune-teller told me we were going to have a war."

"Is that all you care?"

"Yes," Julie said. "All I know about wars is how to be glad if we win, and how to die if I have to."

Espivant looked at her with envy.

"But don't you realize what a terrible war it would be? Worse than the last one?"

She made a gesture of indifference.

"I don't bother my head about it. After all, it's nothing to do with women." She reflected a moment and then went on: "But you're fifty. And you're not—not at the moment—outstandingly fit. . . ."

"My dear, I know I'm not up to much," said Espivant bitterly, "and I don't need reassuring."

"It's not you I'm reassuring," said Julie, "but me."

Espivant fixed his whole attention on her. He seemed to believe her. He kissed her hand and then put an arm round her shoulders. She disengaged herself, cleverly pivoting away from him.

"Palace furniture, Herbert?"

"Yes. Kept, as one might say, in Boulle."

"Are you the culprit?"

"I had accomplices. But don't start on interior decorating again. I haven't the time."

"Nor have I."

Julie stared him in the face with studied insolence, for she was feeling inferior to her normal self—dry-skinned, less rose-complexioned than usual, small-eyed—and she hated it. Espivant shrugged his shoulders.

"It's no day for rows, Youlka. I've only been up a couple of hours."

"But you haven't had any more of those attacks since my visit, have you?"

"Only one. Let's forget about it. My house gets on my nerves. Oh, don't keep listening toward the gallery; nobody's there. Do you know where Marianne is?"

"No."

"She's gone in search of her son."

"In search . . . ? What did you say?"

"Of her son. I wish you'd listen, Youlka! Toni didn't come home last night. My opinion is, he's with some woman. But his mother's off her head with anxiety. After all, seventeen is young to stay out all night, especially without warning. And then, he's too good-looking, much too good-looking. Are you listening? What are you thinking about?"

"What you're saying. Didn't he leave any clue?"

"Yes, an idiotic note for his mother: 'I'll never set foot in this house again,' or something of the kind. Marianne swears nothing had gone wrong between them, but I simply can't believe it."

"Did he take any money with him?"

"Very little. Marianne doesn't give him much. Only in driblets."

"Why?"

"She says that that's the right thing. I slip him five louis now and then."

"Are you on good terms with your stepson?"

"Very good terms. He's not specially communicative, but he's very sweet-tempered, rather difficult to size up—the least troublesome child in the world. He's got a little flat, two and a half rooms on the second floor, and I haven't seen him for . . . let me see, for forty-eight hours. Do you know him?"

"I've caught glimpses of him. You're on good terms with him, but you don't like him. Is that right? No, you don't like him. Of course you don't like him. You've got your hands full with one Marianne; a pair of them would be too much. She and the boy look so much alike that you can hardly stand it. Is that it? Go on, do tell. Surely you can tell *me*?"

She advanced, pushing Espivant with her forefinger, and putting her face close to his, which was exactly on a level with her own; and attacking the hazel of his eyes with the blue of hers, hardening their expression and harassing him as she used to in the old days when she wanted to make him own up to an infidelity in thought or deed. Caught by surprise, he gave way, and took refuge in cynicism.

"Well, as far as that goes, I don't really care a damn one way or the other. If he had been my own son. . . . But I've neither the years nor the temperament for an adoptive father. But I'm worried about this business, for Marianne's sake. Anything that interferes with her normal course of life makes her . . . how shall I put it? When something tiresome happens to either of us, you or me, we just call it tiresome."

"Or even worse."

"While Marianne calls it an unheard-of event, an unimaginable catastrophe."

"She's the sensitive sort."

"No; but she's fundamentally gloomy. And actually, nothing but the most fortunate things ever happen to her."

"Herbert, you're forgetting yourself!"

They both burst out laughing, when the bell of the private telephone interrupted them.

"What is it, Cousteix? They've found the boy? No? But that's too much of a good thing! No; don't go there now. Stay here, and take all incoming calls, but only tell me when there's something urgent. I want to be left in peace. Hang onto Mademoiselle Billecoq and get her to take down anything important from the foreign wireless stations. Thank you. Oh, and Cousteix—give me Billecoq—I want to dictate. There are one or two odds and ends."

While he was dictating, Julie made a tour of the room. "Herbert and I never managed to furnish this study. I'd worked out a rather Balzacian decoration, the furnishings all imaginary, the name of the nonexistent picture written up on the walls. And now it's much too full. That huge Panini! And those Guardis, thirteen to the dozen. And that array of telephones! It's a funny thing, all those symbols of activity; I can never quite believe that Herbert really needs them."

She was striving to distract her mind from an awkward fact. "Toni refuses to set foot here again. Toni has disappeared. It's no business of mine. Really none." Then she remembered the telephone conversation, the tearful and discordant voice, the childish threats. "Toni didn't sleep at home. And he wrote that he *refused* to come back."

Julie wandered about the room, peered at a little picture entirely filled with Venice, stroked with disgusted hands the brass and tortoiseshell of the Boulle while she listened to Espivant's voice dictating into the mouthpiece "*. . . the points, my dear colleague, that you have kindly brought to my notice by no means imply that I must consider. . . .* Are you following,

Mademoiselle Billecoq? For Heaven's sake try and keep up."

"Toni stayed out all night. He doesn't want to set foot in his stepfather's house." She frowned, ferociously calling to mind the faint adolescent face so like Marianne's. "If only he were dead," she exclaimed to herself, "we should be well rid of him!" It escaped her notice that her thoughts had been expressed as "We should" instead of "I should."

"That's all. Take me off the office line, Billecoq. Tell Monsieur Cousteix to put me on only if Madame d'Espivant telephones. Come, Youlka. I'm so sorry."

He pulled up a great, unfriendly crimson armchair for Julie. "Venetian Louis XIV," she thought; "the nastiest style in the world. The whole room stinks of Venice. I loathe rooms furnished according to a single idea. If I know anything of Herbert, he's probably very proud of it." She made her wild-animal grimace and sat down gingerly. Espivant cast a slow glance over her crossed legs and her shoes. His look put her in a good mood at once.

"I've got my pretty shoes on today," she said with a laugh.

"And your pretty legs every day," Herbert answered. "How do you find me, Youlka?"

"Dangerous."

He leaned back in his chair, beaming. "That's the right sort of talk, but it would not be the right sort of behavior."

"Would you like to tie my hands, for safety?"

"You've got so many other weapons."

He contemplated her thoughtfully and without desire.

"Youlka, I want to go to the country."

"I give you my full permission."

"I need some money."

"I've got two hundred and forty francs."

"What did you do with that receipt I gave you, for fun—and also because I was furious—when you sold your diamond necklace during your divorce suit? Before we were married.

You remember. . . . *I hereby testify that I have received from Madame Julius Becker, Baroness of the early pink Dutch variety, the exorbitant sum of . . .*"

"What a memory."

". . . the exorbitant sum of a million, Youlka!"

"That's it. A million that didn't last long, to give it its due."

"What's a million?"

"It was tiny, done up in two rubber bands. . . ."

"Had no staying power, eh?"

They laughed, rubbing shoulders and cold-heartedly provoking each other.

"Did you throw the paper away? Because, my dear child, that comic document is an absolutely genuine receipt. Do you remember I mentioned—idiotically!—that the sum was 'in the nature of a loan'? And I can still see the beautiful sheet of paper, all stamped and engraved, that I consecrated to that masterpiece of prose."

He was consulting his extraordinary memory, which never played him false. "He's like a starling. Léon's right," thought Julie. "When Herbert makes an effort to remember anything he squints a bit."

"You put the paper away in . . ."

"In that lovely box inlaid with mother-of-pearl, a chocolate box, with your other letters and your love letters. I've still got the box, even if I haven't got the stamped paper."

On the alert, she lied in exactly the level and sociable tones she had used in former contests: fencing matches that used to end in sudden sharp squalls. But today, talking as he was only of money, Julie was frightened, not of his violence, but of his diplomacy.

"Have a good hunt for it," he said in a cajoling voice. "I owe you a million, Julie, do you realize?"

"No," Julie said in all sincerity.

"But I do, really. I'd like to pay it back to you. Why don't you claim it? Because I wouldn't give it back? Wrong for once! Marianne can't bear debts, especially mine. Do you get me?"

Julie blushed so much that there was no need to answer.

"Well, don't let's say any more about it. I was only saying . . ."

She bowed her head.

"I quite realize why you said it. But I shouldn't think Marianne's the sort of woman to believe, on the strength of a mere affirmation . . ."

Herbert interrupted her as though he had his answer pat.

"Marianne's the sort of woman who believes what she sees," he said.

He lowered his glance from her eyes the instant he felt that she was about to bridle, and began stroking her shoulders. "You're the only person I enjoy playing dangerous games with, Youlka. I forgot to tell you that the two medical bigwigs, Hattoutant and Giscard, have given me an ultimatum. I've got to quit Paris and political life. The country—and do you see me in the country?"

"I've seen you there. But you don't like it."

He gave her a melancholy smile that had all the appearance of being genuine.

"When we used to go riding at Carneilhan, you used to have your great mane of hair knotted up tight like the tail of a cart horse. It was in a terrible mess sometimes when you got home. . . ."

She thrust the glowing evocation from her with a wave of the hand.

"No, please. Can't you go to the country alone?"

He lowered his head.

"Politics aren't the only thing I've been warned off. You know, in Paris, somehow, the intimacy of married life seems to be a very small part of the twenty-four hours."

"You don't say so!"

"And Deauville wouldn't be too bad either. Everybody goes to bed late. But the country . . ."

Listening reflectively, Julie repressed an awkward temptation to burst out laughing.

"Did they tell your wife there would be . . . certain restrictions?"

"Heavens, no. I put a stop to that. That's the sort of commission I undertake myself."

"What will she say?"

"Oh, nothing. She'll settle in a different room, quite straightforwardly. On nights when there is a full moon or a smell of new-mown hay, she'll get as far away as possible, but not quickly enough for me not to see what her feelings are. Stop laughing, you beast, or I'll chuck the Regent's inkpot at your head. It's a fake, anyhow," he went on coldly.

"And . . . what about divorce?"

"Too soon. I've got absolutely nothing of my own."

He grew angry again and shouted, "Good heavens! After all, I'm not demanding anything extraordinary. That million francs was Becker's money, the proceeds of Becker's presents. You gave it to me, and a fine shindy there would have been if I'd refused it!"

"I agree. But it was my money as well. I had a right to give that. But how can I give Marianne's?"

"Oh, we'd share it," he said naively. "I mean . . . I'd give you some."

Julie smiled in spite of herself.

Espivant, certain now that she would consent, pressed his point home.

"Marianne's money is—ought to be—everybody's. It's gloomy, mysterious money with a somber, Mexican face, and it makes a sound like metal held prisoner underground. A million is only a tiny spangle of all those remote minerals."

She listened, trembling and overswept by a breath from former times. Her practiced ear could single out the spurious anger, the incurable gaiety, the knack of seduction in the very avowal of unworthiness, the gusts of marital hatred and, above all, the positive refusal to be poor again. "I've never hesitated," she thought, "almost flinging myself headlong into poverty, if it was a question of escape. What's he saying? He's still going on about Marianne?"

She saw him break off and press the region of his heart with both hands.

"I swear to you, when I first found myself with that rose-colored body—it was the color of pink wax—in my arms, and that endless mass of hair, so long and thick I was almost frightened when it was all spread out in my bed, I thought I'd overturned the statue barring the entrance—you know, Youlka, it comes in the *Arabian Nights*—the entrance of the underworld with a cave full of emeralds, a cave full of rubies, a cave full of sapphires. And as the statue was fond of me into the bargain—fond, much too fond really—the whole thing seemed easy, agreeable, intoxicating, lasting, and I thought myself an astonishing fellow."

He sat on the arm of Youlka's chair and leaned up against her.

"My poor beautiful darling, my poor, poor beautiful darling. These are things that I ought never to tell you! My poor beautiful darling, if you only knew how cheated of everything I feel. And then I go and send for *you.*"

Leaning against Julie, he tipped up her little black straw boater. She believed not a word he was saying; but, spurred by an overmastering curiosity, she laid her cheek against his velvet jacket. Herbert froze into immobility and Julie knew that he was expecting and fearing one of those gentle but imperious advances—so friendly and so amorous—which he used to call "the Youlka manner." "Always on the lookout for sensuality," she thought, "pleasure-blackmail, pleasure-panacea, pleasure-deathblow. Is that all he knows about or understands?"

Through the cloth of his suit she felt the irregular beating of Herbert's damaged heart, and thenceforward it dominated every other sound. She was scared all of a sudden by the broken rhythm, scared lest the unequal beats should stop, and she sat up straight. A voice that was studiedly, miraculously deep and precise, floated down to her.

"Didn't you like it there, Youlka darling?"

She shook her head to avoid answering and took Herbert by the arm. "Don't sit perched like that on the arm of the chair!"

"Like a bird on a branch!" he said. "By the way, Youlka, has Becker's remittance turned up?"

"No. It comes on the fifteenth. Three notches in the girth, as Léon would say."

"What's Léon's rank in the Army?"

"Captain. The dried-up remains of one, that's to say. Why?"

"Because of the war."

"Oh, really . . ." Julie said with a sigh of boredom.

"Yes, really, just as you say; what does Léon think about it?"

"Well, if war breaks out he's going to sell his pigs. Kill his mare Hirondelle, and join up again."

"How do you mean, kill his mare? Poor wretch! What a brute Léon is. Why?"

Julie looked at him disdainfully.

"If you don't understand, it's no use explaining."

"You Carneilhans are very lucky. You never see further than your noses."

He glanced furtively at his reflection in the brass and tortoiseshell looking glass. Julie realized that he was thinking about his illness and the uncertainty of his life.

"Here, Youlka. I wish you'd have this."

He unclasped from his wrist a watch attached to a platinum curb chain, and handed it to her.

"Is it eatable, Herbert?"

"Yes; when one's got teeth like yours. It's too heavy for me. Everything seems to tire me now. The bracelet presses just where a vein is beating, or an artery. Sell it or pawn it. . . . I'd like it to be a sort of link between us, a sort of something . . ."

"Something on account," said Julie.

He slid the warm chain into her hand.

"Oh, my poor old darling, don't pretend to be tougher than you really are! It doesn't fool me. Let's each of us do what we can for the other. It would be our only virtue! If only I had some money! It's pretty odd, you'll admit, that I never do have any. Would you like to carry off one of the Guardis for breakfast tomorrow? Or would you prefer a Panini three meters by five?" .

"Oh, a little slice of the Panini would be ample, thanks! Do they all belong to you?"

"Nothing here belongs to me. It was a decision I made at the time of my marriage. I stuck to it afterward out of good manners, and now I have to go on, because I've no option. But . . ."

He leaned over Julie, making his brown eyes shine with a more brilliant luster and bringing his sinuous mustached mouth close to her ear. "But I can steal," he said archly.

Julie shook her head.

"You're flattering yourself," she said. "That's what one thinks. But after all, what *can* one carry away from a luxurious marital establishment? I know something about it! It boils down to three trunks full of clothes, some books you don't really care about, a few knickknacks, a necklace, a couple of clips and three rings. And a pair of hideous cufflinks left lying about in a bowl, that you take on principle. Pictures, yes. But rich people haven't owned pictures for very long"—she raised her eyes to the Panini—"and what pictures!"

She opened her hand and looked at the warm chain.

"It certainly looks a very good watch," she said.

"But you must certainly keep the watch!" Espivant cried. "There are two little platinum prongs that fit onto a link of the chain; you press them and the watch comes off. Let's have it a moment. It's beautifully made."

They both sat down, leaning over the watch. A sunbeam turned the nape of Julie's neck into a solid pillar of silver. Herbert's over-silky hair, surrounding a small and carefully hidden tonsure, curled like a woman's. Both of them, quite oblivious of their age, were as fascinated as children with a mechanical toy.

"Marvelous!" said Julie. "What are they called, these sort of fat links, more or less square? They're like a convict's chains."

"I'll give another in exchange," said Espivant.

"Who to?"

"To Marianne, of course, when she's found her lost chick. Hello, that's her. Idiot," he said, laughing. "That's her, calling I mean—that little wooden buzzer ringing under the desk. Hello, Cousteix? Put her through, quick. Hello? Darling, at last! Where are you? Where? But that's miles away! I can't hear at all well."

Julie had withdrawn to the end of the room, and watched him going through the motions of love and concern; questioning with raised eyebrows, pursing his lips into a heart shape and sticking his chin out to underline "very badly" with a note of plaintiveness. "Anyone else would come to bits under the ludicrousness of it all," she thought. "Yet he gets away with it. It's a star turn."

"Found him? Alive? Ah! But why is your voice so tragic, then, my Black Rose?"

He threw Julie a gay little kiss across the telephone with the tips of his fingers. "A star turn with all its execrable taste and all its bounderishness. If he thinks I like it . . ." The mask of the caressing musketeer froze under her eyes and the seductive voice stumbled over the words: "With . . . with what? Veronal? But . . . but is he out of danger? Oh, the idiot child! Neuilly Hospital? Of *course* I understand it's not your fault in any way. But try and talk more clearly, for God's sake. I beg your pardon, darling, but you can imagine that your emotion and mine don't make things easier."

He fell silent and listened for a long time without interrupting. Holding a pencil in his free hand, he began to draw little rabbits, traced in a single outline, on the blotting paper. Julie's piercing eyes counted them automatically. But she gave up counting after the word "Veronal" and lay in wait for some unknown and vaguely threatening event. She breathed in deeply and felt ready for what was to come. "It will be the moment when he stops drawing those little rabbits." He stopped drawing, threw down his pencil and raised his eyes to Julie.

"All right," he said. "The rest isn't particularly important; you'll tell me when you get here," he said into the telephone. "Tomorrow, the whole business will seem no more than a bad dream for both of us. Of course you must leave him there. It's the wisest thing to do. Don't . . . don't hurry, darling; the urgent thing was for me to know where you were. Me too, darling, me too."

He hung up the receiver without lowering his eyes from Julie and lit a cigarette.

"Well, Youlka," he said at last, "so you've developed a taste for young boys."

As she did not answer, he went on:

"To clear up anything that remains obscure, I'd like to inform you that Toni was discovered unconscious at the Hotel Continental. A photograph of you was found beside his bed. Also, a letter saying that he was taking his life voluntarily, and a note from you putting off a rendezvous. That's all. What have you got to say to all that?"

"Nothing," Julie said.

He stood up with violence.

"What do you mean, nothing?"

"Ah, yes, of course! I'd like to know if you'd have preferred the note from me to have been an acceptance of the rendezvous, instead of a refusal. I *didn't put it off.* I *refused* it."

She felt at the top of her form, a condition of which her moral solitude had for a long time robbed her. Once again she was deep in the atmosphere where women, the permanent objects of men's rivalry, bear all their suspicions lightheartedly, listen to their insults, yield under varied assaults and hold their own against masculine presumption and derive from it all a simple and lively pleasure. Her horsewoman's muscles twitched in her thighs and she felt in her breast the rhythm of her full and regular heartbeats. "He's got no idea what to say or do," she thought. "In point of fact, men scarcely ever have. But what's this particular one looking so cross about?"

She was disturbed by her feeling of jubilation. Besides, the presence of several former Julies was blinding her to the implications of the moment. One of her vanished selves was in full flight from good old Becker and flinging herself at the head of a poor but very handsome young officer who was almost demolished by so splendid a catastrophe. Another Julie, naked and golden this time, shivered with cold and impatience between two men who were on the point of coming to blows, but they finally thought better of it. A credulous Julie followed, blindly absorbed by her passion for Espivant, then betrayed, desperate, and, in the end, consoled. They were Julies ready for any drama, provided they were dramas of love. Julies who were only capable of triumph, subtlety, kindness, ferocity, or stoicism if these were the byproducts of love. These and the easy chastity and the physical passion that it engendered were the fruits of Julie's faithful and unflagging appetite for love.

"And when, if I'm not being indiscreet, did this story begin?"

She fixed on Espivant a tenacious blue gaze that overflowed with the spirit of hazard and defiance. "So he's made up his mind," she thought. "Men are not very quick thinkers."

"Your question would be extremely indiscreet if there *were* any story. But there isn't."

"As if I'd believe that!"

"Young Mr. Hortiz wanted to behave like his steppapa. Yes, you don't like that name, do you? I think it's rather fun. It was perfectly natural for him to fall in love with me, at his age and mine. And that's the whole story, as you call it. I've just learned the rest from you. A bit more and it would have been the end."

"I shouldn't advise you to laugh about it!"

"Thanks, I've never needed your advice or permission to laugh. After all, nobody's been killed by the business. And who on earth doesn't commit suicide, more or less, between fifteen and twenty?" She walked up to the desk and took a cigarette from a vase as she would have drawn an arrow from a quiver.

"A light, please, Espivant."

He held out his lighter without a word. The blood was in her cheeks, and she carried herself like a figurehead. Her lips trembled slightly. She surrounded herself with smoke and went on.

"A little fellow less than eighteen years old! A sort of delicate little Borgia! I agree, he's very beautiful. But pff! You ought to know, unless you've quite forgotten what I think of the Italian statuette kind of beauty. I bet he's got two lilac-colored buttons on his chest and a dismal little—"

"That's enough!" Espivant said.

"Enough of what?" Julie innocently asked.

"Enough of all that . . . of all that filth."

"But what filth, Herbert? Here am I cudgeling my brains to tell the truth: I clear myself of the slur of corrupting children—whom I hold, anyway, in holy abomination. I can't bear veal, lamb, or kid, and I can't bear adolescents. If there's anybody who knows my amorous proclivities, surely that person is not very far from here, at this very moment?"

She was longing to overstep the mark, to hear insulting words and slamming doors, to twist her wrists free from somebody's hands again—either a lover's or a stranger's—to measure her strength against that of another, voluptuously, or in a struggle. But Espivant, she saw, was holding himself back and breathing with difficulty. A generous impulse overcame her. "Here we are with only this scrap of nonsense between us," she went on, "and he's not worth all this fuss! You're not really cross, are you?"

"Yes," said Herbert.

"Cross-*cross,* or just cross?"

He answered with a gesture and avoided looking at her.

"Seriously? But really, Herbert, why?"

Herbert remained standing, his eyes lowered. Julie saw that he was rumpling with one hand under his jacket the place where his heart lay. She shoved a chair from behind into the hollow of his knees, briskly enough to jerk him into the seat by surprise.

"Herbert, will you please tell me how I'm to blame in all

this business? Because I really don't see . . ."

"Leave me alone," he cried in a low voice. "I don't see either! But I'm not going to stand your—that in front of me, talking to me—I'm not going to have you discussing any male creature as if you were deciding to use it or not to use it! You're free and I'm married. I quite realize all that. But your liberty doesn't extend to coming here and then, under my very nose, appraising the Hortiz boy's physique."

As Julie merely shrugged her shoulders, he struck the desk with his fist.

"The Hortiz boy or anyone else! You are the field that I've mown and trampled! But I swear that if others have done the same after me, you're not going to come here and shove the marks they've left on you under my nose!"

He looked her up and down, trying to master his irregular breathing, and Julie admired him with a growing anxiety. She felt a danger swelling inside her that she would be unwilling to escape. But Espivant made a gesture of affliction, and only said: "Go away."

"What do you mean, go away?"

"What I say. Go away!"

She pivoted round on her heel, went out and slammed the door behind her. Strangers gazed at her as she crossed the garden, but she did not even see them.

She plunged into the warm street as into a bath. Then, mastering her passion, she called Espivant a cad and a fool. But, deep down in herself, she went over and over the insulting words, weighing up all they contained of promise or of threat. Toward the south, a storm hung heavy over the city. Paris waited for it supinely with all her *concierges* out of doors on the watered and steaming pavements. "This kind of weather," grinned Julie, "must make Marianne curse herself for being a redhead!" For she knew that the strange purplish hair of Mme. d'Espivant owed nothing to dye.

Now and then she accorded a thought, a "poor kid" to Toni Hortiz, coldly summoning up the loosened, prostrate body, the inanimate beauty of the child who had wished to sleep forever. "It was his right. But it was idiotic. At that age, luckily, one's as clumsy at dying as at living. It's hot. A cold river to swim in, that's what I want." She noticed that her bag seemed heavier on her arm. "Of course, the chain. I've got it. I'll sell it tomorrow morning."

She took a cab to *Le Journal.* Under irregular raindrops, each the size of a flower petal, the curiosity aroused by the Beauty Queens had filled the streets. Lucie Albert, in her joy at seeing Julie, made her signs as though she had been shipwrecked, to which Julie gave cold response. But she was determined to enjoy herself to the full. They sat side by side in the hottest part of the room. Bereft of all pity for the exhausted Beauties, Julie sized them up with a whiplike glance, which lashed them from head to heel: she commented on hair falling out of curl, on the delicacy or coarseness of wrist or ankle, the stoop of a shoulder blade, the little constellations of freckles at the top of young arms, the dress from a foreign capital. This cannibal feast only ended when she saw that Lucie Albert was on the point of fainting or being sick.

The storm, lightened by the shower, had drifted by without a downpour and now it was sailing up and away, opening its lips of fire across a pale yellow sunset.

"Come on, my angel. I'll take you out to dinner," Julie said.

The girl looked at her with her enormous eyes—vast globes unaccustomed to the light of day—and said, "Oh no, Julie. I'm feeling sick . . . and it's too expensive."

"Come on. I'm rich. We'll dance afterward to cool ourselves down! "

"And what about Coco Vatard?" suggested Lucie Albert. "You've no idea what the poor fellow said to me when we were going downstairs."

"No," said Julie. "No Coco today, thanks. That'll do."

She made the usual grimace with her nostrils. Her cheeks were hot under their silver down and her blue eyes somber and aggressive. She rubbed the makeup even over her eyelids in a shop-window looking glass.

She fed her little slave in the Place du Tertre. She filled her up with Asti-Spumante, but only drank iced water and coffee herself.

"But you're eating nothing, Julie. What's the matter? Julie, you haven't told me anything about this afternoon. Did you have words with that gentleman?"

"No, my love. He was very nice. But when I'm not hungry I don't eat, that's all."

She went on listening in a vague way to the childish chatter of the simple little creature. Gay and downcast by turns, Lucie would willingly have joined her solitude in all docility to Julie's, had she been given the chance. But this Julie refused to give. She had always scorned the help that one woman gives to another.

"The other night," Lucie was saying, "one of the clients paid his bill with a thousand-franc note, and Gaston brought it to me at the cash desk. It was about three in the morning. It was a new note, but it didn't seem quite smooth enough between the fingers. I didn't want to make a fuss, but . . ."

Julie breathed in the air of the Parisian night, a pleasure costing little, and reserved for people who refuse to stay indoors. A shooting star streaked briefly across the upper sky and soon lost itself in the vaporous zone hanging over Paris.

"Are you sure it's not later than ten, Julie? You know, I've got to be in the nightclub at ten forty-five."

They danced for a few minutes to the accordion, but Julie, still dreaming of violence and free fights, grew tired of leading all the time a partner who was too fragile and submissive.

"You look as though you're on the warpath tonight, Julie! Who have you got your knife into?"

"I'm wondering," Julie said. "Come on. I'll drop you at your nightclub by taxi."

Julie went home, although it was hardly eleven. A little family café next door supplied her with half a bottle of water, which she swallowed at a draught on the deserted terrace, under the reddened leaves of a chestnut tree. The late passersby turned round to look at this fair-haired woman, as she sat smoking all by herself. Her legs were crossed, her face was lost in shadow and a silver reflection played over the nape of her neck and her silk stockings. She allowed herself to be gazed at without displeasure. Her evening, already half over, no longer held any terrors for her.

She undressed slowly, and created a breath of air between the studio and the kitchen before going straight to a little mother-of-pearl fitted box, without a lock, which was hidden in the hanging cupboard. She undid a bundle of letters, picked out a sheet of paper bearing a sixty-centime stamp, and reread it. *"I hereby testify that I have received, in the nature of a loan, from Madame Julius Becker . . ."* She folded it up at once, and put back everything in good order.

She scattered her remaining hundred and forty francs and the platinum chain over her bedside table. Then she put on her damp bathrobe and sat down to make out a list. "Two tailor-made suits. Four blouses. Two v. pretty pullovers. A long overcoat. An afternoon dress. Stockings, gloves, shoes, hats (two only). Underclothes. A very smart mackintosh." She took the chain solemnly into the kitchen to weigh it on the scales; but she could not find the weights. She lay listening to the wind sweeping across the sheet-zinc of the roof, and then turned the lamp on again and picked up the list. Opposite "underclothes" she wrote "For whose benefit?" and then crossed it out and went back to bed.

The days following were measured out to Julie in equal doses of disappointment and intoxication. She went to a dressmaking house where she unearthed an elderly and rebellious saleswoman, who wore a bang of carrot-colored tow on her forehead, told horrifying tales about the days of vitriol-throwing, and smoked in the W.C. But she made the clumsy mistake of saying to Julie, "Ah, in our day, Countess . . . ," and Julie squandered eight out of her ten thousand francs at another dressmaker's.

"But what are you doing?" Lucie Albert complained into the telephone. "Nobody seems to see you anymore."

"I'm working," Julie answered importantly. "Come round if you like and I'll teach you how to knit washable sports-gloves."

Her experimental bent and her skill with her hands had returned to her. She gilded a pair of mules, and tried painting a solution of *vernis-Martin* over an old biscuit box, which turned out like an enormous caramel. Finally, she knitted some gloves and a scarf out of very thick pink string, over which Lucie Albert was lost in admiration. The huge, nocturnal eyes of the little pianist-cashier blinked sleepily as she tried to follow the needles, for she could only manage to relax when sitting at a table in a bar or outside of a café.

"I've seen some lovely washable gloves in the Rue Fontaine," she said. "They've even got some sky-blue ones."

"Knitted by machinery," said Lucie.

"Yes. And what if they are? They're just as good."

Brand-new, dashing, self-centered, dressed up in gray and black, smartly gloved and wearing a pink scarf, Julie went out one morning at eleven o'clock. There was a yellow, end-of-August sun, and she stopped in front of the glass between two shopwindows. "A woman like that," she thought, "can still look a knockout if she's properly dressed. That little felt hat with the wood pigeon's feather is a pure marvel. All the outfit needs is a dark gray man. But that's an expensive accessory."

She was surprised to discover that her new wardrobe filled her with melancholy and a thirst for further luxuries. She found herself standing absentmindedly on the curb and waiting, not for *a* motorcar, but *the* motorcar, *her* motorcar. Only half awake, she would reach out for the cool contact of another body asleep outside the discarded sheets. She fingered the old place of the wedding ring on her fourth finger. Then she remembered that, in her impetuosity and unreason, she had lost the sleeper with the cold knees, the motorcar, the tiresome but charming house, the ring, and the trace of the ring. All that she had frittered away became almost tangible, and she opened her lovely nostrils to the memory of the tonic smell exhaled, when they grew warm to each other's contact, by the copper-red mare she used to ride and her Russia-leather saddle. "A Russia-leather saddle! Heavens, how flash I must have been! A saddle that must have cost—God knows how much! The mare, too. After the mare, I had a little car. Then I had the old Encelade woman instead of my Carneilhan Rocquencourt cousins and my Espivant sister-in-law, and Coco Vatard instead of Puylamare. And anybody who came and told me I had lost on the deal would have caught it hot!" But so far there had been only Julie de Carneilhan to reproach her with the social status of Mme. Encelade (expert in massage and removing tattoo marks and threading pearl necklaces), with the opinionated youth of Coco Vatard and the transparent emptiness of Lucie Albert.

A little later, she thought she had fallen ill. But, inexperienced as she was in illnesses, she thought it might be something to do with the change of life. "Already?" she thought, "And for a sou I should have said I was going strong." But when she questioned her bodily state, she was rewarded with neither instruction nor blame. She thought about Espivant every day, and about Marianne and young Toni, and in all sincerity said to herself, "It's odd how little I think of those people!"

Coco Vatard was the beneficiary of this sudden access of superficial democracy. Recalled and amnestied, he duly admired the hats and the dresses, the bronze-colored stockings stretched tight on legs with small, well-placed muscles. In token of her new gentle dispostion, Julie was "kind" to him, at last, one silent afternoon in the half-darkness of the studio. But he had no chance of putting into words the overwhelming gratitude he felt for the long, fair, and faintly luminous reef lying beside him. At the first word, the tip of a cigarette reddened in the shadows and Julie's muffled voice reached his ears.

"No. I hate talking about it afterward."

Julie could not help noticing that, apart from his effusiveness, Coco was becoming gloomy in the extreme. One day she tried to make him laugh by telling him how, in order to fit herself out with new clothes, she had sold a wristwatch. But he failed to laugh.

"Oh! I was sure you must have done something silly. You never consult me about anything. That wristwatch—which, by the way, I never saw you wearing—you may need it someday. You ought to have sold it only in the event of war. God knows what will happen to you when I'm gone."

"You think a lot about the war, Coco."

"I'm twenty-eight, Julie."

They were just finishing luncheon in the Bois. Julie powdered her nose and strengthened the red on a mouth which was the same pink color inside as her scarf and her cord gloves. The melancholy that she discerned in Coco's wide-open eyes did not disturb her, for she knew that love seldom finds expression in gaiety.

"I'll be recalled to the infantry. But I'll wangle to get into a motorized unit."

As he was talking only about himself and a hypothetical war, she interrupted him without hesitation.

"By the way, Coco. I've fallen out with Monsieur d'Espivant."

"Oh," Coco said. "I don't like that."

She laughed in his face and opened her jacket, showing her gray and pink-edged blouse drawn tight across her bosom.

"Well, I don't want to argue. But may one know why you're so keen, all of a sudden, that my relationship with Monsieur d'Espivant should be marked by cordiality?"

"That's easy. Your falling out, as you say, with that gentleman means that something pretty—well, pretty tough—must have occurred between you."

"We'll admit that. And then?"

"Well, something pretty tough could only be the result of something intimate, so I wonder . . . But you'll jump down my throat again."

"What do you think?"

Coco did not turn his eyes away, although Julie was searching them with a blue, unloving gaze.

"I wonder what you can both have been up to that was so intimate, in your past or your present, for the conversation to turn nasty. Quarreling with a man so 'gravely ill,' as you call it . . . weren't you afraid that it might have done for him?"

She avoided answering him. Her one desire was to be elsewhere, far away from him. Sooner begin the last three years all over again! Three years that had destroyed her bit by bit, with every hour worsening the last hour's work and each month evoking a more facile surrender than the month before, leading to a life that she was too frivolous and too proud to consider vain, a life to which her physical health, like the optimism of strong children, alone gave any value. Haphazard months, needy periods of waiting. Does all this, then, happen in a woman's life because of certain definite infractions and disobediences, through individual omissions, the breach of a companionship with one man, the choice of another, and then the fact of being chosen by yet a third? The long sequence of household cares, of toil with the needle, of turned skirts—"My dear, I swear it's better than right-side out!"—of ingenuities which one pretends are so many little triumphs, are not, then, the result of pure hazard, but of a hostile, of an almost fatalistic power? She thought without gratitude of good old Becker's gratuitous alms-giving. She called to mind those little festivities of the flesh, swiftly conducted and swiftly forgotten, exasperated moments from which a broken masculine voice seemed to rise to Julie's ears. "It's not their real voice," thought Julie, "but the voice of an instant." Three, four years of improvised meals on a card table—"Delicious, these radishes with mustard. Julie's really *full* of ideas!"—and restaurants where one went with one's lips properly made up and a dazzling complexion and a smile that pretended to be shortsighted, but revealed the authentic lady; champagne and caviar, or, perhaps, oysters, and *pâté de foie de porc.* Forty—forty-two—forty-five years old. "Who is that? Why it's the beautiful Madame de Carneilhan. Do you mean to say that name means nothing to you?"

The wind, blowing up the corners of the tablecloth, announced the fact that rain was gathering in the sky, and that the bottom of the shallow lower lake was only mud.

"Julie, you're not feeling ill, are you?"

She shook her head and smiled patiently. "No," she answered within herself. "I'm just waiting for the moment when you are no longer there. Because you're something I've never come across, and something I shan't be able to put up with much longer: a really clear-sighted man. You read through me into another man, and you treat him as an enemy. One would really think that Herbert has no secrets for you. You hate him and understand him. When I think of Espivant you ask me if I'm feeling ill. What good advice you could give me from the height of your twenty-eight years! An honest little counselor, one of those little plebeian marvels that chance sometimes placed at the elbows of queens. But the bitches of queens go to bed with the marvel and turn him into a trumpery duke, an embittered lover and a misunderstood statesman. With you as my adviser I'd never do 'anything silly,' as you so nicely put it."

She emptied her glass of brandy at a gulp, though it was a very old brandy and worth serious attention, a smooth and civilized brandy.

"Alley-oop!" said Julie, putting her glass down.

"Bravo!" said Coco Vatard.

"If he only knew what he was applauding! Nothing silly anymore—that's tantamount to saying I'll never be any use to anyone again—not even to myself. He'd keep me from ruining myself, or from being taken in. People can always ruin themselves again, even when they've got nothing. The clever ones pick them out a mile off. And he is full of scruples. Coco would never try to turn a receipt written as a joke into ready money, for instance. Chance has fortunately placed a good seventeen years between us; to mention only *that* particular distance."

"The brandy makes your eyes shine, Julie. They're so

blue—a frightening blue," Coco said in a low voice. "But you don't say a word to me. Won't you talk to me at least with your eyes?"

By half closing her eyelids, she softened the blue that he found so terrible.

"The clear-sighted little wretch!" she thought. "It makes his company intolerable."

"It's the Carneilhan blue," she said. "My father used to scare us with that blue when we were children. And then my brother and I discovered that we'd inherited it. Léon maintains that that particular blue tames horses."

"Really?" said Coco sarcastically. "And what color does he break in his pigs with?"

Julie did not flicker an eyelid, for Coco's fate was sealed.

"He's impossible," her thoughts continued. "He suspects everything with any likeness to me. I hope he'll soon detest me too."

"You'd much prefer me to have no family, wouldn't you, Coco?"

"I don't wish anybody's death," Coco said.

She looked at him prudently, well aware of the profound distrust that a man feels after a recent act of possession.

"Take me home, my dear, will you? I'm in a bit of a hurry today."

Her companion had the unwisdom to look surprised, a fact that she attributed to his clandestine espionage. The tired summer all round their luncheon table was cruel to her skin, thirsting as it was for the touch of salt water and deprived of the wind which, in the country round Carneilhan, would be ruffling the aspens and scattering the chaff in the threshing yard. The smell of the yawning melon on a neighbor's dessert plate suddenly ruined the smell of her coffee.

"He spies on me. He keeps a check on how I spend my hours and days. He knows I've got nothing to do, apart from all that soaping and darning he finds so reassuring, and knows that Espivant is forbidden fruit for me at the moment. Had I realized that myself?"

She became playful, as if she had some crime to conceal,

throwing crumbs to the sparrows, exclaiming in front of a great barrier of red geraniums. On the way back to the car she picked up a tomtit's feather with a silver tip and stuck it into Coco's buttonhole.

"You should never give feathers away, or birds. It brings bad luck to friendships."

"Throw it away, then."

He laid his hand flat on the little feather as though to protect it.

"No," he said. "What's given is given."

But she put an arm round his shoulders, and, letting her fingers fall, sought and plucked out the tit's feather and abandoned it to the stormy wind. She turned her head away from his grateful glance. "*I* know, I know, you're humbly thankful. But you won't be humble for long. That was the very last thing I shall do for you," she thought. She hummed a tune. She went on humming inside the car so that he shouldn't dare to speak.

"Drop me there, Coco, in front of the chemist's. I've got to pick something up."

She jumped out nimbly before the car had stopped. Taken unawares, Coco bumped against the pavement with the near-side front wheel.

"Your driving's become hopeless these days, my child."

"I know," Coco admitted.

He got out, and touched a scratch on the rim with his finger.

"I'll wait, Julie. Be quick."

"No, no!" she cried. "I'm almost at home."

But at that moment the downpour turned the pavement blue, and Julie ran and bought the first tube of toothpaste she saw, went back to the car, and let herself be driven home. She seemed to hear, resounding through her whole body, the warning drone of a terrible intolerance. Already she was unable to bear Coco approaching her refuge and drawing up outside her door.

"Till this evening . . ." Coco began.

"This evening," Julie said, "I've got my brother coming."

Coco raised his eyebrows and opened his eyes wide.

"Your brother?"

"My brother. Don't ask which. I've only got one. We're dining together."

She thrust the lower part of her face forward, in imitation of Léon, sucking in her cheeks and pulling down over her eyes brows as yellow, under the brown pencil strokes, as the flowers of a willow, and clamped on her features a disfiguring and specifically Carneilhan mask, as if she were loosing dogs on a trespasser.

"All right," Coco said. "You needn't make faces at me like that. We'll telephone each other, then. Wait a moment, Julie! You'll spoil your lovely suit."

But she opened the door and ran across the pavement under the warm lash of the rain. She hid behind the second door in the hall, and only went up in the lift after she had seen the car drive off. Tears and raindrops were running down her cheeks, relaxing the almost convulsive tension of her intolerance.

She allowed the last slanting arrows of the downpour to come into the studio. A pure blue, harbinger of clear skies, was rising in the west. She looked after her wet clothes before telephoning Léon de Carneilhan. As she waited beside the instrument, well-known sounds penetrated the wide and murmurous enclosure at the other end—a sharp whinny, and then the grave bell note of a wooden bucket striking the flagstones. She recalled the stables opening onto the yard, the terrible little office on ground-floor level and the room on the first floor. This was the habitat of the bachelor Léon de Carneilhan; and that was all Julie knew about it. She suspected that her brother had a leaning toward adventures in deserted lanes and open-air village laundries; a tendency that sprang from a certain grossness of appetite and the pride of a man bereft of fortune. Their partcular brand of fraternal relationship shied away from any exchange of confidences. "We're too much relations to be friends," Julie would say. But because she was the younger in age and strength, something deep-rooted in Julie compelled her to respect Léon de Carneilhan and his capacity for living alone.

With her first glance that evening, she noticed his drawn muzzle, his tanned and hollow cheeks, and said nothing. But she asked him about his mare Hirondelle. Carneilhan lowered his eyes.

"I've changed all my ideas," he said. "I don't think we'll be able to avoid war much longer, but I've decided to take Hirondelle to Carneilhan. After all, she's entitled to live out her life in peace. She's nineteen, and still a beauty."

Julie stopped beating the vinaigrette sauce.

"You're taking her? Taking her yourself?"

"Yes. Gayant will ride La Grosse and lead Tullia. They're all I've got left. I've sold out. I couldn't carry on."

"Well done!" Julie said at a venture.

She looked him furtively up and down for any sign of prosperity. But he was not even wearing a new tie. Nothing he wore ever seemed quite able to rise above a certain level of threadbare cleanliness.

"But," Julie asked, "will Hirondelle be able to do the journey?"

He smiled gently, as though the mare were looking at him.

"She'll do it slowly, at her ease. I'm quitting the high road after Le Mans, it's too hard on her feet. She'll be wild with delight. What are you giving us to eat?"

"Beef the way—you know—they used to do it in Périgord. Then salad, cheese, and fruit. Go down and get the rolls, would you? I clean forgot."

She followed him out with her eye. "There's white pack thread showing in his mustache and his nose is getting bigger. That's how the end starts, even with Carneilhans."

After a few short and regulation questions, they began their meal, without talking.

"Has selling out made things any easier?" Julie asked.

"It's given me breathing space," Léon answered. He went

and put the beef back in the oven and returned the compliment with another question.

"And Espivant, still at death's door?"

"He's not so bad," Julie said. "Remind me to tell you about him after dinner."

Carneilhan, with Julie's permission, dined in his shirt-sleeves, drinking away serenely at a nondescript red wine that showed black in the lamplight.

"But," Julie said all of a sudden, "if you're taking the whole lot to Carneilhan—does that mean you're going to stay there?"

"Not that I know."

The ambiguous answer was not enough for Julie. The deep mauvish night closing over Paris warned her of summer's end and made her dread the disappearance of this long-faced, fair-haired man out of the same mold as herself; sitting with grim eyes on his plate, eating with peasant's hands and the movements of a gentleman.

"These are real greengages," he said. "They're excellent."

"Tell me, Léon, when do you think you'll start?"

"Why do you want to know? A week from today."

"As soon as that?"

He surveyed his sister through the smoke of a mediocre cigar that lit unevenly.

"It's not as soon as all that. The nights are getting longer. But it'll be cooler in the daytime."

"Yes. Do you remember when we went to Cabourg with my lovely chestnut mare?"

"Yes. And Espivant too, don't forget! He soon packed up."

"Yes. So your mind's made up?"

"Unless it comes down in buckets that day, of course."

"Yes. Have you any news from Carneilhan? What's the weather like down there?"

"Magnificent."

Julie was afraid of insisting. Nevertheless, there were

twenty questions on the tip of her tongue about the downstairs room, the "blue room," three poultry-yard pheasants, the brood mares and even old Father Carneilhan. She felt a strange weakness in her that sighed for somewhere cut in the rick's side, to lie down in the hay, for the afternoon torpor of that pale and shingly soil. She got up suddenly.

"Stay where you are. I'll go and make the coffee. Will you clear the table?"

When she came back with the brown coffeepot, the cloth had been straightened on the card table, the whiskey and brandy, glasses, and cigarettes and the cups laid out. Julie gave a whistle of approval. Before sitting down she took the stamped sheet of paper out of the box of love letters and laid it down in front of her brother.

"What do you think of that?"

He read it slowly, and, before putting it down, verified the watermark by holding it up to the light.

"I understand your keeping it. It's your affair. But apart from that, I don't think it's specially interesting. Why did you show it to me?"

"But it was you who . . . who told me that you felt there might be a lot of money that Espivant . . ."

Carneilhan interrupted her.

"I meant if he died, and not what advantage might be got out of him during his lifetime. This paper dates from before that ridiculous marriage of yours. Who would dream of stirring up that ugly old story and spattering everyone with mud?"

"Oh, all right," said Julie disconcertedly. "Let's pretend I never mentioned it."

"Once and for all, nothing that puts you in touch with Espivant can do you any good."

"Why, pray?"

"Because you're so weak."

He kept his eyes fixed on his sister. She merely lowered hers, started shelling almonds and burnt her lips with the boiling coffee, while keeping well out of range of his blue irises and their pinhead black pupils.

"But who can have been putting that into your head?"

"Only me, really."

"Or one of your little pals who thought he might get something out of it."

Julie straightened up with a jerk and assumed a lofty tone of voice.

"Really, my dear boy, I may have all sorts of nonsense with 'my little pals,' but not to the extent of telling them my family affairs!"

"Espivant's not part of your family," Carneilhan observed.

"No. But don't let's split hairs. Let's drop the whole thing. My idea was no good. Yours wasn't any better, as Herbert's well again now. Do you know, by the way, that he never saw a penny of that famous dowry? He told me so himself."

"I can quite believe it," grunted Carneilhan. "He's such a fool."

"I agree that he's not a genius, but a fool? . . ."

"Yes. Don't you see that he's done nothing but idiotic things all his life—always in a bright and intelligent manner? That stroke of genius, his last marriage, let's take a look at that! If I married a rich woman, I'd have her cleaning my boots."

"It's always so nice to be at your feet."

"You can always get out of anything," Carneilhan went on. "Anyway, I'd never marry a rich woman." He thought for a moment, and then jerked up his lean head. "If he failed to get hold of 'his' dowry, how can you have thought of asking for all or part of the million back?"

Julie went purple, and feigned stupidity.

"Oh, as for me, you know there's not a single blunder I don't make! But you must give me credit for consulting you first."

"Delighted to do so."

She felt uneasy at his suspicions and tried to put him off the scent by dragging him away from Espivant. She managed to do so by telling him, with exaggerated abandon, the tale of

Toni's attempted suicide, and Carneilhan emitted a hard laugh when he learnt that Espivant had flown off the handle.

"You know how he is," Julie elaborated, "when he hears that a man is after a woman he has known! He feels ever so slightly a cuckold."

When Léon swept the crumbs off the table with the edge of his hand—a gesture that seemed to say, "None of this is of any use to anyone"—Julie breathed again and poured herself out a middling drink. Her stiffness fell away, she beamed in the lamplight and felt the warmth of the alcohol rise to her temples. She felt that her efforts had been crowned with success when she heard Carneilhan, in good spirits at last, say, "I don't know how you manage it, but you don't look a day over thirty tonight." She longed to become even more deserving of this praise and its undertow of silent, fraternal jealousy; so, like a bird trailing a supposedly broken wing, she had to direct attention away from the truth. She burst out with her ringing laugh, shed two tears, and told Carneilhan that she wanted to "ditch Coco Vatard," who was getting on her nerves.

Then she seemed to lose her head, and, with it, all discrimination between what she should and should not confide to a Carneilhan very much on the alert. She pulled to shreds poor harmless little Coco, brandished his scalp, plunged it into dye-steeped vats. "Can you see me, my dear, waking up beside a chap with a violet stomach and a green nose!" Carneilhan did not allow himself to be blinded all at once. While Julie, her lips shining with brandy and her straw-colored hair all uncurled by the rain, deliberately stripped her cast-off playmate down to the skin and beyond, Carneilhan risked, in a level tone of voice, a harmless question: "Didn't Herbert impress you as being rather a sham? And don't you find it slightly odd that Herbert seems to need you so much all of a sudden?" He tired of it in the end, and Julie no longer noticed the name that he kept dropping between her snippets of chatter in the hope of tripping her up. The conversation became a confused noise in her ears, and Julie was suddenly struck down by the need for sleep. She rolled herself up in the blanket of her divan–bed and stopped talking. Léon de Carneilhan pushed the leaves of the french window to, switched off all the lights except the one beside the bed, and turned out the gas in the kitchen. When he left, Julie was asleep under the dark red cover, and the short locks of her hair shone with the same pallor as her skin. She did not so much as tremble at the slam of the hall door.

Next morning she determined to take action, and laid her plans. By "plans" she always meant a series of decisions which seemed quite incoherent to other people, often earning censure from her friends and ridicule from her acquaintances, for she acted in defiance of what either would have advised. On this occasion, she took one precaution—which was to consult the candlewoman. With a new candle tucked into her breast next to the skin, she went and woke up Lucie Albert, to drag her off, pale from fatigue, with gaping eyes and a body in the throes of a kind of walking hypnosis. But that little creature of the night did not forget to take a candle from the piano for herself, one of two pink and faded spirals, which she slipped inside her blouse.

"What, Julie, another taxi?"

"Another taxi. And that's not all. Jump in, and go to sleep until we get to the Avenue Junot."

When the open taxi drove past a looking glass, Julie passed stern judgment on the slender, rocking silhouette, the pallor and the drowsiness of her companion, which made her all the more satisfied with her own upright reflection, her old black-and-white tailor-made (which had just been cleaned yet again), and the pink-and-yellow color of the nosegay formed by her face and her short froth of curly hair. Her secret state of mind and body was patent in her determined expression, her nostrils particularly open to the wind, and her mouth at its largest, painted a challenging red.

At the candlewoman's, an unchanging temperature not unlike the chill of the inside of a church prevailed in the little parlor. Cane-bottomed chairs stood against the wall, and the only decoration was a kind of diploma framed in black.

"I certify," Julie read out loud, *"that Madame Elena did everything in her power to prevent my late lamented daughter Géneviève from leaving on the yacht, having told her that she would be going to her death.* I say, this is a scream."

"Oh, Julie! There's nothing to laugh at! Think of that poor young woman being drowned! It's not funny at all!"

Julie gazed at her little friend.

"How on earth could you know, my poor darling, what's funny or not?"

Mme. Elena came in yawning, wagging her head over the arduous duties of her profession and complaining that she did not get enough sleep: apparently she did not qualify as sleep the sort of permanently torpid state that smeared her eyes with a vague blue haze. The rest of her, from the check apron to the loaflike bun of hair, might have belonged to a self-respecting charwoman. She started on the lighted candle with a knife as though she were scraping a carrot, and mumbled darkly to excite her two consultants. She spelled out, in the pools of hardened wax, that Julie would become involved with a rather unreliable man, that she would go on a journey and, finally, that she would climb a spiral staircase. With Lucie she became even more sibylline, and pronounced, as she pressed the old twisted candle on a sham Rouen plate, vague sentences about a hidden child. But what did the untrustworthy man and the clandestine child matter to Julie and Lucie Albert? All they wanted was to give themselves up to the enjoyment of a mystery that would never be elucidated. Lucie kept on saying, "Yes, yes," nodding her head as though she were memorizing an order. Julie took refuge behind an expression of mute Carneilhan aloofness. She left Mme. Elena's as though she had just been to a masseuse, and settled down outside a café. Lucie Albert managed to wake up at last when faced with a coffee and cream.

"I feel as hungry as I used to be after High Mass at Carneilhan," cried Julie.

"I'm feeling ever so peckish, too!" cried Lucie Albert. "Julie, just think! A hidden baby! It's amazing!"

"But have you got one?"

"Oh no, Julie! But everybody I meet now will make me think of hidden babies; it's fascinating. And do you see yourself in what she told you?"

Julie smiled as she buttered her *croissant.*

"Not at all! So you see how much easier I feel about things! I mean about what I'm going to do."

"But what things?"

Julie buried her teeth in the *croissant*, and swept the Place Clichy with an optimistic glance. Now, in the August heat, it was as dusty and deserted as a crossroads in the provinces.

"Anything, any nonsense. But, you know, *sensible* nonsense for once."

"Julie, you're not going to marry Coco?"

"What did you say?"

Lucie Albert retreated scared to the back of her chair. "It wasn't *my* idea, Julie. Coco's the one who's always saying, 'I'm very much afraid that woman is the woman of my life.' Don't curl your lip up like that; it looks awful. But do you believe what she foretells, Julie?"

"For five minutes. Then I hardly think about it."

She thought it wiser to lie no further. She was gauging the length of the next few days, swept clean of any observant intruder. Even Toni Hortiz, packed off by Marianne to the top of some wretched Alp, was recovering from his first suicide, and Mme. Elena had only read into her destiny those jumbled images of staircases and journeys. Far away from indiscreet surveillance, she was breathing in deeply a new atmosphere of freedom, through which, when the moment came, she could advance alone, and select her blunder, and cherish her last fling of folly. "But why should it be the last?" her pride whispered. Whenever she was in the throes of activity or impatience, she tensed the muscles in her thighs as though she were on horseback.

"You go and sleep," she told Lucie Albert. "When can you sleep till?"

"Four, five o'clock. Specially after having eaten. I only have to dress and make up."

Julie's oversensitive nostrils suspected the little thing of not washing much; her hair had gone lackluster from long hours, night after night, in a fog of cigar and cigarette smoke. Her skin, she thought, looked as pale and damp as chicory.

"Poor kid," she said. "I'll drop you."

The enormous eyes, which betrayed only the signs of accumulated sleepless nights, grew larger still.

"Oh, Julie, Julie! You'll end up by sleeping on straw!"

"On straw? But you've no idea of the price of straw. It's terrible!" Julie laughed. "Good-bye. I might drop in for a glass of something this evening."

"Oh, *do*! *Do* Julie! I'll play that pretty little tune out of *Les Biches* for you in the entr'acte! Do you promise?"

Between eleven and one in the morning, Julie made her way down to the nightclub. Alone, dressed in a new black tailor-made, she sat down in front of a gin-fizz at a table smaller than a tea tray, attracting attention by her fine stature, the sulphur-colored carnation echoing the shade of her hair, and her blue eyes as unabashed as those of the blind. She exchanged smiles now and then with her little friend, who left the cash desk to sit at the piano and play, very prettily, a fragment from *Les Biches*. After midnight, she accompanied the songs of the star who owned the place.

The narrow room differed little from other narrow rooms devoted to songs and alcohol. A layer of smoke clung to the low ceiling, and the size of the room and of the stage left no scope for attempts at eccentric decoration. Lucie waited for a sign from Julie before coming over to sit sideways near her friend and accepting a gin-fizz.

"Oh, Julie, you are beautiful, you know!"

"Have to be," said Julie pensively.

She forced herself to keep up a semblance of conversation. But she was conscious of no reality beyond the thin, dry taste of the gin. All the rest was merely a background to her last actions of the afternoon: removing the stamped paper from the mother-of-pearl box, folding it in a new shape, adding the few words "Do what you like," signing it "Youlka," and sending the whole thing to Herbert d'Espivant. The brevity and the ease of it all left her slightly astonished. She was not regretting her decision; nor did she regret it later during a night of calm insomnia. She only doubted, on the brink of sleep, whether she had really done it, and this doubt woke her up again. She was surprised, in the fine weather of the following morning, to find herself singing, and the morning slipped quickly by. "How easy waiting is, when one's really waiting for something or someone!" She touched the wood under the tabletop three times with her middle finger. After that she had to answer Coco's telephone call. Serene and out of all danger, she dismissed him in affectionate tones.

"No, my dear child, I can't. I really can't. Oh, but it's not a mystery at all, don't be absurd. My brother . . . Yes, him again, as you say. My brother has sold his—what's it called?—his establishment, thanks. Apart from the ducks and the pigs, there's the furniture, which will go for at least a hundred and fifty louis, but poor old Léon hasn't any idea of how to set about it, so I have to. No, really not, not tomorrow. Tomorrow I'll be at Ville d'Avray all day. Telephone me there? My dear, just imagine, it's been cut off for the last three months. He hadn't paid the bill. Ah, my brother's an odd card! Fortunately, I've only got one. What? Come here straight away? Oh no, my dear. No, no . . . I really wouldn't."

An urgent voice at the other end kept saying, "Why? But why?" Julie pondered for a moment and answered in a friendly voice: "Because I'd chuck you downstairs. Yes; that's the gospel truth. Yes. True as I'm standing here."

She put the receiver gently back on its stand and smiled at the world of uncertainty that was opening in front of her. She put on the little felt hat with the wood pigeon's feather and went down to the street to buy eggs and shellfish and fruit. The day drifted by with such a soft and imperturbable flow, and Julie's waiting mood populated every moment so densely that the silence surrounding her was like a continual murmuring. "My letter reached him by the morning post, about nine o'clock. He must have recognized my writing." In imagination she moved across to the Rue Saint-Sabas and installed herself there. "At nine o'clock, the mail was put on the little table outside his room as usual. He may be unfaithful, but in everything else he's a slave to habit. Bath. Hairdresser and manicure at the same time. Marianne? It's true, Marianne's there. Smothered in her purple hair, shaped into fringes and coils and shells, Marianne at that time would be. . . . Anyway, who cares? Marianne can do what she likes." Julie waved Marianne away with her hand and came back to Espivant. "At ten o'clock he must have looked at his nails before dressing and said, 'It's an odd thing, but no manicurist has ever understood the first thing about nails.' Then he opened my letter. Then he called Marianne . . . unless he screwed his eyes up and said, 'Let's see. . . . Better wait a bit!' "

She lowered her head and clasped her hands between her knees because, saying "Better wait," she realized what a stern gymnastic exploit it can be just to wait. At eight she gave up and went and had buckwheat pancakes washed down with cider at a little Breton establishment, and finished her evening at the local cinema.

She was scrubbing herself in the bath next morning when the telephone rang.

"Run, Madame Sabrier, run for Heaven's sake!"

She heard the charwoman answering "Yes, sir," "No, sir," and leapt out of the water. When she saw her naked and dripping, and flowering with crimped yellow seaweed, Mme. Sabrier let out a shocked squawk and fled.

"Hello," said Julie in a high slow voice. "Hello? Who's speaking? Ah! Monsieur Cousteix, of course. How is Monsieur d'Espivant? Today between four and seven? No; I wasn't thinking of going out. Actually I had planned to stay at home. I won't be going out. Good-bye, Monsieur Cousteix."

Drops of water, while she talked, ran down off her hair in parallel lines, hung for a moment on the tip of her breasts, and fell to the floor. Julie trembled with imaginary cold. She caught sight of her hair and her lashes all stuck together. "I'm going to look awful today."

She dressed and put on white canvas shoes and walked up and down in the Bois for an hour and a half. Then she came home and cooked herself a well-chosen beefsteak on the ring. "As thick," she thought, "as a dictionary."

But she left the washing up, and painted her nails red. The hours of the afternoon were faithfully, tritely similar to the swift, exciting hours that precede the arrival of a man one is waiting for. She got ready a tray with two cups and wrapped a bunch of green mint up in a damp cloth to scent the tea made in the Moroccan way. "Moroccan tea doesn't tire the heart." Then she lay down in the oxhide armchair. Now and then she turned toward her reflection and congratulated it with a vague smile on having its hair done neatly, on being dressed in a gray tailor-made and rejuvenated by the lowered shutters. Made for meeting a man and being desired by him, for loving him often and too much, she played with the thought of the man who would soon come in. "I wish he'd come. I can't go on looking ahead like this. Afterward . . . afterward is a long way off."

She gave no free rein, in her mind, to the thought of physical pleasure. The best part of her vigil was a deep passivity and entire ignorance, for never once in her life had she picked up the threads of a broken liaison, regained the taste for a savor she had forgotten. A faint red flush rose to her cheeks and neck at the thought that perhaps at this moment Espivant might be fearing or desiring the amorous conflict of their two bodies. "No, no. Of course there is no question of it. Today's the day when I do my best to get him out of the hole he's in. Today he'll find out that I'm his real ally in spite of all we've said and done and hurled at each other's heads."

The sum of money he coveted, the impudent misuse of a few written lines, no longer tormented her. A "practical joke" either comes off or falls flat. If it's a flop, so much the worse. Nothing had accustomed Julie to thinking of Marianne as a moral creature capable of judging the acts of others. She remained a Marianne whom she had never seen at close quarters, Marianne the millionaire, a precious object calculated to discourage all rivals, a sort of Eastern conquest thrown open to competition once more by widowhood. A slightly sordid mystery did in point of fact surround Marianne. Julie was almost astonished that she knew how to read and write, spoke French, was not a deaf-mute! A woman loaded with so much beauty, with so heavy a fortune. Irritated, Julie gave way to a false little laugh. "It's almost as if she were a cripple or a woman with six toes," she thought.

The school clock chimed four and she leapt from her seat to open the shutter and gaze questioningly at the street and the weather, to make sure that the magnificent day and the light warmth had not changed; to chew a leaf of mint and powder her face. At the timid and uncertain ring of the bell, she laughed. "What punctuality!"—and she gave a finishing touch, before answering the door, to a bunch of cornflowers, and shook loose a sheaf of red poppies that spread round them, along with their dark blue pollen, a smell of dust and opium.

Upright, with her feet together and her mouth slightly open to reveal her white front teeth, she opened the door, "No, it's not him yet . . ."

"Madame? Yes; it's here."

Automatically her features maintained the half-smile over the white front teeth, the look of impertinent false myopia. "But—but it's Marianne . . . Marianne," she said to herself. "No; it can't be Marianne? It mustn't be Marianne!"

"I am Madame d'Espivant," said the stranger.

Julie dropped her free arm, accepted the reality at last, and stepped backward.

"Come in, Madame."

She slipped into her duties as a properly trained woman of the world, and Madame d'Espivant gave all the necessary answers. "Do sit down!" "Thank you." "This chair's rather low." "No. I'm perfectly all right, really. . . ." And then they

both lapsed into silence. Carneilhan frivolity was already at grips with anxiety. "It's Marianne. What a story! Lucie will be knocked sideways. And what about Léon? Here, right in front of my eyes, is the famous Marianne."

"Madame, my presence here must seem . . . strange to you."

"But of course not, Madame."

"We're going to waste a lot of time," thought Julie. "She's got a charming tone of voice. Lovely pitch. And downstairs in his driver's seat, Beaupied must be wondering what's going on!"

"But I only came because my husband asked me to."

"Oh? It was he who . . ."

"Yes. He's ill today. Really ill," she repeated as though Julie were about to protest. "I waited till it was time for his injection before leaving his side."

"I do hope it's not serious," Julie said.

"A very pretty pitch her voice has, soft, with a something acid in the higher registers. But if we go on like this," she thought, "I'll have to ask her to dinner. Fancy going out at four o'clock in a black afternoon dress! And that hat, with its little floating veil! I must say, I don't find the lovely Marianne so staggering after all!"

Then Julie shook off her feminine reactions and began to isolate Marianne from her general renown and from her own private criticism. She searched avidly for "the statue of rose-colored wax" described by Espivant, did not at once discover it, and thought her complexion of untransparent carnation, a complexion with the grain and opacity of marble, had about it a touch of slightly Jewish pallor. "Yes. In broad daylight it must be pink."

"Unfortunately, it is rather serious. I believe my husband himself—so he told me—has informed you that the doctors diagnosed his illness as heart trouble."

"Yes, indeed, Madame, indeed. But the future of an organic ailment depends so much on general conditions, and Espivant is supposed—was supposed—to have plenty of natural resistance."

"And so on and so forth, and what lovely weather we are having," Julie went on to herself. She was regaining her self-control. "Oh! I hadn't seen the plaits! Oh, what hair!"

Mme. d'Espivant had just thrown back her veil, laying bare part of the red-brown mass of her hair, the brilliant swellings and bosses of a diadem of plaits that crossed and recrossed and invaded her ears and tightly clasped her temples and her brow. "It's amazing!" Julie said to herself. "She's a woman, like certain statuettes, made up entirely of precious materials—jade, green-spangled quartz, ivory, amethyst. Can she really be alive? Yes; she is. And here she is in my flat. Here she is, and not trembling at all, and less impressed at having me in front of her than I am to see her here. Let us get to the point, Madame d'Espivant, to the point!"

"I wish I could share your optimism, Madame," said Marianne, "but I feel I must tell you that your recent demand has greatly alarmed my husband."

She turned slightly in her chair and raised her very dark eyes to Julie. They were wide open, like ancient Greek eyes, and armed with lashes on either lid, and the whites were tinted with blue. "Lovely, lovely eyes," thought Julie in admiration. "And how little she uses them! And she's simple. She must be simple to come and see me, even if he's sent her. What was she just saying? My recent demand? I should think it was recent, my letter only having been posted the day before yesterday."

"Were you able to judge in such a short time whether my . . . demand had an adverse effect on Espivant?"

The dark eyes fixed themselves on Julie.

"My husband, Madame, even before his illness, suffered greatly from his nerves." "Thanks for the inside information!" Julie said to herself. The passivity of Marianne, and her gravity, put her out of reach of all irony. ". . . and worry can cause definite ravages on a nervous patient in the space of a fortnight. . . ."

Julie flinched at the word "fortnight." "Look out! Things are beginning to slip and slide, and I don't quite see. A fortnight? Oh, the dirty dog, what's he been telling her?"

She repeated pensively: "A fortnight?"

"Perhaps a little more," said Madame d'Espivant. "It was a fortnight ago, I remember, when I came in and found my husband so terribly upset."

"She's got a rim round her mouth like some pretty Indian woman and a little hollow at the corner of her lips. She's a magnificent creature, without the faintest idea of what she ought to wear."

"Upset, Madame? I don't see my share of blame in this . . . this upset?"

Julie opened her jacket as she was feeling hot, and also, especially, so that Marianne might see her slender throat and the long noble lines of her figure under the gray-and-pink shirt. "There! She must have seen at once that I'm not a complete hunchback myself!" As she was longing to smoke, she offered her case to Marianne, who refused.

"I hope my smoking doesn't bother you. I was forgetting, Herbert smokes, of course. You said that you held me responsible for his getting worse. It's Monsieur d'Espivant's heart that is causing the trouble? His heart. Of course, his habit of hiding his feelings must have overtaxed his heart. . . ."

"I can wear myself out being ironical; she doesn't even appear to understand. Perhaps that's the most touching thing about her, that vague sadness, that widowed look, that warm-blooded womanish apathy. One thing seems obvious—she's sad, so Herbert must be really ill, as she says."

"Madame, please believe me when I say that I came here without pleasure and that I speak with deep regret," Mme. d'Espivant said. "You cannot have forgotten that your demand—the legitimacy of which my husband does not question—was accompanied by certain terms."

"She looks a bit matronly when she bridles," thought Julie. "It's not a question of flesh, because she's still slim. It's lack of breeding. A miraculously beautiful woman, with something unspeakably common about her. She blushed when I called Espivant by his first name. But, my good lady, you must get used to the idea that there used to be 'something,' as they say, between Herbert and me. Second Madame d'Espivant, don't lose your head!"

". . . was accompanied by certain terms that could be interpreted in a disturbing way, that made one foresee a . . . a disagreeable publicity round my husband's name, his personality, his honor, even. Am I mistaken?"

"How! What? Publicity! His honor? I can't ask her to repeat it, she'd think I was either deaf or an idiot. If I were at all reasonable, I'd get up and lead her politely to the door, and the farce of the two Comtesses d'Espivant would be at an end."

"You know, I should quite understand," Marianne insisted, "if necessity or some feeling drove you to use arguments, such as one employs only as a last resort. It's essential that I should not misrepresent what my husband told me, isn't it?"

Julie gazed in stupefaction at this beautiful woman in black who, even in accusing her, displayed such nervousness. "He did that! He's done this to me. He's put the whole thing on me. Everything, he's put everything on my shoulders. He's made her believe that his idea of a kind of blackmail was really mine. Oh! It's not to be borne. I can't have Marianne thinking I'm capable of . . ." But she was already in the grips of a still more prevailing blindness. She shook her head and cleared her throat.

"Espivant told you the truth, Madame."

She turned away, crushed out her cigarette, saw her hand shaking as she heard her voice shake, and felt an extraordinary joy because of it. "It's done now. I've said it! I've said what he wanted me to. I'm drowned, lost, done for, everything has happened as he wanted it to. But she must go now. I must tell her to go."

"So don't think about it anymore. Don't let's think about it, Madame," cried Marianne. "A woman cannot always be equal to circumstances," she added with a touch of plebeian *naiveté*. "You mustn't think about it anymore."

Julie grew gloomy again as a result of all this encouragement. "Don't think about it, indeed! Everybody under the sun seems to take it into their heads to give me advice—Coco Vatard, the beautiful Marianne! Don't think about it! As if I'd be able not to think that Herbert's put the whole dirty business onto me, has rolled me in filth. There's still time for me to say the word and put Marianne wise. She's not sure of him yet. She feels that Herbert's cunning white hand is somehow mixed up in all this, and I can change everything with a word if I want to. That, at least, he can't steal."

A line, written in a jagged, stabbing handwriting, floated in front of her eyes, and she read it through again: *"Youlka, please come."* She could not help herself, the saliva of sudden tears filled her mouth and she burst out into sobs.

"Madame . . . Madame . . ." Marianne's voice was murmuring close beside her. Julie struggled in vain, mopping her eyes with the help of a little handkerchief. She heard her own hiccoughs, but was unable to master them. "Nothing, absolutely nothing worse could have happened to me. In front of her! Crying in front of her! If only she'd go. No, there she is, rooted to the floor. She's watching the damage." All in a muddle, she thought of her swollen eyes, of the tearspots all over her blouse, and Espivant's treachery. "Doing that to me! How sure of me he must be! Surer of me than of his own wife."

She got herself in hand at last, blew her nose and felt no embarrassment in powdering her nose and smoothing out her eyelashes with a damp forefinger.

"I'm making an exhibition of myself," said Julie, "and a very unpleasant exhibition, too. I'm so sorry."

Mme. d'Espivant made a movement with her hand that simultaneously excused itself, put to rights a tulle collar that nothing had disturbed, and felt at her throat for a nonexistent string of pearls. "She took it off to come and see me," thought Julie, always prompt to change her mood.

"Madame," Marianne said. "I was deeply moved by your tears. Yes, yes, deeply moved. You seem so spontaneous, so . . . so impulsive. Seeing you, I can hardly believe my ears and what my husband was forced to tell me."

They were both standing up, with the folding table between them. Marianne's heavy scent assailed her. She recognized the scented air that had its source in the vestibule in the Rue Saint-Sabas, sailed up to the "children's room" where Herbert lay in his pearl gray pajamas, and then dispersed under the icy fan of the ether. She wrinkled her brows which, dabbed now with her handkerchief, had become completely fair. "I can clear myself in a few words," she thought. "It would be over in a moment. She's waiting for it. She practically invited me to. I'll speak, I'll speak!"

She spoke, without asking Marianne to sit down again. "Madame, the action I took needed no publicity; but I thought, for several reasons, that you couldn't be ignorant of it. I resigned myself to doing it under conditions that were . . . painful and offensive to me."

"Why offensive? The decision was entirely yours, if I understood properly."

"Careful," thought Julie. "This middle-class creature knows better than I do myself what I'm talking about, and wants to get me in a muddle. I'd give absolutely anything for a glass of really cold water. Ah, now she's really listening! She'd like to know what sort of man she's married to! Her little ears and her huge eyes are wide open for the truth. But she won't hear it from me. She'll only get a rotten, made-up story out of me, and she'll have to swallow it."

"Monsieur d'Espivant's extreme frankness doesn't put me on a bed of roses, Madame. The demand that your husband thinks is legitimate . . ."

Marianne interrupted her. "He only said that he did not contest its legitimacy."

"I'm delighted for his sake," Julie said. "As Espivant has told you everything, you also know how long this *démarche* was delayed. Putting it off was not always easy for me."

"Oh! I quite understand," said Marianne.

Julie leant toward Marianne, smaller than herself, and managed to smile.

"But there's nothing sure about it, or I do not make myself

properly understood. Living from hand to mouth, and on very little, is a sort of game for certain kinds of character, a bet that one simply has to win once every twenty-four hours. It's very exciting. I'm a bit of a gambler. . . . And so it went on, until the day when I'd lost everything. And what I did then, you know."

As Marianne did not move, and seemed to be waiting for her to go on speaking, Julie said in a low voice: "I think you know as much about it now as I do."

The intonation obliged Mme. d'Espivant to pick up her bag and her gloves and pull her veil down again, while Julie hastened to guide her to the door. On the landing, they both took refuge once more in automatic good manners and the exchange of commonplaces.

"But really, please don't bother . . ."

"The landing's so tiny that one's in danger of falling when one comes out of my door. I'll get the lift."

"No, no, really. I'd rather walk."

"No, I couldn't have managed five minutes more of it! Oh! And 'I hope you don't mind the smoke, Madame,' and 'I quite understand, Madame,' and 'the demands I made, Madame.' Like schoolgirls playing at visiting." Julie slaked her thirst with long gulps. Then, driven by some odd impulse, she went and sprawled in the only chair in the dark and claustrophobic little hall. Her mood grew calmer, and she felt grateful to Marianne for having left, for being so far away and already on the other bank of the Seine. "That woman's superb—or beautiful, actually, rather than superb. She hasn't got that nasty side to her that spoils so many of the Mme. Thingummies one meets. In evening dress, or at home—I'll bet anything she wears tea gowns!—smothered with her hair and her eyes and with silks and satins and harem jewels, she must be tremendous . . . tremendous."

She leaned her head against the rough pink plaster. "Oh dear, I'm no good at that sort of diplomacy. Marianne soon saw that. Nor at any other sort, for the matter of that. I just about got him out of the business by the skin of my teeth, my poor traitor. I'm not quite sure yet whether I did get him out of it."

She suddenly leapt to her feet. "And what about the money, the money he wanted? We're no better off if she doesn't give him the money he wants, if she hasn't given it him yet. Poor Herbert! It hurts him here if he stretches his arms out. Poor Herbert needs the wretched little sum, the chance to be a bachelor, his gamekeeper's pension."

She went and washed her reddened eyes at the tap, telling herself to keep calm. "He'll ring me up. Or I'll call up Cousteix. What was the good woman saying, all honeyed up with plaits and veils and crêpe-de-chine? That Herbert was *really* ill today? After all, perhaps it's true. I'd better wait. If only he'd tell me, or let me know. If it hasn't come off, I'll begin all over again. I'll fix it, whatever happens. Oh Herbert, my greatest love of all, happiest part of my life, and my greatest sorrow!"

She pressed a pad soaked in salt and water on her eyes. Under her eyelids, mixed up with luminous globules and zigzags, little mirages flickered past—a memory, a hope as simple as herself: the small, luxurious table, the fruit, the aromatic fumes of the coffee, a bright sunbeam falling on the burnished silver, and in front of her, pale from his heart attack, the man she was fanning with a napkin soaked in cold ether coming back to life in the hollow of her arm. A rough thirst for rescue work, and unquestioning feminine longing to prove her devotion, assailed her. She made her shoulders and her finger joints crack to test her strength, promising Espivant all her help meanwhile in threatening tones. "You'll have your beastly little million. I'll shove it at you on the table beside the cherries, slap in the middle of the bowl of figs, or in your great footbath of a coffee cup. If that Marianne of yours doesn't cough up, I'll have a thing or two to tell her! And if we pull it off, I won't think twice about whatever share of the swag you toss me! I'll snap it up in midair like a dog! And, who cares, I'll go and telephone."

She ran into the studio where, from the doorway, her eyes fell on an envelope that looked blindingly white and frighteningly thick. "Marianne must have put that there! When did she do it? Oh, of course, when I went in front of her to open the door. Nobody could say Madame d'Espivant is the sort of woman to lose her head."

She felt the packet, weighing it in her hand. "How light it is! Much lighter, I should have said, than that odd million of ours. The address is in Herbert's handwriting."

The top envelope enclosed another in which, wrapped in several thicknesses of tissue paper, was a bundle of blue and pinkish notes that finally emerged, pinned together in trusses of ten, brand new, and smelling faintly of tallow. "Is that all? Why, there are only a hundred thousand francs, and not a word. Not even an impertinent little 'Thank you'—not even the sort of joke a cheerful swindler might scribble, to make me laugh?" She looked questioningly at the door through which Marianne had just left, as though she could call her back. "He split the bundle up into our two stakes with his own hands—those swollen and masterful hands . . . and that's all there is to it. It's the last straw of cruelty. It's . . ."

"It's ten percent; what a middleman or a house agent would get," she said out loud, on what she hoped was a cynical and bantering note. But the sound jarred on her.

She rolled up the notes and slipped an elastic band round them, and then, at a loss what to do with them, she went and put them into the mother-of-pearl box. She came back and leaned idly over the balcony, vaguely marveling at the fact that the approach of evening had already assembled the sparrows in the ivy of a dusty neighboring courtyard.

"Not even a line," she sighed. "Not a single word to break this silence. The last words I heard him say were 'Go away.' An hour before, less than an hour, he'd said 'Didn't you like it there, Youlka?' "

She was inflicting bruises on herself purposely, trying out the two tones of voice, the harsh and the tender, and she proudly decided that the harsh, the insulting tone, was the one she preferred. It had at least a faint smack of the truth about it, of active jealousy, of flattering iniquity. "I'd have liked just one word, a word that would have turned us into accomplices, soft on the ear, and comforting to look at on the white paper. He really might have taken the trouble."

She leaned there, motionless under the approach of the violet hour, until her arms grew numb. Then she pulled down the blind and switched on the top light. Making up her mind to go out, she opened her makeup box. "Oh! No, I daren't show myself this evening." She felt sorry for her poor face. She made do with another of her scratch meals, with soup and meat replaced by sardines and cheese. She sprinkled sugar on yesterday's fruit which was beginning to shrivel, but she felt defeated by the thought of making coffee. She kept turning, as she ate, toward the telephone, as though demanding an explanation for its silence.

She washed up with deft gestures, and carefully avoided plunging her hands into the dishwater. Everything she did seemed easy and even pleasant, but not entirely satisfying. "Haven't I forgotten something?" she wondered. When the plates were in the rack and the bed turned down, she gave herself a clean answer to all this uncertainty: "No; there's nothing I've forgotten. There's no hurry. There's nothing left I can do for him. Or for anybody else."

As the hours passed, she thought out plan after plan—to telephone to Espivant to thank him, to insult him, but most of all, to summon him to her, to beseech him. "But beseech him for what? What I really want from Herbert can't be put into words."

She opened a book. But she had never, in her whole life, succeeded in giving the greatest of books precedence over the most insignificant of worries about love. "Well," she sighed, "I suppose I'd better go to bed. The only thing is, I'm not tired." She lay motionless in bed and listened to the hours striking. As the clock of the neighboring school tolled the succeeding hours she wondered, "How could I have stood that clock chiming the hours and the halves and quarters all this time? I'll never be able to get used to it again. I'll have to move." She fell asleep nevertheless, but woke up with a feeling that something or someone was living in the flat besides herself. At about four o'clock, she got out of bed, slipped into the bathrobe that never quite had time to get dry, and opened the stepladder so that she could climb to the top shelves of the hanging cupboard. There she began reaching and rummaging for things that seldom saw the light of day. After hanging on the back of a chair a beige gabardine coat and a pair of brown whipcord riding breeches, Julie de Carneilhan sat down under the naked bulb of the kitchen lamp and fell to polishing her riding boots.

The alarm clock and the bell in the hall both rang at the same moment. A clear whinnying sound, shrill as a cavalry trumpet, echoed from the street. Julie, booted, dressed in riding breeches and a flannel shirt, was tying a white scarf round her neck.

"Is that you already, Léon?" she shouted through the door. "It may interest you to know I'm all ready to be off."

"No, Madame la Comtesse, it's Gayant. I've come for the bags and things."

She opened the door, and shook the dry and horny hand that was held out to her by a little man on the threshold.

"Do you think it is going to rain today? I'm taking a mackintosh, just in case."

"No rain, Madame la Comtesse. Mist and dew, and then we'll have the wind and the sun between the stroke of a quarter to seven and seven."

"Is that Hirondelle kicking up such a fuss down there?"

"That's it, Madame. She always knows when the least preparations are in the wind. There's been no holding her since yesterday. She's seen the nosebags and straps and everything."

"Give me my jacket, Gayant. Thanks. Gayant, do you think I'm still up to this sort of trip?"

"I think so," said Gayant. "Madame la Comtesse is a horsewoman. How much does your ladyship weigh?"

"Fifty-five kilos."

"That's all right. Last year your ladyship weighed fifty-six and a half. Fifty-five's all to the good."

The little man with the overlong arms sized Julie up, from her boots to her soft felt hat.

"Do you think so?"

"Yes. Better for Tullia."

"Oh, you only bother about the mares, of course. It doesn't matter if I do myself in! Here, take this and this, and this. Take care, that's our breakfast! Go downstairs and tell my brother to come up. His coffee's ready."

She buttoned up her jacket and saw to it that the fork of her riding breeches fitted properly, with that shocking and masculine gesture with which classical dancers adjust their tights. She felt at ease in these clothes. Her boots and gloves fitted her on the large side, and she was securely hatted against the wind. She slapped herself over the thighs and cursed. "All this cash is making my pockets bulge. I'll hand half of it over to Léon."

She gazed at her reflection in the looking glass, festooned with crops and switches: a tall pale figure, with long, clean-cut legs. Her short and sleepless night, devoted by turns to agreeable preparations and sad thoughts, had just come to an end. She was all ready to go, but she still felt uncertain of her departure. Gayant's discreet "Whoa back there!" rose from the silent street, and the sound of Carneilhan lovingly scolding his mare. Julie could hear the horses moving across the road in the direction of departure. She sat down and wrote a few lines to the *concierge* and the charwoman, leaving a tip for each of them. The sight of the envelopes placed so prominently on the card table reminded her of the faked-up parcel padded with white paper. She felt weak and agitated. "I'm not going. No; I won't go! To begin with, I'm no longer up-and-coming enough for this sort of jaunt. And then, nothing decisive has been said yet. Herbert has often played a mouse longer than this, and perhaps today's the day he'll send for me, or even come here. I don't want to leave. I'm not going to leave!"

She leaned over the balcony, and could just descry the somber group formed by the two saddled mares, the little harnessed luggage trap and the two men busy with the three horses. She breathed in the dampness that prevails before daybreak, the smell of ivy, and the impalpable watery powder that hung in the air. She was moved. "How cool," she thought, "this spindrift of fresh water." Her wounded and versatile spirits veered round to the impending journey and sang in double time the songs that are improvised to and maintained by the gait of a horse; drew rein by a stream under the high timbers of a forest. Quenching their thirst, the mares would tread their hoofs and play their muzzles in the running water. "La Grosse and Tullia can be reshod anywhere by the roadside, while Léon will have taken at least four pairs of dancing shoes for Hirondelle. I didn't ask Gayant whether he'd taken the currycomb and the hoof-picker. But Gayant never forgets anything!"

Julie sat down on her unmade bed. It would never be open again for Coco Vatard. "What did that sententious young man say? Ah, yes! That he feared I was the woman of his life. Well, it wasn't so wide of the mark, that shopgirl cliché of his. He didn't say I was his Great Love; he'd get it quite clear; he said I was the Woman of his Life. Coco Vatard will have plenty of mistresses and at least one wife. Each of them will open up a wound, an anxiety of which none of them will be the real cause. I'll recover from Herbert once again, I think. And perhaps another man, not Herbert, will hurt me once again. But it will always be from him, that damned 'Man of my Life,' that I shall draw all my consolation and my desolation."

She thought she had been dreaming a long while, but, when her brother climbed the stairs, the brow of dawn had not yet risen above the neighboring school buildings, nor painted green the ivy leaves in the walled garden.

Instead of ringing, Léon de Carneilhan knocked three times, fairly hard, on the door: a sound which shook away Julie's dreams and set her once more ajangle. "I don't want to go! I won't go! I'll explain to Léon that I've got serious reasons for staying behind. After all, I'm a free agent!"

When Léon came in, she wrinkled her brows, and apostrophized him in the vigorous terms that had become a sort of ritual between them.

"What on earth were you up to down there, taking such a time, I'd like to know?"

"And who do you think's going to tighten the girths? And stow everything that rattles in the bottom of the trap? Including your bags and suitcases? And one of the bins of oats that was leaking through the bottom? Gayant never forgets anything, but he has no idea of how to stow things. If I didn't keep my eyes open, the trap would make as much row as a motorcar, once we got going."

Like Julie, Carneilhan had lowered his reddish eyebrows. He relaxed as he contemplated his sister.

"You know, that kit still suits you, though Lord knows I've never been keen on women riding astride."

Julie could have returned a similar compliment to her brother, who was dressed in some indestructible material. Russet-colored like their owner, his riding clothes had faded over the shoulders, his coarse and thickly planted hair was going white on the crown, and his forehead, owing to the strange cut of his features, was more deeply tanned than his narrow temples. A meager Adam's apple shifted up and down his throat as he swallowed his bowl of hot coffee.

"Shall we go down?"

Julie's blue eyes wavered.

"Listen, Léon, I'd rather . . . I'd rather not go. I'm not feeling well today . . ."

He interrupted her, moving a step toward her.

"Is that true or not true?"

She pulled herself together, and admitted courageously: "It's not true. I wanted to . . . to stay on a few days, to . . . to please somebody."

Carneilhan's glance slid across to the open bed and came back to Julie.

"Do you mean Espivant?"

She quivered, flinging herself against the suspicion.

"No, no! What on earth are you dreaming of?"

Then she laughed and cried tauntingly, "Really, my dear! You've no imagination. Or else too much."

She lowered her eyes in a comic imitation of bashfulness.

"Poor little Coco. He's very nice, you know."

She seemed to change her mind all of a sudden, and started rummaging in her pockets.

"Here, take this off my hands. Put it in your breast pocket."

She tossed him half of the roll of new banknotes.

"What's this?"

"Fifty thousand. Look after them for me while we're on the road. Good old Becker, believe it or not! He sent me that to celebrate his sixtieth birthday."

Carneilhan slowly arranged the notes, fumbling them incredulously.

"Good old Becker. Poor little Coco. It sounds as if you only knock around with saints and martyrs. Espivant will be an archangel soon."

Julie gave a little sigh of exasperation.

"Oh, you can keep that one. He's tougher than a seven-year-old hen. Are we going, Léon, or are we not? We're wasting so much time."

Swift and rose-colored light was already mounting in the sky. Julie's face materialized in the looking glass, her pallor, the rings under her eyes, her faded air.

"Oh!" she said with a start.

"What's wrong now?"

She pointed to her washed-out reflection.

"I don't think I'm up to it, Léon. I'd be under my horse within a mile from here. I didn't sleep last night, I'm not in training, I . . ."

She turned away, dabbing at her eyelashes. Her brother caught hold of her elbow, and made her swing round toward him. "What a great goose you are! You know what an old armchair Tullia is. Your nice, awful old Tullia, dappled like a circus horse; the beautiful remains of my Hirondelle, La Grosse pulling the old trap with half the paint off, Gayant dressed like nothing on earth. Do you want not to come because you're ashamed of joining such a wretched band of gypsies?"

She put her arms on his shoulders, laughing and crying.

"No, no, no! Of course not, I'm not ashamed! Look at my breeches, they've got two moth holes in them! Have you still got *the* trap?"

"You don't suppose I went and bought a new one for Gayant? Of course it's *the* trap. There's not an inch of paint left on it. It's peeling all over like a plane tree losing its bark. But it's still got a smart little umbrella basket, and luckily the rubber on the wheels is still intact. When you're tired, you can get into the trap, and let Gayant ride Tullia."

Julie gazed at the russet-colored muzzle and the piercing blue eyes that were losing their stern and threatening look.

"So I *shall* get tired?" she said sadly. "You see, even you say, already, that I'll get tired!"

"I wouldn't swear to it," said Léon, shaking his head. "But I advise you to. *Be* tired. Come on; let's be off. We're not trying to impress anyone anymore. I've got everything I possess on me. I see you're taking your whole fortune. Don't leave anything behind. The road to Carneilhan will be a one-way journey for me. Do you think you can say the same?"

He tightened his leather belt in order to avoid seeming to wait for a reply. But Julie said nothing.

"Off we go, Julie."

"Yes. Where shall we stop?"

"Wherever you like."

She smiled at such an unexpected statement.

"How long do you think it'll take us to get to Carneilhan?"

For the first time Julie saw her brother make a gesture of uncertainty. He raised his arms and let them drop.

"Three weeks . . . three months . . . all our lives."

He listened in the direction of the mares, who were growing restive. They heard the clink of the horseshoes on the cobblestones below.

"Isn't it an astounding feeling, Julie, having some money and no home, instead of having a home and no money?"

These few words, the lofty voice, the large, quivering nose, the movement of the jaw muscles under the reddened and clean-shaven cheek were accepted by Julie as precious symbols of brotherly affection.

"I want to breathe, Julie. It gets me in the ribs, having no money for oats, no money for straw, for the harness maker's bill and the blacksmith's."

Julie put her hand on her brother's arm to interrupt a litany that she knew by heart. The arm responded. She felt the muscles move, and rejoiced in so much strength. It seemed a token of hope and support.

"The sun's up," said Carneilhan. "We're going the long way round, Julie. The long way will tire the mares least, and also the horsewoman. We'll be far better off in the byways, with grass on either side. Gayant knows some tracks and pathways that are almost Red Indian, they're so remote."

Julie opened her nostrils and her whole body leaned forward in a movement of consent.

"You didn't warn old Père Carneilhan that I was coming too?"

"He'll know soon enough," Léon said, wryly. "If we'd told him, he might have taken to writing again just to stop you starting. Your presence will bother him a lot, at first. He'll have to clear all his stuff out of your blue room, his salt stores and millet cobs, his provisions of dried bread, everything that the damp and the rats can get at."

As he spoke, Julie's recollections passed through a porch, sniffed the cold hall and fumblingly hung a straw hat on a stag's antler. "Shall I still like my home?" she wondered. "Shall I still love my two Carneilhans enough, with their silence, their pride and their frugality?" She reached a blue room discolored by sunlight under a beamed ceiling. "I'll repaint it pink." The white underside of the aspen leaves cast their light over her memory like the reflections of a river, and she leaned out of the window of the blue room. "Unless I repaint it pale yellow!" From her oval room at the top of the tower, Julie de Carneilhan, aged fifteen, with the frontiers of her stubborn forehead marked out by her blond plaits, peered down at the rounded tops of two lime trees casting their shade upon the terrace, at the brood mares resting their heads on the railings of the meadow, at Père Carneilhan in his flat cap with his little hazel switch thrust into his coat pocket. So the network of roads, the staircase "turning like a corkscrew" promised by the candlewoman simply led, as though predestined, to the room she had lived in as a girl?

Careless of the sleep which still enfolded the house, they went downstairs with an indiscreet clatter of boots and talk.

"Do you think I should take the spirit stove?"

"I kept out the first-aid set; it's rolled up in a blanket."

When they appeared, the horses pawed the ground affectionately, and Julie greeted each of them with a lump of sugar to make amends and revive their friendship. The saddles and bridles and the stirrup leathers stretched by long use were shining with age and endless polishing. In order to make much of her dappled mare, such an ugly and meritorious beast, Julie threw her useless quirt into the trap.

Julie, who had been deprived so long of outdoor life and travel, found herself slightly astray among the seasons and the regions; she expected, almost, to gather plums and lilies of the valley on the way, wild strawberries and dog roses. She longed for the towing paths and the resilient turf of the heathland. But, above all, she summoned up remembrance of certain sandy pathways, soft under the horses' feet and hemmed in with prickly burdocks and bitter blackberries, with gorse bushes that plucked at manes and tails, and hollowed out pathways that used to force Julie and another horseman, both happy to ride side by side, close up against each other. "Herbert! And my long hair that used to come down over my shoulders when he tilted back my head." She pressed her forehead for an instant against Tullia's neck, hiding a last fleeting weakness. Then she turned resolutely toward her brother, at the very moment when the tall mare Hirondelle, immaculately gaitered in white, was coming to search out and caress the hand of Carneilhan with her wide, fanatic nostrils.

"Ah," thought Julie, "he, at least, is taking with him what he loves best in the world."

CHÉRI

Translated by Roger Senhouse

GIVE IT ME, Léa, give me your pearl necklace! Do you hear me, Léa? Give me your pearls!"

No answer came from the huge brass-bedecked wrought-iron bedstead that glimmered in the shadows like a coat of mail.

"Why won't you let me have your necklace? It looks every bit as well on me as on you—even better!"

At the snap of the clasp, ripples spread over the lace frilled sheets, and from their midst rose two magnificent thin-wristed arms, lifting on high two lovely lazy hands.

"Leave it alone, Chéri! You've been playing long enough with that necklace."

"It amuses me. . . . Are you frightened I'll steal it?"

He was capering about in front of the sun-drenched rosy pink curtains—a graceful demon, black against a glowing furnace; but when he pranced back toward the bed, he turned white again from top to toe, in his white silk pajamas and white Moorish slippers.

"I'm not frightened," the soft, deep voice answered from the bed. "But you'll wear out the thread. Those pearls are heavy."

"They certainly are," Chéri said with due respect. "Whoever gave you this lot never meant to make light of you!"

He was standing in front of a pier glass framed in the space between two windows, gazing at the reflection of a very youthful, very good-looking young man, neither too short nor too tall, hair with the blue sheen of a blackbird's plumage. He unbuttoned his pajamas, displaying a hard, darkish chest, curved like a shield; and the whites of his dark eyes, his teeth, and the pearls of the necklace gleamed on the overall rosy glow of the room.

"Take off that necklace!" The female voice was insistent. "Do you hear what I say?"

The young man, motionless in front of his image, laughed softly to himself: "Yes, yes, I heard you. I know so well you're terrified I'll make off with it!"

"No, I'm not. But if I did offer it to you, you're quite capable of taking it."

He ran to the bed and bounded into it. "You bet I am! I rise above the conventions. Personally, I think it's idiotic for a man to allow a woman to give him a single pearl for a tiepin, or two for a pair of studs, and then to consider himself beyond the pale if she gives him fifty. . . ."

"Forty-nine."

"Forty-nine—as if I hadn't counted! I dare you to say they don't look well on me! Or that I'm ugly!"

Léa sat up in bed. "No, I won't say that. For one thing, because you'd never believe me. But can't you learn to laugh without crinkling up your nose like that? I suppose you won't be happy till you've wrinkles all up the side of your nose!"

He stopped laughing at once, let the skin on his forehead relax, and drew in the fold under his chin like a coquettish old woman. They looked at each other in open hostility—she, leaning on her elbow in a flurry of frills and lace; he, sitting sidesaddle on the edge of the bed. He was thinking "Who's she to talk of any wrinkles I may have one day?" and she "Why is he so ugly when he laughs?—he who's the very picture of beauty!" She thought for a moment, then finished aloud: "It's because you look so ill-natured when you're joking. You never laugh except unkindly—*at* people, and that makes you ugly. You're often ugly."

"That's not true!" Chéri exclaimed, crossly.

Anger knitted his eyebrows close above his nose, magnified his eyes, glittering with insolence behind a palisade of lashes, and parted the chaste bow of his disdainful mouth. Léa smiled to see him as she loved him best: rebellious only to become submissive, enchained lightly but powerless to free himself. She put a hand on his young head, which impatiently shook off the yoke. Like someone quieting an animal, she murmured, "There, there! What is it? What is it, then?"

He fell upon her big beautiful shoulder, nuzzling and butting his way into his favorite resting place with eyes already shut, seeking his customary long morning sleep in the protection of her arms. But Léa pushed him away. "None of that now, Chéri! You're having luncheon with our national Harpy, and it's already twenty to twelve!"

"Not really? I'm lunching at the old girl's? You too?"

Lazily Léa settled deeper into the bed.

"Not me, I'm off duty. I'll go for coffee at half-past two, or tea at six, or for a cigarette at a quarter to eight. Don't worry; she'll always see enough of me. And besides, I've not been asked."

Chéri's sulky face lit up with malice.

"I know, I know why! We're going to have high society. We're going to have the fair Marie-Laure, and that poisonous child of hers."

Léa brought her big blue wandering eyes to rest.

"Oh, really! The little girl's charming. Less so than her mother, but charming. Now take off that necklace, once and for all."

"Pity," Chéri sighed, as he undid the clasp. "It would look so well in the trousseau."

Léa raised herself on her elbow: "What trousseau?"

"Mine," Chéri said with ludicrous self-importance. "*My* trousseau, full of *my* jewels, for *my* marriage!"

He bounded in the air, executed a perfect *entrechat-six,* returned to earth, butted his way through the door curtains, and disappeared, shouting: "My bath, Rose! And quick about it! I'm lunching at the old girl's!"

"That's that," Léa thought. "We'll have a lake in the

bathroom and eight towels floating in it, and razor scrapings in the basin. If only I had two bathrooms!"

But, as on former occasions, she soon saw that this would mean getting rid of a wardrobe and lopping off a corner of her dressing room, and so concluded, as on former occasions: "I shall simply have to put up with it till Chéri gets married."

She lay down again on her back and noticed that Chéri, undressing the night before, had thrown his socks on the mantelpiece, his pants on the writing table, his tie round the neck of her portrait bust. She could not help smiling at this hasty masculine disorder, and half closed her large tranquil eyes. Their blue was as beautiful as ever, and so were the thick chestnut lashes.

At the age of forty-nine, Léonie Vallon, called Léa de Lonval, was nearing the end of a successful career as a richly kept courtesan. She was a good creature, and life had spared her the more flattering catastrophes and exalted sufferings. She made a secret of the date of her birth; but willingly admitted—with a look of voluptuous condescension for Chéri's special benefit—that she was approaching the age when she could indulge in a few creature comforts. She liked order, fine linen, wines in their prime, and carefully planned meals at home. From an idolized young blond she had become a rich middle-aged *demi-mondaine* without ever attracting any outrageous publicity. Not that she went in for any pretenses. Her friends remembered a Four-in-Hand Meet at Auteuil, about 1895, when the subeditor of *Gil Blas* had addressed her as "dear artist" and she had answered: "Artist! Oh come, my good friend, my lovers must have been telling tales. . . ."

Her contemporaries were jealous of her imperturbable good health, and the younger women, whose figures were padded out in front and behind after the fashion of 1912, scoffed at her opulent bust. Young and old alike envied her the possession of Chéri.

"Though, good heavens!" Léa used to say, "there's no reason why they should. They're welcome to him! I don't keep him on a lead. He goes out by himself."

But in this she was not altogether speaking the truth, for she was proud of a liaison—sometimes, in her weakness for the truth, referring to it as "an adoption"—that had lasted six years.

"Trousseau," Léa said over again. "Marriage for Chéri! It's not possible, it's not . . . human . . . you can't give an innocent girl to Chéri! Why, it would be throwing a doe to the hounds! People don't know what Chéri is!"

As if telling the beads of a rosary, she ran her fingers over the necklace which Chéri had tossed on the bed. She put it away at night now because, with his passion for fine pearls and his fondness for playing with them in the morning, he would have noticed too often that her throat had thickened and was not nearly so white, with the muscles under its skin growing slack. She fastened the pearls round her neck without getting up, and took a hand mirror from the bedside table.

"I look like a gardener's wife," was her unflattering comment, "a market gardener's wife. A market gardener's wife in Normandy, off to the potato fields wearing a pearl necklace. I might as well stick an ostrich feather in my nose—and that's being polite!"

She shrugged her shoulders, severely critical of everything she no longer loved in herself: the vivid complexion, healthy, a little too ruddy—an open-air complexion, well suited to emphasize the pure intensity of her eyes, with their varying shades of blue. Her proud nose still won her approval. "Marie-Antoinette's nose!" Chéri's mother was in the habit of saying, without ever forgetting to add: "and in another two years, our Léa will have a chin like Louis Seize's." Her mouth, with its even row of teeth, seldom opened in a peal of laughter; but she smiled often, a smile that set off to perfection the lazy flutter of her large eyes—a smile a hundred times lauded, sung, and photographed—a deep, confiding smile one never tired of watching.

As for her body—"Everyone knows," Léa would say, "that a well-made body lasts a long time." She could still afford to show her body, pink and white, endowed with the long legs and straight back of a naiad on an Italian fountain; the dimpled hips, the high-slung breasts, "would last," Léa used to say, "till well after Chéri's wedding."

She got out of bed, and, slipping into a wrap, went to draw back the long curtains. The noonday sun poured into the gay, rosy, overdecorated room. Its luxury dated: double lace curtains, rosebud watered silk on the walls, gilded woodwork, and antique furniture upholstered in modern silks. Léa refused to give up either this cosy room or its bed, a massive and indestructible masterpiece of wrought iron and brass, grim to the eye and cruel to the shins.

"Come, come!" Chéri's mother protested, "it's not as bad as all that. Personally, I like this room. It belongs to a period. It has a style of its own. It suggests La Païva."

The remembrance of this dig made Léa smile as she pinned up her hair. She hurriedly powdered her face on hearing two doors slam, and the thud of a male foot colliding with some delicate piece of furniture. Chéri came back into the room in shirt and trousers, his ears white with talcum powder. He was in an aggressive mood.

"Where's my tiepin? What a wretched hole this is! Have they taken to pinching the jewelry?"

"Marcel must have stuck it in his tie to go to the market," Léa gravely replied.

Chéri, who had little or no sense of humor, was brought up short by the little quip like an ant by a lump of coal. He stopped his angry pacing up and down, and found nothing better to say than: "Charming! and what about my boots?"

"Your what?"

"The calf, of course!"

Léa smiled up at him from her dressing table, too affectionately. "You said it, not I," she murmured in caressing tones.

"The day when a woman loves me for my brains," he retorted, "I shall be done for. Meanwhile I must have my pin and my boots."

"What for? You don't wear a tiepin with a lounge suit, and you've got one pair on already."

Chéri stamped his foot. "I've had enough of this! There's nobody here to look after me, and I'm sick of it all."

Léa put down her comb. "Very well, say good-bye to it all for good!"

He shrugged his shoulders, like a young tough. "You wouldn't like it if I did!"

"Be off with you! I hate guests who complain of the cooking and leave bits and pieces all over the place and cream cheese sticking to the mirrors. Go back to your sainted mother, my child, and stay there."

Unable to meet Léa's gaze, he lowered his eyes, and broke out into schoolboy protests. "Soon I shan't be allowed to open my mouth! Anyhow, you'll let me have your motor to go to Neuilly?"

"No."

"Why not?"

"Because I'm going out in it myself at two, and because the chauffeur is having his dinner."

"Where are you going at two?"

"To say my prayers. But if you need three francs for a taxi . . . Idiot," she added tenderly. "At two I'll probably come to your lady mother's for coffee. Does that satisfy you?"

He tossed his head like a young buck. "You bite my head off, you won't give me anything I ask for; they hide my things away, they . . ."

"Will you never learn to dress yourself?"

She took the tie from Chéri's hands and tied it for him.

"There! And that frightful purple tie. . . . However, it's just the thing for the fair Marie-Laure and family. . . . And you wanted to wear a pearl on top of all that! You little dago. . . . Why not earrings into the bargain?"

His defenses were down. Blissful, languid, irresolute, supine, he surrendered again to a lazy happiness and closed his eyes. . . .

"Nounoune darling . . ." he murmured.

She brushed the hair off his ears, combed a straighter parting in the bluish locks of his black hair, dabbed a little scent on his temples, and gave him a quick kiss, unable to resist the tempting mouth so close to her own.

Chéri opened his eyes, and his lips, then stretched out his hands.

She moved away. "No. It's a quarter to one! Be off now, and don't let me see you again!"

"Never?"

"Never," she laughed back at him with uncontrollable tenderness.

Left to herself, she smiled proudly, and a sharp little sigh of defeated desire escaped her as she listened to Chéri's footsteps crossing the courtyard. She saw him open and close the gates, drift away on his winged feet, only to encounter the adoring glances of three shopgirls walking along arm in arm.

"Lawks! He's too good to be true! Let's touch him to see if he's real!"

But Chéri took it all for granted and did not even turn round.

"MY BATH, Rose! Tell the manicurist she can go, it's far too late now. My blue coat and skirt—the new one—the blue hat with the white under brim, and the little shoes with the straps . . . No, wait . . ."

Léa, with one leg across the other, rubbed her ankle and shook her head.

"No, the blue kid laced boots. My legs are a little swollen today. It's the heat."

Her elderly maid, butterfly-capped, raised understanding eyes to Léa. "It's . . . it's the heat," she repeated obediently, shrugging her shoulders as much as to say: "We know . . . Nothing lasts forever. . . ."

With Chéri out of the house, Léa became herself again, very much alive, cheerful, and on the spot. Within an hour, she had been given her bath, followed by a spirit-rub scented with sandalwood, and was ready dressed, hatted, and shod. While the curling tongs were heating, she found time to run through the butler's book and send for Emile, the footman, and call his attention to the blue haze on one of the looking glasses. She ran an experienced eye—rarely taken in—over everything in the room, and lunched in solitary bliss, with a smile for the dry Vouvray and for the June strawberries, served, with their stalks, on a plate of Rubelles enamel as green as a tree frog after rain. Someone in the past who appreciated good food must have chosen the huge Louis Seize looking glasses and the English furniture of the same period for this rectangular dining room: light, airy sideboards, high pedestalled dumb-waiters, spindly yet strong Sheraton chairs, in a dark wood with delicate swags. The looking glasses and the massive silver caught the full light of day, with a touch of green reflected from the trees in the Avenue Bugeaud. Léa, as she ate, examined a fork for any suspicion of pink cleaning powder left in the chasing, and half closed one eye the better to judge the quality of the polish on the dark wood. Standing behind her, the butler watched this performance nervously.

"Marcel!" Léa said, "for the last week or so, the wax on your floors has been smeary."

"Does Madame think so?"

"Madame does think so. Add a little turpentine while you're melting it in a double saucepan; it's quite easy to do again. You brought up the Vouvray a little too soon. Close the shutters as soon as you've cleared the table; we're in for a heat wave."

"Very good, Madame. Will Monsieur Ch—Monsieur Peloux be dining?"

"Probably. . . . No *crème-surprise* tonight. We'll just have a strawberry water ice. Coffee in the boudoir."

As she rose from the table, straight and tall, the shape of her legs visible under a dress that molded her hips, she had ample time to note the "Madame is beautiful" in the butler's discreet glance, and this did not displease her.

"Beautiful," Léa whispered on her way up to the boudoir. "No. . . . No longer. I have now to wear something white near my face, and very pale pink underclothes and tea gowns. Beautiful! Pish. . . . I hardly need to be that any longer."

All the same, she allowed herself no siesta in the painted silk boudoir, when she had finished with coffee and the newspapers. And it was with battle written on her face that she gave her chauffeur the order: "To Madame Peloux's."

The tree-lined road through the Bois, dry beneath the young, already wind-faded June foliage—the tollgate—Neuilly—Boulevard d'Inkermann—"How many times have I come this way?" Léa wondered. She began to count, then tired of counting and softened her step on the gravel outside Madame Peloux's house to overhear any sounds coming from it.

"They're in the garden room," she concluded.

She had put on more powder before approaching the house and tightened the fine-meshed, misty blue veil under her chin. Her answer to the manservant's formal request to pass through the house was: "No; I'd rather go round by the garden."

A real garden—almost a park—completely surrounded the vast white villa, typical of the outer suburbs of Paris. Madame Peloux's villa had been called "a country residence" in the days when Neuilly was still on the outskirts of Paris. This was apparent from the stables, converted into garages, the other offices with their kennels and washhouses, not to mention the size of the billiard room, entrance hall and dining room.

"This is a handsome investment of Madame Peloux's," her female devotees never tired of repeating—the old toadies who, in exchange for a dinner or a glass of brandy, came there to take a hand against her at bezique or poker. And they added: "But then, where has Madame Peloux not got money invested?"

Walking along in the shade of the acacia trees, between trellised roses and huge clumps of rhododendrons in full blaze, Léa could hear the murmur of voices, and, rising above it, Madame Peloux's shrill nasal trumpet notes and Chéri's dry cackle.

"That child's got an ugly laugh," she thought. She paused a moment to listen more attentively to a new feminine note; weak, pleasing, quickly drowned by the redoubtable trumpeting. "That must be the girl," she said to herself, and a few quick steps brought her to the garden room with its glass front, from which Madame Peloux burst out with a "Here comes our beautiful friend!"

A little round barrel of a woman, Madame Peloux—in reality Mademoiselle Peloux—had been a ballet dancer from her tenth to her sixteenth year. Occasionally Léa would search for some trace in Madame Peloux that might recall the once chubby little fair-haired Eros, or the later dimpled nymph, and found nothing except the big implacable eyes, the delicate aggressive nose, and a still coquettish way of standing with her feet in "the fifth position," like the members of the *corps de ballet*.

Chéri, coming to life in the depths of a rocking chair, kissed Léa's hand with involuntary grace and ruined his gesture by exclaiming: "Hang it all! you've put on a veil again, and I loathe veils."

"Will you leave her alone!" Madame Peloux interposed. "You must never ask a woman why she is wearing a veil. We'll never be able to do anything with him," she said to Léa affectionately.

Two women had risen to their feet in the golden shade of a straw blind. One, in mauve, rather coldly offered her hand to Léa, who looked her over from head to foot.

"Goodness, how lovely you are, Marie-Laure! you're perfection itself!"

Marie-Laure deigned to smile. She was a red-haired young woman with brown eyes, whose physical presence alone was enough to take your breath away. She drew attention, almost coquettishly, to the other young woman, by saying: "But would you have recognized my daughter Edmée?"

Léa held out a hand which the girl was reluctant to shake.

"I should have known you, my child, but a schoolgirl alters so quickly, and Marie-Laure alters only to become always more disconcertingly lovely. Are you quite finished with school now?"

"I should hope so, I should hope so," exclaimed Madame Peloux. "You can't go on forever, hiding her under a bushel, such a miracle of grace and charm, and she's nineteen already!"

"Eighteen," said Marie-Laure, sweetly.

"Eighteen, eighteen! . . . Yes of course, eighteen! Léa, you remember? This child was just making her first Communion the year that Chéri ran away from school, surely you remember? Yes, yes, you did, you little good-for-nothing, you ran away and Léa and I were driven nearly out of our wits!"

"I remember perfectly," Léa said, and she exchanged an imperceptible little nod with Marie-Laure—something corresponding to the *"touché"* of a punctilious fencer.

"You must get her married soon, you must get her married soon!" pursued Madame Peloux, who never failed to repeat a basic truth at least twice. "We'll all come to the wedding."

She brandished her little arms in the air, and the young girl glanced at her with ingenuous alarm.

"She's just the daughter for Marie-Laure," thought Léa, gazing at her more closely. "She has all her mother's dazzling qualities, but in a quieter key: fluffy, ash-brown hair, that looks as if it were powdered; frightened, secretive eyes, and a mouth she avoids opening even to speak or smile. . . . Exactly what Marie-Laure needs as a foil—but how she must hate her!"

Madame Peloux insinuated a maternal smile between Léa and the young girl: "You ought to have seen how well these two young people were getting on together in the garden!"

She pointed to where Chéri stood smoking a cigarette on the other side of the glass partition, his cigarette holder clenched between his teeth, and his head tilted back to avoid the smoke. The three women looked at the young man who—forehead held at an angle, eyes half-shut, feet together, motionless—looked for all the world like a winged figure hovering dreamily in the air. Léa did not fail to observe the expression of fright and subjugation in the girl's eyes, and she took pleasure in making her tremble by touching her on the arm. Edmée quivered from head to foot, withdrew her arm, and whispered almost savagely, "What?"

"Nothing," Léa replied, "I dropped my glove."

"Come along, Edmée!" Marie-Laure called, negligently.

Silent and docile, the girl walked toward Madame Peloux, who flapped her wings: "Leaving already? Surely not? We must meet again soon, we must meet again soon!"

"It's late," Marie-Laure said, "and you'll be expecting any

number of people as it's Sunday afternoon. The child is not accustomed to company."

"Of course not, of course not," Madame Peloux said tenderly. "She's had such a sheltered existence . . . such a lonely life!"

Marie-Laure smiled, and Léa gave her a look as much as to say, "That's one for you!"

"But we'll call again soon."

"Thursday, Thursday! Léa, you'll come to luncheon on Thursday?"

"I'll be here," Léa answered.

Chéri had rejoined Edmée at the entrance to the room and stood beside her, disdaining all conversation. He heard Léa's promise, and turned round: "Splendid, then we can go for a run in the motor."

"Yes, yes, just the thing for you young people," Madame Peloux insisted, touched by his proposal. "Edmée can sit in front next to Chéri, at the wheel, and the rest of us will go at the back. Youth at the helm, youth at the helm! Chéri, my love, will you ask for Marie-Laure's motor?"

Her small, stumpy feet kept slipping on the gravel, but she managed to take her two visitors to the corner of the path, where she handed them over to Chéri. On her return, she found that Léa had taken off her hat and was smoking a cigarette.

"Aren't they sweet, those two!" Madame Peloux gasped. "Don't you think so, Léa?"

"Delicious," Léa breathed out in the same puff as her cigarette smoke. "But really, that Marie-Laure!"

"What's Marie-Laure been up to?" asked Chéri, as he rejoined them.

"How lovely she is!"

"Ah! Ah!" Madame Peloux began in formal assent. "That's true, that's true. She has been really lovely."

Chéri and Léa caught each other's eye and laughed.

"Has been?" Léa emphasized the past tense. "But she's the picture of youth. Not a single wrinkle! And she can wear the palest mauve, such a foul color! I loathe it and it loathes me."

Madame Peloux raised her big pitiless eyes and thin nose from her brandy glass.

"The picture of youth, the picture of youth!" yapped Madame Peloux. "Pardon me, pardon me! Marie-Laure had Edmée in 1895, no . . . '94. She'd just run away with a singing teacher, leaving Khalil Bey flat, though he'd given her the famous pink diamond which . . . No, no! Wait! . . . That must have been the year before!"

The trumpet notes were shrill and off-key. Léa put a hand over her ear, and Chéri declared, with some feeling: "Everything would be heavenly on an afternoon like this, if only we could be spared my mother's voice!"

She looked at her son with no sign of anger, accustomed to his insolence. Dignified, feet dangling, she settled herself back in a basket chair too high for her short legs. In one hand she warmed her glass of brandy. Léa, rocking herself gently to and fro, glanced occasionally at Chéri, who lay sprawled on a cool cane settee, coat unbuttoned, a cigarette dying between his lips, a lock of hair over one eyebrow. "He's a handsome young blackguard," she thought admiringly.

There they remained, peacefully side by side, making no effort to talk or be sociable, happy after their own fashion. Years of close familiarity rendered silence congenial, and Chéri slipped back into his lethargy, Léa into her calm. As the afternoon became hotter, Madame Peloux pulled her narrow skirt up to her knees, displaying her tight little sailor's calves, and Chéri ripped off his tie—reproved by Léa in an audible "Tch, tch."

"Oh! leave the child alone," Madame Peloux protested, as from the depths of a dream. "It's much too hot! Would you care for a kimono, Léa?"

"No, thank you. I'm perfectly comfortable."

Their unbuttoned siestas disgusted her. Never once had her young lover caught her untidily dressed, or with her blouse undone, or in her bedroom slippers during the day. "Naked, if need be," she would say, "but squalid, never!"

She picked up her picture paper again, but did not read it. "These Pelouxs—mother and son alike!" she thought dreamily. "They've only to sit themselves down at a good meal or in the heart of the countryside and—snap!—the mother whisks off her stays and the son his waistcoat. They behave like publicans out on a holiday, the pair of them." She cast a vindictive eye on one of the publicans in question, and saw that he had fallen asleep, his eyelashes spread against his pallid cheeks, his mouth closed. His upper lip, lit from below, reflected two silver pinpoints of light at the twin curves of its delicious Cupid's bow, and Léa was forced to admit that he looked far more like a sleeping god than a licensed victualer.

Without moving from her chair, she gently plucked the lighted cigarette from between Chéri's fingers and put it in the ashtray. The hand of the sleeper relaxed and the tapering fingers, tipped with cruel nails, drooped like wilting flowers: a hand not strictly feminine, yet a trifle prettier than one could have wished; a hand she had kissed a hundred times—not in slavish devotion—but kissed for the pleasure of it, for its scent.

From behind her paper, she glanced at Madame Peloux. Was she asleep too? Léa always liked to remain awake while mother and son dozed, allowing her a quiet hour's self-communing in the dappled sunlight of a broiling afternoon. But Madame Peloux was not asleep. She was sitting bolt upright in her wickerwork chair, like a Buddha staring into space, and sipping her *fine-champagne* with the absorption of an alcoholic baby.

"Why doesn't she go to sleep?" Léa wondered. "It's Sunday. She's lunched well. She's expecting her sponging old cronies to drop in for her five o'clock tea. By rights she ought to be having a snooze. If she's not snoozing, it's because she's up to some devilment or other."

They had known each other for twenty-five years. Theirs was the hostile intimacy of light women, enriched and then cast aside by one man, ruined by another: the tetchy affection of rivals stalking one another's first wrinkle or white hair. Theirs was the friendship of two practical women of the world, both adept at the money game; but one of them a miser, and the other a sybarite. These bonds count. Rather late in their day, a stronger bond had come to link them more closely: Chéri.

Léa could remember Chéri as a little boy—a marvel of beauty with long curls. When quite small he was known as Fred, and had not yet been nicknamed Chéri.

Sometimes forgotten and sometimes adored, Chéri grew up among wan housemaids and tall sardonic menservants. Although his birth had mysteriously brought wealth to the house, no "Fräulein," no "Miss" was ever to be seen at Chéri's side; and his mother had preserved him, to the accompaniment of piercing shrieks, from "these ghouls."

"Charlotte Peloux, you belong to another age." The speaker was the moribund, mummified, but indestructible Baron de Berthellemy. "Charlotte Peloux, in you I salute the only light woman who ever had the courage to bring up her son as the son of a tart! You belong to another age! You never read, you never travel, you make a point of knowing your neighbor's business, and you abandon your child to the tender mercies of the servants. How perfect! How absolutely About! . . . Or, better still, how like a novel by Gustav Droz. . . . And to think that you've never heard of either! . . ."

Chéri had enjoyed the full freedom of a profligate upbringing. When barely able to lisp, he was quick to pick up all the backstairs gossip. He shared in the clandestine suppers of the kitchen. His ablutions varied between milky immersions in his mother's orrisroot baths and scanty cat licks with the corner of a towel. He suffered from indigestion after a surfeit of sweets, or from pangs of hunger when no one remembered to give him his supper. He was wretchedly bored at every Battle of Flowers, where Charlotte Peloux would exhibit him—half-naked and catching cold—sitting on drenched roses; but it so happened, when he was twelve, that he had a glorious adventure in an illicit gambling den, when an American woman allowed him to play with a fistful of louis d'or, and called him "a little masterpiece." At about the same time, Madame Peloux imposed a tutor on her son—an Abbé, whom she packed off at the end of ten months "because," she confessed, "whenever I caught sight of that black robe trailing along the passages, it made me think I was housing a female relation, and God knows there are few things more depressing than having a poor relation to stay!"

At the age of fourteen, Chéri had a taste of school. He didn't believe in it. He broke prison and ran away. Madame Peloux not only found the energy to incarcerate him a second time, but also, when faced with her son's tears and insults, took to her heels with hands over her ears screaming, "I can't bear the sight of it! I can't bear the sight of it!" So sincere were her cries that she actually fled from Paris, in the company of a man who was young but far from scrupulous. Two years later she came back, alone. It was the last time she succumbed to an amorous impulse.

She found, on her return, that Chéri had shot up too fast; that his cheeks were hollow and his eyes black-ringed; that he dressed like a stable lad and spoke with a worse accent than ever. She beat her breast, and snatched him back from the boarding school. He utterly refused to work; demanded horses, carriages, jewels; insisted on a substantial monthly allowance; and, when his mother began to beat her breast and shriek like a peahen, he put a stop to her cries by saying: "Madame Peloux, ma'am, don't carry on so. My venerable mother, if no one except me drags you down into the gutter, you're likely to die a comfortable death in your downy bed; I don't altogether fancy a trustee for my estate. Your cash is mine. Let me go my own way! Men friends cost next to nothing—a dinner and a bottle of champagne. As for the fair sex, surely Ma'me Peloux, seeing that I take after you, you can trust me not to treat 'em to more than a trinket—if that!"

He pirouetted about while she shed tears and proclaimed

herself the happiest of mothers. When Chéri began buying motorcars, she trembled once more; but he simply advised her: "Keep an eye on the petrol, Ma'me Peloux, if you please!" and sold his horses. He was not above checking the two chauffeurs' books. His calculations were quick and accurate, and the figures he jotted down on slips of paper—dashed off rapidly, round and regular—were in marked contrast to his rather slow and childish handwriting.

At seventeen he was like a little old man, always fussing over his expenses: still good-looking—but skinny and short-winded. More than once Madame Peloux ran into him on the cellar steps, coming up from checking the bottles in the racks and bins.

"Would you believe it?" she said to Léa. "It's too wonderful."

"Much too wonderful," Léa answered, "he'll come to a bad end. Chéri! Show me your tongue!"

He put out his tongue, made a face, and showed other signs of disrespect. Léa took no notice. She was too intimate a friend, a sort of doting godmother, whom he called by her Christian name.

"Is it true," Léa enquired, "that you were seen last night at a bar, sitting on old Lili's knees?"

"Her knees!" scoffed Chéri. "She hasn't had any for ages. They foundered years ago."

"Isn't it true," Léa persisted with greater severity, "that she made you drink gin laced with pepper? You know gin is bad for the breath!"

On one occasion, Chéri, hurt, snapped back at Léa: "I can't think why you bother me with all these questions. You must have seen what I was up to; you were tucked away in that cubbyhole at the back, with Patron your prizefighter friend."

"That's perfectly correct," Léa answered, unmoved. "There's nothing of the dissipated schoolboy about Patron. He has other attractions, and a good deal more to recommend him than a perky little face and two black rings round his eyes."

That week Chéri had been out on the razzle in Montmartre and les Halles, consorting with ladies of the town who called him "poppet" and "my pet vice," but he had got no kick out of it: he suffered from migraines and a dry cough. Madame Peloux poured out her heart-breaking woes—"Life is nothing but a series of crosses for us mothers"—to her masseuse, to her staymaker, Madame Ribot, to old Lili, to the Baron de Berthellemy, and thus passed painlessly from the state of being the happiest-of-parents to that of the martyr–mother.

A night in June, when Madame Peloux and Léa and Chéri were together in the garden room at Neuilly, was to change the destinies of the young man and the middle-aged woman. Chéri's friends had gone off for the evening—little Baxter, a wholesale wine merchant, and the Vicomte Desmond, a hanger-on of his, barely of age, difficult and arrogant—and so Chéri had returned to the maternal fold, and habit had drawn Léa there also.

For one more evening, in a whole sequence of such occasions, these two women, each suspicious of the other, found themselves together. They had known each other for over twenty years; they shared a past made up of similarly dull evenings; they lacked other friends; and, in their later days, they had become mistrustful, self-indulgent, and cut off from the world, as women are who have lived only for love.

Both were staring in silence at Chéri, who never spoke. Madame Peloux lacked the strength to take her son's health in hand, but hated Léa a little more each time she bent her white neck and glowing cheeks over Chéri's pallid cheek and transparent ear. She would willingly have bled that healthy female neck, already wrinkled by the so-called lines of Venus, in order to give a touch of color to her slim, lily-green son: yet it never occurred to her to take her darling away to the country.

"Chéri, why are you drinking brandy?" Léa scolded.

"Out of politeness to Ma'me Peloux—who would otherwise be drinking alone," Chéri answered.

"What are you going to do tomorrow?"

"Dunno, and you?"

"I'm off to Normandy."

"With?"

"That's none of your business."

"With our friend Spéleïeff?"

"Don't be so stupid. That was over two months ago. You're behind the times. Spéleïeff's in Russia."

"Chéri, darling, what can you be thinking of?" sighed Madame Peloux. "Don't you remember going last month to the charming dinner given by Léa to celebrate the end of the affair? Léa, you've never let me have the recipe for those langoustines I enjoyed so much."

Chéri sat up, his eyes sparkling. "Yes, yes, langoustines, swimming in a creamy sauce! How I'd like some now!"

"You see," Madame Peloux said reproachfully, "he's got no appetite to speak of and yet he's asking for langoustines."

"Shut up!" Chéri snapped. "Léa, are you off to the shady woods with Patron?"

"Certainly not, my boy. Patron and I are merely friends. I'm going on my own."

"Nice to be so rich!" Chéri threw out.

"I'll take you with me, if you like: there'll be nothing to do but eat and drink and sleep. . . ."

"Where is this place of yours?" He had risen to his feet and was standing over her.

"You know Honfleur—the Côte de Grâce—don't you? Sit down; you're green in the face. Now as you go down the Côte de Grâce, you know those farm gates where we always say, in passing, your mother and I . . ."

She turned round to where Madame Peloux was sitting. Madame Peloux had disappeared. The discretion with which she had faded away was something so unlike the normal Charlotte Peloux, that they looked at each other and laughed in surprise.

Chéri sat down close to Léa. "I'm tired," he said.

"You're ruining your health."

He drew himself up in his chair, with offended vanity. "Oh! I'm still in good enough fettle, you know."

"Good enough! For others perhaps . . . but not . . . not for me, I'd have you know."

"Too green?"

"The very word I was looking for. So why don't you come down to the country? No nonsense, of course. Ripe strawberries, fresh cream, cakes, grilled spring chicken . . . that's just what you need—and no women."

He let himself snuggle up to Léa's elbow and shut his eyes.

"No women . . . grand . . . Léa, tell me, you're my pal? You are? Then let's be off. Women indeed! I'm fed up with 'em. Women! I've seen all they've got to show."

These vulgarities were muttered in a drowsy voice. Léa listened to his soft tone, and felt his warm breath against her ear. He had taken hold of her long string of pearls and was rolling the larger ones between his fingers. She slipped her arm under his head and so accustomed was she to treating the boy in this way that, almost without thinking, she pulled him toward her and rocked him in her arms.

"How comfy I am!" he sighed. "You're a good pal. I'm so comfy."

Léa smiled, as though hearing praise she valued intensely. Chéri seemed to be ready to drop off to sleep. She looked very closely at his glistening, almost dewy, eyelashes sunk flat against the cheeks, and then at the cheeks themselves, hollowed by his joyless dissipation. His upper lip, shaved that morning, was already bluish, and the pink lampshades lent his mouth an artificial color.

"No women!" Chéri exclaimed, as though dreaming. "Then . . . kiss me!"

Taken by surprise, Léa made no movement.

"Kiss me, I tell you!"

He rapped out his order, frowning, and Léa felt embarrassed by the rekindled gleam in his eyes. It was as if someone had switched on the light. She shrugged her shoulders and kissed the forehead so close to her lips. He drew his arms tighter around her neck, and pulled her down toward him.

She shook her head only at the very instant that their lips touched, then she remained absolutely motionless, and held her breath like someone listening. When he released his hold, she broke away from him, rose to her feet, took a deep breath, and put a hand up to tidy her unruffled hair. She turned to him, rather pale and with rueful eyes, and said, teasingly: "That was a bright idea!"

He lay far back in the rocking chair, speechless, and scrutinized her with a suspicious, questioning gaze, so that she asked: "What is it?"

"Nothing," Chéri said. "I know what I wanted to know."

She blushed with humiliation, then skillfully defended herself.

"What do you know? That I like your mouth? My poor child, I've kissed uglier. What does that prove? D'you think I'm going to fling myself at your feet and cry, 'Take me!' You talk as if you've known only nice young girls! D'you imagine I'm going to lose my head because of a kiss?"

She grew calmer while speaking and wished to prove her self-control.

"Listen, child," she persisted, as she leaned over him, "d'you think a handsome mouth means anything to me?"

She smiled down at him, completely sure of herself, but unaware that there remained on her face a sort of very faint quiver, an appealing sadness, and that her smile was like a rainbow after a sudden storm.

"I'm perfectly calm. Even if I were to kiss you again, or even if we . . . " She stopped and pouted with scorn. "No, no, I really can't see you and me doing that."

"Nor could you see us doing what we did just now," Chéri said, taking time over his words. "And yet you don't mind doing it, and not in a hurry, either. So now you're thinking of going further, are you? *I* never suggested such a thing."

They faced each other like enemies. Léa was afraid to reveal a desire she had not yet had time to develop or to disguise; she resented this child, so suddenly cold and perhaps derisive.

"You're right," she conceded lightly. "Let's say no more about it. Shall we say instead that I'm offering to put you out to grass! And the food will be good . . . *my* food, in other words."

"We'll see," Chéri answered. "Shall I bring the Renouhard tourer?"

"Of course; you're not going to leave it behind with Charlotte."

"I'll pay for the petrol, but you'll feed the chauffeur."

Léa burst out laughing. "I'll feed the chauffeur! Ha! Ha! There speaks the son of Madame Peloux! Get along with you! You forget nothing. . . . I'm not usually inquisitive, but I should love to eavesdrop when you're making up to a woman."

She sank into a chair and fanned herself. A sphinx moth and a number of long-legged mosquitoes hovered round the lamps; scents of the countryside drifted in from the garden, now that night had fallen. A sudden waft from an acacia burst in upon them, so distinct, so active, that they both turned round, half expecting to see it advancing toward them.

"It's the rose acacia," Léa said.

"Yes," Chéri said. "But tonight it has sipped a draught of orange-flower water."

She stared at him, in vague admiration, astonished that he had hit upon such an idea. He was breathing in the scent in helpless rapture, and she turned away, suddenly fearful lest he might call her; but he did call, and she went to him.

She went to kiss him, on an impulse of resentment and selfishness, and half thinking to chastise him. "Just you wait, my boy. . . . It's all too true that you've a pretty mouth, and, this time, I'm going to take my fill because I want to—and then I'll leave you, I don't care what you may say. Now . . ."

Her kiss was such that they reeled apart, drunk, deaf, breathless, trembling as if they had just been fighting. She stood up again in front of him, but he did not move from the depths of his chair, and she taunted him under her breath, "Well? . . . Well?" and waited for an insult. Instead, he held out his arms, opened his vague beautiful hands, tilted his head back as if he had been struck, and let her see beneath each eyelash the glint of a shining tear. He babbled indeterminate words—a whole animal chant of desire, in which she could distinguish her name—"darling"—"I want you"—"I'll never leave you"—a song to which she listened, solicitous, leaning over him, as if unwittingly she had hurt him to the quick.

WHEN LÉA RECALLED their first summer in Normandy, she would sum it up impartially: "I've had other naughty little boys through my hands, more amusing than Chéri, more likeable, too, and more intelligent. But all the same, never one to touch him."

"It's funny," she confided to the old Baron de Berthellemy, toward the end of the summer of 1906, "but sometimes I think I'm in bed with a Chinee or an African."

"Have you ever had a Chinaman or a Negro?"

"Never."

"Well then?"

"I don't know. I can't explain. It's just an impression."

The impression had grown upon her slowly, also an astonishment she had not always been able to conceal. Her earliest memories of their idyll were abundantly rich, but only in pictures of delicious food, superb fruit, and the pleasure of taking pains over her country larder. She could still see Chéri—paler in the blazing sunlight—dragging along his exhausted body beneath the lime-tree tunnels in Normandy, or asleep on the sun-warmed paving beside a pond.

Léa used to rouse Chéri from sleep to cram him with strawberries and cream, frothy milk, and corn-fed chicken. With wide, vacant eyes, as though dazed, he would sit at dinner watching the mazy motions of the moths round the bowl of roses, and then look at his wristwatch to see whether the time had come to go to bed; while Léa, disappointed but unresentful, pondered over the unfulfilled promises of the kiss at Neuilly and good-naturedly bided her time.

"I'll keep him cooped up in this fattening pen till the end of August, if need be. Then, back in Paris again—ouf!—I'll pack him off to his precious studies."

She went to bed mercifully early, so that Chéri—after nuzzling against her till he had hollowed out a selfishly comfortable position—might get some sleep. Sometimes, when the lamp was out, she would watch a pool of moonlight shimmering over the polished floor, or listen, through the chorus of rustling aspens and shrilling crickets, unceasing by night or day, to the deep, retrieverlike sighs that rose from Chéri's breast.

"Why can't I go to sleep? Is there something wrong with me?" she vaguely wondered. "It's not this boy's head on my shoulder—I've held heavier. The weather's wonderful. I've ordered him a good plate of porridge for tomorrow. Already his ribs stick out less. Then why can't I go to sleep? Yes, of course, I remember. . . . I'm going to send for Patron, the boxer, to give the boy some training. We've plenty of time between us, Patron and I, to spring a surprise on Madame Peloux."

She fell asleep, lying stretched out on her back between the cool sheets, the dark head of her naughty little boy resting on her left breast. She fell asleep, to be aroused sometimes—but all too rarely—by a waking desire of Chéri's toward the break of day.

Patron actually arrived after they had been two months in their country retreat, with his suitcase, his small pound-and-a-half dumbbells, his black tights, his six-ounce gloves, and his leather boxing boots, laced down to the toe. Patron, with his girlish voice, his long eyelashes, and his splendid tanned skin, as brown as the leather of his luggage—he hardly looked naked when he took off his shirt. And Chéri, by turns peevish, listless, or jealous of Patron's smooth strength, started the slow, oft-repeated movements. They were tiresome, but they did him good.

"One . . . sss . . . two . . . sss . . . I can't hear you breathing . . . three . . . sss. . . . Don't think I can't see you cheating there with your knee . . . sss. . . . "

An awning of lime foliage filtered the August sunlight. The bare bodies of instructor and pupil were dappled with purple reflections from the thick red carpet spread out upon the gravel. Léa watched the lessons with keen attention. Sometimes during the quarter of an hour's boxing, Chéri, drunk with newfound strength, lost all control and, red-faced with anger, attempted a foul blow. Rocklike, Patron stood up to his swings, and from the height of his Olympian glory let fall oracular words—words of wisdom that packed more weight than his proverbial punch.

"Steady on now! That left eye's wandering a bit! If I hadn't stopped myself in time, it would have had a nasty taste of the stitches on my right glove."

"I slipped," Chéri said, enraged.

"It's not a question of balance," Patron went on, "it's a question of morale. You'll never make a boxer."

"My mother won't let me, isn't that a pity?"

"Whether your mother lets you or not, you'll never make a boxer, because you've got a rotten temper. Rotten tempers and boxing don't go together. Aren't I right, Madame Léa?"

Léa smiled, and reveled in the warm sun, sitting still and watching the bouts between these two men, both young and both stripped. In her mind she kept comparing them. "How handsome Patron is—as solid as a house! And the boy's shaping well. You don't find knees like his running about the streets every day of the week, or I'm no judge. His back, too, is . . . will be . . . marvelous. Where the devil did Mother Peloux drop her line to fish up a child like that? And the set of his head! quite a statue! But what a little beast he is! When he laughs, you'd swear it's a greyhound snarling!" She felt happy and maternal—bathed in quiet virtue. "I'd willingly change him for anyone else," she said to herself, with Chéri naked in the afternoon beside her under the lime-tree bower, or with Chéri naked in the morning on her ermine rug, or Chéri naked in the evening on the edge of the warm fountain. "Yes, handsome as he is, I'd willingly make a change, if it weren't a question of conscience!"

She confessed her indifference to Patron.

"And yet," Patron objected, "the lad's very nicely made. There's muscles on him now such as you don't see on our French lads; his are more like a colored boy's—though he couldn't look any whiter, I must say. Nice little muscles they are, and not too showy. He'll never have biceps like melons."

"I should hope not, Patron! But then, you know, I didn't take him on for his boxing!"

"Of course not," Patron acquiesced, letting his long lashes droop, "there's—your feelings to be considered."

He was always embarrassed by Léa's unveiled allusions to sex, and by her smile—the insistence of the smiling eyes she brought to bear on him whenever she spoke of love.

"Of course," Patron tried another tack, "if he's not altogether satisfactory . . . "

Léa laughed: "Altogether! no . . . but I find being disinterested is its own reward. Just as you do, Patron."

"Oh! me . . . " He waited in fear and hope for the question that did not fail to follow.

"Always the same, Patron? You still won't give way an inch?"

"I won't give way, Madame Léa, and I've just had a letter from Liane by the midday post. She says she's all alone, that I've no good reasons for refusing, and that her two admirers have left her."

"Well?"

"Well, I don't believe it! I won't give way, because she won't give way. She's ashamed, she says, of a man who works for his living—specially when it pulls him out of bed so early every day for his training—a man who gives boxing lessons and teaches Swedish gymnastics. We've only got to meet, and the row starts all over again. 'Anyone'd think,' she shouts at me, 'that I'm not in a position to support the man I love!' That shows very nice feelings, I don't say it doesn't, but it doesn't fit in with my ideas. Everyone's funny about something. It's just like you said, Madame Léa, it's all a question of conscience."

They were talking in low tones under the trees: he prudish and half naked; she dressed in white, the color flaming in her cheeks. They were enjoying the pleasure of a friendly understanding: they shared the same taste for the simple things of life, good health and a sort of plebeian decency. And yet Léa would not have been shocked had Patron received handsome presents from a beautiful and expensive woman like Liane. "Fair exchange is no robbery." And she did her best to break down Patron's "funny feelings" by arguments based on homespun justice. These leisurely conversations always revealed their worship of the same twin deities—love and money, and would drift away from money and love to come back to Chéri and his deplorable upbringing, to his exceptional good looks ("harmless, after all," as Léa would say) and to his character ("virtually nonexistent," as Léa would say). They had a taste for sharing confidences, and a dislike of new words or ideas, which they satisfied in these long talks. They were often disturbed by the preposterous apparition of Chéri, whom they thought either asleep or motoring down some baking hot road—Chéri, looming into sight, half naked, but equipped with an account book, a stylo behind his ear.

"Look at our Mister Adding Machine," Patron said admiringly. "All got up as a clerk in a bank."

"What can this mean?" Chéri shouted from afar. "Three hundred and twenty francs for petrol? Somebody must be swilling the stuff! We've been out four times in the last fortnight—and seventy-seven francs for oil!"

"The motor goes to the market every day," Léa replied. "And while we're on the subject, it appears your chauffeur had three helpings of the joint for his dinner. Don't you think that's stretching our agreement a bit far? . . . Whenever a bill sticks in your throat, you look just like your mother."

At a loss for an answer, he stood uncertain for a moment, shifting from one slender foot to the other, poised with winged grace like a young Mercury. This always made Madame Peloux swoon with delight and yelp, "Me when I was eighteen! Winged feet! winged feet!" He cast about for some insolent retort, his whole face aquiver, his mouth half open, his forehead jutting forward, in a tense attitude that showed off to advantage the peculiar and diabolic upward twist of his eyebrows.

"Don't bother to think of an answer," Léa said kindly. "I know you hate me. Come and kiss me. Handsome devil. Fallen angel. Silly goose. . . . "

He came, calmed by the softness of her voice, yet ruffled by her words. Seeing them together, Patron once again let the truth flower on his guileless lips.

"As far as first-rate bodies go, Monsieur Chéri, you have one all right. But whenever I look at it, Monsieur Chéri, I feel that if I was a woman I'd say to myself. 'I'll come back again in ten years' time.'"

"You hear, Léa? He says in ten years' time," Chéri said insinuatingly, pushing away the head of his mistress as she leaned toward him. "What do you think of that?"

But she did not deign to listen. The young body owed to her its renewed vigor, and she began patting it all over, touching it anywhere and everywhere, on the cheek, on the leg, on the behind, with the irreverent pleasure of a nanny.

"What d'you get out of being spiteful?" Patron then asked.

Chéri allowed a savage, inscrutable gaze to sweep over every inch of the waiting Hercules before he answered. "I find it comforting. You wouldn't understand."

In fact, Léa herself understood precious little about Chéri after three months' intimacy. If she still talked to Patron, who now came only on Sundays, or to Berthellemy, who arrived without being invited but left again two hours later, about "sending Chéri back to his blessed studies," it was because the phrase had become a kind of habit, and as though to excuse herself for having kept him there so long. She kept on setting a limit to his stay, and then exceeding it. She was waiting.

"The weather is so lovely. And then his trip to Paris last week tired him. And, besides, it's better for me to get thoroughly sick of him."

For the first time in her life, she waited in vain for what had never before failed her: complete trust on the part of her young lover, a self-surrender to confessions, candors, endless secrets—those hours in the depths of the night when, in almost filial gratitude, a young man unrestrainedly pours out his tears, his private likes and dislikes, on the kindly bosom of a mature and trusted friend.

"They've always told me everything in the past," she thought obstinately. "I've always known just what they were worth—what they were thinking and what they wanted. But this boy, this brat . . . No, that would really be the limit."

He was now strong, proud of his nineteen years, gay at meals and impatient in bed; even so he gave away nothing but his body, and remained as mysterious as an odalisque. Tender? Yes, if an involuntary cry or an impulsive hug is an indication of tenderness. But the moment he spoke, he was "spiteful" again, careful to divulge nothing of his true self.

How often at dawn had Léa held him in her arms, a lover soothed, relaxed, with half-closed lids! Each morning his eyes and his mouth returned to life more beautiful, as though every waking, every embrace, had fashioned them anew! How often, at such moments, had she indulged her desire to master him, her sensual longing to hear his confession, and pressed her forehead against his, whispering, "Speak. Say something. Tell me . . . "

But no confession came from those curved lips, scarcely anything indeed but sulky or frenzied phrases woven round "Nounoune"—the name he had given her when a child and the one he now used in the throes of his pleasure, almost like a cry for help.

"Yes, I assure you, he might be a Chinee or an African," she declared to Anthime de Berthellemy, and added, "I can't tell you why." The impression was strong but confused, and she felt lazily incompetent to find words for the feeling that she and Chéri did not speak the same language.

It was the end of September when they returned to Paris. Chéri went straight to Neuilly, the very first evening, to "spring a surprise" on Madame Peloux. He brandished chairs, cracked nuts with his fist, leaped onto the billiard table and played cowboy in the garden at the heels of the terrified watchdogs.

"Ouf!" Léa sighed, as she entered her house in the Avenue Bugeaud, alone. "How wonderful!—a bed to myself!"

But at ten o'clock the following night, she was sipping coffee and trying not to find the evening too long or the dining room too large, when a nervous cry was forced from her lips. Chéri had suddenly appeared, framed in the doorway—Chéri, wafted on silent, winged feet.

He was not speaking or showing any sign of affection, but just running toward her.

"Are you mad?"

Shrugging his shoulders, disdaining all explanations, just running toward her. Never asking "Do you love me?" "Have you already forgotten me?" Running toward her.

A moment later they were lying in the middle of Léa's great brass-encumbered bed. Chéri pretended to be worn out and sleepy. This made it easier to grit his teeth and keep his eyes tight shut, suffering as he was from a furious attack of taciturnity. Yet, through his silence, she was listening as she lay beside him, listening with delight to the distant delicate vibration, to the imprisoned tumult thrumming within a body that sought to conceal its agony, its gratitude and love.

WHY DIDN'T your mother tell me this herself at dinner last night?"

"She thought it better it should come from me."

"No!"

"That's what she said."

"And you?"

"What about me?"

"Do you think it better?"

Chéri raised uncertain eyes to Léa's. "Yes." He appeared to think it over a moment and repeated: "Yes, far better, in fact."

In order not to embarrass him, Léa looked away toward the window.

The August morning was dark with warm rain, which fell vertically on the already rusted foliage of the three plane trees in the garden court.

"It might be autumn," she said, and sighed.

"What's the matter?" Chéri asked.

She looked at him in astonishment. "Nothing, I don't like the rain, that's all."

"Oh! All right, I thought . . ."

"What?"

"I thought something was wrong."

She could not help giving a frank laugh. "Wrong with me,

because you're getting married? No, listen . . . you're . . . you're so funny."

She seldom laughed outright, and her merriment vexed Chéri. He shrugged his shoulders and made the usual grimace while lighting a cigarette, jutting out his chin too far and protruding his lower lip.

"You oughtn't to smoke before luncheon," Léa said.

He made some impertinent retort she did not hear. She was listening to the sound of her own voice and its daily lectures, echoing away down the past five years. "It's like the endless repetition in opposite looking glasses," she thought. Then, with a slight effort, she returned to reality and cheerfulness.

"It's lucky for me that there'll soon be someone else to stop you smoking on an empty stomach."

"Oh! *she* won't be allowed to have a say in anything," Chéri declared. "She's going to be my wife, isn't she? Let her kiss the sacred ground I tread on, and thank her lucky stars for the privilege. And that will be that."

He exaggerated the thrust of his chin, clenched his teeth on his cigarette holder, parted his lips, and, as he stood there in his white silk pajamas, succeeded only in looking like an Asiatic prince grown pale in the impenetrable obscurity of palaces.

Léa drew the folds of her pink dressing gown closer about her—the pink she called "indispensable." She was lazily turning over ideas which she found tiresome, ideas that she decided to hurl, one by one, as missiles against Chéri's assumed composure.

"Well, why are you marrying the child?"

He put both elbows on the table and, unconsciously, assumed the composed features of his mother. "Well, you see, my dear girl . . ."

"Call me Madame or Léa. I'm neither your housemaid nor a pal of your own age."

She sat straight up in her armchair and clipped her words without raising her voice. He wanted to answer back. He looked defiantly at the beautiful face, a little pale under its powder, and at the frank blue light of her searching eyes. But

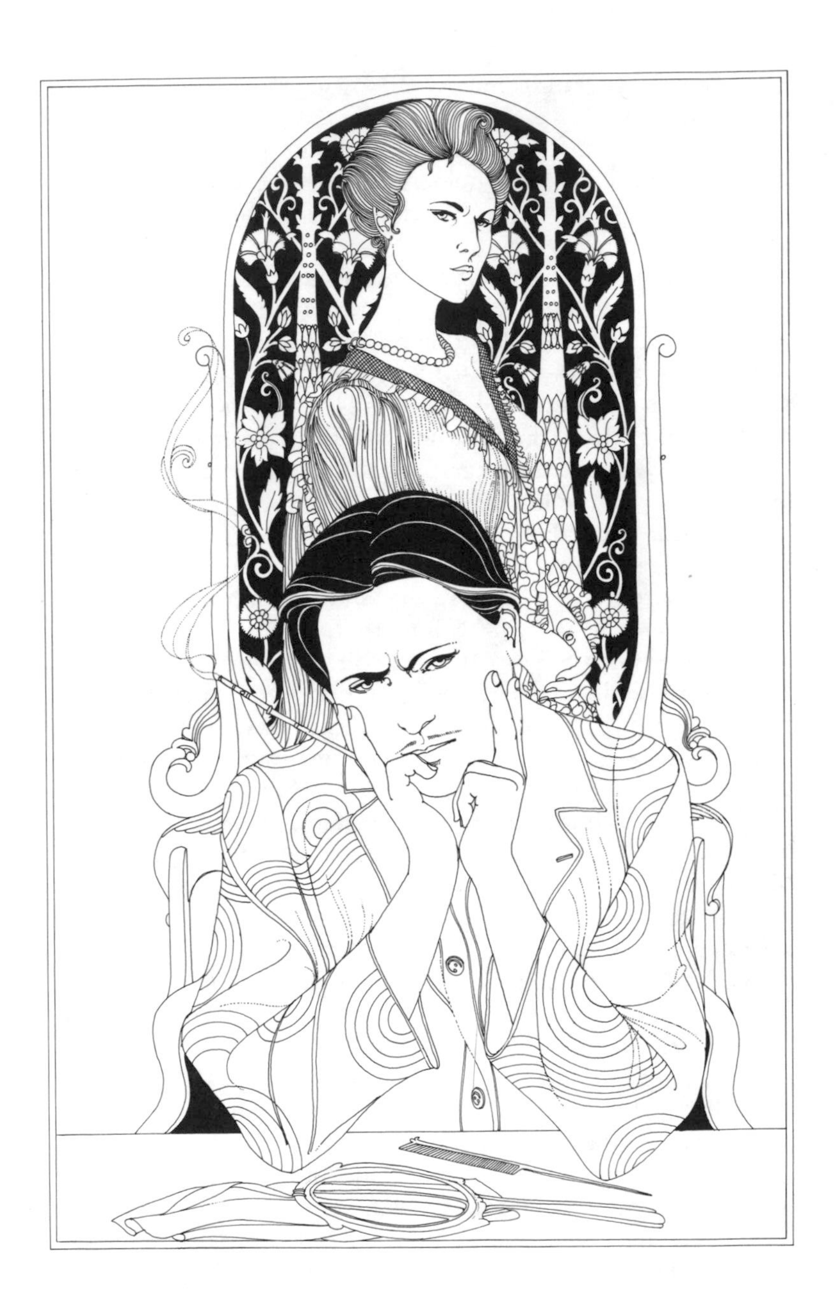

he softened, and conceded, in a tone most unusual for him, "Nounoune, you asked me to explain. . . . It had to come to this in the end. And besides, there are big interests at stake."

"Whose?"

"Mine," he said without a smile. "The girl has a considerable fortune of her own."

"From her father?"

He rocked himself to and fro, his feet in the air. "Oh, how do I know? What a question! I suppose so. You'd hardly expect the fair Marie-Laure to draw fifteen hundred thousand out of her own bank account, would you? Fifteen hundred thousand, and some decent family jewels into the bargain."

"And how much have you?"

"Oh, I've more than that of my own," he said with pride.

"Then you don't need any more money?"

He shook his smooth head and it caught the light like blue watered silk. "Need . . . need . . . ? You know perfectly well we don't look at money in the same way. It's something on which we never see eye to eye."

"I'll do you the justice to say that you've spared me any reference to it during the last five years." She leaned toward him and put her hand on his knee. "Tell me, child, how much have you put by from your income in these five years?"

He cavorted like a clown, laughed, and rolled at Léa's feet, but she pushed him aside with her toe.

"No, tell me the truth . . . fifty thousand a year, or sixty? Tell me, sixty? Seventy?"

He sat down on the carpet facing away from Léa, and laid his head back on her lap. "Aren't I worth it, then?"

He stretched out to his full length, turned his head to look up at her, and opened his eyes wide. They looked black, but their true shade, Léa knew, was a dark almost reddish brown. As though to indicate her choice of what was rarest among so much beauty, she put her forefinger on his eyebrows, his eyelids, and the corners of his mouth. At moments this lover, whom she slightly despised, inspired her with a kind of respect by his outward form. "To be as handsome as that amounts to nobility," she said to herself.

"Tell me, child, how does this young person feel about you?"

"She loves me. She admires me. She never says a word."

"And you—how do you behave with her?"

"I don't," he answered simply.

"Delightful love duets," Léa said, dreamily.

He sat up, crossing his legs tailor-fashion.

"You seem to me to be thinking a lot about her," he said severely. "Don't you think of yourself at all, in this upheaval?"

She gazed at Chéri with an astonishment that made her look years younger—eyebrows raised and lips half open.

"Yes, you, Léa. You, the victimized heroine. You, the one sympathetic character in all this, since you're being dropped."

He had become rather pale, and his tough handling of Léa seemed to be hurting him.

Léa smiled. "But, my darling, I've not the slightest intention of changing my life. Now and then, during the next week, I'll come across a pair of socks, a tie, a handkerchief on my shelves . . . and when I say a week . . . you know in what excellent order my shelves are kept! Oh, yes, and I'll have the bathroom redone, I've got an idea of putting in encrusted glass. . . ."

She fell silent and assumed an almost greedy look as she traced a vague outline with her finger. Chéri continued to look vindictive.

"You aren't pleased! What do you want, then? Do you expect me to go to Normandy to hide my grief? To pine away? To stop dyeing my hair? To have Madame Peloux rushing to my bedside?" And she imitated Madame Peloux, flapping her arms and trumpeting: " 'The shadow of her former self, the shadow of her former self! The poor unfortunate creature has aged a hundred years, a hundred years!' Is that what you want?"

He had been listening with a smile that died on his lips, and a trembling of the nostrils that might be due to emotion. "Yes!" he cried.

Léa rested her smooth, bare, heavy arms on Chéri's shoulders.

"My poor boy! But at that rate, I ought to have died four or five times already! To lose a little lover . . . To exchange one naughty little boy . . ." She added in lower, lighter tones: "I've grown used to it!"

"We all know that," he said harshly. "I don't give a damn—d'you hear me?—I don't give a single damn that I wasn't your first lover. What I should have liked, or rather what would have been . . . fitting . . . decent . . . is to be your last." With a twist of his shoulders, he shrugged off her superb arms. "After all, what I am saying to you now is for your own good."

"I understand perfectly. You think only of me. I think only of your fiancée. That's all very nice, all very natural. It's clear that we both have hearts of gold."

She rose, waiting for some outrageous rejoinder. But he said nothing, and it hurt her to see for the first time a look of discouragement on his face.

She bent over and put her hands under his armpits.

"Now then, come along, get your clothes on. I've only to put on my dress, I'm ready underneath, and what in the world is there to do on a day like this except to go to Schwabe and choose a pearl for you? You see, I must give you a wedding present."

He jumped up, his face aglow: "Top hole! A pearl for my shirtfront! A pale pink pearl. I know the very one!"

"Not on your life! A white one, something masculine for pity's sake! Don't tell me, I know which one just as well as you. It'll ruin me, as usual. However, think of the money I'm going to save when you're out of the way!"

Chéri adopted a more reticent attitude. "Oh, that . . . that depends on my successor."

Léa turned back at the door of her boudoir and gave him her

gayest smile, showing her strong teeth and the fresh blue of her eyes skillfully darkened by bister.

"Your successor? A couple of francs and a packet of cigarettes! And a glass of cassis on Sunday—that's all the job will be worth! And I'll settle money on your children."

THEY BOTH became extremely gay for the next few weeks. Chéri's official duties as a fiancé separated them for a few hours each day, sometimes for a night or two. "We mustn't let them lose confidence," Chéri declared. Léa, kept by Madame Peloux at a safe distance from Neuilly, satisfied her curiosity by plying Chéri with a hundred questions. Whenever he came back to Léa's house, he was full of his own importance and heavy with secrets which he at once divulged. He was like a schoolboy playing truant.

"Oh my sainted aunt!" he shouted one day, cramming his hat down on Léa's portrait bust. "The goings-on at the Peloux Palace Hôtel ever since yesterday!"

She began by scolding him, laughing already in anticipation.

"Take your hat off that, in the first place. And in the second, don't invoke your wretched aunt in my house. Well, what's been happening now?"

"A riot, Nounoune! A riot's broken out among the ladies. Marie-Laure and Ma'me Peloux are scratching each other's eyes out over the marriage settlement!"

"No!"

"Yes! It was a superb sight. (Look out for the olives. . . . I'm going to impersonate Ma'me Peloux as a windmill. . . .) 'Separate bank accounts! Separate bank accounts! Why not a trustee? It's a personal insult, a personal insult. You forget that my son has his own fortune! . . . May I inform you Madame . . .' "

"She called her Madame?"

"She most certainly did. 'Let me tell you, Madame, that my son has never had a penny's-worth of debts since he came of age and the list of his investments bought since 1910 is worth . . .' is worth this, that and the other, including the skin off my nose, plus the fat off my bottom. In short, Catherine de Medici in person! But even more artful, of course!"

Léa's blue eyes glistened with tears of merriment. "Oh Chéri! you've never been funnier in your life! What about the other? The fair Marie-Laure?"

"Her? Oh! terrible, Nounoune. That woman must have at least a dozen corpses in her wake. Dolled up in jade green, red hair, painted to look eighteen, and the inevitable smile. The trumpetings of my revered Mamma failed to make her bat an eyelid. She held her fire till the assault was over, then she came out with: 'It might perhaps be wiser, dear Madame, not to talk too loudly about all the money your son put by in 1910 and the years following. . . .' "

"Bang! Straight between the eyes! . . . Between yours. Where were you while all this was going on?"

"Me? In the large armchair."

"You were actually in the room?" She stopped laughing, and eating. "You were there? What did you do?"

"Cracked a joke, of course. Ma'me Peloux had just seized hold of a valuable piece of bric-à-brac, to avenge my honor, when I stopped her without even getting up. 'My adored mother, calm yourself. Follow my example, follow that of my charming mother-in-law, who's being as sweet as honey . . . as sweet as sugar.' And that's how I managed to arrange that the settlement should apply only to property acquired after marriage."

"I simply don't understand."

"The famous sugar plantations that the poor little Prince Ceste left to Marie-Laure by his will. . . ."

"Yes?"

"Forged will! Fury of the Ceste family! Lawsuit pending! Now d'you get it?"

He crowed.

"I get it. But how did you get hold of the story?"

"Ah! I'll tell you! Old Lili has just pounced with her full weight upon the younger of the Ceste boys, who's only seventeen and religious. . . ."

"Old Lili? What a nightmare!"

"And he babbles family secrets in her ear between every kiss. . . ."

"Chéri! I feel sick!"

"And old Lili tipped me off at Mamma's At Home last Sunday. She simply adores me! Besides, she respects me because I've never wanted to go to bed with her. . . ."

"I should hope not!" Léa sighed. "Yet all the same . . ." She broke off to reflect, and it seemed to Chéri her enthusiasm was flagging.

"Well, you must say it was pretty smart of me, eh?"

He leaned across the table; and the sunshine, playing over the silver and the white tablecloth, lit him up like a row of footlights.

"Yes . . ." "All the same," she was thinking, "that poisonous Marie-Laure simply treated him like a ponce . . ."

"Is there any cream cheese, Nounoune?"

"Yes . . ." ". . . and he showed no more surprise than if she had thrown him a flower. . . ."

"Nounoune, will you let me have that address? the address of the place where you get your cream cheese—for the new cook I've engaged for October?"

"Are you mad? It's homemade. I *have* a cook, you know. Think of the *sauce aux moules* and *vol-au-vent*!" ". . . it's true I've practically kept the boy for the last five years. . . . But all the same he has an income of three hundred thousand francs a year. That's the point. Can you be a ponce with three hundred thousand a year? But why ever not? It doesn't depend on the amount, but on the man. . . . There are some men I could have given half a million to, and that wouldn't make them a ponce. But how about Chéri? After all, I have never actually given him any money. All the same . . ."

"All the same," she broke into speech, "she treated you like a gigolo!"

"Who did?"

"Marie-Laure!"

He brightened at once, like a child.

"Didn't she? Didn't she just, Nounoune? That's what she meant, wasn't it?"

"So it seems to me."

Chéri raised his glass of Château-Chalon, almost the color of brandy. "So here's to Marie-Laure! What a compliment, eh? And if anyone can still say it of me when I'm your age, I shan't ask anything better!"

"If that's enough to make you happy . . ."

She listened to him absentmindedly till the end of luncheon. Accustomed to her half-silences and her worldly wisdom, he asked for nothing better than the usual maternal homilies—"Take the brownest crusts. Don't eat so much new bread. . . . You've never learned how to choose a fruit. . . ." All the time, secretly disgruntled, she was reproaching herself, "I must make up my mind what I want! What would I really have liked him to do? Get up on his hind legs and hiss 'Madame, you have insulted me! Madame, I am not what you take me for!' I'm responsible, when all's said and done. I've spoon-fed him, I've stuffed him with good things. . . . Who in the world would have thought that one day he'd want to play the paterfamilias? It never occurred to me! Even supposing it had—as Patron would say, 'Nature will out.' Even supposing Patron had accepted Liane's proposals, his nature would have come out all right if anyone had hinted at the fact in his hearing. But Chéri . . . has Chéri's nature. He's just Chéri. He's . . ."

"What were you saying, child?" she interrupted her thoughts to ask. "I wasn't listening."

"I was saying that never again—never, do you hear me—

will anything make me laugh so much as my scene with Marie-Laure!"

—"There you are," Léa concluded her thoughts, "it . . . it merely made him laugh."

Slowly she rose to her feet, as though tired. Chéri put an arm round her waist, but she pushed it away.

"What day is your wedding to be, now I come to think of it?"

"Monday week."

His candor and detachment terrified her. "That's fantastic!"

"Why fantastic, Nounoune?"

"You don't look as if you were giving it a thought!"

"I'm not," he said, calmly. "Everything's been arranged. Ceremony at two o'clock, saving us all the fuss and rush of a wedding breakfast. Instead, a tea party at Ma'me Peloux's. After that, sleepers, Italy, the Lakes. . . ."

"Are the Lakes back in fashion?"

"They are. There'll be villas, hotels, motor-drives, restaurants, like Monte Carlo, eh?"

"But the girl! There's always the girl. . . ."

"Of course there's the girl. She's not much, but she's there!"

"And I'm no longer there."

Chéri had not expected her to say this and showed it. His face became disfigured, and he suddenly turned white about the mouth. He controlled his breath to avoid an audible gasp, and became himself again.

"Nounoune, you'll always be there."

"Monsieur overwhelms me."

"There'll always be you, Nounoune . . ." and he laughed awkwardly, "whenever I need you to do something for me."

She did not answer. She bent to pick up a tortoiseshell comb that had fallen to the floor and pushed it back in her hair, humming to herself. She went on humming a little snatch of song in front of the looking glass, pleased with herself, proud of having kept her self-control so easily, covered up so successfully the only emotional moment of their separation, proud of having held back words that must never be said: "Speak . . . beg for what you want, demand it, put your arms round my neck. . . . You have suddenly made me happy. . . ."

MADAME PELOUX must have been talking a great deal and for a long time before Léa appeared. The high color on her cheeks emphasized the sparkle of her large eyes, which expressed only an indiscreet and inscrutable watchfulness. This Sunday she was wearing a black afternoon dress with a very narrow skirt, and nobody could fail to have observed that her feet were tiny and her stays too tight. She stopped talking, took a little sip from the petal-thin brandy glass warming in her hand, and nodded at Léa in lazy contentment.

"Isn't it a lovely day? Such weather, such weather! Would anyone believe we're in the middle of October?"

"Oh, no, never. . . . Most certainly not!" two obsequious voices answered in chorus.

Beside the curving garden path a stream of red salvias wound between the banks of gray-mauve Michaelmas daisies. Golden butterflies flitted as if it were summer and the scent of chrysanthemums, strengthened by the hot sun, was wafted into the garden room. A yellowing birch tree trembled in the wind above beds of tea roses, where the last of the bees still were busy.

"But what's this weather," yelled Madame Peloux, suddenly waxing lyrical, "but what's this weather, when compared to what *they* must be having in Italy?"

"Yes, indeed! . . . Just what I was thinking!" the attendant voices echoed.

Léa turned with a frown in their direction. "If only they would hold their tongues," she thought.

The Baroness de la Berche and Madame Aldonza were sitting at a card table, playing piquet. Madame Aldonza, an aged ballerina, with legs eternally swathed in bandages, was distorted with rheumatism, and wore her shiny black wig a little askew. Opposite her, a head or more taller, the Baroness squared her rigid shoulders like a country priest's. Her face was large and had grown alarmingly masculine with age. She was a bristling bush of hair—hair in her ears, tufts in her nostrils and on her lip, and rough hairs between her fingers.

"Baroness, don't forget I made ninety," Madame Aldonza bleated like a goat.

"Score it, score it, my good friend! All I want is to see everyone happy."

An endless flow of honied words masked her savage cruelty. Léa looked at her closely as if for the first time, felt disgusted, and turned back to Madame Peloux. "Charlotte, at least, *looks* human," she thought.

"What's the matter with you, my Léa? You don't seem your usual self?" Madame Peloux enquired tenderly.

Léa drew up her handsome figure and answered: "Of course I am, Lolotte dear . . . it's so comfortable here in your house, I was merely relaxing," thinking all the while, "Careful now . . . she's just as cruel as the other," and she at once assumed an expression of flattering contentment, of dreamy repletion, and accentuated it by sighing, "I lunched too well. . . . I really must get thinner. I shall start a strict diet from tomorrow."

Madame Peloux flapped her hands and simpered.

"Isn't a broken heart enough to do that?"

"Oh, oh, oh! Ha-ha! Ho-ho!" guffawed Madame Aldonza and the Baroness de la Berche. "Ha-ha-ha!"

Léa rose to her full height in her autumn dress of somber green, handsome under her satin hat trimmed with sealskin, youthful among these old ruins over whom she cast a gentle eye. "Oh, la-la, my dears! Give me a dozen such heartbreaks, if that would help me to lose a couple of pounds!"

"Léa, you're astounding," the old Baroness shot at her in a puff of smoke. "Madame Léa, think of me, please, when you throw away that hat," old Madame Aldonza begged. "Madame Charlotte, you remember your blue one? It lasted me two years. Baroness, when you've quite finished ogling Madame Léa, perhaps you'll be kind enough to deal the cards to me."

"Very well, my sweet, and may they bring you luck!"

Léa stopped for a moment by the door, then stepped out into the garden. She picked a tea rose, which shed its petals. She listened to the breeze in the birch, to the trams in the avenue, to the whistle of the local train. The bench she sat on was warm, and she closed her eyes, letting her shoulders enjoy the warmth of the sun. When she opened her eyes again, she hurriedly turned her head in the direction of the house, feeling positive that she was going to see Chéri standing in the garden entrance with his shoulder against the doorway.

"What can be the matter with me?" she wondered. Piercing screams of laughter and a little chorus of greeting from indoors brought her, trembling slightly, to her feet. "Can I be suffering from nerves?"

"Ah, here they are, here they are!" Madame Peloux trumpeted, and the deep bass of the Baroness chimed in "Here come the happy pair!"

Léa shivered, ran as far as the door and stopped short: there, in front of her, were old Lili and her adolescent lover, Prince Ceste, just arriving.

Perhaps seventy years of age, with the corpulence of a eunuch held in by stays, old Lili was usually referred to as "passing all bounds," without these "bounds" being defined. Her round pink painted face was enlivened by a ceaseless girlish gaiety, and her large eyes and small mouth, thin-lipped and shrunken, flirted shamelessly. Old Lili followed the fashion to an outrageous degree. A striking blue-and-white striped skirt held in the lower part of her body, and a little blue jersey gaped over her skinny bosom crinkled like the wattles of a turkey-cock; a silver fox failed to conceal the neck, which was the shape of a flowerpot and the size of a belly. It had engulfed the chin.

"It's terrifying," Léa thought. She was unable to tear her eyes away from details that were particularly sinister—a white sailor hat, for instance, girlishly perched on the back of a short-cut, strawberry-roan wig; or, again, a pearl necklace visible one moment and the next interred in a deep ravine which once had been termed a *"collier de Vénus."*

"Léa, Léa, my little chickabiddy!" old Lili exclaimed as she did her best to hasten toward Léa. She walked with difficulty on round swollen feet, tightly swaddled in high-heeled laced boots with paste buckles on the ankle straps, and was the first to congratulate herself on this performance: "I waddle like a duckling! it is a special little way I have. Guido, my passion, you remember Madame de Lonval? Don't remember her too well or I'll tear your eyes out. . . ."

A slim youth with Italian features, enormous empty eyes and a weak receding chin, kissed Léa's hand hastily and retired into the shadows without a word. Lili caught him in flight, pulled his head down to her scaly chest, calling the onlookers to witness: "Do you know what this is, Madame, do you what this is? This, ladies, is the love of my life!"

"Restrain yourself, Lili!" Madame de la Berche advised in her masculine voice.

"But why? But why?" from Charlotte Peloux.

"For the sake of decency," said the Baroness.

"Baroness, that's not nice of you! I think they're so sweet. Ah!" she sighed, "they remind me of my own children."

"I was thinking of them," Lili said, with a delighted smile. "It's our honeymoon too, Guido's and mine. Indeed, we've just come to ask about the other young couple! We want to hear all about them."

Madame Peloux became stern. "Lili, you don't expect me to go into details, do you?"

"Oh yes, yes, I do," Lili cried, clapping her hands. She tried to skip, but succeeded only in raising her shoulders and hips a little. "That's always been my besetting sin, and always will be! I adore spicy talk! I'll never be cured of it. That little wretch there knows how I adore it."

The silent youth, called to bear witness, did not open his mouth. The black pupils of his eyes moved up and down against the whites, like frantic insects. Léa watched him, rooted to the spot.

"Madame Charlotte told us all about the wedding ceremony," bleated Madame Aldonza. "The young Madame Peloux was a dream in her wreath of orange blossom!"

"A madonna! A madonna!" Madame Peloux corrected at the top of her voice, with a burst of religious fervor. "Never, never, has anyone looked so divine. My son was in heaven! In heaven, I tell you! . . . What a pair they made, what a pair!"

"You hear that, my passion? Orange blossom!" Lili murmured. "And tell me, Charlotte, what about our mother-in-law, Marie-Laure?"

Madame Peloux's pitiless eyes sparkled: "Oh her! Out of place, absolutely out of place. In tight-fitting black, like an eel wriggling out of the water—you could see everything, breasts, stomach—everything!"

"By Jove!" muttered the Baroness de la Berche with military gusto.

"And that look of contempt she has for everybody, that look of having a dose of cyanide up her sleeve and half a pint of chloroform inside her handbag! As I said, out of place—that exactly describes her. She behaved as if she could only spare us five minutes of her precious time—she'd hardly brushed the kiss off her lips before she said, 'Au revoir, Edmée, au revoir, Fred,' and off she flew."

Old Lili was breathing hard, sitting on the edge of her chair, her little grandmotherly mouth, with its puckered corners, hanging half open. "And who gave the usual advice?" she threw out.

"What advice?"

"The little talk—oh, my passion, hold my hand while I say it!—instruction for the young bride. Who gave her that?"

Charlotte Peloux took offense and stared at her. "Things may well have been done in that way when you were young, but the practice has fallen into disuse."

The sprightly old girl plumped her fists on her thighs: "Disuse? Disuse or not, how would you know anything about it, my poor Charlotte? There's so little marrying in your family!"

"Ha-ha-ha!" the two toadies imprudently guffawed.

But a single glance from Madame Peloux made them tremble. "Peace, peace, my little angels! You're each enjoying your paradise on earth, so what more do you want?" The Baroness stretched out a strong arm, like a policeman keeping order, between the purple faces of Lili and Madame Peloux. But Charlotte scented battle like a war-horse. "If you're looking for trouble, Lili, you don't have to look further than me! Because of your age, I must treat you with respect, and if it weren't for that . . ."

Lili shook with laughter from chin to thigh. "If it weren't for that, you'd get married yourself just to give me the lie? I know—it's not so hard to get married! Why, I'd marry Guido like a shot, if only he were of age!"

"Not possible!" gasped Charlotte, so taken aback that she forgot her anger.

"But, of course . . . Princess Ceste, my dear! *la piccola principessa! Piccola principessa,* that's what my little Prince always calls me!"

She nipped hold of her skirt, and, in turning, displayed a gold curb chain where her ankle ought to have been. "Only," she continued mysteriously, "his father . . ."

By now out of breath, she made a sign to the silent young man, who took up the tale in a low rapid voice as if he were reciting his piece: "My father, the Duke of Parese, threatens to put me in a convent if I marry Lili."

"In a convent!" Charlotte Peloux squealed. "A man in a convent!"

"A man in a convent!" neighed Madame de la Berche in her deep bass, "Egad! if that isn't exciting!"

"They're barbarians," Aldonza lamented, joining her misshapen hands together.

Léa rose so abruptly that she upset a glass.

"It's uncolored glass," Madame Peloux observed with satisfaction. "You'll bring good luck to my young couple. Where are you running off to? Is your house on fire?"

Léa managed to squeeze out a sly little laugh: "On fire? In a sense, perhaps. Ssh! no questions! It's a secret."

"What? Already? It's not possible!" Charlotte Peloux cheeped enviously. "I was just saying to myself that you looked as if . . ."

"Yes, yes! You must tell us! Tell us everything," yapped the three old women.

Lili's quilted fists, old Aldonza's deformed stumps, Charlotte Peloux's hard fingers had seized upon her wrist, her sleeve, her gold mesh bag. She snatched her arm away from all these claws and succeeded in laughing again, teasingly: "No, it's far too early in the day, it would spoil everything! It's my secret." And she rushed away to the hall.

But the door opened in front of her and a desiccated old fellow, a sort of playful mummy, took her into his arms: "Léa, lovely creature, a kiss for your little Berthellemy, or he won't let you pass!"

She gave a cry of fright and impatience, struck off the gloved bones retarding her progress, and fled.

Neither in the avenues of Neuilly, nor on the roads through the Bois, turning to blue in the fast-falling twilight, did she allow herself a moment's reflection. She shivered slightly and pulled up the windows of the motorcar. She felt restored by the sight of her clean house, the comfort of her pink bedroom and boudoir, overcrowded with furniture and flowers.

"Quick, Rose, light the fire in my room!"

"But, Madame, the pipes are already at their winter temperature. Madame should not have gone out with only a fur round her neck. The evenings are treacherous."

"A hot-water bottle in my bed at once, and for dinner a cup of thick chocolate beaten up with the yolk of an egg, some toast, and a bunch of grapes. . . . Hurry, dear, I'm freezing. I caught cold in that junk shop at Neuilly. . . ."

Once under the sheets, she clenched her teeth to stop them chattering. The warmth of the bed eased her stiffened muscles, but still she did not altogether relax, and she went through the chauffeur's expense book till the chocolate arrived. This she drank at once, frothy and scalding. She chose her *chasselas* grapes one by one, the long, greenish-amber bunch dangling by its stem against the light.

Then she turned out the bedside lamp, settled herself in her favorite position, flat on her back, and gave way.

"What can be the matter with me?"

She succumbed again to anxiety and started to shiver. She was obsessed by the vision of an empty doorway, with clumps of red salvia on either side. "I can't be well," she thought, "one doesn't get into a state like this over a door!" Again she saw the three old women, Lili's neck, and the beige rug that Madame Aldonza had trailed about with her for the past twenty years. "Which of them am I going to look like in ten years' time?"

Though she did not feel alarmed at this prospect, her anxiety increased still further. She let her mind wander from one incident of her past life to another, from this scene to that, trying to rid her thoughts of the empty doorway framed by red salvia. She was growing restless in her bed and trembled slightly. Suddenly she jumped as though shot, racked by a pain so deep that at first she thought it must be physical, a pain that twisted her lips and dragged from them, in a raucous sob, a single name: "Chéri!"

Tears followed, beyond all control at first. As soon as she had regained her self-control, she sat up, wiped her face, and turned on the lamp again. "Ah! That's what it is! Now I understand!"

She took a thermometer from the drawer of her bedside

table and put it under her arm. "My temperature's normal, so it's nothing physical. I see. I'm just unhappy. Something must be done about it."

She drank some water, got out of bed, bathed her inflamed eyes, put on a little powder, poked the fire, and went back to bed. She was on her guard, full of mistrust for an enemy she had never known: grief. She had just said good-bye to thirty years of easy living: years spent pleasantly, intent often on love, sometimes on money. This had left her, at almost fifty, still young and defenseless.

She made fun of herself, ceased to feel her grief, and smiled. "I think I was out of my mind just now. There's nothing wrong with me any longer."

But a movement of her left arm, which bent automatically to hold and shelter a sleeping head, brought back all her agony, and she sat up with a jump. "Well, this *is* going to be fun!" she said out loud and sternly.

She looked at the clock and saw that it was barely eleven. Overhead passed the slippered tread of the elderly Rose, on her way up the stairs to the attic floor. Then there was silence. Léa resisted the impulse to call out for help to the deferential old body. "Don't give the servants anything to gossip about. We mustn't have that."

She left her bed again, wrapped herself up warm in a quilted silk dressing gown and toasted her feet. Then she half opened her window and listened for she knew not what. A moist and milder wind had brought clouds in its wake, and the lingering leaves in the neighboring Bois sighed with every gust. Léa shut the window again, picked up a newspaper and looked at the date—"October the twenty-sixth. Exactly a month since Chéri was married?" She never said "Since Edmée was married."

Following Chéri's example, she did not yet count his young wraith of a wife as really alive. Chestnut-brown eyes, ashy hair which was very lovely with the vestige of a crimp in it—all the rest melted away in her memory like the contours of a face seen in a dream.

"At this very moment, of course, they'll be in each other's arms in Italy. And . . . and I don't mind that in the least."

She was not boasting. The picture of the young couple she had called up, the familiar attitudes it evoked—even Chéri's face, as he lay exhausted for a minute, with the white line of light between his tired eyelids—aroused in her neither curiosity nor jealousy. On the other hand, an animal convulsion again racked her body, bending her double, as her eye fell on a nick in the pearl gray wainscot—the mark of some brutality of Chéri's. "The lovely hand which here has left its trace has turned away from me forever," she said. "How grandly I'm talking! Soon grief will be turning me into a poet!"

She walked about, she sat down, she went to bed again and waited for daylight. At eight o'clock Rose found her writing at her desk, and this upset the old lady's maid.

"Is Madame not well?"

"So-so, Rose. Age, you know. . . . Doctor Vidal thinks I ought to have a change of air. Will you come with me? It promises to be a cold winter here in Paris. We'll go south to the sun, and eat meals cooked in oil."

"Whereabouts will that be?"

"You want to know too much. Simply have my trunks brought down, and give my fur rugs a good beating."

"Madame will be taking the motorcar?"

"I think so. I'm sure of it, in fact. I'll need all my creature comforts now, Rose. Just think of it, this time I'm going all on my own. It's going to be a pleasure trip."

During the next five days Léa rushed all over Paris; wrote, telegraphed, and received telegrams and answers from the south. And she said good-bye to Paris, leaving behind a short letter addressed to Madame Peloux which she started no less than three times:

My dear Charlotte,

You'll forgive me if I go away without saying good-bye to you, and keep my little secret to myself. I'm making a perfect fool of myself . . . and why not? It's a short life, let's make it a gay one.

I send you an affectionate kiss. Remember me to the child when he comes back.

Your incorrigible
Léa.

P.S.—Don't trouble to come and interview my butler or concierge; no member of my household knows anything at all about it.

DO YOU KNOW, my adored treasure, I don't think you're looking very well."

"It's the night in the train," Chéri answered shortly.

Madame Peloux did not dare to say just what she thought. She found her son changed. "He's . . . yes, he's sinister!" she decided; and she ended by exclaiming enthusiastically, "It's Italy!"

"If you like," Chéri conceded.

Mother and son had just finished breakfasting together, and Chéri had condescended to praise with an oath his cup of "housemaid's coffee," made with creamy milk, well sugared, slowly reheated, with buttered toast crumbled into it and browned till it formed a succulent crust.

He felt cold in his white woolen pajamas and was clasping his knees to his chest. Charlotte Peloux, anxious to look pretty for her son, had put on a brand new marigold négligée, and a boudoir cap fitting tight across the forehead. This made her face stand out, bare and macabre.

Finding her son's eye fixed upon her, she simpered: "You see, I've adopted the grandmother style. Very soon, I'll powder my hair. Do you like this cap? Rather eighteenth-century, don't you think? Du Barry or Pompadour? How do I look in it?"

"Like an old convict," Chéri said witheringly. "Next time you must run up a warning signal."

She groaned, then shrieked with laughter: "Ha-ha-ha. You've a sharp tongue in your head and no mistake!"

But he did not laugh. He was staring out at the lawn powdered with snow after last night's fall. His nervous state was visible only in the spasmodic twitching of his jaw muscles. Madame Peloux was intimidated. She, too, was silent. The faint tinkle of a bell sounded.

"That's Edmée, ringing for her breakfast," said Madame Peloux.

Chéri did not answer. "What's wrong with the heating? It's freezing in here!" he said a moment later.

"It's Italy!" Madame Peloux repeated lyrically. "You come back here, your eyes and your heart full of the warm sun of the south, and find you've landed at the Pole—at the North Pole. There hasn't been a flower on the dahlias for the last week. But don't worry, my precious! Your love nest will soon be finished. If the architect hadn't gone down with paratyphoid, it would be ready for you now. I warned him. If I told him once, I told him twenty times: 'Monsieur Savaron . . .' "

Chéri, who was standing by the window, turned round sharply. "What was the date on that letter?"

Madame Peloux opened her large childlike eyes: "What letter?"

"The letter from Léa you showed me."

"She put no date on it, my love; but I got it the night before my last Sunday At Home in October."

"I see. And you don't know who it is?"

"Who what is, my paragon?"

"Whoever it was she went away with, of course."

Malice clothed Madame Peloux's stark features. "No. Would you believe it, nobody has an idea! Old Lili is in Sicily, and none of my set has a clue! A mystery, an enthralling mystery! However, you know me, I've managed to pick up a few scraps here and there . . ."

Chéri's dark eyes expanded: "What's the tattle?"

"It seems it's a young man . . ." Madame Peloux whispered. "A young man not . . . not particularly desirable, if you know what I mean . . . very well made, of course!" She was lying, careful to insinuate the worst.

Chéri shrugged his shoulders.

"Well made, did you say? Don't make me laugh! My poor Léa! I can see him from here—a hefty little fellow from Patron's training quarters—black hairs on his wrists and clammy hands. . . . Well, I'm going back to bed now; you make me tired."

Trailing his bedroom slippers, he went back to his room, dawdling in the long corridors and on the spacious landings of the house he seemed to be discovering for the first time. He ran into a pot-bellied wardrobe, and was amazed. "Damned if I knew that thing was there. . . . Oh, yes, I vaguely remember. . . . And who the devil's this chap?" He was addressing an enlarged photograph, in a deep black frame, hanging funereally near a piece of colored pottery, equally unfamiliar to Chéri.

Madame Peloux had been installed in this house for the last twenty-five years, and had kept every unfortunate result of her bad taste and acquisitiveness. "Your house looks just like the nest of a magpie gone batty," was old Lili's reproachful comment. She herself had a hearty appetite for modern pictures, and still more for modern painters. To this Madame Peloux had replied: "I believe in letting well enough alone."

If the muddy green paint—"The green of hospital corridors," Léa called it—flaked off in one of the passages, Madame Peloux would have it repainted a similar muddy green; or if the maroon velvet on a chaise-longue needed replacing, she was careful to choose the same maroon velvet.

Chéri paused by the open door of a dressing room. Embedded in the dark red, marble-topped washstand were jug and basin of plain white with a monogram, and over the two electric-light fittings were lily-shaped bead shades. Chéri shuddered as though caught in a violent draft—"Good God, how hideous, what an old junk shop!"

He hurried away. At the end of the passage, he came upon a

window edged with small pieces of red and yellow stained glass. "That's the last straw!" he said grumpily.

He turned to the left and roughly opened a door—the door of his nursery—without knocking. A little cry came from the bed where Edmée was just finishing her breakfast. Chéri closed the door and stared at his wife without going any closer.

"Good morning," she said with a smile. "You do look surprised to see me here!"

She lay bathed in a steady blue light reflected from the snow outside. Her crimped ashy chestnut hair was down, but barely covered her prettily curved shoulders. With her pink-and-white cheeks matching her nightgown, and her rosy lips paler than usual from fatigue, she looked like a light-toned picture, not quite finished and rather misty.

"Aren't you going to say good morning to me, Fred?" she insisted.

He sat down close beside his wife and took her in his arms. She fell back gently, dragging him with her. Chéri propped himself on his elbow to look down more closely at her. She was so young that even when tired she still looked fresh. He seemed astonished by the smoothness of her fully rounded lower eyelids, and by the silvery softness of her cheeks.

"How old are you?" he asked suddenly.

Edmée opened her eyes, which she had closed voluptuously. Chéri stared at the brown of their pupils and at her small square teeth.

"Oh, come! I shall be nineteen on the fifth of January, and do try and remember it."

He drew his arm away roughly and the young woman slipped into the hollow of the bed like a discarded scarf.

"Nineteen, it's prodigious! Do you know that I'm over twenty-five?"

"But of course I know that, Fred. . . ."

He picked up a pale tortoiseshell mirror from the bed table and gazed at himself. "Twenty-five years old!"

Twenty-five years of age and a face of white marble that

seemed indestructible. Twenty-five, but at the outer corners of the eye and beneath it—delicately plagiarizing the classical design of the eyelid—were two lines, visible only in full light, two incisions traced by the lightest, the most relentless, of fingers.

He put back the mirror: "You're younger than I am. That shocks me."

"Not me!"

She had answered in a biting voice, full of hidden meaning. He took no notice.

"Do you know why my eyes are beautiful?" he asked in all seriousness.

"No," Edmée said. "Perhaps because I love them?"

"Stuff!" Chéri said, shrugging his shoulders. "It's because they're shaped like a sole."

"Like what?"

"Like a sole."

He sat down near her to give a demonstration.

"Look—here—the corner next the nose is the head of the sole. And then—the upper curve, that's the back of the sole; whereas the lower line runs perfectly straight and that's its belly. And the other corner that tapers up to my temples, that's the sole's tail."

"Oh?"

"Yes, but if I had an eye shaped like a flounder, that's to say, with the lower part as much curved as the top, then I should look silly. See? You've passed your matric., and you didn't know that?"

"No, I must admit . . ."

She broke off, feeling guilty, because he had spoken sententiously and with exaggerated passion, like someone with a mania. "There are moments when he looks like a savage," she thought, "like a man from the jungle. Yet he knows nothing about plants or animals, and sometimes he doesn't seem even to know about human beings."

Sitting close beside her, Chéri put one arm round her shoulders and with his free hand began to finger the small, evenly matched, very round and very beautiful, pearls of her necklace. Intoxicated by the scent which Chéri used too much of, she began to droop like a rose in an overheated room.

"Fred! Come back to sleep! We're both tired. . . ."

He seemed not to have heard. He was staring at the pearls with obsessed anxiety.

"Fred!"

He shivered, leaped to his feet, furiously tore off his pajamas and jumped naked into bed, seeking the place to rest his head on a shoulder where the delicate collarbone was still youthfully sharp. The whole of Edmée's body obeyed his will as she opened her arms to him. Chéri closed his eyes and never moved. She took care to remain awake, a little smothered under his weight, and thinking him asleep. But almost at once he turned over away from her with a sudden pitch, imitating the groans of someone fast asleep, and rolled himself up in the sheet at the other side of the bed.

"He always does that," Edmée noted.

All through the winter, she was to awaken in this square room with its four windows. Bad weather delayed the completion of the new house in the Avenue Henri-Martin—bad weather, and Chéri's whims. He wanted a black bathroom, a Chinese drawing room, a basement fitted up with a swimming pool and gymnasium. To the architect's objections he would answer: "I don't care a damn. I pay, I want the work done. To hell with the cost." But every now and again he would cast a ruthless eye over an estimate and proclaim "You can't bamboozle young Peloux." Indeed, he held forth on standardization, fibro-cement, and colored stucco with unexpected glibness and a memory for exact figures that compelled the contractor's respect.

Rarely did he consult his young wife, although he paraded his authority for her benefit and took pains, when occasion arose, to cover his deficiencies by giving curt commands. She was to find that he possessed an instinctive eye for color, but had only contempt for beauty of shape and period differences.

"You simply clutter up your head with all that stuff and

nonsense, what's your name, yes, you, Edmée. An idea for the smoking room? All right, here's one: Blue for the walls—a ferocious blue. The carpet purple—a purple that plays second fiddle to the blue of the walls. Against that you needn't be afraid of using as much black as you like and a splash of gold in the furniture and ornaments."

"Yes, you're right, Fred. But it will be rather drastic with all those strong colors. It's going to look rather charmless without a lighter note somewhere . . . a white vase or a statue."

"Nonsense," he interrupted, rather sharply. "The white vase you want will be me—me, stark naked. And we musn't forget a cushion or some thingumabob in pumpkin red for when I'm running about stark naked in the smoking room."

Secretly attracted and at the same time disgusted, she cherished these fanciful ideas for turning their future home into a sort of disreputable palace, a temple to the greater glory of her husband. She offered little resistance, just gently requested "some little corner" for a small and precious set of furniture upholstered with needlework on a white ground—a present from Marie-Laure.

This gentleness masked a determination that was young yet far from inexperienced; it stood her in good stead during the four months of camping out in her mother-in-law's house. It enabled her to evade, throughout these four months, the enemy stalking her, the traps laid daily to destroy her equanimity, her still susceptible gaiety, and her tact. Charlotte Peloux, overexcited at the proximity of so tender a victim, was inclined to lose her head and squander her barbs, using her claws indiscriminately.

"Keep calm, Madame Peloux," Chéri would throw out from time to time. "What bones will there be left for you to pick next winter, if I don't stop you now?"

Edmée raised frightened, grateful eyes to her husband, and did her best not to think too much, not to look too much at Madame Peloux. Then one evening, Charlotte, almost heedlessly, three times tossed across the chrysanthemum table piece Léa's name instead of Edmée's.

Chéri lowered his satanic eyebrows: "Madame Peloux, I believe your memory is giving way. Perhaps a rest cure is indicated?"

Charlotte Peloux held her tongue for a whole week, but Edmée never dared to ask her husband: "Did you get angry on my behalf? Was it me you were defending? Or was it that other woman, the one before me?"

Life as a child and then as a girl had taught her patience, hope, silence; and given her a prisoner's proficiency in handling these virtues as weapons. The fair Marie-Laure had never scolded her daughter: she had merely punished her. Never a hard word, never a tender one. Utter loneliness, then a boarding school, then again loneliness in the holidays and frequent relegations to a bedroom. Finally, the threat of marriage—any marriage—from the moment that the eye of a too beautiful mother had discerned in the daughter the dawn of a rival beauty, shy, timid, looking a victim of tyranny, and all the more touching for that. In comparison with this inhuman, gold-and-ivory mother, Charlotte Peloux and her spontaneous malice seemed a bed of roses.

"Are you frightened of my respected parent?" Chéri asked her one evening.

Edmée smiled and pouted to show her indifference: "Frightened? No. You aren't frightened when a door slams, though it may make you jump. It's a snake creeping under it that's frightening."

"A terrific snake, Marie-Laure, isn't she?"

"Terrific."

He waited for confidences that did not come and put a brotherly arm round his wife's slender shoulders: "We're sort of orphans, you and I, aren't we?"

"Yes, we're orphans, and we're so sweet!"

She clung to him. They were alone in the big sitting room, for Madame Peloux was upstairs concocting, as Chéri put it, her poisons for the following day. The night was cold and the window panes reflected the lamplight and furnishings like a pond. Edmée felt warm and protected, safe in the arms of this unknown man. She lifted her head and gave a cry of alarm.

He was staring up at the chandelier above them with a look of desperation on his magnificent features, and two tears hung glistening between the lids of his half-closed eyes.

"Chéri, Chéri, what's the matter with you?" On the spur of the moment she had called him by the too endearing nickname she had never meant to pronounce. He answered its appeal in bewilderment and turned his eyes down to look at her.

"Chéri, oh God! I'm frightened. What's wrong with you?"

He pushed her away a little, and held her facing him.

"Oh! Oh! You poor child, you poor little thing! What are you frightened of?"

He gazed at her with his eyes of velvet, wide-open, peaceful, inscrutable, all the more handsome for his tears. Edmée was about to beg him not to speak, when he said, "How silly we are! It's the idea that we're orphans. It's idiotic. It's so true."

He resumed his air of comic self-importance, and she drew a breath of relief, knowing that he would say no more. He began switching off all the lights with his usual care, and then turned to Edmée with a vanity that was either very simple or very deceitful: "Well, why shouldn't I have a heart like everybody else?"

"WHAT are you doing there?"

He had called out to her almost in a whisper, yet the sound of Chéri's voice struck Edmée so forcibly that she swayed forward as if he had pushed her. She was standing beside a big open writing desk and she spread her hands over the papers scattered in front of her.

"I'm tidying up . . ." she said in a dazed voice. She lifted a hand and it remained poised in midair as though benumbed. Then she appeared to wake up, and stopped lying.

"It's like this, Fred. You told me that when we came to move house you'd hate to be bothered over what you'd want to take with you, all the things in this room . . . the furniture. I honestly wanted to tidy, to sort things. Then the poison, temptation came . . . evil thoughts . . . one evil thought. . . . I implore your forgiveness. I've touched things that don't belong to me. . . ."

She trembled bravely and waited.

He stood with his forehead jutting forward, his hands clenched in a threatening attitude; but he did not seem to see his wife. His eyes were strangely veiled, and ever after she was to retain the impression of having spoken with a man whose eyes were deathly pale.

"Ah, yes," he said at length. "You were looking . . . you were looking for love letters." She did not deny it. "You were hunting for my love letters."

He laughed his awkward, constrained laugh.

Edmée felt hurt, and blushed. "Of course you must think me a fool. As if you were the kind of man not to lock them away in a safe place or burn them! And then, anyhow, they're none of my business. I've only got what I deserved. You won't hold it too much against me, Fred?"

Her pleading had cost her a certain effort, and she tried deliberately to make herself look appealing, pouting her lips a little and keeping the upper half of her face shadowed by her fluffy hair. But Chéri did not relax his attitude, and she noticed for the first time that the unblemished skin of his cheeks had taken on the transparence of a white rose in winter, and that their oval contour had shrunk.

"Love letters," he repeated. "That's howlingly funny."

He took a step forward, seized a fistful of papers and scattered them: postcards, restaurant bills, tradespeople's announcements, telegrams from chorus girls met one night and never seen again, *pneumatiques* of four or five lines from sponging friends; and several close-written pages slashed with the saberlike script of Madame Peloux.

Chéri turned round again to his wife: "I have no love letters."

"Oh!" she protested. "Why do you want . . ."

"I have none," he interrupted; "you can never understand. I've never noticed it myself until now. I can't have any love letters because———" He checked himself. "But wait, wait. . . . Yes, there was one occasion, I remember, when I didn't want to go to La Bourboule, and it . . . Wait, wait."

He began pulling out drawers and feverishly tossing papers to the floor.

"That's too bad! What can I have done with it? I could have sworn it was in the upper left-hand . . . No. . . ."

He slammed back the empty drawers and glowered at Edmée.

"You found nothing? You didn't take a letter which began 'But what do you expect, I'm not in the least bored. There's nothing better than to be separated one week in every month,' and then went on to something else. I don't remember what, something about honeysuckle climbing high enough to look in at the window."

He broke off, simply because his memory refused to come to his aid, and he was left gesticulating in his impatience.

Slim and recalcitrant, Edmée did not quail before him. She took refuge in caustic irritability. "No, no, I *took* nothing. Since when have I been capable of *taking* things? But if this letter is so very precious to you, how is it you've left it lying about? I've no need to inquire whether it was one of Léa's?"

He winced, but not quite in the manner Edmée had expected. The ghost of a smile hovered over his handsome, unresponsive features; and, with his head on one side, an expectant look in his eyes, and the delicious bow of his mouth taut-stretched, he might well have been listening to the echo of a name.

The full force of Edmée's young and ill-disciplined emotions burst forth in a series of sobs and tears, and her fingers writhed and twisted as if ready to scratch. "Go away! I hate you! You've never loved me. I might not so much as exist, for all the notice you take of me! You hurt me, you despise me, you're insulting, you're, you're . . . You think only of that old woman! It's not natural, it's degenerate, it's . . . You don't love me! Why, oh why, did you ever marry me? . . . You're . . . you're . . ."

She was tossing her head like an animal caught by the neck, and as she leaned back to take a deep breath, because she was suffocating, the light fell on her string of small, milky, evenly matched pearls. Chéri stared in stupefaction at the uncontrolled movements of the lovely throat, at the hands clasped together in appeal, and above all at the tears, her tears. . . . He had never seen such a torrent of tears. For who had ever wept in front of him, or wept because of him? No one. Madame Peloux? "But," he thought, "Madame Peloux's tears don't count." Léa? No. Searching his memory, he appealed to a pair of honest blue eyes; but they had sparkled with pleasure only, or malice, or a rather mocking tenderness. Such floods of tears poured down the cheeks of this writhing young woman.

What could be done about all these tears? He did not know. All the same, he stretched out an arm, and as Edmée drew back, fearing some brutality perhaps, he placed his beautiful, gentle, scented hand on her head and patted her ruffled hair. He did his best to copy the tone and speech of a voice whose power he knew so well: "There, there. . . . What's it all about? What's the matter, then? There . . . there. . . ."

Edmée collapsed suddenly, fell back huddled in a heap on a settee, and broke out into frenzied and passionate sobbing that sounded like yells of laughter or howls of joy. As she lay doubled up, her graceful body heaved and rocked with grief, jealousy, fury and an unsuspected servility. And yet, like a wrestler in the heat of a struggle, or a swimmer in the hollow of a wave, she felt bathed in some strange new atmosphere, both natural and harsh.

She had a good long cry, and recovered by slow degrees, with periods of calm shaken by great shudders and gasps for breath. Chéri sat down by her side and continued to stroke her hair. The crisis of his own emotion was over, and he felt bored. He ran his eyes over Edmée as she lay sideways upon the unyielding settee. This straggling body, with its wrinkled-up frock and trailing scarf, added to the disorder of the room; and this displeased him.

Soft as was his sigh of boredom, she heard it and sat up. "Yes," she said, "I'm more than you can stand. . . . Oh! it would be better to . . ."

He interrupted her, fearing a torrent of words: "It's not that. It's simply that I don't know what you want."

"What I want? How d'you mean, what I . . ."

She lifted her face, still wet with tears.

"Now listen to me." He took her hands.

She tried to free herself. "No, no, I know that tone of voice. You're going to treat me to another of those nonsensical outbursts. When you put on that tone of voice and face, I know you're going to prove that your eye is shaped like a striped super-mullet, or that your mouth looks like the figure three on its side. No, no, I can't stand that!"

Her recriminations were childish, and Chéri relaxed, feeling that after all they were both very young. He pressed her warm hands between his own.

"But you must listen to me! . . . Good God! I'd like to know what you've got to reproach me with! Do I ever go out in the evenings without you? No! Do I often leave you on your own during the day? Do I carry on a secret correspondence?"

"I don't know—I don't think so——"

He turned her this way and that like a doll.

"Do I have a separate room? Don't I make love to you well?"

She hesitated, smiling with exquisite suspicion. "Do you call that love, Fred?"

"There are other words for it, but you wouldn't appreciate them."

"What you call love . . . isn't it possible that it may be, really, a . . . kind . . . of alibi?" She hastened to add, "I'm merely generalizing, Fred, of course . . . I said '*may* be,' in certain cases. . . ."

He dropped Edmée's hands. "That," he said coldly, "is putting your foot right in it."

"Why?" she asked in a feeble voice.

He whistled, chin in air, as he moved back a step or two. Then he advanced upon his wife, looking her up and down as if she were a stranger. To instill fear a fierce animal has no need to leap. Edmée noticed that his nostrils were dilating and that the tip of his nose was white.

"Ugh!" he breathed, looking at his wife. He shrugged his shoulders, turned, and walked away. At the end of the room he turned round and came back again. "Ugh!" he repeated, "Look what's talking!"

"What are you saying?"

"Look what's talking, and what it says. Upon my word, it actually has the cheek to . . ."

She jumped up in a rage. "Fred," she said, "don't dare to speak to me again in that tone! What do you take me for?"

"For a woman who knows exactly how to put her foot in it, as I've just had the honor of informing you."

He touched her on the shoulder with a rigid forefinger, and this hurt her as much as if he had inflicted a serious bruise. "You've matriculated; isn't there somewhere some kind of a proverb which says, 'Never play with knives or daggers' or whatever it may be?"

"Cold steel," she answered automatically.

"That's right. Well, my child, you must never play with cold steel. That's to say, you must never be wounding about a man's . . . a man's favors, if I may so express it. You were wounding about the gifts, about the favors, I bestow on you."

"You . . . you talk like a cocotte," she gasped.

She blushed, and her strength and self-control deserted her. She hated him for remaining cool and collected, for keeping his superiority: its whole secret lay in the carriage of his head, the sureness of his stance, the poise of his arms and shoulders.

The hard forefinger once more pressed into Edmée's shoulder.

"Excuse me, excuse me. . . . It'll probably come as a great surprise when I state that, on the contrary, it's you who have the mentality of a tart. When it comes to judging such matters, there's no greater authority than young Peloux. I'm a connoisseur of 'cocottes,' as you call them. I know them inside out. A 'cocotte' is a lady who generally manages to receive more than she gives. Do you hear what I say?"

What she heard above all was that he was now addressing her like a stray acquaintance.

"Nineteen years old, white skin, hair that smells of vanilla; and then, in bed, closed eyes and limp arms. That's all very pretty, but is there anything unusual about it? Do you really think it so very unusual?"

She had started at each word, and each sting had goaded her toward the duel of female versus male.

"It may be very unusual," she said in a steady voice. "How could *you* know?"

He did not answer, and she hastened to take advantage of a

hit. "Personally, I saw much handsomer men than you when we were in Italy. The streets were full of them. My nineteen years are worth those of any other girl of my age, just as one good-looking man is as good as the next. Don't worry, everything can be arranged. Nowadays, marriage is not an important undertaking. Instead of allowing silly scenes to make us bitter . . ."

He put a stop to what she had to say by an almost pitying shake of the head.

"My poor kid, it's not so simple as that."

"Why not? There's such a thing as quick divorce, if one's ready to pay."

She spoke in the peremptory manner of a runaway schoolgirl, and it was pathetic. She had pushed back the hair off her forehead, and her anxious, intelligent eyes were made to look all the darker by the soft contours of her cheeks now fringed with hair: the eyes of an unhappy woman, eyes mature and definitive in a still undeveloped face.

"That wouldn't help at all," Chéri said.

"Because?"

"Because . . ." He leaned forward with his eyelashes tapered into pointed wings, shut his eyes and opened them again as if he had just swallowed a bitter pill. "Because you love me."

She noticed that he had resumed the more familiar form of addressing her, and above all the fuller, rather choked tones of their happiest hours. In her heart of hearts she acquiesced: "It's true, I love him. At the moment, there's no remedy."

The dinner bell sounded in the garden—a bell which was too small, dating from before Madame Peloux's time, a sad clear bell reminiscent of a country orphanage. Edmée shivered. "Oh, I don't like that bell. . . ."

"No?" said Chéri, absentmindedly.

"In our house, dinner will be announced. There'll be no bell. There'll be no boardinghouse habits in our home—you'll see."

She spoke these words without turning round, while

walking down the hospital-green corridor, and so did not see, behind her, either the fierce attention Chéri paid to her last words, or his silent laughter.

HE WAS WALKING along with a light step, stimulated by the early spring, perceptible in the moist gusty wind and the exciting earthy smells of squares and private gardens. Every now and again a fleeting glimpse in a glass would remind him that he was wearing a becoming felt hat, pulled down over the right eye, a loose-fitting spring coat, large light-colored gloves and a terra-cotta tie. The eyes of women followed his progress with silent homage, the more candid among them bestowing that passing stupefaction which can be neither feigned nor hidden. But Chéri never looked at women in the street. He had just come from his house in the Avenue Henri-Martin, having left various orders with the upholsterers: orders contradicting one another, but thrown out in a tone of authority.

On reaching the end of the avenue, he took a deep breath of the good spring scents carried up from the Bois on the heavy moist wing of the west wind, and then hurried on his way to the Porte Dauphine. Within a few minutes he had reached the lower end of the Avenue Bugeaud, and there he stopped. For the first time in six months his feet were treading the familiar road. He unbuttoned his coat.

"I've been walking too fast," he said to himself. He started off again, then paused and, this time, trained his eyes on one particular spot fifty yards or so down the road: bareheaded, chamois leather in hand, Ernest the concierge—Léa's concierge—was "doing" the brasswork of the railings in front of Léa's house. Chéri began to hum, realized from the sound of his voice that he never did hum, and stopped.

"How are things, Ernest? Hard at work as usual?"

The concierge brightened respectfully.

"Monsieur Peloux! It's a pleasure to see Monsieur again. Monsieur has not changed at all."

"Neither have you, Ernest. Madame is well, I hope?"

He turned his head away to gaze up at the closed shutters on the first floor.

"I expect so, Monsieur, all we've had has been a few postcards."

"Where from? Was it Biarritz?"

"I don't think so, Monsieur."

"Where is Madame?"

"It wouldn't be easy for me to tell you, Monsieur. We forward all letters addressed to Madame—and there's none to speak of—to Madame's solicitor."

Chéri pulled out his billfold, and cocked an eye at Ernest.

"Oh, Monsieur Peloux, money between you and me? Don't think of it. A thousand francs won't make a man tell what he doesn't know. But if Monsieur would like the address of Madame's solicitor?"

"No thanks, there's no point. And when does she return?"

Ernest threw up his hands: "That's another question that's beyond me. Maybe tomorrow, maybe in a month's time. . . . I keep everything in readiness, just the same. You have to watch out where Madame is concerned. If you said to me now, 'There she comes round the corner of the avenue,' I shouldn't be surprised."

Chéri turned round and looked toward the corner of the avenue.

"That's all Monsieur Peloux wants? Monsieur just happened to be walking by? It's a lovely day. . . ."

"Nothing else, thank you, Ernest. Good-bye, Ernest."

"Always at Monsieur's service."

Chéri walked up as far as the Place Victor-Hugo, swinging his cane as he went. Twice he stumbled and almost fell, like people who imagine their progress is being followed by hostile eyes. On reaching the balustraded entrance to the Métro, he leaned over the ramp to peer down into the pink-and-black recesses of the underground, and felt utterly exhausted. When he straightened his back, he saw that the lamps had been lighted in the square and that the blue of dusk colored everything around him.

"No, it can't be true. I'm ill."

He had plumbed the depths of cavernous memories and his return to the living world was painful. The right words came to him at last. "Pull yourself together, Peloux, for God's sake! Are you losing your head, my boy? Don't you know it's time to go back home?"

This last word recalled a sight that one hour had sufficed to banish from his mind: a large square room—his own nursery; an anxious young woman standing by the window; and Charlotte Peloux, subdued by a martini.

"Oh, no," he said aloud. "Not that! That's all over."

He signaled to a taxi with his raised stick.

"To the . . . er . . . to the Restaurant du Dragon Bleu."

Chéri crossed the grillroom to the sound of violins in the glare of the atrocious electric light, and this had a tonic effect. He shook the hand of a maître d'hôtel who recognized him. Before him rose the stooping figure of a tall young man. Chéri gave an affectionate gasp. "Desmond, the very man I wanted to see! Howdydo?"

They were shown to a table decorated with pink carnations. A small hand and a towering aigrette beckoned toward Chéri from a neighboring table.

"It's La Loupiote," Vicomte Desmond warned him.

Chéri had no recollection of La Loupiote, but he smiled toward the towering aigrette and, without getting up, touched the small hand with a paper fan lying on his table. Then he put on his most solemn "conquering hero" look, and swept

his eyes over an unknown couple. The woman had forgotten to eat since he had sat down in her vicinity.

"The man with her looks a regular cuckold, doesn't he?"

He had leaned over to whisper into his friend's ear, and his eyes shone with pleasure as if with rising tears.

"What d'you drink, now you're married?" Desmond asked, "Camomile tea?"

"Pommery," Chéri said.

"And before the Pommery?"

"Pommery, before and after." And, dilating his nostrils, he sniffed as he remembered some sparkling, rose-scented old champagne of 1889 that Léa kept for him alone.

He ordered a meal that a shopgirl out on the spree might choose—cold fish *au porto,* a roast bird, and a piping hot soufflé which concealed in its innards a red ice, sharp on the tongue.

"Hello!" La Loupiote shouted, waving a pink carnation at Chéri.

"Hello," Chéri answered, raising his glass.

The chimes of an English wall clock struck eight. "Blast!" Chéri grumbled, "Desmond, go and make a telephone call for me."

Desmond's pale eyes were hungry for revelations to come.

"Go and ask for Wagram 17–08, tell them to put you through to my mother, and say we're dining together."

"And supposing young Madame Peloux comes to the telephone?"

"Say the same thing. I'm not tied to her apron strings. I've got her well trained."

He ate and drank a lot, taking the greatest care to appear serious and blasé; but his pleasure was enhanced by the least sound of laughter, the clink of glasses, or the strains of a syrupy valse. The steely blue of the highly glazed woodwork reminded him of the Riviera, at the hour when the too blue sea grows dark around the blurred reflection of the noonday sun. He forgot that very handsome young men ought to pretend indifference; he began to scrutinize the dark girl opposite, so that she trembled all over under his expert gaze.

"What about Léa?" Desmond asked suddenly.

Chéri did not jump: he was thinking of Léa. "Léa? She's in the south."

"Is all over between you?"

Chéri put his thumb in the armhole of his waistcoat.

"Well, of course, what d'you expect? We parted in proper style, the best of friends. It couldn't last a lifetime. What a charming, intelligent woman, old man! But then, you know her yourself! Broadminded . . . most remarkable. My dear fellow, I confess that if it hadn't been for the question of age. . . . But there *was* the question of age, and you agree . . ."

"Of course," Desmond interrupted.

This young man with lackluster eyes, though he knew just how to perform the wearing and difficult duties of a parasite, had just yielded to curiosity and blamed himself for such rashness. Chéri, circumspect and at the same time highly elated, never stopped talking about Léa. He made all the right remarks, showed all the sound sense of a married man. He spoke in praise of marriage, while giving Léa's virtues their due. He extolled the submissive sweetness of his young wife, and thus found occasion to criticize Léa's independence of character. "Oh, the old devil, she had her own ideas about everything, I can tell you!"

He went a step further in his confidences, speaking of Léa with severity, and even impertinence. He was sheltering behind idiotic words, prompted by the suspicions of a deceived lover, and at the same time enjoying the subtle pleasure of being able to speak of her without danger. A little more, and he would have sullied her name, while his heart was rejoicing in his own memories of her: sullied the soft sweet name which he had been unable to mention freely during the last six months, and the whole gracious vision he had of Léa, leaning over him with her two or three irreparable wrinkles, and her beauty, now lost to him, but—alas—ever present.

About eleven o'clock they rose to go, chilled by the emptiness of the almost deserted restaurant. However, at the next table, La Loupiote was busy writing letters and had called for telegraph forms. She raised her white, inoffensive, sheep-like head as the two friends passed by. "Well, aren't you even going to say good evening?"

"Good evening," Chéri condescended to say.

La Loupiote drew her friend's attention to Chéri's good looks. "Would you believe it! And to think that he's got such pots of money. Some people have everything!"

But when Chéri merely offered her an open cigarette case, she became vituperative. "They have everything, except the knowledge of how to make proper use of it. Go back home to your mother, dearie!"

"Look here," Chéri said to Desmond when they were outside in the narrow street, "Look here, I was about to ask you, Desmond . . . Wait till we get away from this beastly crowd. . . ."

The soft damp evening air had kept people lingering in the streets, but the theatergoers from the Rue Caumartin onward had not yet packed the boulevard. Chéri took his friend by the arm: "Look here, Desmond . . . I wanted you to make another telephone call."

Desmond stopped, "Again?"

"You'll ask for Wagram . . ."

"17–08."

"You're marvelous. . . . Say that I've been taken ill in your flat. Where are you living?"

"Hôtel Morris."

"Splendid—and that I won't be back till morning, and that you're making me some mint tea. Go on, old man. Here, you can give this to the telephone girl, or else keep it yourself. But come back quickly. I'll be sitting waiting for you outside Weber's."

The tall young man, arrogant and serviceable, went off crumpling the franc notes in his pocket, without permitting himself a comment. When Desmond rejoined him, Chéri was slouched over an untouched orangeade in which he appeared to be reading his fortune.

"Desmond . . . Who answered you?"

"A lady," the laconic messenger replied.

"Which?"

"Dunno."

"What did she say?"

"That it was all right."

"In what tone of voice?"

"Same as I'm speaking to you in."

"Oh, good. Thanks."

"It was Edmée," thought Chéri.

They were walking toward the Place de la Concorde and Chéri linked arms with Desmond. He did not dare to admit that he was feeling dog-tired.

"Where do you want to go?" Desmond asked.

"Well, old man," Chéri sighed in gratitude, "to the Morris; and as soon as we can. I'm fagged out."

Desmond forgot to be impassive. "What? It can't be true. To the Morris? What d'you want to do? No nonsense! D'you want to . . ."

"To go to bed," Chéri answered. And he closed his eyes as though on the point of dropping off, then opened them again. "Sleep, I want to sleep, got it?"

He gripped his friend's arm too hard.

"Let's go there, then," Desmond said.

Within ten minutes they were at the Morris. The sky blue and white bedroom and the imitation Empire furniture of the sitting room smiled at Chéri like old friends. He took a bath, borrowed one of Desmond's silk nightshirts which was too tight for him, got into bed, and, wedged between two huge soft pillows, sank into dreamless bliss, into the dark depths of a sleep that protected him from all attacks.

HE BEGAN to count the shameful days as they went by. "Sixteen . . . seventeen . . . When three weeks are up, I'll go back to Neuilly." He did not go back. Though he saw the situation quite clearly, he no longer had the strength to cure it. At night, and in the morning sometimes, he flattered himself that he would get over his cowardice within an hour or two. "No strength left? . . . Please, please, I beg of you . . . Not yet strength enough. But it's coming back. What's the betting I'll be in the Boulevard d'Inkermann dining room at the stroke of twelve? One, two . . ." The stroke of twelve found him in the bath, or else driving his motor, with Desmond at his side.

At every mealtime, he felt optimistic for a moment about his marriage. This feeling was as regular as a recurrent fever. As he sat down facing Desmond at their bachelor table, the ghost of Edmée would appear, and plunge him into silent thoughts of his young wife's inconceivable deference. "Really, that young thing's too sweet! Did you ever see such a dream of a wife? Never a word, never a complaint! I'll treat her to one of those bracelets when I get back. . . . Upbringing, that's what does it! Give me Marie-Laure every time for bringing up a daughter!" But one day in the grillroom at the Morris, abject terror was written on his face when he caught sight of a green dress with a chinchilla collar just like one of Edmée's dresses.

Desmond found life wonderful and was getting a little fat.

He reserved his arrogance for moments when Chéri—encouraged by him to pay a visit to some "prodigious English girl, riddled with vice," or to some "Indian potentate in his opium palace"—refused point blank or else consented with unconcealed scorn. Desmond had long since despaired of understanding Chéri's ways; but Chéri was paying—and better than during the best of their bachelor days together. They ran across the blond La Loupiote a second time, when they visited a friend of hers, a woman who boasted such an ordinary name that nobody ever remembered it; "What's-her-name . . . you know perfectly well . . . that pal of La Loupiote's."

The Pal smoked opium, and gave it to others. The instant you came into her modest, ground-floor flat, you smelled escaping gas and stale drugs. She won the hearts of her guests by a tearful cordiality and by a constant incitement to self-pity—both objectionable traits. She treated Desmond, when he paid her a visit, as "a great big desperately lonesome boy," . . . and Chéri as "a beauty who has got everything and it only makes him more miserable." Chéri never touched the pipe; he looked at the small box of cocaine with the repugnance of a cat about to be dosed, and spent most of the night with his back against the cushioned dado, sitting up on a straw mat between Desmond, who went to sleep, and the Pal, who never stopped smoking. For most of the night he breathed in the fumes that satisfy all hunger and thirst, but his self-control and distrust persisted. He appeared to be perfectly happy, except that he stared now and then, with pained and questioning intensity, at the Pal's withered throat—a skinny, far too red throat, round which shimmered a string of false pearls.

Once, he stretched out a hand and with the tip of his fingers touched the henna-tinted hair on the nape of her neck. He judged the weight of the big light hollow pearls with his hand, then snatched it back with the nervous shiver of someone who catches his fingernail on a piece of frayed silk. Not long after, he got up and went.

"Aren't you sick to death of all this," Desmond asked

Chéri, "sick of these poky holes where we eat and drink and never have any girls? Sick of this hotel with the doors always slamming? Sick of the nightclubs where we go in the evenings, and of dashing in that fast car of yours from Paris to Rouen, Paris to Compiègne, Paris to Ville d'Avray? . . . Why not the Riviera for a change? The season down there isn't December and January, it's March, April, or . . ."

"No, " said Chéri.

"Then what?"

"Then nothing."

Chéri affected to become amiable and put on what Léa used to call "his air of worldly superiority."

"Dear old boy . . . you don't seem to appreciate the beauty of Paris at this time of the year. . . . This . . . er . . . indecisive season, this spring that doesn't seem willing to smile, the softness of the light . . . as opposed to the commonplace Riviera. . . . No, don't you see, I like it here."

Desmond all but lost his lackey patience. "Yes, and besides, it may be that the young Peloux's divorce will . . ."

Chéri's sensitive nostrils blenched. "If you've arranged to touch a commission from some lawyer friend, you can drop the idea at once. There'll be no such thing as 'young Peloux's divorce.' "

"My dear fellow! . . ." Desmond protested, doing his best to look hurt. "You have a very curious way of behaving to a man who has been a friend since your childhood, and who has always . . ."

Chéri was not listening. Instead, he pushed toward Desmond's face a pointed chin and a mouth pursed like a miser's. For the first time in his life he had heard a stranger disposing of his possessions.

He began to reflect. Young Peloux's divorce? Many nights and days had he spent in thinking over these words till they had come to spell liberty, a sort of second boyhood, perhaps something even better. But Desmond's voice, with its affected nasal twang, had just called up the image he had been looking for: Edmée, resolute in her little hat with its long motoring veil, moving out of the house at Neuilly on her way to an unknown house to join an unknown man. "Of course, that would settle everything," and his Bohemian side was delighted. At the same time a surprisingly timorous Chéri jibbed, "That's not the sort of way one behaves!" The image became focused in sharper color and movement. Chéri could hear the heavy musical note of the iron gate swinging to, and could see beyond it fingers wearing a gray pearl and a white diamond. "Farewell," the small hand said.

Chéri jumped up, pushing back his seat. "Those are mine, all of them! The woman, the house, the rings . . . they all belong to me!"

He had not spoken out loud, but his features expressed such savage violence that Desmond thought his last hour of prosperity had struck. Chéri spoke to him pityingly but without kindness.

"Poor pussycat, did I scare you? What it is to be descended from the Crusaders! Come along, and I'll buy you pants as fine as my shirts, and shirts as fine as your pants. Desmond, is today the seventeenth?"

"Yes, why?"

"The seventeenth of March. In other words, spring. Desmond, people who think themselves smart, I mean those in the height of fashion, women or men—can they afford to wait any longer before buying their spring wardrobes?"

"Hardly——"

"The seventeenth, Desmond! Come along at once; everything's all right. We're going to buy a huge bracelet for my wife, an enormous cigarette holder for Madame Peloux, and a tiny tiepin for you."

On more than one such occasion he had felt an overwhelming presentiment that Léa was on the point of returning; that she was already back in her house; that the first-floor shutters had been opened, allowing a glimpse of the flowered pink net curtains across the windows, the lace of the full-length curtains at each side and the glint of the looking glasses. . . . The fifteenth of April went by and still there was no sign of Léa.

The mournful monotony of Chéri's existence was tempered by several provoking incidents. There was a visit from Madame Peloux, who thought she was breathing her last when she found Chéri looking as thin as a greyhound, eyes wandering and mouth tight shut. There was the letter from Edmée: a letter all in the same surprising tone, explaining that she would stay on at Neuilly "until further orders," and had undertaken to pass on to Chéri "Madame de la Berche's best regards." . . . He thought she was laughing at him, did not know what to answer, and ended by throwing away the enigmatic screed; but he did not go to Neuilly.

April advanced, leafy, cold, bright, and scenting all Paris with tulips, bunches of hyacinths, paulownias and laburnums like dropping wells of gold. Chéri buried himself all the deeper in austere seclusion. The harassed, ill-treated, angry but well-paid Vicomte Desmond was given his orders: now to protect Chéri from familiar young women and indiscreet young men; now to recruit both sections and form a troop, who ate, drank, and rushed screaming at the top of their voices between Montmartre, the restaurants in the Bois, and the cabarets on the left bank.

One night the Pal was alone in her room, smoking opium and bewailing some shocking disloyalty of La Loupiote's, when her door opened to reveal the young man, with satanic eyebrows tapering toward his temples. He begged for "a glass of really cold water" to allay some secret ardor that had parched his beautiful lips. He showed not the slightest interest in the Pal and the woes she poured out. She pushed toward him the lacquer tray with its pipe: he would accept nothing, and took up his usual position on the mat, to share with her the semiobscurity in silence. There he stayed till dawn, moving as little as possible, like a man who fears that the least gesture may bring back his pain. At dawn, he questioned the Pal: "Why weren't you wearing your pearls today; you know, the big ones?" and politely took his leave.

Walking alone at night was becoming an unconscious habit with him. With rapid lengthy strides he would make off toward some positive but inaccessible goal. Soon after midnight he would escape from Desmond, who discovered him again only toward daybreak, asleep on his hotel bed, flat on his stomach, his head pillowed on his folded arms, in the posture of a fretful child.

"Oh, good, he's here all right," Desmond would say with relief. "One can never be sure with such a crackpot."

One night, when out on a tramp, his eyes wide open in the darkness, Chéri had felt compelled to walk up the Avenue Bugeaud; for during the day he had disregarded the superstition that made him return there once every twenty-four hours. There are maniacs who cannot go to sleep without having first touched the doorknob three times; a similar obsession made him run his hand along the railings, then put his finger to the bellpush, and call out Hullo! under his breath, as if in fun, before making off in haste.

But one night, that very night, as he stood before the railings, his heart jumped almost into his mouth: there, in the court, the electric globe shone like a mauve moon above the front door steps, the back door stood wide open shedding a glow on the paved courtyard, while, on the first floor, the bedroom lights filtered through the shutters to make a golden comb. Chéri supported himself against the nearest tree and lowered his head.

"It can't be true. As soon as I look up, it will all be dark again."

He straightened up at the sound of a voice. Ernest, the concierge, was shouting in the passage: "At nine tomorrow, Marcel will help me carry up the big black trunk, Madame."

Chéri turned round in a flash and ran as far as the Avenue du Bois. There he sat down. In front of his eyes danced the image of the electric globe he had been staring at—a dark purple ball fringed with gold, against a black group of trees in bud. He pressed his hand to his heart, and took a deep breath. Early lilac blossom scented the night air. He threw his hat away, undid the buttons of his overcoat and, leaning back on a seat, let himself go, his legs outstretched and his hands hanging feebly by his sides. A crushing yet delicious weight had just fallen upon him. "Ah!" he whispered, "so this is what they call happiness. I never knew."

For a moment he gave way to self-pity and self-contempt. How many good things had he missed by leading such a pointless life—a young man with lots of money and little heart! Then he stopped thinking for a moment, or possibly for an hour. Next, he persuaded himself there was nothing in the world he wanted, not even to go and see Léa.

When he found himself shivering in the cold, and heard the blackbirds caroling the dawn, he got up and, stumbling a little but lighthearted, set off toward the Hôtel Morris without passing through the Avenue Bugeaud. He stretched himself, filled his lungs with the morning air, and overflowed with goodwill to all.

"Now," he sighed, the devil driven out of him, "now . . . Oh now you'll see just how nice to the girl I shall be."

Shaved, shod, and impatient—he had been up since eight—Chéri shook Desmond. Sleep gave him a swollen look, livid and quite frightful, like a drowned man. "Desmond! Hey, Desmond! Up you get. . . . You look too hideous when you're asleep!"

The sleeper woke, sat up, and turned toward Chéri, eyes the color of clouded water. He pretended to be fuddled with sleep so that he could make a long and close examination of Chéri—Chéri dressed in blue, pathetic, superb, and pale under the lightest coat of powder.

There were still moments when Desmond felt painfully aware of the contrast between his ugly mask and Chéri's good looks. He pretended to give a long yawn. "What's he up to now?" he wondered; "The idiot is in far better looks than yesterday—especially his eyelashes, and what eyelashes he has . . ." He was staring at the lustrous sweep of Chéri's thick lashes and the shadow they shed on the dark pupils and bluish whites of his eyes. Desmond noticed also that, this morning, the contemptuously arched lips were moist and fresh, and that he was breathing through them as if he had just that moment finished making love.

Quickly he relegated his jealousy to the back of his mind—where he kept his personal feelings—and asked Chéri in tones of weary condescension: "May one inquire whether you are going out at this hour of the morning, or just coming in?"

"I'm going out," Chéri said. "Don't worry about me. I'm off shopping. I'm going to the florist's, the jeweler's, to my mother's, to my wife's, to . . ."

"Don't forget the Papal Nuncio!"

"I know what's what," Chéri answered. "He shall have some imitation gold studs and a sheaf of orchids."

It was rare for Chéri to respond to jokes: he usually accepted them in stony silence. His facetious reply proved that he was pleased with himself, and revealed this unaccustomed mood to Desmond. He studied Chéri's reflection in the looking glass, noted the pallor of his dilated nostrils, observed that his eyes were continually on the rove, and ventured to put the most discreet of questions.

"Will you be coming back for luncheon? . . . Hey, Chéri, I'm speaking to you. Are we lunching together?"

Chéri answered by shaking his head. He whistled softly, arranging himself in front of the pier glass so that it framed his figure exactly like the one between the two windows in Léa's room—the one which would soon frame in its heavy gold, against a sunny pink background, the reflection of his body—naked or loosely draped in silk—the magnificent picture of a young man, handsome, loved, happy, and pampered, playing with the rings and necklaces of his mistress. "Perhaps her young man's reflection is already there, in Léa's looking glass!" This sudden thought cut so fiercely into his exhilaration that it dazed him, and he fancied he had heard it actually spoken.

"What did you say?" he asked Desmond.

"I never said a word," his well-trained friend said stiffly. "It must have been someone talking outside in the courtyard."

Chéri went out, slamming the door behind him, and returned to his own rooms. They were filled with the dim continual hubbub of the fully awakened Rue de Rivoli, and Chéri, through the open window, could see the spring foliage, the leaves stiff and transparent like thin jade knives against the sun. He closed the window and sat down on a useless little chair which stood against the wall in a dingy corner between his bed and the bathroom door.

"How can it be? . . ." he began in a low voice, and then said no more. He did not understand why it was that during the last six and a half months he had hardly given a thought to Léa's lover. *"I'm making a perfect fool of myself,"* were the actual words of the letter so piously preserved by Charlotte Peloux.

"A perfect fool?" Chéri shook his head. "It's funny, but that's not how I see her at all. What sort of a man can she be in love with? Somebody like Patron—rather than like Desmond, of course. An oily little Argentine? Maybe. Yet all the same . . ." He smiled a simple smile. "Apart from me, who is there she could possibly care for?"

A cloud passed over the sun and the room darkened. Chéri leaned his head against the wall. "My Nounoune . . . My Nounoune . . . Have you betrayed me? Are you beastly enough to deceive me? . . . Have you really done that?"

He tried to give a sharper edge to his suffering by a misuse of his imagination: the words and sights it presented left him more astonished than enraged. He did his best to evoke the elation of early morning delights when he was living with Léa, the solace of the prolonged and perfect silences of certain afternoons, with Léa—the delicious sleepy hours in winter spent in a warm bed in a freshly aired room, with Léa . . . ; but, all the time, in the suffused, cherry-colored afternoon light aflame behind the curtains of Léa's room, he saw in Léa's arms one lover and one lover only—Chéri. He jumped up, revived by a spontaneous act of faith. "It's as simple as that! If I'm unable to see anyone but myself beside her, then it's because there is no one else to see."

He seized the telephone, and was on the point of ringing her up, when he gently replaced the receiver. "No nonsense. . . ."

He walked out into the street, erect, with shoulders squared. He went in his open motor to the jeweler's, where he became sentimental over a slender little bandeau of burning blue sapphires invisibly mounted on blue steel, "so exactly right for Edmée's hair, " and took it away with him. He bought some stupid, rather pompous flowers. As it had only just struck eleven, he frittered away a further half-hour, drawing money from the bank, turning over English illustrated papers at a kiosk, visiting his scent shop and a tobacconist's that specialized in Oriental cigarettes. Finally, he got back into his motor, and sat down between his sheaf of flowers and a heap of little beribboned parcels.

"Home."

The chauffeur swiveled round on his basket seat.

"Monsieur? . . . What did Monsieur say? . . ."

"I said Home—Boulevard d'Inkermann. D'you require a map of Paris?"

The motor went full speed toward the Champs-Elysées. The chauffeur drove much faster than usual and his thoughts could almost be read in his back. He seemed to be brooding uneasily over the gulf which divided the flabby young man of the past months—with his "As you like," and his "Have a glass of something, Antonin?"—from young Monsieur Peloux, strict with the staff and mindful of the petrol.

"Young Monsieur Peloux" leaned back against the morocco leather, hat on knees, drinking in the breeze and exerting all his energy in an effort not to think. Like a coward, he closed his eyes between the Avenue Malakoff and the Porte Dauphine to avoid a passing glimpse of the Avenue Bugeaud, and he congratulated himself on his resolution.

The chauffeur sounded his horn in the Boulevard d'Inkermann for the gate to be opened, and it sang on its hinges with a heavy musical note. The capped concierge hurried about his business, the watchdogs barked in recognition of their returning master. Very much at his ease, sniffing the green smell of the newly mown lawns, Chéri entered the house and with a master's step climbed the stairs to the young woman whom he had left behind three months before, much as a sailor from Europe leaves behind, on the other side of the world, a little savage bride.

LÉA SAT at her bureau, throwing away photographs from the last trunk to be unpacked. "Heavens, how hideous people are! The women who had the nerve to give me these! And they think I'm going to put them up in a row on the mantelpiece—in plated frames or little folding cases. Tear them all up quick, and straight into the wastepaper basket!"

She picked up the photographs again and, before throwing them away, subjected each to the closest scrutiny of which her blue eyes were capable. A postcard with a dark background of a powerful lady encased in full-length stays, doing her best to veil her hair and the lower part of her face with a wisp of tulle, in the teeth of a strong sea breeze. *"To dearest Léa, in memory of exquisite hours spent at Guéthary. Anita."* Another photograph, stuck on the middle of a piece of cardboard with a surface like dried mud, portrayed a large and lugubrious family. They might have been a penal colony, with a dumpy, heavily painted grandmother in charge. Holding above her head a tambourine tricked out with favors, she was resting one foot on the bent knee of what looked like a robust and crafty young butcher boy. "That should never have seen the light of day," Léa said decisively, crumpling the rough-cast cardboard.

She smoothed out an unmounted print, to disclose two old provincial spinsters. An eccentric, loud-voiced and aggressive couple, they were to be found every morning on a bench somewhere along a promenade, and every evening between a glass of Cassis and their needlework frames, on which they were embroidering black pussycats, fat toads, or a spider. *"To our beautiful fairy! From her little friends at Le Trayas, Miquette and Riquette."*

Léa destroyed these souvenirs of her travels—and brushed a hand across her forehead. "It's horrible. And there'll be dozens and dozens more after these, just as there were dozens before them, all much the same. There's nothing to be done about it. It's life. Maybe wherever a Léa is to be found, there at once spring from the earth a myriad creatures like Charlotte Peloux, de la Berche, and Aldonza, or old horrors who were once handsome young men, people who are . . . well, who are impossible, impossible, impossible. . . ."

She heard, so fresh was her memory, voices that had called out to her from the top of hotel steps or hailed her with a "Hoo-hoo" from afar, across golden sands, and she lowered her head in anger like a bull.

She had returned, after an absence of six months, thinner, more flabby, less serene. Now and again a nervous twitch of the jaw jerked her chin down against her neck, and careless henna-shampooing had left too orange a glint in her hair; but her skin had been tanned to amber by sea and wind. This gave her the glowing complexion of a handsome farmer's wife, and she might have done without rouge. All the same, she would have to arrange something carefully round her neck, not to say cover it up completely; for it had shrunk and was encircled with wrinkles that had been inaccessible to sunburn.

Still seated, she dawdled over tidying away her various odds and ends, and her eyes began to glance round the room, as if some chair were missing. But what she was looking for was her old energy, the old anxiety to see at once that everything was as it should be in her comfortable home.

"Oh! That trip!" she sighed. "How could I? How exhausting it all is!"

She frowned, once again with that irritable jerk of her chin, when she noticed the broken glass of a little picture by Chaplin which she thought perfectly lovely—the head of a young girl, all silver and rose.

"And I could put both hands through that tear in the lace

curtains. . . . And that's only the beginning. . . . What a fool I was to stay away so long! And all in *his* honor! As if I couldn't just as well have nursed my grief here, in peace and comfort!"

She rose, disgruntled, and, gathering up the flounces of her tea gown, went over to ring the bell, saying to herself, "Get along with you, you old baggage!"

Her maid entered, under a heap of underclothes and silk stockings.

"Eleven o'clock, Rose. And my face hasn't been done yet. I'm late."

"There's nothing to be late for. There aren't any old maids now to drag Madame off on excursions, or turn up at crack of dawn to pick every rose in the place. There's no Monsieur Roland to drive Madame mad by throwing pebbles through her window. . . ."

"Rose, there's only too much to keep us busy in the house. The proverb may well be true that three moves are as bad as a fire, but I'm quite convinced that being away from home for six months is as bad as a flood. I suppose you've noticed the hole in the curtain?"

"That's nothing. . . . Madame has not yet seen the linen room: mouse droppings everywhere and holes nibbled in the floor. And it's a funny thing that I left Émerancie with twenty-eight glass cloths and I come back to find twenty-two."

"No!"

"It's the truth—every word I say, Madame."

They looked at each other, sharing the same indignation, both of them deeply attached to this comfortable house, muffled in carpets and silks, with its well-stocked cupboards and its shiny white basement. Léa gave her knee a determined slap.

"We'll soon change all that, my friend. If Ernest and Émerancie don't want their week's notice, they'll manage to find those six glass cloths. And did you write to Marcel, and tell that great donkey which day to come back?"

"He's here, Madame."

Léa dressed quickly, then opened the window and leaned

out, gazing complacently at her avenue of trees in bud. No more of those fawning old maids, and no more of Monsieur Roland—the athletic young heavyweight at Cambo. . . . "The idiot," she sighed.

She forgave this passing acquaintance his silliness, and blamed him only for having failed to please her. In her memory—that of a healthy woman with a forgetful body—Monsieur Roland was now only a powerful animal, slightly ridiculous and, when it came to the point, so very clumsy. Léa would now have denied that, one rainy evening when the showers were falling in fragrance on the rose geraniums, a flood of blinding tears had served to blot out Monsieur Roland behind the image of Chéri.

This brief encounter had left Léa unembarrassed and unregretful. In the villa she had taken at Cambo, the "idiot" and his frolicking old mother would have been made just as welcome as before. They could have gone on enjoying the well-arranged meals, the rocking chairs on the wooden balcony, all the creature comforts that Léa dispensed with such justifiable pride. But the idiot had felt sore and gone away, leaving Léa to the attentions of a stiff, handsome officer, graying at the temples, who aspired to marriage with "Madame de Lonval."

"Our years, our fortunes, the taste we both have for independence and society, doesn't everything show that we were destined for each other?" murmured the colonel, who still kept his slim waist.

She laughed, and enjoyed the company of this dry, dapper man, who ate well and knew how to hold his liquor. He mistook her feelings and he read into the lovely blue eyes, and the trustful, lingering smiles of his hostess, the acceptance he was expecting. The end of their dawning friendship was marked by a decisive gesture on her part: one she regretted in her heart of hearts and for which she was honest enough to accept the blame. "It's my own fault. One should never treat a Colonel Ypoustègue, descendant of an ancient Basque family, as one would treat a Monsieur Roland. I've never given anyone such a snub. All the same, it would have been gentlemanly, and intelligent too, if he had come back as usual the next day in his dogcart, to smoke his cigar, meet the two old girls and pull their legs."

She failed to understand that a middle-aged man could accept his dismissal, but not certain glances—glances appraising his physique, comparing him in that respect so unmistakably with another, unknown and invisible. Léa, caught in his sudden kiss, had subjected him to the searching, formidable gaze of a woman who knows exactly where to find the telltale marks of age. From the dry, well-cared-for hands, ribbed with veins and tendons, her glance rose to the pouched chin and furrowed brows, returning cruelly to the mouth entrapped between double lines of inverted commas. Whereupon all the aristocratic refinement of the "Baroness de Lonval" collapsed in an "Oh, la la," so insulting, so explicit, so common, that the handsome figure of Colonel Ypoustègue passed through her door for the last time.

"The last of my idylls," Léa was thinking, as she leaned out over her window ledge. But the weather over Paris was fine, her echoing courtyard was dapper, with its trim bay trees rising ball-shaped in green tubs, and from the room behind her a breath of scented warmth came playing over the nape of her neck: all this gradually helped her to recover her good humor, and her sense of mischief. She watched the silhouettes of women passing on their way down to the Bois. "So skirts are changing again," Léa observed, "and hats are higher." She planned sessions with her dressmaker, others with her milliner; the sudden desire to look beautiful made her straighten her back. "Beautiful? For whom? Why, for myself, of course. And then to aggravate old Ma Peloux!"

Léa had heard about Chéri's flight, but knew no more than that. While disapproving of Madame Peloux's private-detective methods, she did not scruple to listen to a young *vendeuse,* who would show her gratitude for all Léa's kindnesses by pouring gossip in her ear at a fitting, or else by sending it to her, with "a thousand thanks for the delicious chocolates" on a huge sheet of paper embossed with the letterhead of her establishment. A postcard from Lili, forwarded to Léa at Cambo—a postcard scribbled by the dotty old harridan in a trembling hand without commas or full stops—had recounted an incomprehensible story of love and flight and a young wife kept under lock and key at Neuilly.

"It was weather like this," Léa recalled, "the morning I read Lili's postcard in my bath at Cambo."

She could see the yellow bathroom, the sunlight dancing on the water and ceiling. She could hear the thin-walled villa reechoing with a great peal of laughter—her own laughter, rather ferocious and none too spontaneous—then the cries that followed it: "Rose! Rose!"

Breasts and shoulders out of water, dripping, robust, one magnificent arm outstretched, looking more than ever like a naiad on a fountain, she had waved the card with the tips of her wet fingers. "Rose, Rose! Chéri . . . Monsieur Peloux has done a bunk! He's left his wife!"

"That doesn't surprise me, Madame," Rose had said. "The divorce will be gayer than the wedding, when the dead seemed to be burying the dead."

All through that day Léa had given way to unseemly mirth. "Oh! that fiendish boy. Oh! the naughty child! Just think of it!"

And she shook her head, laughing softly to herself, like a mother whose son has stayed out all night for the first time.

A bright, varnished park phaeton flashed past her gates, sparkled behind its prancing high-steppers and vanished almost without a sound on its rubber wheels.

"There goes Spéleïeff," Léa observed; "he's a good sort. And there goes Merguillier on his piebald: eleven o'clock. It won't be long before that dried-up old Berthellemy passes on his way to thaw out his bones on the Sentier de la Vertu. Curious how people can go on doing the same thing day after day! I could almost believe I'd never left Paris, except that Chéri isn't here. My poor Chéri! He's finished with, for the present. Nightlife, women, eating at any hour, drinking too much. It's a pity. He might have turned into a decent sort, perhaps, if he'd only had pink chaps like a pork butcher and flat feet. . . ."

She left the window, rubbing her numbed elbows, and shrugged her shoulders. "Chéri could be saved once, but not a second time." She polished her nails, breathed on a tarnished ring, peered closely at the disastrous red of her hair and its graying roots, and jotted down a few notes on a pad. She did everything at high speed and with less composure than usual, trying to ward off an attack of her old insidious anxiety. Familiar as this was, she denied its connection with her grief and called it "her moral indigestion." She began wanting first one thing, then suddenly another—a well-sprung victoria with a quiet horse appropriate to a dowager; then a very fast motorcar; then a suite of Directoire furniture. She even thought of doing her hair differently; for twenty years she had worn it high, brushed straight off the neck. "Rolled curls low on the neck, like Lavallière? Then I should be able to cope with this year's loose-waisted dresses. With a strict diet, in fact, and my hair properly hennaed, I can hope for ten—no, let's say five years more of . . ."

With an effort she recovered her good sense, her pride, her lucidity. "A woman like me would never have the courage to call a halt? Nonsense, my beauty, we've had a good run for our money." She surveyed the tall figure, erect, hands on hips, smiling at her from the looking glass. She was still Léa.

"Surely a woman like that doesn't end up in the arms of an old man? A woman like that, who's had the luck never to soil her hands or her mouth on a withered stick! Yes, there she stands, the 'vampire,' who needs must feed off youthful flesh."

She conjured up the chance acquaintances and lovers of her early days: always she had escaped elderly lechers; so she felt pure, and proud of thirty years devoted to radiant youths and fragile adolescents.

"And this youthful flesh of theirs certainly owes me a great debt. How many of them have me to thank for their good health, their good looks, the harmlessness of their sorrows! And then their eggnogs when they suffered from colds, and the habit of making love unselfishly and always refreshingly! Shall I now, merely to fill my bed, provide myself with an old gentleman of . . . of . . ." She hunted about and finished up with majestic forgetfulness of her own age, "An old gentleman of forty?"

She rubbed her long shapely hands together and turned away in disgust. "Pooh! Farewell to all that! It's much prettier. Let's go out and buy playing cards, good wine, bridge scorers, knitting needles—all the paraphernalia to fill a gaping void, all that's required to disguise that monster, an old woman."

In place of knitting needles, she bought a number of dresses, and négligées like the gossamer clouds of dawn. A Chinese pedicure came once a week, the manicurist twice, the masseuse every day. Léa was to be seen at plays, and before the theater at restaurants where she never thought of going in Chéri's time.

She allowed young women and their friends—as well as Kühn, her former tailor, now retired—to ask her to their box or to their table. But the young women treated her with a deference she did not appreciate; and when Kühn, at their first supper together, called her "my dear friend," she retorted: "Kühn, I assure you it doesn't suit you at all to be a customer."

She sought refuge with Patron, now a referee and boxing promoter. But Patron was married to a young person who ran a bar, a little creature as fierce and jealous as a terrier. To join the susceptible athlete, Léa went as far out as the Place d'Italie, at considerable risk to her dark sapphire-blue dress, heavy with gold embroidery, to her birds of paradise, her impressive jewels, and her new rich red-tinted coiffure. She had had enough after one sniff of the sweat, vinegar and turpentine exuded by Patron's "white hopes," and she left, deciding never to venture again inside that long, low, gas-hissing hall.

An unaccountable weariness followed her every attempt to get back into the bustling life of people with nothing to do.

"What can be the matter with me?"

She rubbed her ankles, a little swollen by evening, looked at her strong teeth, and gums that had hardly begun to recede; and thumped her strong ribs and healthy stomach as if sounding a cask. Yet some undefinable weight, now that the chock had been knocked from under her, was shifting within her, and dragging her down. It was the Baroness de la Berche—met by chance in a "public bar" where she was washing down two dozen snails with cabbies' white wine—who in the end informed her of the prodigal's return to the fold, and of the dawn of a crescent honeymoon in the Boulevard d'Inkermann. Léa listened calmly to this Moral Tale; but she turned pale with emotion the following day when she recognized the blue limousine outside her gates and saw Charlotte Peloux on her way to the house.

"At last, at last! Here you are again, Léa, my beauty! . . . Lovelier than ever! Thinner than last year! Take care, Léa, we mustn't get too thin at our age! So far, and no further! And yet . . . But what a treat it is to see you!"

Never had that bitter tongue sounded so sweet to Léa. She let Madame Peloux prattle on, thankful for the breathing space afforded by this acid stream. She had settled Charlotte Peloux into a deep armchair, in the soft light of the little pink-paneled salon, as in the old days. Automatically she had herself taken the straight-backed chair, which forced her to lift her shoulders and keep up her chin, as in the old days. Between them stood the table covered by a cloth of heavy embroidery, and on it, as in the old days, the large cut-glass decanter half full of old brandy, the shimmering petal-thin goblets, iced water, and shortbread biscuits.

"My beauty, now we'll be able to see each other again in peace, in peace. You know my motto: 'When in trouble, shun your friends: let them only share your luck!' All the time

Chéri was playing truant, I purposely didn't show you any sign of life, you understand. Now that all's well and my children are happy again, I shout it aloud, I throw myself into your arms, and we start our pleasant existence all over again. . . ." She broke off and lit a cigarette, as clever with her pauses as an actress, ". . . without Chéri, of course."

"Of course," Léa acquiesced with a smile.

She was watching and listening to her old enemy in satisfied astonishment. The huge inhuman eyes, the chattering lips, the restless, tight little body—all that was facing her across the table had come simply to test her powers of resistance, to humiliate her, as in the old days, always as in the old days. But, as in the old days, Léa knew when to answer, when to be scornful, when to smile, and when to retaliate. Already that sorry burden, which had weighed so heavily the day before and the days before that, was beginning slowly to lift. The light seemed normal once more, and familiar, as it played over the curtains and suffused the little drawing room.

"Here we are again," Léa thought, in lighter vein. "Two women, both a little older than a year ago, the same habits of backbiting and the same stock phrases; good-natured wariness at meals shared together; the financial papers in the morning, scandalmongering in the afternoon: all this will have to be taken up again, since it's Life, my life. The Aldonzas and the de la Berches, the Lilis and a few homeless old gentlemen: the whole lot squeezed round a card table, with the packs jostling the brandy glasses, and perhaps, thrown in, a pair of little woolen shoes, begun for a baby who's soon to be born. . . . We'll start all over again, since it is ordained. Let's enter on it cheerfully. After all, it's only too easy to sink back into the grooves of the old life."

And she settled back, eyes bright and mouth relaxed, to listen to Charlotte Peloux, who was greedily expatiating upon her daughter-in-law.

"My Léa, you should know, if anyone, that what I've always longed for is peace and quiet. Well now, I've got them. Chéri's escapade, you see, was nothing more than sowing a few wild oats. Far be it from me to reproach you, Léa dear, but as you'll be the first to admit, from eighteen to twenty-five he really never had the time to lead the life of a bachelor! And now he's done it with a vengeance!"

"It's a very good thing that he did," Léa said, without the flicker of a smile; "it acts as a sort of guarantee to his wife for the future."

"The very word, the very word I was hunting for!" barked Madame Peloux, beaming. "A guarantee! And ever since that day—one long dream! And, you know, when a Peloux does come home again after being properly out on the spree, he never goes off again!"

"Is that a family tradition?" Léa asked.

But Charlotte took no notice.

"And what's more, he was very well received when he did return home. His little wife—ah, there's a little wife for you, Léa!—and I've seen a fair number of little wives in my time, you know, and I don't mind telling you I've never seen one to hold a candle to Edmée!"

"Her mother is so remarkable," Léa said.

"Think, just think, my beauty—Chéri left her on my hands for very nearly three months! and between you and me she was very lucky to have me there."

"That's exactly what I was thinking," Léa said.

"And then, my dear, never a word of complaint, never a scene, never a tactless word! Nothing, nothing! She was patience itself, and sweetness . . . and the face of a saint, a saint!"

"It's terrifying," Léa said.

"And then, what d'you suppose happened when our young rascal walked in one morning, all smiles, as though he'd just come in from a stroll in the Bois? D'you suppose she allowed herself a single comment? Not one. Far from it. Nothing. As for him, though at heart he must have felt just a little ashamed . . ."

"Oh, why?" Léa asked.

"Well, really! After all . . . He was welcomed with open arms, and the whole thing was put right in their bedroom—in two ticks—just like that—no time lost! Oh, I can assure you, for the next hour or so there wasn't a happier woman in the world than me."

"Except, perhaps, Edmée," Léa suggested.

But Madame Peloux was all exaltation, and executed a superb soaring movement with her little arms: "I don't know what you can be thinking of. Personally, I was only thinking of the happy hearth and home."

She changed her tune, screwed up her eyes and pouted: "Besides, I can't see that little girl frantic with passion, or sobbing with ecstasy. Twenty, and skinny at that. . . . Pah! at that age they stammer and stutter. And then, between ourselves, I think her mother's cold."

"Aren't you being carried away by your sense of family?" Léa said.

Charlotte Peloux expanded her eyes to show their very depths, but absolutely nothing was to be read there.

"Certainly not, certainly not! Heredity, heredity! I'm a firm believer in it. Look at my son, who is fantasy incarnate. . . What? You don't know that he's fantasy incarnate?"

"It must have escaped my memory," Léa apologized.

"Well, I have high hopes for my son's future. He'll love his home as I love mine, he'll look after his fortune, he'll love his children, as I loved him. . . ."

"For goodness' sake, don't paint such a depressing picture," Léa begged. "What's it like, the young people's home?"

"Sinister!" shrieked Madame Peloux. "Positively sinister. Purple carpets. Purple! A black-and-gold bathroom. A salon with no furniture in it, full of Chinese vases larger than me! So, what happens is that they're always at Neuilly. Besides, without being conceited, I must say that girl adores me."

"Her nerves have not been upset at all?" Léa asked, anxiously.

Charlotte Peloux's eyes brightened. "No danger of that! She plays her hand well, and we must face the fact."

"Who d'you mean by 'we'?"

"Forgive me, my beauty, pure habit. We're dealing here

with what I call a brain, a real brain. You should see the way she gives orders without raising her voice, and takes Chéri's teasing, and swallows the bitterest pills as if they were lollipops. . . . I begin to wonder, I really begin to wonder, whether there is not positive danger lying ahead for my son. I'm afraid, Léa dear, I'm afraid she may prove a damper on his originality, on his . . ."

"What? Is he being an obedient little boy?" Léa interrupted. "Do have some more of my brandy, Charlotte, it comes from Spéleïeff and it's seventy-four years old—you could give it to a newborn babe."

" 'Obedient' is hardly the right word, but he's . . . inter—impertur . . ."

"Imperturbable?"

"That's the word! For instance, when he knew I was coming to see you . . ."

"Did he know, then?"

An impetuous blush leapt to Léa's cheeks, and she cursed her hot blood and the bright daylight of the little drawing room. Madame Peloux, a benign expression in her eyes, fed on Léa's confusion.

"But of course he knew. That oughtn't to bring a blush to your cheeks, my beauty. What a child you are!"

"In the first place, how did you know I was back?"

"Oh, come, Léa, don't ask such foolish questions. You've been seen about everywhere."

"Yes, but Chéri—did you tell him I was back?"

"No, my beauty, it was he who told me."

"Oh, it was he who . . . That's funny."

She heard her heart beating in her voice and dared not risk more than the shortest answers.

"He even added: 'Madame Peloux, you'll oblige me by going to find out news of Nounoune.' He's still so fond of you, the dear boy."

"How nice!"

Madame Peloux, crimson in the face, seemed to abandon herself to the influence of the old brandy and talked as in a dream, wagging her head from side to side. But her russet eyes remained fixed and steely, and she kept a close watch on Léa, who was sitting bolt upright, armed against herself, waiting for the next thrust.

"It's nice, but it's quite natural. A man doesn't forget a woman like you, Léa dear. And . . . if you want to know what I really think, you've only to lift a finger and . . ."

Léa put a hand on Charlotte Peloux's arm. "I don't want to know what you really think," she said gently.

The corners of Madame Peloux's mouth fell: "Oh, I can understand, I approve," she sighed in a passionless voice. "When one has made other arrangements for one's life, as you have . . . I haven't even had a word with you about yourself!"

"But it seems to me that you have."

"Happy?"

"Happy."

"Divinely happy? A lovely trip? Is *he* nice? Where's his photo?"

Léa, relieved, sharpened her smile and shook her head. "No, no, you'll find out nothing, search where you will. Have your detectives let you down, Charlotte?"

"I rely on no detectives," Charlotte answered. "It's certainly not because anyone has told me . . . that you'd been through another heartbreaking desertion . . . that you'd been terribly worried, even over money. . . . No, no, you know what small attention I pay to gossip!"

"No one knows it better than me. My dear Lolotte, you can go back home without any fears on my behalf. And please reassure our friends, and tell them that I only wish they had made half what I did out of oil shares between December and February."

The alcoholic cloud screen, which softened the features of Madame Peloux, lifted in a trice; a clear, sharp, thoroughly alert face emerged. "You were in on oil? I might have known it! And you never breathed a word to me."

"You never asked me about it. . . . You were thinking only

of your family, as was natural. . . ."

"Fortunately, I was thinking of compressed fuel at the same time." The muted trumpet resembled a flute.

"Ah! and you never let on to me either!"

"Intrude upon love's young dream? Never! Léa, my dear, I'm off now, but I'll be back."

"You'll come back on Thursday, because at present, my dear Lolotte, your Sundays at Neuilly . . . they're finished for me. Would you like it if I started having a few people here on Thursdays? Nobody except old friends, old Ma Aldonza, our Reverend-Father-the-Baroness—poker for you, knitting for me. . . ."

"Do you knit?"

"Not yet, but it will soon come. Well?"

"I jump for joy at the idea! See if I'm not jumping! And you may be sure I won't say a word about it at home. That bad boy would be quite capable of coming and asking for a glass of port on one of your Thursdays. Just one more little kiss, my beauty. . . . Heavens, how good you smell. Have you noticed that as the skin gets less firm, the scent sinks in better and lasts much longer? It's really very nice."

"Be off, be off . . ." Quivering, Léa stood watching Madame Peloux as she crossed the courtyard. "Go on your mischievous way! Nothing can stop you. You twist your ankle, yes—but it never brings you down. Your chauffeur is careful not to skid, so you'll never crash into a tree. You'll get back safely to Neuilly, and you'll choose your moment—today, or tomorrow, or one day next week—to come out with words that should never pass your lips. You'll try and upset those who, perhaps, are happy and at peace. The least harm you'll do is to make them tremble a little, as you made me, for a moment. . . ."

She was trembling at the knees, like a horse after a steep pull, but she was not in pain. She felt overjoyed at having kept so strict a control over herself and her words. Her looks and her color were enhanced by her recent encounter, and she went on pulping her handkerchief to release her bottled-up energy.

She could not detach her thoughts from Madame Peloux. "We've come together again," she said to herself, "like two dogs over an old slipper which both have got used to chewing. How queer it is! That woman is my enemy, and yet it's from her I now draw my comfort. How close are the ties that bind us!"

Thus, for a long time, she mused over her future, veering between alarm and resignation. Her nerves were relaxed, and she slept for a little. As she sat with one cheek pressed against a cushion, her dreams projected her into her fast-approaching old age. She saw day follow day with clockwork monotony, and herself beside Charlotte Peloux—their spirited rivalry helping the time to pass. In this way she would be spared, for many years, the degrading listlessness of women past their prime, who abandon first their stays, then their hair dye, and who finally no longer bother about the quality of their underclothes. She had a foretaste of the sinful pleasures of the old—little else than a concealed aggressiveness, daydreams of murder, and the keen recurrent hope for catastrophes that will spare only one living creature and one corner of the globe. Then she woke up, amazed to find herself in the glow of a pink twilight as roseate as the dawn.

"Ah, Chéri!" she sighed.

But it was no longer the raucous hungry cry of a year ago. She was not now in tears, nor was her body suffering and rebellious, because threatened by some sickness of the soul. Léa rose from her chair, and rubbed her cheek, embossed by the imprint of the embroidered cushion.

"My poor Chéri! It's a strange thought that the two of us—you by losing your worn old mistress, and I by losing my scandalous young lover—have each been deprived of the most honorable possession we had upon this earth!"

Two days went by after the visit of Charlotte Peloux: two gray days that passed slowly for Léa. She faced this new life with the patience of an apprentice. "Since this is going to be my new life," she said to herself, "I'd better make a start." But she set about it clumsily, altogether too conscientiously, so that it was a strain on her perseverance. On the second day, about eleven in the morning, she was seized with a desire to go for a walk through the Bois as far as the Lakes.

"I'll buy a dog," she thought. "He'll be a companion, and force me to walk." And Rose had to hunt through the bottom of the summer cupboards for a pair of strong-soled brown boots and a tweed coat and skirt, smelling of alpine meadows and pine forests. Léa set off with the resolute stride proper to the wearer of heavy footwear and rough country clothes.

"Ten years ago, I should not have feared to carry a stick," she said to herself. When still quite near the house, she heard behind her a brisk, light tread, which she thought she recognized. She became unnerved, almost paralyzed by a compelling fear; and before she could recover she let herself unwittingly be overtaken, and then passed, by an unknown young man. He was in a hurry, and never even glanced at her.

"I really am a fool," she breathed in her relief.

She bought a dark carnation to pin on her jacket and started off again. But thirty yards ahead of her, looming out of the diaphanous mist above the grass verges of the avenue, the silhouette of a man was waiting.

"This time I do recognize the cut of that coat and that way of twirling a cane. . . . Oh, no thank you, the last thing I want is for him to see me shod like a postman and wearing a thick jacket that makes me look stocky. If I must run into him, I'd far rather he saw me in something else . . . and he never could stand me in brown, anyhow. . . . No, no . . . I'm off home. . . . I . . ."

At that moment the waiting man hailed an empty taxi, stepped in, and drove past Léa: he was a young man with fair hair and a small, close-clipped mustache. But this time Léa did not smile or feel relief. She turned on her heel and walked back home.

"One of my off-days, Rose. . . . Bring me the peach-blossom tea gown, the new one, and the big embroidered cloak. I'm stifling in these woolen things."

"It's no good being obstinate," Léa thought. "Twice in succession it's turned out not to be Chéri: the third time it would have been. I know the little jokes Fate plays on one. There's nothing to be done about it. I've no fight left in me today, I'm feeling limp."

She spent the rest of the day once more trying patiently to learn to be alone. After luncheon she enjoyed a cigarette and a look at the papers, and welcomed with a short-lived joy a telephone call from Baroness de la Berche, then another from Spéleïeff, her former lover, the handsome horse dealer, who had seen her in the street the previous evening and offered to sell her a spanking pair.

There followed an hour of complete and frightening silence. "Come, come . . ." She began to walk up and down, with her hands on her hips, her arms free of the heavy gold rose-embroidered cloak, its magnificent train sweeping the floor behind her.

"Come, come. . . . Let's try to take stock. This isn't the moment to become demoralized—now that I'm no longer in love with the boy. I've been living on my own now for six months. I managed perfectly well when I was in the south. To start with, I moved about from place to place. And the people I got to know on the Riviera or in the Pyrenees did me good; I felt positively refreshed each time any of them went away. Starch poultices may not cure a burn, but they do bring relief when constantly renewed. My six months of keeping on the move reminds me of the story of that hideous Sarah Cohen, who married a monster of ugliness. Each time I look at him, I think that I am pretty.

"But I knew what it was like to live alone before these last six months. What sort of life did I lead after I'd left Spéleïeff, for instance? Oh yes, I went chasing round bistros and bars with Patron, and then all of a sudden Chéri came into my life. But before Spéleïeff, there was little Lequellec: when his family dragged him away from me to lead him to the altar, his beautiful eyes were brimming with tears, poor boy. . . . After him, I was all alone for four months, I remember. The first month, I cried a great deal. Oh, no, it was for Bacciocchi I cried so much. But when I was through with my tears, there was no holding me. It was delightful to find myself alone. Yes, but at the Bacciocchi time I was twenty-eight, and thirty after Lequellec, and in between these two, I had known . . . Well, no matter. After Spéleïeff, I became disgusted—so much money so ill spent. Whereas now, after Chéri, I'm . . . I'm fifty, and I was unwise enough to keep him for six whole years!"

She wrinkled her forehead, and looked ugly with her mouth in a sulky droop.

"It serves me right. At my age, one can't afford to keep a lover six years. Six years! He has ruined all that was left of me. Those six years might have given me two or three quite pleasant little happinesses, instead of one profound regret. A liaison of six years is like following your husband out to the colonies: when you get back again nobody recognizes you and you've forgotten how to dress."

To relieve the strain, she rang for Rose, and together they went through the contents of the little cupboard where she kept her lace. Night fell, set the lamps blossoming into light, and called Rose back to the cares of the house.

"Tomorrow," Léa said to herself, "I'll order the motor and drive out to Spéleïeff's stud farm in Normandy. I'll take old La Berche, if she wants to come: it will remind her of the past glories of her own carriages. And, upon my word, should the younger Spéleïeff cast an eye in my direction, I'm not saying I . . ."

She carefully smiled a mysterious and provocative smile, to delude what ghosts there might be hovering round the dressing table or round the formidable bed, glimmering in the shadows. But she felt entirely frigid, and full of contempt for the pleasures other people found in love.

She dined off grilled sole and pastries, and found the meal a recreation. She chose a dry champagne in place of the Bordeaux, and hummed as she left the table. Eleven o'clock caught her by surprise, still taking the measurements of the space between the windows in her bedroom, where she planned to replace the large looking glasses with old painted panels of flowers and balustrades. She yawned, scratched her head, and rang for her maid to undress her. While Rose knelt to take off her silk stockings, Léa reviewed her achievements of the day already slipping into the pages of the past, and was as pleased with her performance as if she had polished off an imposition. Protected for the night against the dangers of idleness, she could look forward to so many hours of sleep, so many when she would lie awake. Under cover of night, the restless regain the privilege of yawning aloud or sighing, of cursing the milkman's cart, the street cleaners, and the early morning sparrows.

During her preparations for the night, she thought over a number of mild projects that would never come into being.

"Aline Mesmacker has a restaurant bar and is simply coining money. . . . Obviously, it gives her something to do, as well as being a good investment. . . . But I can't see myself sitting at a cash desk; and if one employs a manageress, it's no longer worthwhile. Dora and that fat Fifi run a nightclub together, Mother La Berche told me. Everybody's doing it now. And they wear stiff collars and dinner jackets, to attract a special clientèle. Fat Fifi has three children to bring up—they're her excuse. . . . Then there's Kühn, who's simply kicking his heels, and would gladly take some of my capital to start a new dressmaker's." Naked, and brick-pink from the reflection of her Pompeian bathroom, she sprayed herself with her favorite sandalwood, and, without thinking about it, enjoyed unfolding a long silk nightgown.

"All that's so much poppycock! I know perfectly well that I dislike working. To bed with you, Madame! You'll never have any other place of business, and all your customers are gone!"

The colored lining of the white gandoura she put on was suffused with a vague pink. She went back to her dressing table, and combed and tugged at the hairs stiffened by dye, lifting both her arms, and thus framing her tired face. Her arms were still so beautiful, from the full deep hollow of the armpit up to the rounded wrists, that she sat gazing at them in the looking glass.

"What lovely handles for so old a vase!"

With a careless gesture she thrust a pale tortoiseshell comb into the back of her hair, and, without much hope, picked a detective story from the shelf of a dark closet. She had no taste for fine bindings and had never lost the habit of relegating books to the bottom of a cupboard, along with cardboard boxes and empty medicine bottles.

As she stood smoothing the cool linen sheets on her huge uncovered bed, the big bell in the courtyard rang out. The full, solemn, unwonted peal jarred on the midnight hour.

"What in the world . . . ?" she said out loud.

She held her breath while listening, her lips parted. A second peal sounded even louder than the first, and Léa, with an instinctive movement of self-preservation and modesty, ran to powder her face. She was about to ring for Rose when she heard the front door slam, followed by footsteps in the hall and on the stairs, and the sound of two voices mingling—her maid's and someone else's. She had no time to make up her mind: the door of her room was flung open by a ruthless hand. Chéri stood before her—his topcoat unbuttoned over evening clothes, his hat on his head—pale and angry-looking.

He leaned back against the door now shut behind him, and did not move. He looked not so much at Léa as all round the room, with the quick shifting glance of a man about to be attacked.

Léa, who that morning had trembled at the half-surmised outline of a figure in the mist, felt at first only the resentment of a woman caught at her toilet. She drew her wrap more closely about her, settled her comb, and with one foot hunted for a missing slipper. She blushed, yet by the time the high color died down she had already recovered the semblance of calm. She raised her head and appeared taller than the young man who was leaning, all in black, against the white of the door.

"That's a nice way to come into a room," she said in a rather loud voice. "You might at least take your hat off and say good evening."

"Good evening," Chéri said in surly tones.

The sound of his voice seemed to astonish him. He looked all round less like an angry animal, and a sort of smile drifted from his eyes down to his mouth, as he repeated a gentler "Good evening."

He took off his hat and came forward a few steps.

"May I sit down?"

"If you like," Léa said.

He sat down on a pouffe and saw that she remained standing.

"Are you in the middle of dressing? Aren't you going out?"

She shook her head, sat down far away from him, picked up her nail buffer and never said a word. He lit a cigarette, and asked her permission only after it was alight.

"If you like," Léa repeated indifferently.

He said nothing more and dropped his gaze. Noticing that his hand with the cigarette in it was shaking, he rested it on the edge of a table. Léa continued polishing her nails deliberately and from time to time cast a brief glance at Chéri's face, especially at his lowered eyelids and the dark fringe of his lashes.

"It was Ernest who opened the front door to me as usual," Chéri said at last.

"And why shouldn't it have been Ernest? Ought I to have changed my staff because you got married?"

"No. . . I mean, I simply said that . . ."

Again silence fell, broken by Léa.

"May I know whether you intend to remain for some time, sitting on that pouffe? I don't even ask why you take the liberty of entering my house at midnight. . . ."

"You may ask me why," he said quickly.

She shook her head. "It doesn't interest me."

He jumped up precipitately, sending the pouffe rolling away behind him, and bore down upon Léa. She felt him bending over her as if he were going to strike her, but she did not flinch. The thought came to her: "What in this world is there for me to be frightened of?"

"So you don't know what brings me here! You don't want to know what brings me here!"

He tore off his coat and sent it flying on to the chaise longue, then he crossed his arms, and shouted quite close to Léa's face, in a strained but triumphant voice, "I've come back!"

She was using a delicate pair of tweezers, and these she carefully put away before wiping her fingers. Chéri dropped into a chair, as though his strength was completely exhausted.

"Good," Léa said. "You've come back. That's very nice! Whose advice did you take about that?"

"My own," Chéri said.

She got up in her turn, the better to dominate him. Her surging heartbeats had subsided, allowing her to breathe in comfort. She wanted to play her role without a mistake.

"Why didn't you ask me for my advice? I'm an old friend who knows all your clownish ways. Why did it never occur to you that your coming here might well embarrass . . . someone?"

Lowering his head, he searched every corner of the room from under his eyebrows—the closed doors, the bed, metal-girt and heaped with luxurious pillows. He found nothing exceptional, nothing new, and shrugged his shoulders.

Léa expected more than that and drove home her point. "You understand what I mean?"

"Perfectly," he answered. " 'Monsieur' has not come in yet? 'Monsieur' is sleeping out?"

"That's none of your business, child," she said calmly.

He bit his lip and nervously knocked off his cigarette ash into a jewel tray.

"Not in that, I keep on telling you!" Léa cried. "How many times must I . . . ?"

She broke off to reproach herself for having unconsciously

adopted the tone of their old familiar quarrels. But he did not appear to have heard and went on examining one of Léa's rings—an emerald she had purchased on her recent trip.

"What's . . . what's this?" he stammered.

"That? It's an emerald."

"I'm not blind. What I mean is, who gave it to you?"

"No one you know."

"Charming!" Chéri said bitterly.

The note in his voice was enough to restore Léa's authority, and she pressed her advantage, taking pleasure in leading him still further astray.

"Isn't it charming? I get compliments on it wherever I go. And the setting, you've seen it . . . the filigree of diamonds . . ."

"Enough!" bawled Chéri furiously, smashing his fist down on the fragile table.

A few roses shed their petals at the impact, and a china cup slithered without breaking onto the thick carpet. Léa reached for the telephone, but Chéri caught her hand in a rough grasp. "What are you going to do with that telephone?"

"Call the police," Léa said.

He took hold of both her arms, pretending to be up to some playful nonsense as he pushed her away from the instrument.

"Oh go on with you, that's all right. Don't be silly! Can't I even open my mouth without your getting all melodramatic?"

She sat down and turned her back on him. He remained standing, with nothing in his hands: his parted lips were swollen, giving him the look of a sulky child; one black lock hung down over his eyebrow. Surreptitiously, Léa watched him in a looking glass, till his reflection vanished when he sat down. In her turn, Léa was embarrassed when she felt him staring at her back, broadened by the loose folds of her gandoura. She returned to her dressing table, smoothed her hair, rearranged her comb, and, as if for want of something better to do, began unscrewing the top of a scent bottle. Chéri turned his head as the first whiff reached his nostrils.

"Nounoune!" he called.

She did not answer.

"Nounoune!"

"Beg my pardon," she ordered, without turning round.

"Not likely!" he sneered.

"I can't force you. But you'll leave the house. And at once. . . ."

"I beg your pardon," he said at once, peevishly.

"Better than that."

"I beg your pardon," he repeated, quite low.

"That's better."

She went over to him and ran her hand lightly over his bowed head. "Come, tell me all about it."

He shivered, trembling under her touch. "What do you want me to tell you? It's not very complicated. I've come back, that's all."

"Tell me! Come along, tell me!"

He rocked backward and forward on his seat, pressing his hands between his knees, and raised his head toward Léa without meeting her eyes. She watched the quivering of his nostrils, and she heard him trying to control his rapid breathing. She had only to say once more, "Come, tell me all about it," and give him a prod with her finger, as if to push him over. At once he cried out, "Nounoune darling! Nounoune darling!" and threw all his weight upon her, clasping her long legs, so that they gave way under her.

Once seated, she let him slither to the floor and sprawl over her with tears, and inarticulate words, and groping fingers that caught at her lace and her pearls and hunted feverishly under her dress for the shape of her shoulder and under her hair to touch her ears.

"Nounoune darling! We're together again, my Nounoune! Oh, my Nounoune! your shoulder, and your scent, and your pearls, my Nounoune, oh, it's so stunning . . . and that little burnt taste your hair has, oh, it's . . . it's stunning. . . ."

He leaned back to breathe out this silly word with what might have been the last breath of his body: then, still on his knees, he clasped Léa in his arms, offering her a forehead shadowed under tousled hair, a trembling mouth moist with tears, and eyes bright with weeping and happiness. She was so lost in contemplating him, so perfectly oblivious of everything that was not Chéri, that she never thought of kissing him. She twined her arms round his neck and gently hugged him to her, rocking him to the rhythm of murmured words.

"My pet . . . my naughty boy . . . You're here . . . You've come back again. . . . What have you been up to now? You're so naughty . . . my pretty. . . ."

He was moaning softly, keeping his lips together and hardly speaking, as he listened to Léa. He rested his cheek on her breast and begged her to go on, if for a moment she ceased her tender lullaby. And Léa, fearful that her own tears would flow, went on with her scolding.

"Wicked monster . . . heartless little devil . . . Get along with you, you great slut!"

He looked at her in gratitude: "That's right . . . Go on slanging me! Oh, Nounoune!"

She held him at arm's length to see him properly. "So you love me, then?"

He lowered his eyes in childish confusion: "Yes, Nounoune."

A little burst of uncontrollable laughter warned Léa that she was on the verge of giving way to the most terrible joy of her life. An embrace, followed by collapse, the uncovered bed, two bodies joined together like the two living halves of an animal that has been cut through. "No, no," she said to herself, "not yet, oh, not yet. . . ."

"I'm thirsty," Chéri sighed. "Nounoune, I'm thirsty."

She rose quickly and put a hand on the now tepid jug of water; hardly had she hurried from the room before she was back again. Chéri, curled up in a ball, was lying with his head on the pouffe. "Rose will bring you some lemonade," Léa said. "Don't stay there. Come and sit on the chaise longue. Does the lamp hurt your eyes?"

She was trembling with delight in her imperious solicitude. She sat down at the other end of the chaise longue and Chéri half stretched out to nestle against her.

"Perhaps now you'll tell me a little . . ."

They were interrupted by the entry of Rose. Chéri, without getting up, languidly turned his head in her direction: "Evening, Rose."

"Good evening, Monsieur," Rose said, discreetly.

"Rose, tomorrow at nine, I'd like . . ."

"Brioches and chocolate," Rose finished for him.

Chéri shut his eyes again with a sigh of contentment. "And that's that. . . . Rose, where am I going to dress tomorrow morning?"

"In the boudoir," Rose answered accommodatingly. "Only I had better take the settee out, I suppose, and put back the shaving mirror, as it used to be?"

She sought confirmation in the eye of Léa, who was proudly displaying her spoilt child, supported by her arm as he drank.

"If you like," Léa said. "We'll see. You can go, Rose."

Rose retired, and during the ensuing moment's silence nothing could be heard except the vague murmuring of the wind and the cry of a bird bewildered by the brightness of the moon.

"Chéri, are you asleep?"

He gave one of his long-drawn sighs like an exhausted retriever. "Oh, no, Nounoune, I'm too happy to sleep."

"Tell me, child . . . You haven't been unkind over there?"

"At home? No, Nounoune, far from it. I swear to you."

He looked up at her, without raising his trusting head.

"Of course not, Nounoune. I left because I left. The girl's very nice. There was no fuss at all."

"Ah!"

"I wouldn't swear that she didn't have an inkling all the same. This evening she was wearing what I call her 'orphanage look,' you know, pathetic dark eyes under her pretty head of hair. . . . You know how pretty her hair is?"

"Yes."

She threw out these monosyllables in a whisper as if intent on the words of someone talking in his sleep.

"I even think," Chéri continued, "that she must have seen me going through the garden."

"Oh?"

"Yes. She was on the balcony, in her white sequin dress, congealed whiteness. Oh! I don't like that dress. . . . Ever since dinner it had been making me long to cut and run."

"No."

"Yes it had, Nounoune. I can't say whether she saw me. The moon wasn't up. It came up while I was waiting."

"Where were you waiting?"

Chéri waved a vague hand in the direction of the avenue. "There. I was waiting, don't you understand. I wanted to see. I'd waited a long time."

"But what for?"

He hastily jumped away and sat further off. He resumed his expression of primitive distrust. "I wanted to be sure there was nobody here."

"Oh, yes. . . . You thought that . . ."

She could not resist a scornful laugh. A lover in her house! A lover while Chéri was still living! It was grotesque. "How stupid he is!" she thought in her enthusiasm.

"You're laughing?"

He stood up in front of her and put his hand on her forehead, forcing back her head. "You're laughing! You're making fun of me. You're . . . Then you have a lover! There is someone!"

He leaned over her as he spoke, pushing her head back against the end of the chaise longue. She felt the breath of an insulting mouth on her eyelids, and made no effort to be free of the hand that was crushing her hair against her forehead.

"I dare you to say you have a lover!"

She fluttered her eyelids, dazzled by the radiance of the face bearing down on her, and finally, in a toneless voice, she said: "No, I have no lover. I . . . love you. . . ."

He relaxed his hold and began pulling off his dinner jacket and waistcoat; his tie whistled through the air and ended up round the neck of Léa's bust—up on the mantelpiece. Meanwhile, he never moved away from her, and kept her, wedged between his knees, where she sat on the chaise longue.

When she saw him half-naked, she asked, with a note of sadness: "Do you really want to? . . . Do you? . . . "

He did not answer, carried away by the thought of his approaching pleasure and the consuming desire to take her again. She gave way and served her young lover like a good mistress, with devout solicitude. Nevertheless, she anticipated with a sort of terror the moment of her own undoing; she endured Chéri as she might a torture, warding him off with strengthless hands, and holding him fast between strong knees. Finally, she seized him by the arm, uttered a feeble cry and foundered in the deep abyss, whence love emerges pale and in silence, regretful of death.

They remained enfolded in their close embrace and no words troubled the prolonged silence of their return to life. The upper part of his body had slipped down and he lay across Léa's thigh, his pendent head, with eyes closed, resting upon the sheets as if he had been stabbed to death over the body of his mistress. She, meanwhile, partly turned away from him, bore almost the full weight of this unsparing body. She breathed softly but unevenly. Her left arm ached, crushed beneath her. Chéri could feel the back of his neck growing numb. Both were waiting, concentrated and motionless, for the abating tempest of their pleasure to recede.

"He's asleep," Léa thought. With her free hand, she was still clinging to Chéri's wrist and she squeezed it gently. One of her knees was being crushed by a knee—how well she knew its lovely shape! About the level of her own heart she could feel the steady muffled beating of another. Chéri's favorite scent—insistent, clinging, reminding her of fat waxy flowers and exotic glades—was all pervasive. "He is here!" she whispered, immersed in a feeling of blind security. "He is here forever!" her senses reechoed. The well-ordered prudence, the happy common sense that had been her guide through life, the humiliating vagaries of her riper years and the subsequent renunciations, all beat a retreat and vanished into thin air before the presumptuous brutality of love. "He is here!" she thought. "He has left his own home and his pretty silly little wife to come back, to come back to me! Who can take him from me now? Now at last I'll be able to organize our existence. He doesn't always know what he wants; but I do. No doubt we shall have to go away. We shan't go into hiding, but we'll look for somewhere peaceful. For I must find time to look at him. When I was unaware I loved him, I can't ever have looked at him properly. I must find a place where there'll be room enough for his whims and my wishes. I'll do the thinking for both of us—let him do the sleeping."

While she was painstakingly withdrawing her left arm, cramped and pricking with pins and needles, and her numbed shoulder, she glanced at Chéri's averted face and found that he was not asleep. She could see the whites of his eyes and the flutter of the little black wings of his long eyelashes.

"Why, you're not asleep!"

She felt him tremble against her, before he turned over in a single movement.

"But you're not asleep, either, Nounoune!"

He stretched a hand out to the bedside table and switched on the lamp: a flood of rosy light covered the big bed, throwing the patterns of the lace into high relief, hollowing out shadowed valleys between swelling hills in the quilted folds of the eiderdown. Chéri, stretched out at full length, surveyed the field of his victory and of his peace. Léa, leaning on one elbow beside him, stroked his beloved, long eyebrows, and swept back the rebellious locks. Lying with his hair disheveled over his forehead, he looked as if he had been blown over by a raging wind.

The enamel clock struck. Chéri straightened himself at a bound and sat up. "What time is it?"

"I don't know. What difference can it make to us?"

"Oh, I just asked. . . ."

He gave a short laugh, and did not immediately lie down again. Outside, the first milkcart clinked out its tinkling carillon, and he made a vague movement in the direction of the avenue. The strawberry-colored curtains were slit through by the cold blade of dawning day. Chéri turned back to look at Léa, and stared at her with the formidable intensity of a suspicious dog or a puzzled child. An undecipherable thought appeared in the depths of his eyes; their shape, their dark wallflower hue, their harsh or languorous glint, were used only to win love, never to reveal his mind. From sheets crumpled as though by a storm, rose his naked body, broad-shouldered, slim-waisted; and his whole being breathed forth the melancholy of perfect works of art.

"Ah, you . . ." sighed the infatuated Léa.

He did not smile, accustomed as he was to accepting personal praise.

"Tell me, Nounoune. . . ."

"What, my pretty?"

He hesitated, fluttered his eyelids, and shivered. "I'm tired . . . and then tomorrow, how will you manage about——"

Léa gave him a gentle push and pulled the naked body and drowsy head down to the pillows again.

"Don't worry. Lie down and go to sleep. Isn't Nounoune here to look after you? Don't think of anything. Sleep. You're cold, I'm sure. . . . Here, take this, it's warm. . . ."

She rolled him up in the silk and wool of a little feminine garment, retrieved from somewhere in the bed, and put out the light. In the dark, she lent him her shoulder, settled him happily against her side, and listened till his breathing was in rhythm with her own. No desires clouded her mind, but she did not wish for sleep. "Let him do the sleeping; it's for me to do the thinking," she repeated to herself. "I'll contrive our flight with perfect tact and discretion; I believe in causing as little suffering and scandal as possible. . . . For the spring we shall like the south best. If there were only myself to be considered, I'd rather stay here, in peace and quiet; but there's Ma Peloux and the young Madame Peloux. . . ." The vision of a young wife in her nightgown, anxiously standing beside a window, checked Léa only long enough for her to shrug her shoulders with cold impartiality. "I can't help that. What makes one person's happiness . . ."

The black silky head stirred on her breast, and her sleeping lover moaned in his dream. With a zealous arm, Léa shielded him against nightmares, and rocked him gently so that—without sight, without memory, without plans for the future—he might still resemble that "naughty little boy" never born to her.

HE HAD LAIN AWAKE for some little while, taking great care not to stir. Cheek on folded arms, he tried to guess the time. Under a clear sky, the avenue must be vibrating with heat too insistent for early morning, since no shadow of a cloud passed across the lambent rose-red curtains. "Ten o'clock, perhaps?" He was tormented by hunger; he had eaten little the previous evening. A year ago he would have bounded out of bed and roughly aroused Léa from sleep by ferocious shouts for cream-frothed chocolate and butter off the ice.

He did not stir. He was afraid, did he move, of crumbling away what remained to him of his rapture, the visual pleasure he derived from the shining curtains and from the steel and brass spirals of the bed, twinkling in the colored aura of the room. Last night's great happiness had dwindled, it seemed, had melted, and sought refuge in the dancing iridescence of a cut-glass jug.

On the landing, Rose trod the carpet with circumspect step; a discreet besom was sweeping the courtyard; and Chéri heard the tinkle of china coming from the pantry. "How the morning drags on," he said to himself. "I'll get up." But he remained without moving a muscle, for, behind him, Léa yawned and stretched her legs. He felt the touch of a gentle hand on his back. He shut his eyes again, and, for no good reason, his whole body began to act a lie, feigning the limpness of sleep. He was aware of Léa leaving the bed and of her dark silhouette between him and the curtains, which she drew half apart. She turned round to look at him, and with a toss of the head smiled in his direction—in no sense a smile of triumph, but a resolute smile, ready to accept all dangers. She was in no hurry to leave the room, and Chéri kept watch on her through hardly parted eyelashes. He saw her open a railway timetable and run her finger down the columns; then she seemed absorbed in some calculation, brow puckered and face upturned. Not yet powdered, a meager twist of hair at the back of her head, double chin and raddled neck, she was exposing herself rashly to the unseen observer.

She moved away from the window, and, taking her checkbook from a drawer, wrote and tore out several checks. Then she put a pair of white pajamas at the foot of the bed, and silently left the room.

Alone, Chéri took several deep breaths, realizing that he had hardly dared to breathe since Léa had left the bed. He got up, put on the pajamas, and opened a window. "It's stifling in here," he gasped. He had the vague uncomfortable feeling of having done something reprehensible. "Because I pretended to be asleep? But I've watched Léa a hundred times just after she's got out of bed. Only, this time, I made the pretense of being asleep."

The dazzling light restored the rose-pink glow of the room, and the delicate nacreous tints of the picture by Chaplin smiled down at him from the wall. Chéri bowed his head and shut his eyes, in an effort to remember the room as it had looked the night before—the mysterious color, like the inside of a watermelon, the enchanted dome of lamplight, and, above all, his exaltation when reeling under the intensity of his pleasures.

"You're up! The chocolate's already on its way."

He was pleased to note that it had taken Léa only these few moments to do her hair, touch up her face, and spray herself with the familiar scent. The room seemed suddenly to be filled with the cheerful sound of her lovely voice, and with the smell of chocolate and hot toast. Chéri sat down beside the two steaming cups and was handed the thickly buttered toast by Léa. She did not suspect that he was trying to find something to say, for she knew that he was seldom talkative, especially when he was eating. She enjoyed a good breakfast, eating with the haste and preoccupied gaiety of a woman who, her trunks packed, is ready to catch her train.

"Your second piece of toast, Chéri?"

"No, thank you, Nounoune."

"Not hungry anymore?"

"Not hungry."

With a smile, she shook her finger at him. "You know what you're in for! You're going to swallow down two rhubarb pills!"

He wrinkled his nose, shocked. "Listen, Nounoune. You've got a mania for fussing . . ."

"Ta ti ta ta! That's my look out. Put out your tongue. You won't show it me! Then wipe off your chocolate mustache, and let's have a quick sensible talk. Tiresome subjects can't be dealt with too quickly."

She stretched across the table to take Cheri's hand and hold it between her own.

"You've come back. That was our fate. Do you trust yourself to me? I'll be responsible for you."

She could not help breaking off, and closed her eyes as if hugging her victory. Chéri noticed the flush on his mistress's face.

"Oh!" she continued in a lower voice, "When I think of all that I never gave you, all that I never said to you! When I think that I believed you merely a passing fancy, like all the others—only a little more precious than all the others! What a fool I was not to understand that you were my love, *the* love, the great love that comes only once!"

When she opened her blue eyes, they seemed to have become bluer, gaining depth in the shade of her eyelids, and her breathing was uneven.

"Oh," Chéri prayed inwardly, "Don't let her ask me a

question, don't let her expect an answer from me now! I couldn't speak a single word."

She gave his hand a little shake. "Come along, let's be serious. As I was saying—we're leaving, we've already left. What will you do about *over there*? Let Charlotte arrange all the settlement details—it's much the wisest—and make her be generous, I beg of you. How will you let them know *over there*? A letter, I imagine. None too easy, but the less ink spilled, the better. We'll see about that between us. Then there's the question of your luggage. I've none of your things here anymore. Such little details are far more upsetting than a major decision, but don't worry too much. . . . Will you kindly stop tearing the skin off the side of your toe all the time! That's the way to get an ingrowing toenail!"

Automatically, he let his foot drop to the floor. Under the weight of his sullen taciturnity, he found it a strain to focus his jaded attention on what Léa was saying. He stared at his mistress's happy, animated, imperious features, and asked himself vaguely: "Why does she look so happy?"

His bewilderment became so obvious that Léa stopped in the middle of her monologue on their chances of buying old Berthellemy's yacht from him. "Could anyone believe that you've not got one word of advice to give? Oh, you might still be twelve!"

Chéri, snatched from his stupor, put a hand to his forehead and looked at Léa, his eyes filled with melancholy.

"Being with you, Nounoune, is likely to keep me twelve for half a century."

She blinked her eyes several times as if he had breathed on their lids, and let silence settle again.

"What are you trying to say?" she asked at last.

"Nothing, except what I did say, Nounoune. Nothing but the truth. And can you deny it, you, the most honest person alive?"

She decided to laugh, but her gaiety masked a terrible fear.

"But half your charm lies in your childishness, stupid! Later on it will be the secret of your eternal youth. Why complain of it? And you have the cheek to complain of it to *me*!"

"Yes, Nounoune. Do you expect me to complain to anyone but you?" and he caught hold of the hand she had taken away. "My own Nounoune, dearest, darling Nounoune, I'm not only complaining of myself: I'm accusing you!"

She felt the grip of his firm hand. Instead of looking away, his large dark eyes with lashes gleaming clung pitifully to hers. She was determined not to tremble, yet. "It's nothing, it's nothing," she thought. "It calls only for two or three sharp words and he'll become insulting, then sulky, and then I'll forgive him. . . . It's no more than that." But she failed to find the quick rebuke which would change the expression on his face. "Come, come, child . . . You know quite well there are certain jokes I will not tolerate." But at the same moment she knew her voice to be sounding false and feeble. "How badly I said that . . . bad theater. . . ."

It was half-past ten, and the sun was now shining on the table between them. Léa's polished nails twinkled in its beams; but the light fell also on the soft flabby skin on the back of her well-shaped hands and on her wrists. This emphasized—like criss-crossings on a clay soil when heavy rain is followed by a dry spell—the complicated network of tiny concentric grooves and miniature parallelograms. Léa rubbed her hands absentmindedly, turning her head to make Chéri look out of the window; but he persisted in his miserable, hangdog moodiness. The two hands were pretending, as if in disgrace, to toy with a loop of her belt. Brusquely he pounced upon them, kissed and kissed them again, then pressed his cheek against them, murmuring "My Nounoune. . . . Oh, my poor Nounoune . . ."

"Let me alone," she cried with inexplicable anger, snatching her hands away from him.

She took a moment to regain her control, frightened of her weakness, for she had been on the verge of tears. As soon as she was able, she smiled and spoke.

"So now it's me you're sorry for! Why did you accuse me a moment ago?"

"I was wrong," he said, humbly. "For me you have been always . . ." He made a gesture to express his inability to find words worthy of her.

"*You have been*?" she underlined in a biting voice. "That sounds like an obituary notice, my good child!"

"You see . . ." he began reproachfully.

He shook his head, and she saw only too well that she could not rouse any anger in him. She tightened all her muscles, and reined in her thoughts with the help of those few words, ever the same, and inwardly repeated again and again: "Here he is, in front of my eyes. I've only to look to see he's still there. He's not out of reach. But is he still here, with me, really and truly?"

Her thoughts escaped from the domination of these repeated phrases, only to sink into a great unvoiced lament. "Oh! if only, if only I could somehow be returned to the moment when I was saying, 'Your second piece of toast, Chéri!' for that moment's only just round the corner—it's not yet lost and gone forever! Let's start again from there. The little that's taken place since won't count—I'll wipe it out, I'll wipe it out. I'm going to talk to him as though we're back where we were a moment ago. I'm going to talk to him about our departure, our luggage."

She did, in fact, speak, and said, "I see . . . I see I cannot treat as a man a creature who, from sheer feebleness of character, can drive two women to distraction. Do you think that I don't understand? You like your journeys short, don't you? Yesterday at Neuilly, here today, but tomorrow! Tomorrow, where? Here? No, no, my child, no need to lie, that guilty look would never take in even a woman stupider than I am, if there is one like that over there. . . ."

She threw out an arm to indicate Neuilly with so violent a gesture that she upset a cake stand, which Chéri picked up again. Her words had sharpened her grief into anguish, an angry jealous anguish pouring forth like a young wife's outburst. The rouge on her cheek turned to the deep purple of wine lees; a strand of her hair, crimped by the curling tongs, wriggled down her neck like a small dry snake.

"And even the woman over there, even your wife, won't be found waiting there every time you choose to come back home! A wife, my child, may not always be easy to find, but she's much easier to lose! You'll have yours kept under lock and key by Charlotte, eh? That's a marvelous idea! Oh, how I'll laugh, the day when . . ."

Chéri got up, pale and serious. "Nounoune! . . ."

"Why Nounoune? What d'you mean, Nounoune? Do you think you're going to frighten me? You want to lead your own life, do you? Go ahead! You're bound to see some pretty scenes, with a daughter of Marie-Laure's. She may have thin arms and a flat behind, but that won't prevent her from . . ."

"I forbid you, Nounoune!"

He seized her by the arm; but she rose, vigorously shook herself free, and broke into hoarse laughter: "Why, of course, 'I forbid you to say a word against my wife!' Isn't that it?"

He walked round the table, trembling with indignation, and went straight up to her. "No, I forbid you—d'you hear me?—I forbid you to spoil my Nounoune!" She retreated to the end of the room, babbling, "What's that? What's that?" He followed her as though bent on chastising her. "You heard what I said. Is that the way for Nounoune to speak? What do you mean by such behavior? Cheap little jibes like Madame Peloux's, is that what you go in for? To think they could come from you, Nounoune, from you. . . ."

Arrogantly he threw back his head. "I know how Nounoune should speak. I know how she ought to think. I've had time to learn. I've not forgotten the day when you said to me, just before I married, 'At least don't be cruel. Try not to make her suffer. I have the feeling that a doe is being thrown to a greyhound.' Those were your words. That's really you. And the night before I married, when I ran away to come and see you, I remember you said to me . . ."

He could not go on, but all his features were bright with the memory.

"Darling, pull yourself together." He put his hands on Léa's shoulders. "And even last night," he went on, "it wasn't the first time you asked me whether I might not have hurt somebody *over there*! My Nounoune, I knew you as a fine woman, and I loved you as a fine woman, when we first started. If we have to make an end of it, must you start behaving like all the other women?"

She dimly felt the cunning behind the compliment and sat down, hiding her face in her hands.

"How hard you are, how hard," she stammered. "Why did you come back? . . . I was so calm on my own, getting so used to . . ."

She heard herself lying and stopped.

"Well, *I* wasn't!" Chéri said quickly. "I came back because . . . because . . ."

He raised his arms, let them drop and lifted them again. "Because I couldn't go on without you, there's no point in looking for any other explanation."

For a moment no word was spoken.

Quite overcome, she looked at this impatient young man, who with light feet and open arms, as white as a seagull, seemed poised for flight.

Chéri let his dark eyes rove all over her body.

"Oh, you can be proud of yourself," he said suddenly. "You can be proud of yourself for having made me—and what's more for three months—lead such a life, such a life!"

"I did?"

"Who else, if it wasn't you? If a door opened, it was Nounoune; the telephone rang, Nounoune; a letter in the garden postbox, perhaps Nounoune. . . . In the very wine I drank, I looked for you, and I never found a Pommery to equal yours. And then at nights . . . Oh, heavens above!"

He was walking up and down the carpet with rapid, noiseless steps. "I know now what it is to suffer for a woman, and no mistake! After you, I know what all the other women will be . . . dust and ashes! Oh, how well you've poisoned me!"

She drew herself up slowly in her chair, and, letting her body turn now this way, now that, followed Chéri's movements. Her cheeks were dry, rather shiny, and their fevered flush made the blue of her eyes almost intolerable. He was walking up and down, head lowered, and he never stopped talking.

"Imagine Neuilly with you not there, the first days after my return! For that matter, everything—with you not there! I almost went mad. One night, the child was ill—I no longer remember what it was, headache, pains, something. I felt sorry for her, but I had to leave the room; otherwise nothing in the world could have stopped me saying, 'Wait, don't cry, I'll go and fetch Nounoune and she'll make you well'—and you would have come, wouldn't you, Nounoune? Great heavens, what a life it was. . . . I took on Desmond at the Hôtel Morris, paid him well into the bargain, and sometimes at night I would tell him stories. . . . I used to speak as if you were unknown to him. 'Old boy, there's never been a skin like hers. . . . Take one look at that cabochon sapphire of yours, and then hide it away forever, because no light can turn the blue of *her* eyes to gray!' I used to tell him how you could be tough when you wanted to be; and that no one had ever got the better of you, least of all me! I used to say, 'That woman, old boy, when she's wearing just the right hat—the dark blue one with the white wing, Nounoune, last summer's—and with the way she has of putting on her clothes—you can match her against any other woman you may choose—and she'll put every one of them in the shade!' And then that wonderful manner you have of walking—of talking—your smile—the erect way you hold yourself, I used to say to him—to Desmond: 'Ah! A woman like Léa *is* something!' "

He snapped his fingers with proprietary pride and stopped, quite out of breath from his talking and walking. "I never said all that to Desmond," he thought, "and yet I'm not telling lies. Desmond understood all right."

He wanted to go on and glanced at Léa. She was still ready to listen. Sitting bolt upright now, she exposed to him in the full light her noble face in its disarray, the skin shining like wax where the hot tears had dried. Her cheeks and chin were pulled down by an invisible weight, and this added a look of sadness to the trembling corners of her mouth. Chéri found intact amidst this wreckage of beauty the lovely commanding nose and the eyes as blue as a blue flower.

"And so you see, Nounoune, after months of that sort of life, I come back here, and . . ." He pulled himself up, frightened by what he had nearly said.

"You come back here, and find an old woman," Léa said calmly, in a whisper.

"Nounoune! Listen, Nounoune!"

He threw himself on his knees beside her, looking like a guilty, tongue-tied child no longer able to hide his misdemeanor.

"And you find an old woman," Léa repeated. "So what are you afraid of, child?"

She put her arms round his shoulders, and felt his body rigid and resistant, in sympathy with the hurt she was suffering. "Come, cheer up, my Chéri. Don't cry, my pretty. . . . What is it you're afraid of? Of having hurt me? Far from it: I feel so grateful to you."

He gave a sob of protestation, finding no strength to gainsay her.

She put her cheek against his tousled black hair. "Did you say all that, did you really think all that of me? Was I really so lovely in your eyes, tell me? And so kind? At the age when a woman's life is so often over, was I really the loveliest for you, the most kind, and were you really in love with me? How grateful I am to you, my darling! The finest, did you say? . . . My poor child."

He let himself go, while she supported him in her arms.

"Had I really been the finest, I should have made a man of you, and not thought only of the pleasures of your body, and my own happiness. The finest! Oh no, my darling, I certainly wasn't that, since I kept you to myself. And now it's almost too late. . . ."

He seemed to be asleep in Léa's arms; but his obstinately tight-shut eyelids quivered incessantly, and with one lifeless hand he was clutching hold of her négligée and slowly tearing it.

"It's almost too late, it's almost too late. But all the same . . ." She leaned over him. "Listen to me, my darling. Wake up, my pretty, and listen to me with your eyes open. Don't be afraid of looking at me. I am, after all, the woman you were in love with, you know, the finest woman . . ."

He opened his eyes, and his first tearful glance was already filled with a selfish, mendicant hope.

Léa turned away her head. "His eyes . . . Oh, we must get this over quickly. . . ." She put her cheek against his forehead.

"It was I, child, it was my real self who said to you, 'Don't cause unnecessary pain; spare the doe. . . .' I had quite forgotten, but luckily you remembered. You are breaking away from me very late in the day, my naughty little boy; I've been carrying you next to my heart for too long, and now you have a load of your own to carry: a young wife, perhaps a child. . . . I am to blame for everything you lack. . . . Yes, yes, my pretty, here you are, thanks to me, at twenty-five, so lighthearted, so spoiled, and at the same time so sad. . . . I'm very worried about you. You're going to suffer and make others suffer. You who have loved me. . . ."

His fingers tightened their grip on her négligée, and Léa felt the sharp nails of her "naughty child" bite into her breast.

"You who have loved me," she went on after a pause, "will you be able to? . . . I don't know how to explain what I mean. . . ."

He drew back in order to listen: and she could barely restrain herself from saying, "Put your hand back on my breast and your nails where they have left their mark; my strength abandons me as soon as your flesh is parted from mine." Instead, she leaned over him as he knelt in front of her, and continued: "You have loved me, and you will regret . . . "

She smiled at him, looking down into his eyes.

"What vanity, eh! . . . But you will regret me! I beg of you, when you're tempted to terrify the girl entrusted to your care and keeping, do restrain yourself! At such moments, you must find for yourself the wisdom and kindness you never learned from me. I never spoke to you of the future. Forgive me, Chéri—I've loved you as if we were both destined to die within the same hour. Because I was born twenty-four years before you, I was doomed, and I dragged you down with me. . . ."

He was listening very attentively, which made his face look hard. She put her hand on his forehead to smooth the furrows of anxiety.

"Can you see us, Chéri, going out to lunch together at Armenonville! . . . Can you see us inviting Monsieur and Madame Lili! . . ."

She gave a sad little laugh, and shivered.

"Oh, I'm just about as done for as that old creature. . . . Quick, quick, child, run off after your youth! Only a small piece of it has been snipped off by aging women: all the rest is there for you and the girl who is waiting for you. You've now had a taste of youth! It never satisfies, but one always goes back for more. Oh, you had started to make comparisons before last night. . . . And what am I up to now, doling out all this advice and displaying the greatness of my soul! What do I know of you two? She loves you: it's her turn to tremble; but her misery will come from passion and not from perverted mother love. And you will talk to her like a master, not capriciously, like a gigolo. Quick, quick, run off. . . ."

She spoke in tones of hasty supplication. He listened, standing planted before her, his chest bare, his hair tempestuous: and so alluring, that she had to clasp her hands to prevent their seizing hold of him. He guessed this, perhaps, and did not move away. For an instant they shared a lunatic hope—do people feel like this in midair when falling from a tower?—then the hope vanished.

"Go," she said in a low voice. "I love you. It's too late. Go away. But go away at once. Get dressed!"

She rose and fetched him his shoes, spread out his crumpled shirt and his socks. He stood helpless, moving his fingers awkwardly as if they were numb. She had to find his braces and his tie; but she was careful not to go too close to him and offered him no further help. While he was dressing, she glanced into the courtyard several times, as if she were expecting a carriage at the door.

He looked even paler when he was dressed, and a halo of fatigue round his eyes made them seem larger.

"You don't feel ill?" she asked him. And she added timidly, lowering her eyes, "You could always lie down for a little." But at once she pulled herself together and came over to him, as though he were in great danger. "No, no, you'll be better at home. Hurry, it's not yet midday; a good hot bath will soon put you to rights, and then the fresh air . . . Here are your gloves. . . . Your hat? On the floor, of course. Put your coat on, there's a nip in the air. Au revoir, my Chéri, au revoir. That's right. And tell Charlotte that . . ." She closed the door behind him, and silence put an end to her vain and desperate words. She heard Chéri stumble on the staircase and she ran to the window. He was going down the front steps and then he stopped in the middle of the courtyard.

"He's coming back! He's coming back!" she cried, raising her arms.

An old woman, out of breath, repeated her movements in the long pier glass, and Léa wondered what she could have in common with that crazy creature.

Chéri continued on his way toward the street. On the pavement he buttoned up his overcoat to hide his crumpled shirt. Léa let the curtain fall back into place; but already she had seen Chéri throw back his head, look up at the spring sky and the chestnut trees in flower, and fill his lungs with the fresh air, like a man escaping from prison.

THE LAST OF CHÉRI

Translated by Roger Senhouse

CHÉRI CLOSED the iron gate of the little garden behind him and sniffed the night air: "Ah! it's nice out here!" In the same breath, he changed his mind: "No, it isn't."

The thickly planted chestnut trees weighed heavily upon the heat pent up beneath. A dome of rusted leaves vibrated above the nearest gaslamp. The Avenue Henri-Martin, close-set with greenery, was stifling; only with the dawn would a breath of fresh air come up from the Bois de Boulogne.

Bareheaded, Chéri turned back to look at the house, empty now but still lit up. He heard the clink of roughly handled glass, followed by the clear ring of Edmée's voice, sharp with reproof. He saw his wife come to the window of the gallery on the first floor and lean out. The frosted beads on her evening dress lost their snowy whiteness, caught for a moment a greenish glint from the lamp, then flamed into yellow as she touched the gold lamé curtains.

"Is that you on the pavement, Fred?"

"Who else could it be?"

"You didn't take Filipesco home, then?"

"No, I didn't; he'd hopped it already."

"All the same, I'd rather have liked . . . Oh well, it doesn't matter. Are you coming in now?"

"Not just yet. Far too hot. I'll just stretch my legs."

"But . . . Oh well, just as you like."

She broke off a moment, and must have been laughing, for he could see the quiver of her frost-spangled dress.

"All I can see of you from here is a white shirtfront and a white face cut out on black. Exactly like a poster for a night-club. It looks devastating."

"How you adore my mother's expressions!" he said reflectively. "You can tell everyone to go to bed. I've got my key."

She waved a hand in his direction. He watched the lights go out one by one in all the windows. One particular light—a dull blue gleam—told Chéri that Edmée was going through her boudoir into their bedroom, which looked out on the garden at the back of the house.

"The boudoir will soon come to be known as the study, and no mistake," he thought.

The clock of Janson-de-Sailly began to strike and Chéri cocked his ear to catch the chiming notes in flight, like drops of rain. "Midnight! She's in a hurry to get to bed. . . . Yes, of course, she has to be at her hospital by nine tomorrow morning." He took a few nervous steps, shrugged his shoulders, and grew calmer.

"It's as if I'd married a ballet dancer. Nine o'clock sharp, the class: it's sacrosanct. It has to come before everything else."

He walked on as far as the entrance to the Bois. The day's dust, hanging in the pallid sky, dimmed the brightness of the stars. Step for step, a second tread echoed Chéri's: he stopped and waited for it to catch up with him. He disliked anyone walking behind him.

"Good evening, Monsieur Peloux," said the night watchman, touching his cap.

Chéri answered by raising a finger to his forehead with the condescension of an officer—a trick he had picked up during the war from his fellow quartermaster sergeants—and walked on past the night watchman, who was trying the locks on the iron gates to the little private gardens.

From a couple of lovers on a bench just inside the Bois, came the rustle of crushed clothes and the whisper of smothered endearments. Chéri listened for an instant to the clasped bodies and invisible lips, a sound like the ripple of a ship's prow cleaving calm waters.

"The man's a soldier," he noticed. "I've just heard him unbuckle his belt."

He was not thinking, which left his every sense on the alert. On many a calm night during the war Chéri had derived complex pleasure and subtle terror from his primitive keenness of hearing; his fingers, even when caked with mud and pocket fug, had been quick to distinguish the image on medal or coin, and to tell, by leaf or stalk, plants whose name he did not know. "Hi, there, Peloux lad, just tell us what I've got ahold of here?" Chéri recalled the ginger-headed lad who, under cover of darkness, would push into his hand a dead mole, a small snake, a tree frog, an overripe fruit, or some piece of filth, and then exclaim, "Blimey, he gets it every time!" The memory made him smile, but with no pity for the ginger-headed lad, now dead. Yet he was haunted sometimes by the picture of his pal Pierquin, lying there on his back asleep forever, with a look of distrust still on his face. He often spoke of him.

This very evening, at home, when dinner was over, Edmée had deftly steered the conversation round to the pathetic little tale, put together with such studied clumsiness. Chéri had it off by heart and it ended with the words: "And then Pierquin said to me, 'I had a dream about cats, old lad; and then I'd another dream about our river at home and it looked fair mucky. . . . The meaning of that's pretty clear. . . .' It was at this very moment he was picked off, by the smallest scrap of shrapnel. I wanted to carry him back. They found the two of us, him on the top of me, not a hundred yards from the spot. I tell you about him because he was a rare good sort . . . and he had quite a lot to do with my being given this."

And, as he ended on this modest note, Chéri had lowered his eyes to his green-and-red riband and knocked the ash off his cigarette, as though to keep himself in countenance. He considered it nobody's business that a chance explosion had thrown one of them across the other's shoulders, leaving

Chéri alive and Pierquin dead. The truth—more ambiguous than falsehood—was that the terrific weight of a Pierquin, suddenly struck dead, had kept Chéri alive and half-suffocated, indignant and resentful. Chéri still bore a grudge against Pierquin. And, further, he had come to scorn the truth ever since the day when, years ago, it had suddenly fallen from his mouth like a belch, to spatter and wound one whom he had loved.

But at home this evening, the Americans—Majors Marsh-Meyer and Atkins, and Lieutenant Wood—had not appeared to listen to him. With the vacant faces of athletic first-communicants, with fixed and expressionless eyes, they had simply been waiting to go to a nightclub, waiting with almost painful anxiety. As for Filipesco! "Needs watching," Chéri decided laconically.

The lake in the Bois was encircled with a fragrant mist that rose rather from the scythed slopes of its banks than from the stagnant water. Chéri was about to lean against a tree, when, from the shadows, a woman boldly brushed against him. "Good evening, kid . . ." The last word made him start; it was uttered in a low, parched voice, the very voice of thirst, of dusty roads, of this dry hot night. . . . He made no answer, and the dim figure came a step nearer on soft-soled shoes. But he caught a whiff of black woolens, soiled linen, dank hair, and turned back with long springy strides toward his own home.

The dull blue light was still on: Edmée had not yet left her boudoir–study. In all probability she would still be seated at her desk, signing chits for drugs and dressings, reading through the day's notes and the short reports made by her secretary. Her pretty schoolmarm head, crimped hair with a reddish tint, would be bent over her papers.

Chéri pulled out the small flat key on the end of its thin gold chain. "Here we go. In for another carefully measured dose of love. . . ."

As was his habit, he entered his wife's boudoir without knocking. Edmée showed no sign of surprise, but went on with her telephone conversation. Chéri listened.

"No, not tomorrow. . . . You won't want me there for that. The General knows you perfectly well. And at the Ministry of Commerce, there's . . . What do you mean? 'Have I got Lémery?' No, certainly not! He's charming, but . . . Hullo? . . . Hullo? . . ." She laughed, showing her small teeth. "Oh come! that's going too far. . . . Lémery makes up to every woman, provided she's not blind or lame. . . . What? Yes, he's come in, he's here at my elbow. No, no, I'll be very discreet. . . . Good-bye. . . . See you tomorrow. . . ."

A plain white wrap, the white of her pearl necklace, was slipping off one shoulder. She had taken the pins from her chestnut hair, which, slightly frizzed by the dry atmosphere, followed every movement of her head.

"Who was that?" Chéri asked, as she put back the receiver and turned to ask him:

"Fred, you'll let me have the Rolls tomorrow morning, won't you? It will look better for bringing the General back here to lunch."

"What General?"

"General Haar."

"Is he a Boche?"

Edmée frowned. "Really, Fred, you're too old for such jokes! General Haar is coming to inspect my hospital tomorrow. Then he can go back to America and tell them all that my hospital can compare with any effort of the sort over there. Colonel Beybert will be showing him round, and they'll both come back here for luncheon afterward."

Chéri took off his dinner jacket and sent it flying in the direction of a chair.

"I don't give a damn! I'm lunching out."

"What d'you mean? What's all this?"

A spasm of rage crossed Edmée's face; but she smiled, picked up the dinner jacket with care, and changed her tone of voice. "Didn't you ask me a moment ago who that was on the telephone? Your mother."

Chéri collapsed into an armchair and said nothing. His features were set in their most beautiful and impassive mold.

Over his forehead hovered an air of serene disapproval. This was apparent, too, on his lowered eyelids, faintly shadowed now at the approach of his thirtieth year, and on his mouth, which he was careful never to compress too tightly, keeping his lips gently apart as in sleep.

"You know," Edmée continued, "she wants Lémery, of the Ministry of Commerce, to do something about her three cargo loads of leather. There are three ships filled with leather, at present held up in harbor at Valparaiso. There is something in the idea, you know! The only thing is that Lémery won't grant the necessary import license . . . at least, that's what he says. Do you know how much money the Soumabis offered your mother as a minimum commission?"

With a wave of the hand, Chéri brushed aside ships, leather, and commission.

"Not interested," he said simply.

Edmée dropped the subject, and affectionately approached her husband.

"You will have luncheon here tomorrow, won't you? There'll probably be Gibbs—the reporter from *Excelsior,* who's going to photograph the hospital—and your mother."

Chéri shook his head with no sign of impatience.

"No," he said. "General Hagenbeck . . ."

"Haar."

". . . and a Colonel, and my mother in her uniform. Her tunic—what d'you call it? her jacket?—with its little leather buttons; her elastic uplift belt; epaulettes; high colonel's collar and her chin cascading over . . . and her cane. No, really, I don't pretend to be braver than I am. I'd rather go out."

He was laughing quietly to himself, and his laugh seemed mirthless. Edmée put a hand, already trembling with irritation, upon his arm; but her touch was light.

"You can't mean that seriously?"

"Certainly I can. I shall go for lunch to *Brekekekex,* or somewhere else."

"With whom?"

"With whom I choose."

He sat down and kicked off his pumps. Edmée leaned

against a black lacquer cabinet and racked her brain for words to make him behave sensibly. The white satin front of her dress rose and fell in rhythm to the quickened pace of her breathing, and she crossed her hands behind her back like a martyr. Chéri looked at her with an air of pretended indifference. "She really does look a lady," he thought. "Hair all anyhow, in her chemise, on her way to the bath—she always looks a lady."

She lowered her eyes, caught Chéri's, and smiled.

"You're teasing me," she said plaintively.

"No," Chéri replied. "I shan't lunch here tomorrow, that's all."

"But why?"

He rose, walked as far as the open door into their room—which was in darkness and filled with night scents from the garden—and then came back to her.

"Because I shan't. If you compel me to explain myself, I shall speak out and perhaps be rude. You'll burst into tears, and 'in your distress,' as the saying goes, you'll let your wrap slip to the floor and . . . and unfortunately it won't have the slightest effect on me."

Another spasm of rage passed over his wife's features, but her much-tried patience was not yet exhausted. She smiled and shrugged the one bare shoulder peeping from under her hair.

"It's quite easy to *say* that it won't have any effect on you."

He was walking to and fro, clad in nothing but his short white silk pants. All the time he was testing the elasticity of his instep and calf muscles, and kept rubbing his hand over the twin brown scars under his right breast, as if to preserve their fading hue. Lean, with less flesh on his body than he had had at twenty, at the same time in better shape and training, he liked to parade up and down in front of his wife as a rival rather than a lover. He knew himself to be the more perfect specimen and, as a connoisseur, could condescend to admire in her the slim hips, the small breasts, and the graceful, almost imperceptible lines which Edmée knew so well how to clothe in tubular frocks and slinky tunics. "Are you fading away, then?" he would sometimes ask her, just for the fun of annoying her. He would watch her whole body writhe in anger, and note its sudden and unsuspected vigor.

This reply of his wife's was distasteful to him. He wanted her to look well bred, and to be silent, if not unresponsive, in his arms. He came to a halt, puckered his brow, and looked her up and down. "Pretty manners, I must say. Do you learn them from your physician-in-charge? The war, Madame!"

She shrugged her bare shoulder.

"What a child you are, my poor Fred! It's lucky we're by ourselves. To go on at me like that just because of a little joke . . . which was really a compliment. And for you to try and teach me manners, you . . . you! And after seven years of marriage!"

"Where do you get the seven years from?"

He sat down, naked as he was, as though for a prolonged discussion, his legs wide apart with all the ostentation of an athlete.

"Well . . . really . . . nineteen-thirteen . . . nineteen-nineteen . . . "

"Excuse me! it's clear that we don't reckon by the same calendar. Now, I count from . . ."

Edmée arched a knee, taking the weight of her body on the other leg, a confession of her weariness; but Chéri interrupted her with: "Where's all this talk leading us? Come on, let's go to bed. You've got your ballet class at nine tomorrow, haven't you?"

"Oh! Fred!"

Edmée crushed a rose from a black vase and threw away its petals. Chéri fanned the flames of anger still smoldering in her eyes, now moist with tears, by saying: "That's the name I give that job lot of wounded, when I'm not thinking."

Without looking at him, she murmured through trembling lips: "You brute . . . you brute . . . you loathsome monster!"

He laughed, quite untouched.

"What d'you want me to say? As far as you're concerned,

we all know you're carrying out a sacred mission. But what about me? You might just as well *have* to go to the Opéra every day and practice in the Rotunda, for all the difference it would make. That would leave me just as much . . . just as much out of it. And those men I called your 'job lot,' well, they're wounded, aren't they? wounded who are a little luckier than others, perhaps. I've got absolutely nothing to do with them either. With them, too, I'm . . . out of it."

She turned round to face him so impulsively that it made her hair fly out from her temples: "My darling, don't be so unhappy! You're not out of it at all, you're above all that!"

He got up, drawn toward a jug of iced water, on the sides of which the moisture was slowly condensing into bluish tears. Edmée hurried forward: "With or without lemon, Fred?"

"Without, thanks."

He drank, she took the empty glass from his hands, and he went toward the bathroom.

"By the way," he said. "About that leak in the cement of the bathing pool. It ought . . ."

"I'm having it seen to. The man who makes those glass mosaics happens to be a cousin of Chuche, one of my wounded, and he won't need to be asked twice, believe me."

"Good." Then, as he was moving away, he turned round. "Tell me, this business of the Ranch shares we were talking about yesterday morning, ought we to sell or not? Supposing I went to see old Deutsch about them tomorrow morning, and had a chin-wag with him?"

Edmée gave a shriek of schoolgirl laughter.

"Do you think I waited for you about that? Your mother had a stroke of genius this morning, while we were giving the Baroness a lift home."

"You mean that old La Berche woman?"

"Yes, the Baroness. Your mother, as you so elegantly put it, had a chin-wag with her. The Baroness is one of the original shareholders, and never leaves the Chairman of the Board alone for a moment. . . ."

"Except to cover her face in flour."

"Must you interrupt me the whole time? . . . and by two o'clock, my dear, the whole lot had been sold—every bit of it! The little flare-up on the Bourse this afternoon—it lasted only a very short time—raked us in something like two hundred and sixteen thousand francs, Fred! That'll pay for piles of medicine and bandages. I wanted to keep the news till tomorrow, and then give you one of these topping billfolds. Kiss?"

He stood, naked and white-skinned, holding back the folds of the door curtain, and looking closely at the expression on his wife's face.

"That's all very well . . ." he said at last, "but where do I come in?"

Edmée gave a mischievous shake of the head: "Your power of attorney still stands, my love. 'The right to sell, purchase, draw up, or sign an agreement made out in my name . . . etcetera'—which reminds me, I must send the Baroness something as a souvenir."

"A briar pipe," said Chéri, after pretending to have given the matter his attention.

"No, don't laugh. The good soul is so valuable to us."

"And who are 'us'?"

"Your mother and me. The Baroness knows how to talk to the men in a way they understand. She speaks their language. She tells them rather risqué stories, but in such a way . . . They dote on her."

The strangest of laughs trembled on Chéri's lips. He let go his hold on the dark curtain, and it fell back into place behind him, thus obliterating him completely, as sleep obliterates the figment of a dream. He walked along a passage dimly lit by a blue globe, without making a sound, like a figure floating on air; for he had insisted upon having thick carpets laid on every floor, from top to bottom of the house. He loved silence, and furtiveness, and never knocked at the door of the boudoir, which his wife, since the war, called her study. She showed no annoyance, and sensing Chéri's presence, never jumped when he came into the room.

He took a shower bath without lingering under the cool water, sprayed himself with scent absentmindedly, and returned to the boudoir.

He could hear the sound of someone rumpling the sheets in the bedroom next door, and the tap of a paper knife against a cup on the bedside table. He sat down and rested his chin in his hand. On the little table beside him, he caught sight of the morrow's menu, duly made out for the butler, according to daily routine. On it he read: *"Homard Thermidor, Côtelettes Fulbert-Dumonteil, Chaud-froid de canard, salade Charlotte, Soufflé au curaçao, Allumettes au Chester."* . . . "No alteration required," he murmured to himself. *"Six places?"*—"Ah, yes, that I must alter." He corrected the number, and once more cupped his chin in his hand.

"Fred, do you know what time it is?"

He did not answer the soft voice, but went into their room and sat down facing the bed. With one shoulder bare and the other half-hidden by a wisp of white nightgown, Edmée was smiling, despite her tired state, aware that she looked prettier in bed than out. But Chéri remained seated, and once again cupped his chin in his hand.

"Rodin's *Penseur,*" said Edmée, to encourage him to smile or to move.

"There's many a true word spoken in jest," he answered sententiously.

He pulled the folds of his Chinese dressing gown closer over his knees and savagely crossed his arms.

"What the hell am I doing here?"

She did not understand, or had no wish to do so.

"That's what I'd like to know, Fred. It's two o'clock, and I get up at eight. Tomorrow's going to be another of those pleasant little days. . . . It's unkind of you to dawdle like this. Do come along; there's a nice breeze rising. We'll go to bed with it on our faces, and imagine we're sleeping out of doors."

He weakened, and hesitated only an instant before hurling his silk wrap to a far corner of the room, while Edmée switched out the remaining light. She nestled up against him in the dark, but he neatly turned her over with her back to him and held her round the waist with strong arms, murmuring, "Like that. That's like being on a bobsled," and fell asleep.

The following day, from the little window of the linen room where he was hidden, he watched them leave. The duck's-egg green motor and another long American automobile were purring very quietly in the avenue under the thick overhanging chestnut trees. The green shade and the recently watered pavement exuded a pretense of freshness, but Chéri knew very well that in the garden at the back of the house the heat of this June morning—the month that scorches Paris—was already shriveling the lovely deep blue of a pool of forget-me-nots within their edging of pinks.

His heart began to beat with a sort of nervousness when he saw, approaching the iron gates to his house, two figures in khaki, with gold stars on their breast and crimson velvet bands round their caps.

"In uniform, of course, the crackpot!"

This was the nickname Chéri had bestowed on the physician-in-charge at Edmée's hospital, and without really knowing it, he loathed the man and his red-gold hair and the caressing tones he put into technical terms when talking to Edmée. He muttered vague hearty curses, against the Medical Corps in particular, and against all who insisted on wearing uniform in peacetime. The American officer was growing fat, so Chéri sneered: "I thought the Americans went in for sport. What's he doing with a belly like that?" but he said not a word when Edmée, in a white dress and white shoes, vivaciously held out her white-gloved hand to the doctor. She greeted him in loud, quick, cheerful tones. Chéri had not missed a single word that fell from her red mouth, which parted in a smile over such tiny teeth. She had walked out as far as the motors, come back to tell a footman to fetch a notebook she had forgotten and stood chatting while she waited for it. She had spoken in English to the American colonel, and lowered her voice, in automatic deference, when replying to Doctor Arnaud.

Chéri was keeping a sharp lookout from behind the muslin curtains. His characteristic mistrust and slyness froze his features into immobility directly he concealed a strong emotion, and he kept a strict watch on himself, even when alone. His eyes traveled from Edmée to the doctor, and then from the American colonel back to Edmée, who had more than once looked up to the first floor, as though she knew of his hiding place.

"What are they waiting for?" he grumbled under his breath. "Ah, so this is it. . . . God in heaven!"

Charlotte Peloux had arrived, in a sportscar driven by an impersonal and impeccable young chauffeur. Bursting out of her gabardine uniform, she held her head stiffly upright under its little tight-fitting hat with a military peak, and the ends of her bobbed red hair could be seen popping out at the back. She did not set foot to ground, but suffered them to come and pay their respects to her. She received Edmée's kiss and apparently asked after her son, for she too raised her head in the direction of the first floor, thus unveiling her magnificent eyes, over which drifted, as over the huge eyes of an octopus, some dark inhuman dream.

"She's wearing her little military cap," Chéri murmured.

He gave a curious shudder, which made him angry with himself, and smiled when the three motors drove away. He waited patiently until his "bachelor's runabout" drew up against the curb punctually at eleven o'clock, and he kept it waiting for some considerable time. Twice he stretched out his hand to lift the receiver of the telephone, and twice he let it fall again to his side. His sudden impulse to invite Filipesco soon vanished and he thought he would like to collect young Maudru and his girl. "Or, better still, Jean de Touzac. . . . But at this hour he'll still be furiously snoring. Gosh! all that lot . . . not one of them, I must be fair, a patch on Desmond. . . . Poor old boy."

He regarded Desmond as a war casualty; but with greater

compassion than he ever vouchsafed the dead. Desmond, who was alive yet lost to him, had the power of inspiring him with an almost tender melancholy, as well as with the jealous respect due to a man with a "job." Desmond ran a nightclub, and sold antiques to Americans. A gutless washout during the whole of the war, when he had carried anything and everything but a rifle—official papers, billycans, any dirty hospital receptacle—Desmond had bitten deep into peacetime with a warlike fervor, and rich had been his immediate reward, very much to Chéri's astonishment. *Desmond's* had been started in quite a small way in a private house in the Avenue d'Alma, and now it sheltered frenzied and silent couples behind its heavy ashlar masonry, beneath ceilings decorated with swallows and hawthorn, and hemmed in by the bulrushes and flamingoes of its stained-glass windows. They danced at *Desmond's,* night and day, as people dance after war: the men, young and old, free from the burden of thinking and being frightened—empty-minded, innocent; the women, given over to a pleasure far greater than any more definite sensual delight, to the company of men: that is to say, to physical contact with them, their smell, their tonic sweat, the certain proof of which tingled in every inch of their bodies—the certainty of being the prey of a man wholly alive and vital, and of succumbing in his arms to rhythms as personal, as intimate, as those of sleep.

"Desmond will have got to bed at three, or three-thirty," Chéri reckoned. "He'll have had enough sleep."

But once again he let drop the hand he had stretched out to the telephone. He went down the stairs in double quick time, aided by the springy thick pile that covered every floorboard in his house. As he passed by the dining room he looked without anger at the five white plates set in a diadem round a black crystal bowl, in which floated pink water lilies, matching the pink of the tablecloth; and he did not pause till face to face with the looking glass, fixed to the back of the heavy door of the reception room on the ground floor. He feared, yet was attracted by, this looking glass, which drew what little light it had from the french windows immediately facing it across the corridor, their opaque blue panes further obscured by the dark foliage of the garden. Every time he bumped into his own image, Chéri was brought up sharp by a slight shock when he recognized it as his own. He never could understand why this glass did not reflect the faithful image of a young man of twenty-four. He could not detect the precise points where time, with invisible finger, marks first the hour of perfection on a handsome face, and then the hour of that more blatant beauty, the herald of a majestic decline.

To Chéri's mind, there could be no question of a decline, and he could never have noticed it on his own features. He had just happened to bump into a thirty-year-old Chéri and failed to recognize him; and he sometimes asked himself "What's wrong with me?" as though he were feeling a little off-color or had thrown his clothes on anyhow. Now he hurried past the reception-room door, and thought no more about it.

Desmond's, being a properly organized establishment, was up and doing by midday, despite the late hours it kept. The concierge was hosing the paved courtyard, a waiter was sweeping the steps clean, brushing away a heap of high-class rubbish—fine light dust, silver paper, corks with metal caps, stub-ends of gold-tipped cigarettes, and crumpled drinking straws—rubbish which bore daily witness to the prosperity of *Desmond's.*

Chéri cleared at a bound the residue of last night's brisk business; but the smell inside the house barred further progress like a rope stretched across his path. Forty couples, packed like sardines, had left behind the smell—the memory of their sweat-soaked clothes—stale, and tainted with tobacco fumes. Chéri plucked up courage and leapt up the staircase, narrowed by heavy oak banisters supported on caryatids. Desmond had wasted no money on changing the stuffy sumptuosities of 1880. After removing two dividing walls, installing a refrigerator in the basement, engaging a jazz band regardless of cost, no further outlay would be necessary for at least another year. "I'll bring it up to date to attract customers," so Desmond said, "when dancing isn't such a rage."

He slept on the second floor, in a room where convolvulus ran riot on the walls and storks on the stained-glass windows; his bath was of enameled zinc, bordered by a tiled frieze of river plants, and the ancient heating apparatus wheezed like a bulldog past its prime. But the telephone shone as brightly as a weapon kept polished by daily use, and Chéri, after bounding up four steps at a time, discovered his friend, lips to the chalice, apparently imbibing the murky breath of its mouthpiece. His wandering glance came down to earth, and hardly settled on Chéri before it was off and up again to the convolvulus-wreathed cornice. His yellow-gold pajamas cast a blight over a morning-after-the-night-before face, but Desmond was inflated by prosperity and no longer worried about being ugly.

"Good morning," said Chéri. "I came through all right. What a stench there is on your stairs. Worse than a dugout."

". . . You'll never get *Desmond's* custom at twelve," Desmond was saying to an invisible listener. "I have no difficulty in buying Pommery at that price. And for my private cellar, Pommery ought to be eleven when minus labels . . . hullo . . . yes, the labels that came off in the general rumpus. That's what I want . . . hullo?"

"You're coming out to lunch. I've got the runabout at the door," Chéri said.

"No, and twice times no," said Desmond.

"What?"

"No, and a thousand times no. Hullo? . . . Sherry! What d'you take me for? This isn't a bar. Champagne, or nothing. Don't go on wasting your time and mine. Hullo. . . . That's quite possible. Only I'm all the rage at the moment. Hullo. . . . At two o'clock precisely. A very good day to you, Monsieur."

He stretched himself, before offering a limp hand. He still

looked like Alfonso XIII, but thirty summers and the war had rooted this uncertain creature in the soil he needed. To have come through the war without firing a shot, to have eaten regularly, taken every advantage of it, and malingered in general, were so many personal victories from which he had emerged strengthened and self-confident. Assurance and a full pocket had made him less ugly, and you could be sure that, at sixty, he would give the illusion of having once passed for a handsome man with a large nose and long legs. He looked at Chéri condescendingly, but with a friendlier eye. Chéri turned away his head and said: "What! Are you reduced to this? Come on, old boy. It's midday and you're not up yet."

"In the first place, I *am* ready," Desmond replied, unbuttoning his pajamas to show a white silk shirt and a bronze-colored bow tie. "And in the second, I'm not going to lunch out."

"So that's it," said Chéri. "Well, of all . . . I'm speechless. . . ."

"But if you like I can give you two fried eggs, and half my ham, my salad, my stout, and my strawberries. No extra charge for coffee."

Chéri looked at him in impotent fury. "Why?"

"Business," said Desmond, with a deliberately nasal twang. "Champagne! You heard what I was saying a moment ago. Oh! these wine merchants! If one didn't put on the screw . . . But I'm a match for them."

He knotted his fingers and the knuckle joints cracked with commercial pride.

"Yes or no?"

"Yes, you swine."

Chéri chucked his soft felt hat at his head; but Desmond picked it up and brushed it with his forearm, to show that this was not the moment for childish jokes. They had eggs in aspic, ham and tongue, and good black stout with coffee-colored foam on it. They spoke little, and Chéri, gazing out onto the paved courtyard, was politely bored.

"What am I doing here? Nothing, except that I'm not at

home, sitting down to cutlets Fulbert-Dumonteil." He visualized Edmée in white, the baby-faced American colonel, and Arnaud, the physician-in-charge, in whose presence she acted the docile little girl. He thought of Charlotte Peloux's epaulettes, and a sort of fruitless affection for his host was coming over him, when the latter asked him an abrupt question:

"Do you know how much champagne was drunk here last night, between four o'clock yesterday and four o'clock this morning?"

"No," said Chéri.

"And do you know how many bottles were returned empty from those delivered here between May the first and June the fifteenth?"

"No," said Chéri.

"Say a number."

"No idea," Chéri grunted.

"But say something! Say a number! Have a guess, man! Name some figure!"

Chéri scratched the tablecloth as he might during an examination. He was suffering from the heat, and from his own inertia.

"Five hundred," he got out at last.

Desmond threw himself back in his chair and, as it swerved through the air, his monocle shot a piercing flash of sunlight into Chéri's eye.

"Five hundred! You make me laugh!"

He was boasting. He did not know how to laugh: his nearest approach was a sort of sob of the shoulders. He drank some coffee, to excite Chéri's curiosity, and then put down his cup again.

"Three thousand, three hundred and eighty-two, my boy. And do you know how much that puts in my pocket?"

"No," Chéri interrupted, "and I don't give a damn. That's enough. My mother does all that for me if I want it. Besides . . ." He rose, and added in a hesitant voice: "Besides, money doesn't interest me."

"Strange," said Desmond, hurt. "Strange. Amusing."

"If you like. No, can't you understand, money doesn't interest me . . . doesn't interest me anymore."

These simple words fell from his lips slowly. Chéri spoke them without looking up, and kicked a biscuit crumb along the carpet; his embarrassment at making this confession, his secretive look, restored for a fleeting instant the full marvel of his youth.

For the first time Desmond stared at him with the critical attention of a doctor examining a patient, "Am I dealing with a malingerer?" Like a doctor, he had recourse to confused and soothing words.

"We all go through that. Everyone's feeling a little out of sorts. No one knows exactly where he stands. Work is a wonderful way of putting you on your feet again, old boy. Take me, for instance. . . ."

"I know," Chéri interrupted. "You're going to tell me I haven't enough to do."

"Yes, it's your own fault." Desmond's mockery was condescending in the extreme. "For in these wonderful times . . ." He was going on to confess his deep satisfaction with business, but he pulled himself up in time. "It's also a question of upbringing. Obviously, you never learned the first thing about life under Léa's wing. You've no idea how to manage people and things."

"So they say." Chéri was put out. "Léa herself wasn't fooled. You mayn't believe me, but though she didn't trust me, she always consulted me before buying or selling."

He thrust out his chest, proud of the days gone by, when distrust was synonymous with respect.

"You've only got to apply yourself to it again—to money matters," Desmond continued, in his advisory capacity. "It's a game that never goes out of fashion."

"Yes," Chéri acquiesced rather vaguely. "Yes, of course. I'm only waiting."

"Waiting for what?"

"I'm waiting. . . . What I mean is . . . I'm waiting for an opportunity . . . a better opportunity. . . ."

"Better than what?"

"What a bore you are. An excuse—if you like—to take up again everything the war deprived me of years ago. My fortune, which is, in fact . . ."

"Quite considerable?" Desmond suggested. Before the war, he would have said "enormous," and in a different tone of voice. A moment's humiliation brought a blush to Chéri's cheek.

"Yes . . . my fortune. Well, the little woman, my wife, now makes that her business."

"Oh, no!" exclaimed Desmond, in shocked disapproval.

"Oh, yes, I promise you. Two hundred and sixteen thousand in a little flare-up on the Bourse the day before yesterday. So, don't you see, the question now arises, 'How am I to interfere?' . . . Where do I stand, in all this? When I suggest taking a hand, they say . . ."

"They? Who are 'they'?"

"What? Oh, my mother and my wife. They start saying: 'Take it easy. You're a warrior. Would you like a glass of orangeade? Run along to your shirtmaker, he's making you look a fool. And while you are going the rounds, you might call in and collect my necklace, if the clasp's been mended . . .' and so on, and so forth."

He was growing excited, hiding his resentment as best he could, though his nostrils were quivering, and his lips as well.

"So must I now tout motorcars, or breed Angora rabbits, or direct some high-class establishment? Have I got to engage myself as a male nurse or accountant in that bargain basement, my wife's hospital?" He walked as far as the window, and came back to Desmond precipitately. "Under the orders of Doctor Arnaud, physician-in-charge, and pass the basins round for him? Must I take up this nightclub business? Can't you *see* the competition!"

He laughed in order to make Desmond laugh; but Desmond, no doubt a little bored, kept a perfectly straight face.

"How long ago did you start thinking of all this? You certainly had no such ideas in the spring, or last winter, or before you were married."

"I had no time for it," Chéri answered quite simply. "We went off on our travels, we began furnishing the house, we bought motors just in time to have them requisitioned. All that led up to the war. Before the war . . . before the war I was . . . a kid from a rich home. I was rich, damn it!"

"You still are."

"I still am," Chéri echoed.

He hesitated once more, searching for words. "But now, it's not at all the same thing. People have got the jitters. And work, and activity, and duty, and women who serve their country—not half they don't—and are crazy about oof . . . they're such thorough-going businesswomen that they make you disgusted with the word *business.* They're such hard workers it's enough to make you loathe the sight of work." He looked uncertainly at Desmond, "Is it really wrong to be rich, and take life easy?"

Desmond enjoyed playing his part and making up for past subservience. He put a protective hand on Chéri's shoulder.

"My son, be rich and live your own life! Tell yourself that you're the incarnation of an ancient aristocracy. Model yourself on the feudal barons. You're a warrior."

"Merde," said Chéri.

"Now you're talking like a warrior. Only, you must live and let live, and let those work who like it."

"You, for instance."

"Me, for instance."

"Obviously, you're not the sort to let yourself be messed about by women."

"No," said Desmond curtly. He was hiding from the world a perverse taste for his chief cashier—a gentle creature with brown hair scraped well back, rather masculine and hairy. She wore a religious medallion round her neck, and smilingly confessed, "For two pins I'd commit murder: I'm like that."

"No. Emphatically, no! Can't you mention anything without sooner or later dragging in 'my wife, women,' or else 'in Léa's time'? Is there nothing else to talk about in 1919?"

Beyond the sound of Desmond's voice, Chéri seemed to be listening to some other, still unintelligible sound. "Nothing else to talk about," he repeated to himself. "Why should there be?" He was daydreaming, lulled by the light and the warmth, which increased as the sun came round into the room. Desmond went on talking, impervious to the stifling heat, and as white as winter endive. Chéri caught the words "little birds" and began to pay attention.

"Yes, I've a whole heap of amusing connections, with whom, of course, I'll put you in touch. And when I say 'birds,' I'm speaking far too frivolously of what amounts to a unique collection, you understand, utterly unique. My regulars are tasty pieces, and all the tastier for the last four years. Just you wait and see, old boy! When my capital is big enough, what a restaurant I'll show the world! Ten tables, at most, which they'll fall over each other to book. I'll cover in the courtyard. . . . You may be sure my lease provides for all additions I make! Cork-lino in the middle of the dance floor, spotlights. . . . That's the future! It's out there. . . ."

The tango merchant was holding forth like a founder of cities, pointing toward the window with outstretched arm. Chéri was struck by the word *future*, and turned to face the spot indicated by Desmond, somewhere high up above the courtyard. He saw nothing, and felt limp. The reverberations of the two o'clock sun smote glumly down upon the little slate roof of the old stables, where the concierge of *Desmond's* had his lodging. "What a ballroom, eh?" said Desmond with fervor, pointing to the small courtyard. "And it won't be long now before I get it!"

Chéri stared intently at this man who, each day, expected and received his daily bread. "And what about me?" he thought, inwardly frustrated.

"Look, here comes my swipes merchant," Desmond shouted. "Make yourself scarce. I must warm him up like a bottle of Corton."

He shook Chéri's hand with a hand that had changed its character: from being narrow and boneless, it had become broad, purposeful, disguised as the rather firm hand of an honest man. "The war . . ." thought Chéri, tongue in cheek.

"You're off? Where?" Desmond asked.

He kept Chéri standing on top of the steps long enough to be able to show off such a decorative client to his wine merchant.

"Over there," said Chéri, with a vague gesture.

"Mystery," murmured Desmond. "Be off to your seraglio!"

"Oh no," said Chéri, "you're quite wrong."

He conjured up the vision of some female—moist flesh, nakedness, a mouth. He shuddered with impersonal disgust, and, repeating "You're quite wrong" under his breath, got into his runabout.

He carried away with him an all too familiar uneasiness, the embarrassment and irritation of never being able to put into words all that he really wanted to say; of never meeting the person to whom he would have to confide a half-formed admission, a secret that could have changed everything, and which, for instance, this afternoon would have dispersed the ominous atmosphere from the bleached pavements and the asphalt, now beginning to melt under a vertical sun.

"Only two o'clock," he sighed, "and, this month, it stays light till well after nine."

The breath of wind raised by the speed of his motor was like a hot dry towel being flapped in his face, and he yearned for the make-believe night behind his blue curtains, to the accompaniment of the simple drip-drop-drip of the Italian fountain's sing-song in the garden.

"If I slip quickly through the hall, I'll be able to get in again without being seen. *They'll* be having coffee by now."

He could almost catch a whiff of the excellent luncheon, of the lingering smell of the melon, of the dessert wine which Edmée always had served with the fruit; and, ahead of time, he saw the verdigrised reflection of Chéri closing the door lined with plate glass.

"In we go!"

Two motors were dozing in the shade of the low-hanging branches just inside the gates, one his wife's and the other American, both in the charge of an American chauffeur who was himself taking a nap. Chéri drove on as far as the deserted Rue de Franqueville, and then walked back to his own front door. He let himself in without making a sound, took a good look at his shadowy form in the green-surfaced mirror, and softly went upstairs to the bedroom. It was just as he had longed for it to be—blue, fragrant, made for rest. In it he found everything that his thirsty drive had made so desirable: and more besides, for there was a young woman dressed in white, powdering her face and tidying her hair in front of a long looking glass. Her back was turned to Chéri, and she did not hear him enter. Thus he had more than a moment to observe in the glass how flushed luncheon and the hot weather had made her, and to note her strange expression of untidiness and triumph and her general air of having won an emotionally outrageous victory. All at once Edmée caught sight of her husband and turned to face him without saying a word. She examined him critically from top to toe, waiting for him to speak first.

Through the half-open window facing the garden floated up the baritone notes of Doctor Arnaud's voice, singing, *"Oy Marie, Oy Marie."*

Edmée's whole body seemed to incline toward this voice, but she restrained herself from turning her head in the direction of the garden.

The slightly drunken courage visible in her eyes might well forebode a serious situation. Out of contempt or cowardice, Chéri, by putting a finger to his lips, enjoined silence upon her. He then pointed to the staircase with the same imperative finger. Edmée obeyed. She went resolutely past him, without being able to repress, at the moment when she came closest to him, a slight twist of the hips and quickening of the step, which kindled in Chéri a sudden impulse to strike her. He leaned over the banisters, feeling reassured, like a cat that has reached safety at the top of a tree; and, still thinking of punishing, smashing, and taking flight, he waited there, ready to be wafted away on a flood of jealousy. All that came to him was a mediocre little feeling of shame, all too bearable, as he put his thoughts into words, "Punish her, smash up the whole place! There's better to do than that. Yes, there's better to do." But what, he did not know.

Each morning, for him, whether he woke early or late, was the start of a long day's vigil. At first he paid but scant attention, believing it to be merely the persistence of an unhealthy habit picked up in the army.

In December, 1918, after putting his kneecap out of joint, he had eked out in his bed at home a short period of convalescence. He used to stretch himself in the early morning and smile. "I'm comfortable. I'm waiting for the time when I feel much better. Christmas this year is really going to be worthwhile."

Christmas came. When the truffles had been eaten, and the holly twig dipped in brandy set alight on a silver platter, in the presence of an ethereal Edmée, very much the wife, and to the acclamations of Charlotte, of Madame de La Berche, and members of the nursing staff of the hospital, together with a sprinkling of Rumanian officers and athletic adolescent American colonels, Chéri waited. "Oh, if only those fellows would go away! I'm waiting to go to sleep, head in the cool air and feet warm, in my own good bed!" Two hours later, he was still waiting for sleep, laid out as flat as a corpse, listening to the mocking call of the little winter owls in the branches—a challenge to the blue light of his unshuttered room. At last he fell asleep; but a prey to his insatiable vigilance from the peep of dawn, he began to wait for his breakfast, and gave utterance to his hearty impatience: "What the hell do they think they're doing with the grub downstairs?" He did not realize that whenever he swore or used "soldiers' slang," it always went with an affected state of mind. His jolliness was a method of escape. Breakfast was brought to him by Edmée; but in his wife's bustling movements he never failed to discern haste and the call of duty, and he would ask for more toast, or for another hot roll which he no longer really wanted, simply from a malicious wish to delay Edmée's departure, to delay the moment when he would once more, inevitably, resume his period of waiting.

A certain Rumanian lieutenant used to be sent off by Edmée to look for concentrated disinfectant and absorbent cotton wool, or again to press a demand upon ministers—"What the government refuses point-blank to a Frenchman, a foreigner gets every time," she affirmed. He used to bore Chéri stiff by cracking up the duties of a soldier, fit or nearly fit, and the paradisal purity of the Coictier Hospital. Chéri went along there with Edmée, sniffed the smells of antiseptics which relentlessly suggest underlying putrefaction, recognized a comrade among the "Trench Feet" and sat down on the edge of his bed, forcing himself to assume the cordiality prescribed by war novels and patriotic plays. He knew well enough, all the same, that a man in sound health, who had come through unscathed, could find no peer or equal among the crippled. Wherever he looked, he saw the fluttering white wings of the nurses, the red-brick color of the faces and hands upon the sheets. An odious sense of impotence weighed upon him. He caught himself guiltily stiffening one of his arms as if held in a sling, or dragging one of his legs. But the next moment he could not help taking a deep breath and picking his way between the recumbent mummies with the light step of a dancer. He was forced reluctantly to reverence Edmée, because of her authority as a noncommissioned angel, and her aura of whiteness. She came across the ward, and, in passing, put a hand on Chéri's shoulder; but he knew that the desire behind this gesture of tenderness and delicate possession was to bring a blush of envy and irritation to the cheek of a young dark-haired nurse who was gazing at Chéri with the candor of a cannibal.

He felt bored, and consumed by the feeling of weariness that makes a man jib at the serried ranks of masterpieces before him as he is being dragged round a museum. The plethora of whiteness, thrown off from the ceiling and reflected back from the tiled floor, blotted out all corners, and he felt sorry for the men lying there, to whom shade would have been a charity, though no one offered it. The noonday hour imposes rest and privacy upon the beasts of the field, and the silence of deep woodland undergrowth upon the birds of the air, but civilized men no longer obey the dictates of the sun. Chéri took a few steps toward his wife, with the intention of saying: "Draw the curtains, install a punkah, take away that macaroni from the poor wretch who's blinking his eyes and breathing so heavily, and let him eat his food when the sun goes down. Give them shade, let them have any color you like, but not always and everywhere this eternal white." With the arrival of Doctor Arnaud, he lost his inclination to give advice and make himself useful.

The doctor, with his white linen belly and his red-gold hair, had taken no more than three steps across the ward before the hovering noncommissioned angel glided to earth again, to minister as a humble seraph, rosy with faith and zeal. Chéri thereupon turned to Filipesco, who was distributing American cigarettes, shouted "Are you coming?" in contemptous tones, and bore him away; but not before he had bidden farewell to his wife, to Doctor Arnaud, to nurses male and female, with the haughty affability of an official visitor. He crossed the rough gravel of the little courtyard, got into his car, and allowed himself no more than a dozen words' soliloquy: "It's the regular thing. The correct move for the physician-in-charge."

Never again did he cross the threshold of the hospital, and thereafter Edmée invited him on State occasions only, out of official courtesy, much as one might, at a dinner party, politely offer the snipe to a vegetarian guest.

He was now given over to reflection, and a prey to idleness. Before the war his idleness had been so light and varied, with the resonant ring of a flawless empty glass. During the war, too, he had endured periods of inertia under military discipline, inertia modified by cold, mud, risk, patrols, and even, on occasion, a little fighting. Conditioned to indolence by his upbringing and the life of a sensual young man, he had watched, himself untouched, the fresh young vulnerable companions all round him pine away in silence, solitude, and frustration. He had witnessed the ravages inflicted on intelligent people by the lack of newspapers as if they were being deprived of a daily drug. Whereas he had relapsed into contemplative silence—like a cat in a garden at night—content with a short letter, a postcard, or a cunningly packed parcel, other men, so-called superior men, had appeared to him to be showing every symptom of ruinous mental starvation. Thus he had learned to take pride in bolstering up his patience, and had brooded over two or three ideas, over two or three persistent memories, as highly colored as a child's, and over his inability to imagine his own death.

Time and again, throughout the war, on coming out of a long dreamless sleep or a fitful bout of spasmodically interrupted rest, he would awake to find himself somewhere outside the present time and, his more recent past sloughed off, restored to the days of his boyhood—restored to Léa. Later, Edmée would suddenly rise up from the past, distinct and clear in every detail, and this evocation of her form, no less than its almost immediate disappearance, had always put Chéri in good spirits. "That gives me two of them," he reckoned. Nothing came to him from Léa; he did not write to her. But he received postcards signed by the crabbed fingers of old mother Aldonza, and cigars chosen by the Baroness de La Berche. Sometimes he dreamed of a long, soft-wool scarf, as blue as a pair of blue eyes with a very faint suggestion of the scent associated with it throughout long hours of warmth and slumber. He had loved this scarf and hugged it to him in the dark, until it had lost its fragrance and the freshness of the blue eyes, and he had thought of it no more.

For four years he had not bothered his head about Léa. Her trusty old cronies, had occasion arisen, would have forwarded news of any events in her life. He never imagined anything happening to her. What had Léa in common with sickness, or Léa with change?

In 1918 he could not believe his ears when the Baroness de La Berche casually mentioned "Léa's new flat."

"Has she moved, then?"

"Where have you sprung from?" the Baroness answered.

"The whole world knows it. The sale of her house to the Americans was a brilliant deal, you bet! I've seen her new flat. It's small, but it's very cosy. Once you sit down in it, you never want to get up again."

Chéri clung to the words "small, but cosy." Unable to imagine anything different, he supplied an overall rose-pink background, threw in that huge galleon of gold and steel—the bed with its lace rigging—and hung Chaplin's pearly breasted nymph from some floating cloud.

When Desmond began looking about for a sleeping partner for his nightclub, Chéri had spasms of alarm and anxiety. "The blackguard's certain to try and tap Léa, or get her mixed up in some fishy business . . . I'd better tip her off on the telephone." He did nothing of the sort, however. Telephoning to a discarded mistress is riskier far than holding out your hand in the street to a nervous enemy who tries to catch your eye.

He went on biding his time, even after surprising Edmée in front of the looking glass, after that flagrant exhibition of overexcitement, flushed cheeks, and untidiness. He let the hours slip by, and did not put into words—and so accentuate—his certainty that a still almost chaste understanding existed between his wife and the man who had been singing *"Oy Marie!"* For he felt much lighter in spirit, and for several days stopped uselessly consulting his wristwatch as soon as daylight began to fade. He developed the habit of sitting out under the trees in a basket chair, like a newly arrived guest in a hotel garden. There he marveled to see how the oncoming night blotted out the blue of the monkshood, producing in its stead a hazier blue into which the shapes of the flowers were fused, while the green of their leaves persisted in distinct clumps. The edging of rose-colored pinks turned to rank mauve, then the color ebbed rapidly and the July stars shone yellow between the branches of the weeping ash.

He tasted at home the pleasures enjoyed by a casual passerby who sits down to rest in a square, and he never noticed how long he remained there, lying back with his hands dangling. Sometimes he gave a fleeting thought to what he called "the looking-glass scene" and the atmosphere in the blue room when it had been secretly troubled by a man's sudden appearance, theatrical behavior, and flight. He whispered over and over, with foolish mechanical regularity, "That's one point established. That's what's called a point-t-established," running the two words together into one.

At the beginning of July he bought a new open motor, and called it his Riviera Runabout. He drove Filipesco and Desmond out along drought-whitened roads, but returned to Paris every evening, cleaving alternate waves of warm and cool air, which began to lose their good smells the nearer the motor drew to Paris.

One day he took out the Baroness de La Berche, a virile companion, who, when they came to the barriers of the Octroi, raised her forefinger to the little felt hat pulled well down on her head. He found her agreeable, sparing of words, interested in wayside inns overgrown with wistaria, and in village wineshops with their cellar smell and wine-soaked sand. Rigid and in silence, they covered two hundred miles or more, without ever opening their mouths except to smoke or feed. The following day Chéri again invited Camille de La Berche with a curt "Well, how about it, Baroness?" and whisked her off without further ado.

The trusty motor sped far afield through the green countryside, and came back at nightfall to Paris like a toy at the end of a string. That evening, Chéri, while never taking his eye off the road, could distinguish on his right side the outline of an elderly woman, with a man's profile as noble as that of an old family coachman. It astonished him to find her worthy of respect because she was plain and simple, and when he was alone in her company for the first time and far away from town life, it began to dawn on him that a woman burdened with some monstrous sexual deformity needs must possess a certain bravura and something of the dignified courage of the condemned.

Since the war this woman had found no further use for her unkindness. The hospital had put her back in her proper place, that is to say, among males, among men just young enough, just tamed enough by suffering, for her to live serenely in their midst, and forget her frustrated femininity.

On the sly, Chéri studied his companion's large nose, the graying hairy upper lip, and the little peasant eyes which glanced incuriously at ripe cornfields and scythed meadows.

For the first time he felt something very like friendship for old Camille, and was led to make a poignant comparison: "She is alone. When she's no longer with her soldiers or with my mother, she's alone. She too. Despite her pipe and her glass of wine, she's alone."

On their way back to Paris, they stopped at a "hostelry" where there was no ice, and where, trained against the plinths of columns and clinging to ancient baptismal fonts dotted about the lawn, the rambler roses were dying, frizzled by the sun. A neighboring copse screened this dried-up spot from any breeze, and a small cloud, scorched to a cherry hue, hung motionless, high in the heavens.

The Baroness knocked out her short briar pipe on the ear of a marble fawn.

"It's going to be grilling over Paris tonight."

Chéri nodded in agreement, and looked up at the cloud. The light reflected from it mottled his white cheeks and dimpled chin, like touches of pink powder on an actor's face.

"Yes," he said.

"Well, you know, if the idea tempts you, let's not go back till tomorrow morning. Just give me time to buy a piece of soap and a toothbrush. . . . And we'll telephone your wife. Then, tomorrow morning we can be up and on our way by four o'clock, while it's fresh."

Chéri sprang to his feet in unthinking haste. "No, no, I can't."

"You can't? Come, come!"

Down near his feet he saw two small mannish eyes, and a pair of broad shoulders shaking with laughter.

"I didn't believe that you were still held on such a tight rein," she said. "But, of course, if you are . . ."

"Are what?"

She had risen to her feet again, robust and hearty, and clapped him vigorously on the shoulder.

"Yes, yes. You run around all day long, but you go back to your kennel every night. Oh, you're kept well in hand."

He looked at her coldly: already he liked her less. "There's no hiding anything from you, Baroness. I'll fetch the car, and in under two hours we'll be back at your front door."

Chéri never forgot their nocturnal journey home, the sadness of the lingering crimson in the west, the smell of the grasses, the feathery moths held prisoner in the beam of the headlamps. The Baroness kept watch beside him, a dark form made denser by the night. He drove cautiously; the air, cool at faster speeds, grew hot again when he slowed down to take a corner. He trusted to his keen sight and his alert senses, but he could not help his thoughts running on the queer, massive old woman motionless at his right side, and she caused him a sort of terror, a twitching of the nerves, which suddenly landed him within a few inches of a wagon carrying no rear lamp. At that moment a large hand came lightly to rest on his forearm.

"Take care, child!"

He certainly had not expected either the gesture or the gentle tone of the voice. But nothing justified the subsequent emotion, the lump like a hard fruit stone in his throat, "I'm a fool, I'm a fool," he kept repeating. He continued at a slower speed, and amused himself by watching the refraction of the beams, the golden zigzags and peacock's feathers, that danced for a moment round the headlamps when seen through the tears that brimmed his eyes.

"She told me that it had a hold on me, that I was held well in hand. If she could see us, Edmée and me. . . . How long is it since we took to sleeping like two brothers?" He tried to count: three weeks, perhaps more? "And the joke about the whole business is that Edmée makes no demands, and wakes up smiling." To himself, he always used the word "joke" when he wished to avoid the word "sad." "Like an old married couple, what! like an old married couple . . . Madame and her physician-in-charge, Monsieur . . . and . . . his car. All the same, old Camille said that I was held. Held. Held. Catch me ever taking that old girl out again. . . ."

He did take her out again, for July began to scorch Paris. But neither Edmée nor Chéri complained about the dog days. Chéri used to come home, polite and absentminded, the backs of his hands and the lower part of his face nut-brown. He walked about naked between the bathroom and Edmée's boudoir.

"You must have been roasted today, you poor townees!" Chéri jeered.

Looking rather pale and almost melting away, Edmée straightened her pretty odalisque back and denied that she was tired.

"Oh well, not quite as bad as that, you know. There was rather more air than yesterday. My office down there is cool, you know. And then, we've had no time to think about it. My young man in bed twenty-two, who was getting on so well . . ."

"Oh yes!"

"Yes, Doctor Arnaud isn't too pleased about him."

She didn't hesitate to make play with the name of the physician-in-charge, much as a player moves up a decisive piece on the chessboard. But Chéri did not bat an eyelid, and Edmée followed his movements, those of a naked male body dappled a delicate green from the reflected light of the blue curtains. He walked to and fro in front of her, ostentatiously pure, trailing his aura of scent, and living in another world. The very self-confidence of this naked body, superior and contemptuous, reduced Edmée to a mildly vindictive immobility. She could not now have claimed this naked body for her own except in a voice altogether lacking the tones and urgency of desire—that is, in the calm voice of a submissive mate. Now she was held back by an arm covered with fine gold hairs, by an ardent mouth behind a golden mustache, and she gazed at Chéri with the jealous and serene security of a lover who covets a virgin inaccessible to all.

They went on to talk about holidays and traveling arrangements, in lighthearted and conventional phrases.

"The war hasn't changed Deauville enough, and what a crowd . . ." Chéri sighed.

"There's simply no place where one can eat a good meal, and it's a huge undertaking to reorganize the hotel business!" Edmée affirmed.

One day, not long before the Quatorze Juillet, Charlotte Peloux was lunching with them. She happened to speak of the success of some business deal in American blankets, and complained loudly that Léa had netted a half-share of the profits. Chéri raised his head, in astonishment. "So you still see her?"

Charlotte Peloux enveloped her son in the loving glances induced by old port, and appealed to her daughter-in-law as witness: "He's got an odd way of putting things—as if he'd been gassed—hasn't he? . . . It's disturbing at times. I've never stopped seeing Léa, darling. Why should I have stopped seeing her?"

"Why?" Edmée repeated.

He looked at the two women, finding a strange flavor in their kindly attention.

"Because you never talk to me about her . . ." he began, ingenuously.

"Me!" barked Charlotte. "For goodness' sake . . . Edmée, you hear what he says? Well at least it does credit to his feelings for you. He has so completely forgotten about everything that isn't you."

Edmée smiled without answering, bent her head, and adjusted the lace that edged the low-cut neck of her dress by tweaking it between her fingers. The movement drew Chéri's attention to her bodice, and through the yellow lawn he noticed that the points of her breasts and their mauve aureolas looked like twin bruises. He shuddered, and his shudder made him realize that the conventional beauty and all the most secret details of her charming body, that the whole of this young woman, in fact, so close and so disloyal, no longer aroused in him anything but positive repugnance. Nonsense, nonsense; but he was whipping a dead horse. And he listened to Charlotte's ever-flowing stream of nasal burblings.

". . . and then again, the day before yesterday, I was saying in your presence, that motor for motor, well—I'd far rather have a taxi, a taxi, any day, than that prehistoric old Renault of Léa's—and if it wasn't the day before yesterday, it was yesterday, that I said—speaking of Léa—that if you're a woman living on your own and you've got to have a manservant, you might just as well have a good-looking one. And then Camille was saying, only the other day when you were there, how angry she was with herself for having sent a second barrel of Quarts-de-Chaumes round to Léa instead of keeping it for herself. I've complimented you often enough on your fidelity, my darling; I must now scold you for your ingratitude. Léa deserved better of you. Edmée will be the first to admit that!"

"The second," Edmée corrected.

"Never heard a word of it," Chéri said.

He was gorging himself with hard pink July cherries, and flipping them from beneath the lowered blind at the sparrows in the garden, where, after too heavy a watering, the flower beds were steaming like a hot spring. Edmée, motionless, was cogitating on Chéri's comment, "Never heard a word of it." He certainly was not lying, and yet his offhand assumed schoolboyishness, as he squeezed the cherry stones and took aim at a sparrow by closing his left eye, spoke clearly enough to Edmée. "What can he have been thinking about, if he never heard a word?"

Before the war, she would have looked for the woman in the case. A month earlier, on the day following the looking-glass scene, she would have feared reprisals, some Red Indian act of cruelty, or a bite on the nose. But no . . . nothing . . . he lived and roamed about innocently, as quiet in his freedom as a prisoner in the depths of a jail, and as chaste as an animal brought from the Antipodes, which does not bother to look for a kindred female in our hemisphere.

Was he ill? He slept well, ate according to his fancy—that

is, delicately, sniffing all the meat suspiciously, and preferring fruit and newly laid eggs. No nervous twitch disfigured the lovely balance of his features, and he drank more water than champagne. "No, he's not ill. And yet he's . . . something. Something that I should guess, perhaps, if I were still in love with him. But . . ." Once again she fingered the lace round the neck of her bodice, inhaled the warmth and fragrance that rose up from between her breasts, and as she bent down her head she saw the precious twin pink and mauve discs through the material of her dress. She blushed with carnal pleasure, and dedicated the scent and the mauve shadows to the skillful, condescending, red-haired man whom she would be meeting again in an hour's time.

"They've spoken of Léa in front of me every day, and I didn't hear. Have I forgotten her, then? Yes, I have forgotten her. But then what does it mean, 'to forget'? If I think of Léa, I see her clearly, I remember the sound of her voice, the scent which she sprayed herself with and rubbed so lavishly into her long hands." He took such a deep breath that his nostrils were indented and his lips curled up to his nose in an expression of exquisite pleasure.

"Fred, you've just made the most horrible face; you were the spit and image of that fox Angot brought back from the trenches."

It was the least trying hour of the day for the pair of them, awake and in bed with breakfast over. After a refreshing shower bath, they were gratified to hear the drenching rain—three months ahead of the proper season—falling in sheets that stripped the false Parisian autumn of its leaves and flattened the petunias. They did not bother to find an excuse, that morning, for having willfully remained behind in town. Had not Charlotte Peloux hit upon the proper excuse the previous evening? She had declared, "We're all good Parigots, born and bred, aren't we! True blue one and all! We and the concierges can claim that we've had a real taste of the first postwar summer in Paris!"

"Fred, are you in love with that suit? You never stop wearing it. It doesn't look fresh, you know."

THE LAST OF CHÉRI

Chéri raised a finger in the direction of Edmée's voice, a gesture which enjoined silence and begged that nothing should divert his attention while he was in the throes of exceptional mental labors.

"I should like to know if I have forgotten her. But what is the real meaning of 'forgotten'! A whole year's gone by without my seeing her." He felt a sudden little shock of awakening, a tremor, when he found that his memory had failed to account for the war years. Then he totted up the years and, for an instant, everything inside him stopped functioning.

"Fred, shall I never get you to leave your razor in the bathroom, instead of bringing it in here!"

Almost naked and still damp, he took his time in turning round, and his back was silver flecked with dabs of talcum powder.

"What?"

The voice, which seemed to come from afar, broke into a laugh.

"Fred, you look like a cake that's been badly sugared. An unhealthy looking cake. Next year, we won't be as stupid as we have been this. We'll take a place in the country."

"Do you want a place in the country?"

"Yes. Not this morning, of course."

She was pinning up her hair. She pointed with her chin to the curtain of rain, streaming down in a gray torrent, without any sign of thunder or wind.

"But next year, perhaps . . . Don't you think?"

"It's an idea. Yes, it's an idea."

He was putting her politely at arm's length, in order to return to his surprising discovery. "I really did think that it was only one year since I'd seen her. I never took the war into reckoning. I haven't seen her for one, two, three, four, five years. One, two, three, four. . . . But, in that case, have I really forgotten her? No! Because these women have spoken of her in front of me, and I've never jumped up and shouted, 'Hold on! If that's true—then what about Léa?' Five years . . . How old was she in 1914?"

He counted once more, and ran up against an unbelievable total. "That would make her just about sixty today, wouldn't it? . . . How absurd!"

"And the important thing," Edmée went on, "is to choose it carefully. Let's see, a nice part of the world would be . . . "

"Normandy," Chéri finished for her, absentmindedly.

"Yes, Normandy. Do you know Normandy?"

"No . . . Not at all well. . . . It's green. There are lime trees, ponds . . ."

He shut his eyes, as though dazed.

"Where do you mean? In what part of Normandy?"

"Ponds, cream, strawberries, and peacocks. . . ."

"You seem to know a lot about Normandy! What grand country it must be! What else d'you find there?"

He appeared to be reading out a description as he leaned over the round mirror in which he made sure of the smoothness of chin and cheeks after shaving. He went on, unmoved, but hesitatingly. "There are peacocks. . . . Moonlight on parquet floors, and a great big red carpet spread on the gravel in front of . . ."

He did not finish. He swayed gently, and slithered onto the carpet. His fall was checked halfway by the side of the bed. As his head lay against the rumpled sheets, the overlying tan of his pallid cheeks had the greenish tinge of an old ivory.

Hardly had he reached the floor when Edmée, without uttering a sound, threw herself down beside him. With one hand she supported his drooping head, and with the other held a bottle of smelling salts to his nostrils, from which the color was visibly ebbing. But two enfeebled arms pushed her away.

"Leave me alone. . . . Can't you see I'm dying?"

He was not dying, however, and under Edmée's fingers his pulse retained its rhythm. He had spoken in a subdued whisper, with the glib, emphatic sincerity of very young would-be suicides who, at one and the same moment, both court death and fight shy of it.

His lips were parted over gleaming teeth and his breathing

was regular; but he was in no haste to come right back to life. Safely ensconced behind his tightly shut eyes, he sought refuge in the heart of that green domain, so vivid in his imagination at the instant of his fainting fit—a flat domain, rich in strawberry beds and bees, in pools of moonbeams fringed with warm stones. . . . After he regained his strength, he still kept his eyes shut, thinking "If I open my eyes, Edmée will then see the picture in my mind."

She remained on one knee, bending over him. She was looking after him efficiently, professionally. She reached out with her free hand, picked up a newspaper and used it to fan his forehead. She whispered insignificant but appropriate words, "It's the storm. . . . Relax. . . . No, don't try to move. . . . Wait till I slip this pillow under you. . . . "

He sat up again, smiling, and pressed her hand in thanks. His parched mouth longed for lemons or vinegar. The ringing of the telephone snatched Edmée away from him.

"Yes, yes. . . . What? Yes, of course I know it's ten. Yes. What?"

From the imperious brevity of her replies, Chéri knew that it was someone telephoning from the hospital.

"Yes, of course I'm coming. What? In . . ." With a rapid glance she estimated Chéri's term of recovery. "In twenty-five minutes. Thanks. See you presently."

She opened the two glass doors of the french windows to their fullest extent, and a few peaceful drops of rain dripped into the room, bringing with them an insipid river smell.

"Are you better, Fred? What exactly did you feel? Nothing wrong with your heart, is there? You must be short of phosphates. It's the result of this ridiculous summer we're having. But what can you expect?"

She glanced at the telephone furtively, as she might at an onlooker.

Chéri stood up on his feet again without apparent effort. "Run along, child. You'll be late at your shop. I'm quite all right."

"A mild grog? A little hot tea?"

"Don't bother about me. . . . You've been very sweet. Yes, a little cup of tea—ask for it on your way out. And some lemon."

Five minutes later she was gone, after giving him a look, which she believed expressed solicitude only. She had searched in vain for a true sign, for some explanation of so inexplicable a state of affairs. As though the sound of the door shutting had severed his bonds, Chéri stretched himself and found that he felt light, cold, and empty. He hurried to the window and saw his wife crossing the small strip of garden, her head bowed under the rain. "She's got a guilty back," he pronounced, "she's always had a guilty back. From the front, she looks a charming little lady. But her back gives the show away. She's lost a good half hour by my having fainted. But 'back to our muttons,' as my mother would say. When I got married, Léa was fifty-one—at the very least—so Madame Peloux assures me. That would make her fifty-eight now, sixty perhaps. . . . The same age as General Courbat? No! That's too rich a joke!"

He tried his hardest to associate the picture of Léa at sixty with the white bristling mustache and crannied cheeks of General Courbat and his ancient cab-horse stance. "It's the best joke out!"

The arrival of Madame Peloux found Chéri still given over to his latest pastime, pale, staring out at the drenched garden, and chewing a cigarette that had gone out. He showed no surprise at his mother's entrance, "You're certainly up with the lark, my dear mother."

"And you've got out of bed the wrong side, it would seem," was her rejoinder.

"Pure imagination. There are, at least, extenuating circumstances to account for your activity, I presume?"

She raised both eyes and shoulders in the direction of the ceiling. A cheeky little leather sports hat was pulled down like a visor over her forehead.

"My poor child," she sighed, "if you only knew what I'm engaged on at this moment! If you knew what a gigantic task . . . "

He took careful stock of the wrinkles on his mother's face, the inverted commas round her mouth. He contemplated the small flabby wavelet of a double chin, the ebb and flow of which now covered, now uncovered, the collar of her mackintosh. He started to weigh up the fluctuating pouches under her eyes, repeating to himself: "Fifty-eight . . . Sixty . . ."

"Do you know the task I've set myself? Do you know?" She waited a moment, opening wider her large eyes outlined by black pencil. "I'm going to revive the hot springs at Passy! *Les Thermes de Passy!* Yes, that means nothing to you, of course. The springs are there under the Rue Raynouard, only a few yards away. They're dormant; all they need is to be revived. Very active waters. If we go the right way about it, it will mean the ruination of Uriage, the collapse of Mont Dore, perhaps—but that would be too wonderful! Already I've made certain of the cooperation of twenty-seven Swiss doctors. Edmée and I have been getting to work on the Paris Municipal Council. . . . And that's exactly why I've come—I missed your wife by five minutes. . . . What's wrong with you? You're not listening to me. . . ."

He persisted in trying to relight his damp cigarette. He gave it up, threw the stub out upon the balcony, where large drops of rain were rebounding like grasshoppers; then he gravely looked his mother up and down.

"I am listening to you," he said. "Even before you speak I know what you're going to say. I know all about this business of yours. It goes by the varying names of company promotion, wheezes, commissions, founders' shares, American blankets, bully beef, etcetera. . . . You don't suppose I've been deaf or blind for the last year, do you? You are nasty, wicked women, that's all there is to it. I bear you no ill will."

He stopped talking and sat down, by force of habit rubbing his fingers almost viciously over the little twin scars beneath his right breast. He looked out at the green, rain-battered garden, and on his relaxed features weariness battled with youth—weariness, hollowing his cheeks and darkening his eye sockets, youth perfectly preserved in the ravishing curve and full ripeness of his lips, the downiness of his nostrils, and the raven-black abundance of his hair.

"Very well, then," said Charlotte Peloux at length. "That's a nice thing to hear, I must say. The devil turned preacher! I seem to have given birth to a Censor of Public Morals."

He showed no intention of breaking the silence, or of making any movement whatever.

"And by what high standards do you presume to judge this poor corrupt world? By your own honesty, I don't doubt!"

Buckled into a leather jerkin, like a yeoman of old, she was at the top of her form and ready for the fray. But Chéri appeared to be through with all fighting, now and forever.

"By my honesty? . . . Perhaps. Had I been hunting for the right word, I should never have hit upon that. You yourself said it. Honesty will pass."

She did not deign to reply, postponing her offensive until a later moment. She held her tongue that she might give her full attention to her son's peculiar new aspect. He was sitting with his legs very wide apart, elbows on knees, his hands firmly locked together. He continued to stare out at the garden laid flat by the lashing rain, and after a moment he sighed without turning his head: "Do you really call this a life?"

As might be expected, she asked: "What life?"

He raised one arm, only to let it fall again. "Mine. Yours. Everything. All that's going on under our eyes."

Madame Peloux hesitated a moment. Then she threw off her leather coat, lit a cigarette, and she too sat down.

"Are you bored?"

Coaxed by the unusual sweetness of a voice that sounded ethereally solicitous, he became natural and almost confidential.

"Bored? No, I'm not bored. What makes you think I'm bored? I'm a trifle . . . what shall I say? . . . a trifle worried, that's all."

"About what?"

"About everything. Myself. . . . Even about you."

"I'm surprised at that."

"So am I. These fellows . . . this year . . . this peace." He stretched his fingers apart as though they were sticky or tangled in overlong hair.

"You say that as we used to say 'this war' . . ." She put a hand on his shoulder and tactfully lowered her voice. "What is the matter with you?"

He could not bear the questioning weight of this hand; he stood up, and began moving about in a haphazard way. "The matter is that everyone's rotten. No!" he begged, seeing an artificial look of indignation on the maternal countenance, "No, don't start all over again. No, present company *not* excluded. No, I do *not* accept the fact that we are living in splendid times, with a dawn of this, a resurrection of that. No, I am *not* angry, don't love you any less than before, and there is nothing wrong with my liver. But I do seriously think that I'm nearly at the end of my tether."

He cracked his fingers as he walked about the room, sniffing the sweet-smelling spray of the heavy rain as it splashed off the balcony. Charlotte Peloux threw down her hat and her red gloves, a gesture intended as a peace offering.

"Do tell me exactly what you mean, child. We're alone." She smoothed back her sparse hennaed hair, cut boyishly short. Her mushroom-colored garb held in her body as an iron hoop clamps a cask. "A woman. . . . She has been a woman. . . . Fifty-eight. . . . Sixty. . . . " Chéri was thinking. She turned on him her lovely velvety eyes, brimming with maternal coquetry, the feminine power of which he had long forgotten. This sudden charm of his mother's warned him of the danger lying ahead, and the difficulty of the confession toward which she was leading him. But he felt empty and listless, tormented by what he lacked. The hope of shocking her drove him on still further.

"Yes," he said, in answer to his own question. "You have your blankets, your macaroni and spaghetti, your légions d'honneur. You joke about the meetings of the Chambre des Députés and the accident to young Lenoir. You are thrilled by

Madame Caillaux, and by the hot springs at Passy. Edmée's got her shopful of wounded and her physician-in-charge. Desmond dabbles in dance halls, wines and spirits, and white slavery. Filipesco bags cigars from Americans and hospitals, to hawk them round nightclubs. Jean de Touzac . . . is in the surplus-store racket. What a set! What . . ."

"You're forgetting Landru," Charlotte put in edgeways.

His eyes twinkled as he gave the slyest of winks, in silent tribute to the malicious humor that rejuvenated his old pugilist of a mother.

"Landru? That doesn't count, there's a prewar flavor about that. There's nothing odd about Landru. But as for the rest—well . . . well, to cut it short, there's not one who's not a rotter and . . . and I don't like it. That's all."

"That's certainly short, but not very clear," Charlotte said, after a moment. "You've a nice opinion of us. Mind you, I don't say you're wrong. Myself, I've got the qualities of my defects, and nothing frightens me. Only, it doesn't give me an inkling of what you're really after."

Chéri swayed awkwardly on his chair. He frowned so furiously that the skin on his forehead contracted in deep wrinkles between his eyes, as though trying to keep a hat on his head in a gusty wind.

"What I'm really after . . . I simply don't know. I only wish people weren't such rotters. I mean to say, weren't *only* rotten. . . . Or, quite simply, I should like to be able not to notice it."

He showed such hesitancy, such a need of coming to terms with himself, that Charlotte made fun of it. "Why notice it, then?"

"Ah, well. . . . That's just the point, you see."

He gave her a helpless smile, and she noticed how much her son's face aged as he smiled. "Someone ought constantly to be telling him hard-luck stories," she said to herself, "or else making him really angry. Gaiety doesn't improve his looks . . ." She blew out a cloud of smoke and in her turn allowed an ambiguous commonplace to escape her. "You didn't notice anything of that before."

He raised his head sharply. "Before? Before what?"

"Before the war, of course."

"Ah, yes . . ." he murmured, disappointed. "No, before the war, obviously. . . . But before the war I didn't look at things in the same way."

"Why?"

The simple word struck him dumb.

"I'll tell you what it is," Charlotte chided him, "you've turned honest."

"You wouldn't think of admitting, by any chance, that I've simply remained so?"

"No, no, don't let's get that wrong." She was arguing, a flush on her cheeks, with the fervor of a prophetess. "Your way of life before the war, after all—I'm putting myself in the position of people who are not exactly broad-minded and who take a superficial view of things, understand!—such a way of life, after all, has a name!"

"If you like," Chéri agreed. "What of it?"

"Well then, that implies a . . . a way of looking at things. Your point of view was a gigolo's."

"Quite possibly," said Chéri, unmoved. "Do you see any harm in that?"

"Certainly not," Charlotte protested, with the simplicity of a child. "But, you know, there's a right time for everything."

"Yes . . ." He sighed deeply, looking out toward a sky masked by cloud and rain. "There's a time to be young, and there's a time to be less young. There's a time to be happy . . . d'you think it needed you to make me aware of that?"

She seemed suddenly to be upset, and walked up and down the room, her round behind tightly molded by her dress, as plump and brisk as a little fat bitch. She came back and planted herself in front of her son.

"Well, darling, I'm afraid you're heading for some act of madness."

"What?"

"Oh! there aren't so many. A monastery. Or a desert island. Or love."

Chéri smiled in astonishment. "Love? You want me . . . in love with . . ." He jerked his chin in the direction of Edmée's boudoir, and Charlotte's eyes sparkled.

"Who mentioned her?"

He laughed, and from an instinct of self-preservation became offensive again.

"*You* did, and in a moment you'll be offering me one of your American pieces."

She gave a theatrical start. "An American piece? Really? And why not a rubber substitute as provided for sailors into the bargain?"

He was pleased with her jingoistic and expert disdain. Since childhood he had had it dinned into him that a French woman demeans herself by living with a foreigner, unless, of course, she exploits him, or he ruins her. And he could reel off a list of outrageous epithets with which a native Parisian courtesan would brand a dissolute foreign woman. But he refused the offer, without irony. Charlotte threw out her short arms and protruded her lower lip, like a doctor confessing his helplessness.

"I don't suggest that you should work . . ." she risked shamefacedly.

Chéri dismissed this importunate suggestion with a shrug of the shoulders.

"Work," he repeated . . . "work, what you mean by that is hobnobbing with fellows. You can't work alone, short of painting picture postcards or taking in sewing. My poor mother, you fail to realize that, if fellows get my goat, women can hardly be said to inspire me either. The truth is, that I have no further use for women at all," he finished courageously.

"Good heavens!" Charlotte caterwauled. She wrung her hands as though a horse had slipped and fallen at her feet; but harshly her son enjoined silence with a single gesture, and she was forced to admire the virile authority of this handsome young man, who had just owned up to his own particular brand of impotence.

"Chéri! . . . my little boy! . . ."

He turned to her with a gentle, empty, and vaguely pleading look in his eyes.

She gazed into the large eyes that shone with an exaggerated brilliance, due, perhaps, to their unblemished white, their long lashes and the secret emotion behind them. She longed to enter through these magnificent portals and reach down to the shadowed heart which had first started to beat so close to her own. Chéri appeared to be putting up no defense and to enjoy being balked, as if under hypnosis. Charlotte had, in the past, known her son to be ill, irritable, sly; she had never known him unhappy. She felt, therefore, a strange kind of excitement, the ecstasy that casts a woman at a man's feet at the moment when she dreams of changing a despairing stranger into an inferior stranger—that is to say, of making him rid himself of his despair.

"Listen, Chéri," she murmured very softly. "Listen. . . . You must . . . No, no, wait! At least let me speak. . . ."

He interrupted her with a furious shake of the head, and she saw it was useless to insist. It was she who broke their long exchange of looks, by putting on her coat again and her little leather hat, making toward the door. But as she passed the table, she stopped, and casually put her hand out toward the telephone.

"Do you mind, Chéri?"

He nodded his consent, and she began in a high-pitched nasal shrill like a clarinet. "Hullo . . . Hullo . . . Hullo . . . Passy, two nine, two nine. Hullo . . . Is that you, Léa? But of course it's me. What weather, eh! . . . Don't speak of it. Yes, very well. Everyone's very well. What are you doing today? Not budging an inch! Ah, that's so like you, you self-indulgent creature! Oh, you know, I'm no longer my own mistress. . . . Oh no, not on that account. Something altogether different. A vast undertaking. . . . Oh, no, not on the telephone. . . . You'll be in all day then? Good. That's very convenient. Thank you. Good-bye, Léa darling!"

She put back the receiver, showing nothing but the curve of

her back. As she moved away, she inhaled and exhaled puffs of blue smoke, and vanished in the midst of her cloud like a magician whose task is accomplished.

WITHOUT HURRYING, he climbed the single flight of stairs up to Léa's flat. At six in the evening, after the rain, the Rue Raynouard reechoed, like the garden of a boarding school, with the chirrup of birds and the cries of small children. He glanced quickly, coldly, at everything, refusing to be surprised at the heavy looking glasses in the entrance hall, the polished steps, the blue carpet, or the lift cage lavishly splashed with as much lacquer and gold as a sedan chair. On the landing he experienced, for a moment, the deceptive sense of detachment and freedom from pain felt by a sufferer on the dentist's doorstep. He nearly turned away, but, guessing that he might feel compelled to return later, he pressed the bell with a determined finger. The maid, who had taken her time in coming to the door, was young and dark, with a butterfly cap of fine lawn on her bobbed hair: her unfamiliar face took from Chéri his last chance of feeling moved.

"Is Madame at home?"

The young servant, apparently lost in admiration of him, could not make up her mind.

"I do not know, Monsieur. Is Monsieur expected?"

"Of course," he said, with a return of his old harshness.

She left him standing there, and disappeared. In the half-light, he was quick to take in his surroundings, with eyes blurred by the gloom, and alert sensitive nostrils. There was nowhere a vestige of that light golden scent, and some ordinary pine essence sputtered in an electric scent burner. Chéri felt put out, like someone who discovers that he is on the wrong floor. But a great peal of girlish laughter rang out, its notes running down a deep descending scale. It was muffled by some curtain or other, but at once the intruder was cast into a whirlpool of memories.

"Will Monsieur please come to the drawing room."

He followed the white butterfly, saying over to himself as he went: "Léa's not alone. She's laughing. She can't be alone. So long as it's not my mother." Beyond an open door, he was being welcomed by rosy pink daylight and he waited, standing there, for the rebirth of the world heralded by this dawn.

A woman was writing at a small table, facing away from him. Chéri was able to distinguish a broad back and the padded cushion of a fat neck beneath a head of thick gray vigorous hair, cut short like his mother's. "So I was right, she's not alone. But who on earth can this good woman be?"

"And, at the same time, write down your masseur's address for me, Léa, and his name. You know what I'm like about names. . . ."

These words came from a woman dressed in black, also seated, and Chéri felt a preliminary tremor of expectation running through him: "Then . . . where is Léa?"

The gray-haired lady turned round, and Chéri received the full impact of her blue eyes.

"Oh, good heavens, child—it's you!"

He went forward as in a dream, and kissed an outstretched hand.

"Monsieur Frédéric Peloux—Princess Cheniaguine."

Chéri bent over and kissed another hand, then took a seat.

"Is he your . . . ?" queried the lady in black, referring to him with as much freedom as if he had been a deaf-mute.

Once again the great peal of girlish laughter rang out, and

Chéri sought for the source of this laugh here, there, and everywhere—anywhere but in the throat of the gray-haired woman.

"No, no, he isn't! Or rather, he isn't any longer, I should say. Valérie, come now, what are you thinking of?"

She was not monstrous, but huge, and loaded with exuberant buttresses of fat in every part of her body. Her arms, like rounded thighs, stood out from her hips on plump cushions of flesh just below her armpits. The plain skirt and the nondescript long jacket, opening on a linen blouse with a jabot, proclaimed that the wearer had abdicated, was no longer concerned to be a woman, and had acquired a kind of sexless dignity.

Léa was now standing between Chéri and the window, and he was not horrified at first by her firm, massive, almost cubic, bulk. When she moved to reach a chair, her features were revealed, and he began to implore her with silent entreaties, as though faced with an armed lunatic. Her cheeks were red and looked overripe, for she now disdained the use of powder, and when she laughed her mouth was packed with gold. A healthy old woman, in short, with sagging cheeks and a double chin, well able to carry her burden of flesh and freed from restraining stays.

"Tell me, child, where have you sprung from? I can't say I think you're looking particularly well."

She held out a box of cigarettes to Chéri, smiling at him from blue eyes which had grown smaller, and he was frightened to find her so direct in her approach, and as jovial as an old gentleman. She called him "child," and he turned away his eyes, as though she had let slip an indecent word. But he exhorted himself to be patient, in the vague hope that this first picture would give place to a shining transfiguration.

The two women looked him over calmly, sparing him neither goodwill nor curiosity.

"He's got rather a look of Hernandez . . . " said Valérie Cheniaguine.

"Oh, I don't see that at all," Léa protested. "Ten years ago perhaps . . . and, anyhow, Hernandez had a much more pronounced jaw!"

"Who's that?" Chéri asked, with something of an effort.

"A Peruvian who was killed in a motor accident about six months ago," said Léa. "He was living with Maximilienne. It made her very unhappy."

"Didn't prevent her finding consolation," said Valérie.

"Like anyone else," Léa said. "You wouldn't have wished her to die of it, surely?"

She laughed afresh, and her merry blue eyes disappeared, lost behind wide cheeks bulging with laughter. Chéri turned away his head and looked at the woman in black. She had brown hair and an ample figure, vulgar and feline like thousands and thousands of women from the south. She seemed in disguise, so very carefully was she dressed as a woman in good society. Valérie was wearing what had long been the uniform of foreign princesses and their ladies—a black tailor-made of undistinguished cut, tight in the sleeve, with a blouse of extremely fine white batiste, showing signs of strain at the breast. The pearl buttons, the famous necklace, the high stiff whalebone collar, everything about Valérie was as royal as the name she legitimately bore. Like royalty, too, she wore stockings of medium quality, flat-heeled walking shoes and expensive gloves, embroidered in black and white.

From the cold and calculating way she looked him over, Chéri might have been a piece of furniture. She went on with her criticisms and comparisons at the top of her voice.

"Yes, yes, there is something of Hernandez, I promise you. But, to hear Maximilienne today, Hernandez might never have existed . . . now that she has made quite certain of her famous Amerigo. And yet! And yet! I know what I'm talking about. I've seen him, her precious Amerigo. I'm just back from Deauville. I saw the pair of them!"

"No! Do tell us!"

Léa sat down, overflowing the whole armchair. She had acquired a new trick of tossing back her thick gray hair; and at each shake of the head, Chéri saw a quivering of the lower part of her face, which looked like Louis XVI's. Ostensibly, she was giving Valérie her full attention, but several times Chéri noticed a mischievous faltering in one of the little shrunken blue eyes, as they sought to catch those of the unexpected visitor.

"Well, then," Valérie started on her story, "she had hidden him in a villa miles outside Deauville, at the back of beyond. But that did not suit Amerigo at all—as you will readily understand, Monsieur!—and he grumbled at Maximilienne. She was cross, and said: 'Ah! that's what the matter is—you want to be on view to the world and his wife, and so you shall be!' So she telephoned to reserve a table at the Normandy for the following evening. Everyone knew this an hour later, and so I booked a table as well, with Becq d'Ambez and Zahita. And we said to ourselves: 'We're going to be allowed to see this marvel at last!' On the stroke of nine there was Maximilienne, all in white and pearls, and Amerigo. . . . Oh, my dear, what a disappointment! Tall, yes, that goes without saying . . . in point of fact, rather too tall. You know what I always say about men who are too tall. I'm still waiting to be shown one, just one, who is well put together. Eyes, yes, eyes, I've got nothing to say against his eyes. But—from here to there, don't you see (she was pointing to her own face), from here to there, something about the cheeks which is too rounded, too soft, and the ears set too low. . . . Oh, a very great disappointment. And holding himself as stiff as a poker."

"You're exaggerating," said Léa. "The cheeks—well what about cheeks?—they aren't so very important. And, from here to there, well really it's beautiful, it's noble; the eyelashes, the bridge of the nose, the eyes, the whole thing is really too beautiful! I'll grant you the chin: that will quickly run to flesh. And the feet are too small, which is ridiculous in a boy of that height."

"No, there I don't agree with you. But I certainly noticed that the thigh was far too long in proportion to the leg, from here to there."

They went on to thrash out the question, weighing up, with a wealth of detail and point by point, every portion of the fore and hind quarters of this expensive animal.

"Judges of pedigree fat cattle," Chéri thought. "The right place for them is the Commissariats."

"Speaking of proportions," Léa continued, "you'll never come across anything to touch Chéri. . . . You see, Chéri, you've come at just the right moment. You ought to blush. Valérie, if you can remember what Chéri was like only six, or say seven years ago . . ."

"But certainly, of course, I remember clearly. And Monsieur has not changed so very much, after all. . . . And you were so proud of him!"

"No," said Léa.

"You weren't proud of him?"

"No," said Léa with perfect calm, "I was in love with him."

She maneuvered the whole of her considerable body in his direction, and let her gay glance rest upon Chéri, quite innocently. "It's true I was in love with you, very much in love, too."

He lowered his eyes, stupidly abashed before these two women, the stouter of whom had just proclaimed so serenely that she and he had been lovers. Yet at the same time the voluptuous and almost masculine tone of Léa's voice besieged his memory, torturing him unbearably.

"You see, Valérie, how foolish a man can look when reminded of a love which no longer exists? Silly boy, it doesn't upset me in the least to think about it. I love my past. I love my present. I'm not ashamed of what I've had, and I'm not sad because I have it no longer. Am I wrong, child?"

He uttered a cry, almost as if someone had trodden on his big toe. "No, no, of course not! The very reverse!"

"It's charming to think you have remained such good friends," said Valérie.

Chéri waited for Léa to explain that this was his first visit to her for five years, but she just gave a good-humored laugh and winked with a knowing air. He felt more and more upset. He did not know how to protest, how to shout out loud that he laid no claim to the friendship of this colossal woman, with the cropped hair of an elderly cellist—that, had he but known, he would never have come upstairs, never crossed her threshold, set foot on her carpet, never collapsed in the cushioned armchair, in the depths of which he now lay defenseless and dumb.

"Well, I must be going," Valérie said. "I don't mean to wait for crush hour in the Métro, I can tell you."

She rose to face the strong light, and it was kind to her Roman features. They were so solidly constructed that the approach of her sixtieth year had left them unharmed: the cheeks were touched up in the old-fashioned way, with an even layer of white powder, and the lips with a red that was almost black and looked oily.

"Are you going home?" Léa asked.

"Of course I am. What d'you suppose my little skivvy would get up to if left to herself!"

"Are you still pleased with your new flat?"

"It's a dream! Especially since the iron bars were put across the windows. And I've had a steel grid fixed over the pantry fanlight, which I had forgotten about. With my electric bells and my burglar alarms . . . Ouf! It's been long enough before I could feel at all safe!"

"And your old house?"

"Bolted and barred. Up for sale. And the pictures in store. My little entresol flat is a gem for the eighteen hundred francs it costs me. And no more servants looking like hired assassins. You remember those two footmen? The thought of them still gives me the creeps!"

"You took much too black a view, my dear."

"You can't realize, my poor friend, without having been through it all. Monsieur, delighted to have met you. . . . No, don't you move, Léa."

She enfolded them both in her velvety barbaric gaze, and was gone. Chéri followed her with his eyes until she reached the door, yet he lacked the courage to follow her example. He remained where he was, all but snuffed out by the conversation of these two women who had been speaking of him in the past tense, as though he were dead. But now Léa was coming back into the room, bursting with laughter. "Princess Cheniaguine! Sixty millions! and a widow!—and she's not in the least bit happy. If that can be called enjoying life, it's not my idea of it, you know!"

She clapped her hand on her thigh as if it were a horse's crupper.

"What's the matter with her?"

"Funk. Blue funk, that's all. She's not the sort of woman who knows how to carry such wealth. Cheniaguine left her everything. But one might say that it would have done her less harm if he'd taken her money instead of leaving her his. You heard what she said?"

She subsided into the depths of a well-upholstered armchair, and Chéri hated to hear the gentle sigh of its cushions as they took the weight of her vast bulk. She ran the tip of her finger along the grooved molding of the chair, blew away the few specks of dust, and her face fell.

"Ah! things are not at all what they were, not even servants. Eh?"

He felt that he had lost color, and that the skin round his mouth was growing tighter, as during a severe frost. He fought back an overwhelming impulse to burst out in rancor mingled with entreaties. He longed to cry out loud: "Stop! Show me your real self! Throw off your disguise! You must be somewhere behind it, since it's your voice I hear. Appear in your true colors! Arise as a creature reborn, with your hair newly hennaed this morning, your face freshly powdered: put on your long stays again, the blue dress with its delicate jabot, the scent like a meadow that was so much a part of you. In these new surroundings I search for it in vain! Leave all this behind, and come away to Passy—never mind the showers—Passy with its dogs and its birds, and in the Avenue Bugeaud we'll be sure to find Ernest polishing the brass bars on your front door." He shut his eyes, utterly worn out.

"And now, my child, I'm going to tell you something for

your own good. What you need is to have your urine tested. Your color's shocking and you've got that pinched look round your lips—sure signs, both of them: you're not taking proper care of your kidneys."

Chéri opened his eyes again, and they took their fill of this placid epitome of disaster seated in front of him. Heroically he said: "D'you really think so? It's quite possible."

"You mean, it's certain. And then, you've not got enough flesh on you. . . . It's no use telling me that the best fighting cocks are scraggy. You could do with a good ten pounds more on you."

"Give them to me," he said with a smile. But he found his cheeks singularly recalcitrant and opposed to smiling, almost as though his skin had stiffened with age.

Léa burst into a peal of happy laughter, and Chéri tasted a pleasure which he could not have borne for long; he listened again to its full and rounded tones, the very laugh which in the old days used to greet some outrageous impertinence on the part of the "naughty little boy."

"That I could well afford! I've certainly been putting on weight, haven't I? Eh? Look . . . here . . . would you believe it? . . . and again here!"

She lit a cigarette, exhaled a double jet of smoke through her nostrils, and shrugged her shoulders. "It's age!"

The word flew out of her mouth so lightly that it gave Chéri a sort of extravagant hope. "Yes: she's only joking. In a flash she'll reappear as her real self." For an instant she seemed to take in the meaning of the look he gave her.

"I've changed a lot, haven't I, child? Fortunately, it doesn't much matter. As for you, I don't like the look of you at all. . . . You've been fluttering your wings too much, as we used to say in the old days. Eh?"

He detested this new "Eh?" with which she peppered her sentences so freely. But he stiffened at each interrogation, and each time mastered his rising excitement, preferring to remain in ignorance of both its reason and its aim.

"I don't ask whether you have any troubles at home. In the

first place, it's none of my business; and besides, I know your wife as if I were her mother."

He listened to the sound of her voice without paying much attention. He noticed, above all, that when she stopped smiling or laughing, she ceased to belong to any assignable sex. Despite her enormous breasts and crushing backside, she seemed by virtue of age altogether virile and happy in that state.

"And I know your wife to be thoroughly capable of making a man happy."

He was powerless to hide his inward laughter, and Léa quickly went on to say.

"What I said was 'a man,' and not 'any man.' Here you are in my house, without a word of warning. You've not come, I take it, just to gaze into my beautiful eyes, eh?"

She turned on Chéri those once "beautiful blue eyes," now so diminished, marbled with tiny red veins, quizzical, neither kind nor unkind, alert and bright certainly, but . . . but where was now the limpid freshness that had laved their whites with palest blue? Where the contour of their orbs, with the roundness of fruit, breast, or hemisphere, and blue as a land watered by many a river?

Jestingly, he said, "Pooh! aren't you sharp! A real detective!" And it amazed him to find that he had fallen into such a carefree posture, with his legs crossed, like a handsome young man with bad manners. For inwardly he was watching his other self, hopelessly distracted and on his knees, waving his arms, baring his breast, and shrieking incoherently.

"I'm not a particularly stupid woman. But you must admit that you don't present me today with a very difficult problem!"

She drew in her chin and its lower folds spread over her neck: the kneeling ghost of his other self bowed its head like a man who has received a death blow.

"You show every known sign of suffering from the disease of your generation. No, no, let me go on. Like all your soldier friends, you're looking everywhere for your paradise, eh! the paradise they owe you as a war hero: your own special Victory Parade, *your* youth, *your* lovely women. . . . They owe you all that and more, for they promised you everything, and, dear God, you deserved it. And what do you find? A decent ordinary life. So you go in for nostalgia, listlessness, disillusion, and neurasthenia. Am I wrong?"

"No," said Chéri, for he was thinking that he would give his little finger to stop her talking.

Léa clapped him on the shoulder, letting her hand with its large rings rest there. As he bent his head down toward it, he could feel on his cheek the heat of this heavy hand.

"Oh!" Léa continued, raising her voice. "You're not the only one! I've come across dozens of boys, since the war ended, exactly in your state of . . ."

"Where?" Chéri interrupted.

The suddenness of the interruption and its aggressive character put an end to Léa's parsonic eloquence. She withdrew her hand.

"They're to be met with everywhere, my child. Is it possible to be so vain? You seem to think you're unique because you find the postwar world insipid. Don't flatter yourself to that extent!"

She gave a low chuckle, and a toss to her sportive gray hair, and then a self-important smile like a judge who has a nice taste in wine. "And you do flatter yourself, you know, always imagining that you're the only one of your kind."

She took a step back and narrowed her gaze, adding, perhaps a little vindictively: "You were unique only for . . . for a time."

Behind this veiled but carefully chosen insult, Chéri discovered something of her femininity at last. He sat bolt upright, delighted to find himself suffering less acutely. But by this time Léa had reverted to her milk and honey.

"But you didn't come here to have that said about you. Did you make up your mind on the spur of the moment?"

"Yes," said Chéri.

He could have wished that this monosyllable might have been the last word between the two of them. Shyly, he let his gaze wander to all the things that surrounded Léa. From the nearest plate he took a dry cake shaped like a curved tile, and then put it back, convinced that it would turn to brick-red grit in his mouth were he to take a bite out of it. Léa noticed this action, and the painful way he swallowed his saliva.

"Tut, tut, so we're suffering from nerves, are we? Peeky chin, and dark lines under the eyes. That's a pretty state of affairs!"

He closed his eyes, and like a coward decided to listen and not look.

"Listen to me, child, I know a little restaurant in the Avenue des Gobelins. . . ."

He looked up at her, in the full hope that she was going mad, that in this way he would be able to forgive her for both looking and behaving like an old woman.

"Yes, I know a little restaurant . . . Let me speak! Only, you must be quick, before the smart set and the newspapers take it into their heads to make it fashionable, and the good woman herself is replaced by a chef. She does all the cooking at present, and, my dear . . ." She brought thumb and forefinger together on the tip of her lips, and blew an imitation kiss. Chéri turned away to look out of the window, where the shadow thrown by a branch flicked at the steady shaft of sunlight, impatiently but at regular intervals, much as a bent reed or river plant appears to strike at the ripples of a regularly flowing current.

"What an odd sort of conversation . . ." he ventured in strained tones.

"No more odd than your presence in my house," Léa snapped back at him.

With a wave of the hand he made it clear that he wanted peace, only peace, with as few words spoken as possible, and preferably none at all. He felt defeated in face of this elderly woman's boundless reserves of energy and appetite. Léa's quick blood was now rising and turning her bulging neck and her ears to purple. "She's got a crop like an old hen," he thought, with something of his old enjoyment of cruelty.

"And that's the truth!" she hurled at him excitedly. "You

drag yourself round here, for all the world like an apparition, and when I do my best to find some way of putting things to rights, I who, when all's said and done, do happen to know you rather well . . ."

He smiled at her despondently, "And how in the world should she know me? When far shrewder people than she, and even than I myself . . ."

"A certain kind of sickness of the soul, my child, of disillusion, is just a question of stomach. Yes, yes, you may laugh!" He was not laughing, but she might well think he was. "Romanticism, nerves, distaste for life: stomach. The whole lot, simply stomach. Love itself! If one wished to be perfectly sincere, one would have to admit there are two kinds of love—well-fed and ill-fed. The rest is pure fiction. If only I knew how to write, or to make speeches, my child, what things I could say about that! Oh, of course, it wouldn't be anything new, but I should know what I was talking about, and that would be a change from our present-day writers."

Something worse than this obsession with the kitchen was upsetting Chéri: the affectation, the false tone of voice, the almost studied joviality. He suspected Léa of putting on an act of hearty and sybaritic geniality, just as a fat actor, on the stage, plays "jovial" characters because he has developed a paunch.

As though defiantly, she rubbed her shiny, almost blotchy red nose with the back of her first finger, and fanned the upper part of her body with the aid of the two revers of her long jacket. In so doing, she was altogether too cheerfully inviting Chéri to sit in judgment on her appearance, and she even ran her hand through her thick gray locks as she shook them free of her head.

"Do you like my hair short?"

He deigned to reply only by a silent shake of the head, just like someone brushing aside an idle argument.

"Weren't you saying something just now about a little restaurant in the Avenue des Gobelins . . . ?"

It was now her turn to brush aside an irrelevance. She was

beginning to understand, and he could see from the quivering of her nostrils that at last she was piqued. His animal instincts, which had been shocked into dullness, were now on the alert and it was as though a weight had been lifted from his mind. He intended somehow to find a way past this shameless flesh, the graying curls and "merry friar" joviality, and reach the being concealed behind them, to whom he was coming back, as to the scene of a crime. He remained close to this buried treasure, burrowing toward it spontaneously. "How in the world did old age come upon her? All of a sudden, on waking up one morning? or little by little? And this surplus fat, this extra avoirdupois, under the weight of which armchairs groan? Was it some sudden shock that brought about this change and unsexed her? Could it, perhaps, have been grief on my account?" But he asked these questions of no one but himself, and without voicing them. "She is piqued. She's on the way to understanding me. She's just going to tell me. . . ."

He watched her rise to her feet, walk over to the bureau, and start to tidy the papers lying on the open hinged flap. He noticed that she was holding herself more upright than when he had first entered the room, and that, under his following eye, she straightened her back still more. He accepted the fact that she was really colossal, her body seeming to run absolutely straight from armpit to hip. Before turning round again to face Chéri, she arranged a white silk scarf tightly round her neck, despite the heat of the room. He heard her take a deep breath, before she came toward him with the slow rolling gait of a ponderous animal.

She smiled at him. "I am not doing my duty as a hostess, it would seem. It's not very polite to welcome someone by giving them advice, especially useless advice."

From under a fold of her white scarf peeped insinuatingly a twisting, coiling, resplendent string of pearls, which Chéri at once recognized.

Held captive beneath the translucent skin, the seven colors of the rainbow flickered with some secret fire of their own all over the surface of each precious sphere. Chéri recognized the pearl with a dimple, the slightly egg-shaped pearl, and the biggest pearl of the string, distinguishable by its unique pink. "These pearls, these at least, are unchanged! They and I remain unchanged."

"So you've still got your pearls," he said.

She was astonished by the foolish phrase, and looked as though she wanted to interpret it.

"Yes, in spite of the war. Are you thinking that I could, or should, have sold them? Why should I have sold them?"

"Or 'for whom?' " he answered jokingly, in a tired voice.

She could not restrain a rapid glance toward the bureau and its scattered papers; and Chéri, in his turn, felt he knew the thought behind it, guessing that it was aimed at some yellowish postcard-photograph, probably the frightened features of a beardless boy in uniform. Disdainfully, he considered this imaginary face and said to himself, "That's none of my concern," adding a moment later, "But what is there here that does concern me?"

The agitation which he had brought in his heart was now excited by everything around him; everything added to it—the setting sun, the cries of insect-chasing swallows, and the ember-glowing shafts of light stabbing through the curtains. He remembered that Léa carried with her wherever she went this incandescent rose-pink, as the sea, on its ebb tide, carries with it far out from shore the earthy smells of pastures and new-mown hay.

No word passed between them for a while, and they were kept in countenance by pretending to listen to the clear fresh notes of a child singing. Léa had not sat down again. Standing massively in front of him, she carried her irretrievable chin higher than before, and betrayed some vague distress by the frequent fluttering of her eyelids.

"Am I making you late? Have you to go out this evening? Do you want to dress?" The questions were abrupt, and forced Léa to look at Chéri.

"Dress? Good Lord, and in what do you wish me to dress? I *am* dressed—irrevocably—once and for all."

She laughed her incomparable laugh, starting on a high note and descending the scale by leaps of equal interval till she got to the deep musical reaches reserved for sobs and amorous moans. Chéri unconsciously raised a hand in supplication.

"Dressed for life, I tell you! And how convenient that is! Blouses, fine linen, and this uniform on top, and here I am in full fig. Equally ready for dinner either at Montagné's or somewhere modest, ready for the cinema, for bridge, or for a stroll in the Bois."

"And what about love—which you're forgetting to mention?"

"Oh, child!"

She blushed and, though her face was dark with the chronic red of sufferers from arthritis, the blush could not be concealed. Chéri, after the first caddish satisfaction of having said something outrageous, was seized with shame and remorse at the sight of this maidenly reaction.

"I was only joking," he said, in some confusion. "Have I gone too far?"

"Of course not. But you know very well I have never cared for certain kinds of impropriety or for jokes that are not really funny."

She strove to control her voice, but her face revealed that she was hurt, and every coarsened feature gave signs of a distress that could perhaps be outraged modesty.

"Dear God, if she takes it into her head to cry!" and he imagined the catastrophic effect of tears coursing down each cheek into the single deep ravine near the mouth, and of her eyelids reddened by the salt of tears.

He hastened to intercept: "No, no, you mustn't think that! How could you! I never meant . . . Please, Léa. . . ."

From her quick reaction he realized suddenly that this was the first time he had spoken her name. Proud, as in the old days, of her self-control, she gently stopped him.

"Don't worry, child. I'm not offended. But I've only got you here for a few minutes, so don't spoil them by saying anything I shouldn't care to remember."

Her gentle tone left him cold, and her actual words seemed

offensively tactful to him. "Either she's lying, or she really has become the sort of person she pretends. Peace, purity, and the Lord knows what! She might as well wear a ring in her nose! Peace of heart, guzzling, and the cinema. . . . Lies, lies, all lies! She wants to make me think that women find growing old comfortable, positively enjoyable. How can she expect *me* to swallow that? Let her bore anyone else she likes with her fine talk about how cozy life is, and the little restaurants with the most delicious country dishes. I'm not having any! Before I could toddle, I knew all there is to know about reducing. I was *born* among aging beauties! All my life I've watched them, my painted pixies, squabbling about their wrinkles, and, well into their fifties, scratching each other's eyes out over some wretched gigolo!"

"You sit there saying nothing, and I'm not used to it anymore. I keep on thinking that there's something you want to say to me."

On her feet, separated from Chéri by an occasional table with a decanter and port glasses, she made no effort to defend herself against the severe inspection to which she was being subjected; but from the almost invisible tremors that passed over her body, Chéri noted the muscular effort required to keep in her spreading stomach. "How many times must she have put on her full-length corset again, left it off, then valiantly put it on again, before abandoning it forever? . . . How often of a morning must she have varied the shades of her face powder, rubbed a new rouge on her cheeks, massaged her neck with cold cream and a small lump of ice tied up in a handkerchief, before becoming resigned to the varnished hide that now shines on her cheeks!" Impatience alone, perhaps, had made her tremble, yet this faint tremor led him to expect—so stubbornly blind was he to reality—some miraculous new blossoming, some complete metamorphosis.

"Why don't you say something?" Léa persisted.

Little by little she was losing her poise, though she was careful not to move. She was playing with her rope of large pearls, knotting and unknotting, round her big well-manicured and wrinkled fingers, their luminous, indescribably bedewed and everlasting luster.

"Perhaps it's simply because she's frightened of me," Chéri mused. "A man who says nothing must always seem a bit cranky. She's thinking of Valérie Cheniaguine's terrors. If I put my hand out, would she scream for help? My poor Nounoune!" He lacked the courage to pronounce this name out loud, and, to protect himself from even a moment's sincerity, he spoke:

"What are you going to think of me?"

"It all depends," Léa answered guardedly. "At the moment you remind me of people who bring along a little box of cakes and leave it in the hall, saying to themselves: 'There'll be plenty of time to produce these later,' and then pick them up again when they go."

Reassured by the sound of their voices, she had begun to reason like the Léa of old, quick on the uptake, and as wily as a sharp-witted peasant. Chéri rose to his feet, walked round the table which separated him from Léa, and the daylight streaming through the pink curtains struck him full in the face. This made it easy for her to compute the passage of days and years from his features, which were all of them in danger, though still intact. There was something about so secret a falling away to tempt her pity and trouble her memory, and perhaps extract from her the word or gesture that would precipitate Chéri into a frenzy of humiliation. As he stood there, a sacrifice to the light, with eyes lowered as if he were asleep, it seemed to him this was his last chance of extorting from her one last affront, one last prayer, one final act of homage.

Nothing happened, so he opened his eyes. Once more he had to accept the true picture—in the shape of his stalwart old friend, who, prudently keeping her distance, was bestowing on him a certain degree of benevolence from small and slightly suspicious blue eyes.

Disillusioned and bewildered, he looked all over the room

for her, except in the very spot where she stood. "Where is she? Where is she? This old woman is hiding her from me. She's bored by me, and she's waiting for me to go, thinking it all an infernal nuisance, these crowding memories and this returning ghost. . . . But if by any chance I did ask for her help, if I beg her to give me back Léa . . ." Deep inside him, his kneeling double was still palpitating, like a body from which the lifeblood is being drained. With an effort of which he would never have deemed himself capable, Chéri tore himself away from this tortured image.

"I must be going," he said out loud, and he added on a note of rather cheap wit, "and I'm taking my box of cakes with me."

Léa's exuberant bosom heaved with a sigh of relief. "As you like, my child. But I'm always here, you know, if you're in any little trouble."

Though she seemed so obliging, Chéri could sense an underlying resentment. Within that vast edifice of flesh crowned with silvery thatch, femininity had for a moment reasserted itself in tones resounding with an intelligent harmony. But Chéri could not respond: like a ghost he had come, and with the shyness of a ghost he must vanish, in his own despite.

"Of course," Chéri replied, "and I thank you."

From that moment on, he knew, unerringly and spontaneously, exactly how to manage his exit. All the right words sprang to his lips, fluently, mechanically.

"You do understand, don't you, I came here today . . . why not sooner, you may ask? I know I ought to have come a long while ago. . . . But you will forgive me. . . ."

"Of course," Léa said.

"I'm even more harebrained than before the war, you know, so that . . ."

"I understand, I understand."

And because of this interruption, he thought that she must be impatient to see the last of him. A few words were exchanged during Chéri's retreat, in the intervals of bumping into some piece of furniture, crossing a strip of sunshine from the courtyard window—after the pink light in the drawing room it seemed by comparison almost blue—kissing a puffy hand bulging with rings when it was raised to his lips. Another of Léa's laughs, which broke off abruptly halfway down its usual scale, just like a fountain when the jet is turned off and the crest of the plume, suddenly bereft of its stem, falls back to earth in a myriad separate pearls. . . . The staircase seemed to glide away under Chéri's feet like a bridge connecting two dreams, and once more he was in the Rue Raynouard. Even the street was unfamiliar.

He noticed that the rosy tints of the sky were wonderfully reflected in the rain-filled gutters and on the blue backs of the low-skimming swallows. And now, because the evening was fresh, and because all the impressions he was bringing away with him were slipping back perfidiously into the recesses of his mind—there to assume their final shape and intensity—he came to believe that he had forgotten all about them, and he felt happy.

ONLY THE SOUND of an old woman's bronchial cough, as she sat over her glass of crème-de-menthe, disturbed the peace of the barroom where the murmur of the Place de l'Opéra died away, as though muffled in an atmosphere too thick to carry any eddies of sound. Chéri ordered a long drink and mopped his brow: this precaution was a carryover from the days when he had been a little boy and sat listening to the babble of female voices, as, with biblical gravity, they bandied such golden rules as: "If you want your milk of cucumber with real cucumber in it, you must make it yourself . . . " or, "Never rub the perspiration into your face when you're overheated, or the perspiration will get under your skin and ruin it."

The silence, and the emptiness of the bar, created an illusion of coolness, and at first Chéri was not conscious of the couple who, with heads bent close together across a narrow table, were lost in inaudible whisperings. After a few moments his attention was drawn to this unknown man and woman by an occasional hissing sibilant which rose above the main stream of their chatter, and by the exaggerated expressions on their faces. They looked like servants, underpaid, overworked, and patient.

He took a mouthful or two of the fizzy iced drink, leaned his head back against the yellow plush of the banquette, and was delighted to feel a slackening of the mental strain which, for the last fortnight, had been sapping his strength. The dead weight of the present had not accompanied him across the threshold of the bar, which was old-fashioned, with red walls, gilt festoons, plaster roses, and a large open hearth. The cloakroom attendant could be half-seen in her tiled kingdom, counting every stitch as she mended the linen, her white hair bowed beneath a green lamp.

A passerby dropped in. He did not trespass upon the yellow room, but took his drink standing at the bar as though to be discreet, and left without a word. The Odol odor of the crème-de-menthe was the only thing distasteful to Chéri, and he frowned in the direction of the dim old woman. Under a black and battered soft hat, he could distinguish an old face, accentuated here and there by rouge, wrinkles, kohl, and puffiness—all jumbled together—rather like a pocket into which have been popped, higgledy-piggledy, handkerchief, keys, and loose change. A vulgar old face, in short—and commonplace in its vulgarity, characterized, if at all, only by the indifference natural to a savage or a prisoner. She coughed, opened her bag, blew her nose vaguely, and replaced the seedy black reticule on the marble-topped table. It had an affinity with the hat, for it was made of the same black cracked taffeta, and equally out of fashion.

Chéri followed her every movement with an exaggerated repugnance; during the last two weeks he had been suffering, more than he could reasonably be expected to bear, from everything that was at once feminine and old. That reticule sprawling over the table almost drove him from the spot. He wanted to avert his eyes, but did nothing of the sort: they were riveted by a small sparkling arabesque, an unexpected brilliance fastened to the folds of the bag. His curiosity surprised him, but half a minute later he was still staring at the point of sparkling light, and his mind became an absolute blank. He was roused from his trance by a subconscious flash of triumphant certainty, and this gave him back the freedom to think and breathe. "I know! It's the two capital L's interlaced!"

He enjoyed a moment of calm satisfaction, not unlike the sense of security on reaching a journey's end. He actually forgot the cropped hair on the nape of that neck, the vigorous gray locks, the big nondescript coat buttoned over a bulging stomach; he forgot the contralto notes of the peal of youthful laughter—everything that had dogged him so persistently for the past fortnight, that had deprived him of any appetite for food, any ability to feel that he was alone.

"It's too good to last!" he thought. So, with a brave effort, he returned to reality. He looked more carefully at the offending object, and was able to reel off: "The two initials, set in little brilliants, which Léa had designed first for her suede bag, then for her dressing-table set of light tortoise-shell, and later for her writing paper!" Not for a moment would he admit that the monogram on the bag might represent some other name.

He smiled ironically. "Coincidence be blowed! I wasn't born yesterday! I came upon this bag by chance this evening, and tomorrow my wife will go and engage one of Léa's old footmen—again by chance. After that I shan't be able to go into a single restaurant, cinema, or tobacconist's without running up against Léa at every turn. It's my own fault. I can't complain. I ought to have left her alone."

He put some small change beside his glass, and got up before summoning the barman. He faced away from the old woman as he slipped between the two tables, holding himself in under his waistcoat, like a tomcat squeezing under a gate. This he managed so adroitly that the edge of his coat only just brushed against the glass of green crème-de-menthe. Murmuring an apology, he made a dash for the glass door, to escape into the fresh air beyond. Horrified, but not really in the least surprised, he heard a voice call out after him, "Chéri!"

He had feared—known indeed—that this was coming. He turned to find that there was nothing about the raddled old ruin to help him recall her name; but he made no second attempt to escape, realizing that everything would be explained.

"Don't you recognize me? You don't? But how could you? More women were aged by the war than men were killed by it and that's a fact. All the same, it's not for me to complain; I didn't risk losing anyone in the war. . . . Eh! Chéri! . . ."

She laughed; and recognition was complete, for he saw that what he had taken for decrepitude was only poverty and natural indifference. Now that she was holding herself upright and laughing, she did not look more than her age—sixty or thereabouts—and the hand with which she sought Chéri's was certainly not that of a doddering old grandmother.

"The Pal!" Chéri murmured, almost in tones of admiration.

"Are you really pleased to see me?"

"Oh, yes. . . ."

He was not telling a lie. He was gaining assurance step by step and thinking, "It's only her . . . Poor old Pal . . . I'd begun to fear . . . "

"Will you have a glass of something, Pal?"

"Just a whiskey and soda, my pretty. My! haven't you kept your looks!"

He swallowed the bitter compliment which she tossed to him from the peaceful fringes of old age.

"And decorated, too," she added out of pure politeness. "Oh! I knew all about it, you may be sure! We all knew about it."

The ambiguous plural failed to wrest a smile from Chéri, and the Pal thought she had shocked him.

"When I say 'we,' I'm speaking of those of us who were your real friends—Camille de La Berche, Léa, Rita, and me. You may be sure Charlotte would never have told me a word about it. As far as she's concerned, I don't exist. But—and I may as well say so—she doesn't exist for me, either." She stretched out across the table a pale hand that had long forgotten the light of day. "You must understand that Charlotte will never again be anything to me but the woman who contrived to get poor little Rita arrested and detained for twenty-four hours. . . . Poor Rita, who had never known a word of German. Was it Rita's fault, I ask you, if she happened to be Swiss?"

"I know, I know. I know the whole story," Chéri broke in precipitately.

The Pal raised her huge dark watery eyes toward him, full of inveterate complicity and a compassion that was always misplaced. "Poor kid," she sighed. "I understand you. Forgive me. Ah! you've certainly had your cross to bear!"

He questioned her with a look, no longer accustomed to the overstatements that added a rich funereal tone to the Pal's vocabulary, and he feared she might be going to talk to him about the war. But she was not thinking of the war. Perhaps she never had, for it is the concern of two generations only.

She went on to explain. "Yes, I was saying that to have such a mother must have been a heavy cross to bear for a son like you—for a boy, that's to say, with a blameless life, both before marriage and after! A nice, quiet boy and all that; not one to sow his wild oats all over the place, or to squander his inheritance."

She wagged her head, and bit by bit he began to piece together the past. He rediscovered her, though she had the mask of a ravaged tragedy queen. Her old age was without nobility, yet bore no signs of illness, no telltale trace that betrayed her addiction to opium. The drug is merciful to those unworthy of it.

"Have you quite given up the pipe?" asked Chéri sharply.

She raised a white untended hand. "What do you suppose? That kind of foolishness is all very well when you're not all on your own. In the days when I used to shock you young men, yes. . . . You remember when you used to come back at nights? Ah! you were very fond of that. . . . 'Dear old Pal,' you used to say to me, 'just let me have another little pipeful, and pack it well!' "

Without turning a hair, he accepted this humble flattery, as he might from an old retainer, who fibs in order to fawn. He smiled knowingly, and scrutinized the folds of black tulle round her neck, looking in the shadows under the faded hat for a necklace of large fake pearls.

Almost mechanically and sip by sip, he drank the whiskey which had been put in front of him by mistake. He did not care for spirits as a rule, but this evening he enjoyed the whiskey, for it helped him to smile easily and softened to his touch unpolished surfaces and rough materials; it enabled him to listen kindly to an old woman for whom the present did not exist. They met again on the further side of the superfluous war years and the young, importunate dead: the Pal spanned the gap by throwing across to Chéri a bridge of names—names of old men who bore charmed lives, of old women revitalized for the struggle or turned to stone in their ultimate shape, never to alter again. She recounted in detail a hard-luck story of 1913, some unhappiness that had taken place before August 1914, and something trembled in her voice when she spoke of La Loupiote—a woman now dead—"The very week of your wedding, dear boy! you see what a coincidence it was? the hand of Fate was upon us, indeed"—dead after four years of a pure and peaceful friendship.

"We slanged each other day in, day out, dear boy, but only in front of other people. Because, don't you see, it gave them the impression that we were 'a couple.' Who would have believed it, if we hadn't gone for each other hammer and tongs? So we called each other the most diabolical names, and the onlookers chuckled: 'Have you ever seen such a devoted pair?' Dear boy, I'll tell you something else that will knock you flat—surely you must have heard about the will Massau was supposed to have made. . . ."

"What Massau?" Chéri asked, languidly.

"Oh, come. You knew him as well as you know yourself! The story of the will—so called—that he handed to Louise MacMillar. It was in 1909, and at the time I am speaking of, I was one of the Gérault pack, his pack of 'faithful hounds'—and there were five of us he fed every evening at *La Belle Meunière* down at Nice; but on the Promenade des Anglais, you must remember, we only had eyes for you—dolled up in white like an English baby, and Léa all in white as well. . . . Ah! what a pair you made! You were the sensation—a miracle, straight from the hands of the Creator! Gérault used to tease Léa: 'You're far too *young*, girlie, and what's worse you're too proud. I shan't take you on for fifteen or twenty years at least. . . . ' And to think that such a man had to be taken from us! Not a tear at his funeral that wasn't genuine, the whole nation was in mourning. And now let me get on with the story of the will. . . ."

Chéri was deluged with a perfect flood of incidents, a tide of bygone regrets and harmless resurrections, all declaimed with the ease and rapidity of a professional mourner. The two of them formed a symmetrical pattern as they leaned toward each other. The Pal lowered her voice when she came to the dramatic passages, giving out a sudden laugh or exclamation; and he saw in one of the looking glasses how closely they seemed to resemble the whispering couple whose place they had taken. He got up, finding it imperative to put an end to this resemblance. The barman imitated his movement, but from afar, like a discreet dog when its master comes to the end of a visit. "Ah! well . . . yes . . . " said the Pal, "well, I'll finish the rest another time."

"After the next war," said Chéri, jokingly. "Tell me, those two capital letters. . . . Yes, the monogram in little brilliants. . . . It's not yours, Pal?"

He pointed at the black bag with the tip of his forefinger, extending it slowly while withdrawing his body, as though the bag were alive.

"Nothing escapes you," the Pal said in admiration. "You're quite right. She gave it to me, of course. She said to me: 'Such bits of finery are far too frivolous for me nowadays!' She said: 'What the devil do you suppose I'd be doing with those mirrors and powder and things, when I've a great face like a country policeman's?' She made me laugh. . . ."

To stem the flood, Chéri pushed the change from his hundred franc note toward the Pal. "For your taxi, Pal."

They went out onto the pavement by the tradesman's entrance, and Chéri saw from the fainter lamplight that night was coming on.

"Have you not got your motor?"

"My motor? No. I walked; it does me good."

"Is your wife in the country?"

"No. Her hospital keeps her in Paris."

The Pal nodded her invertebrate hat. "I know. She's a big-hearted woman. Her name's been put forward for a decoration, I understand from the Baroness."

"What?"

"Here, stop that taxi for me, dear boy, the closed one. . . . And Charlotte's going big guns in her support; she knows people round Clemenceau. It will make up a little for the story about Rita . . . a little, not very much. She's as black as sin itself, is Charlotte, my boy."

He pushed her into the oven of the taxi, where she sank back and became enveloped in the shadow. She ceased to exist. It was as though he had never met her, now that he heard her voice no longer. He took stock of the night, filling his lungs with the dust-laden air that foretold another scorching day. He pictured, as in a dream, that he would wake up at home, among gardens watered every evening, among the scent of Spanish honeysuckle and the call of birds, resting alongside his wife's straight hips. . . . But the Pal's voice rose up from the depths of the taxi: "Two hundred and fourteen, Avenue de Villiers! Remember my address, Chéri! And you know that I often dine at the *Giraffe*, Avenue de Wagram, don't you, if ever you should want me. . . . You know, if ever you should be looking for me."

"That's really the limit," thought Chéri, lengthening his step. " 'If I should ever be looking for her.' I ask you! Next time I come across her, I'll turn round and walk the other way."

Cooled off and calmer, he strode without effort along the *quais* as far as the Place de l'Alma, and from there took a taxi back to the Avenue Henri-Martin. The eastern sky was already burnished with dull copper-colored tints, which seemed rather to betoken the setting of some planet than the dawn of a summer day. No clouds streaked the vault of the heavens, but a haze of particles hung heavy and motionless over Paris, and would presently flare up and smolder with the somber glow of red-hot metal. As dawn breaks, the dog days drain great cities and their suburbs of the moist pinks, floral mauves, and dewy blues that suffuse the sky above open country where plant life flourishes in profusion.

Nothing was stirring in the house when Chéri came to turn the tiny key in the lock. The flagged hall still smelled of the previous evening's dinner, and the cut branches of syringa, arranged by the armful in white vases tall enough to hide a man, filled the air with unbreathable poison. A stray gray cat slipped past him, stopped dead in the middle of the passage, and coldly inspected the intruder.

"Come here, little clerk of the Courts," Chéri called in a low voice. The cat glared at him almost insultingly and did not budge. Chéri remembered that no animal—no dog, horse or cat—had ever shown him any signs of affection. He could hear, across a span of fifteen years, Aldonza's raucous voice prophesying: "A curse lies on those from whom animals turn away." But when the cat, now wide awake, began to play with a small green chestnut, bowling it along with its front paw, Chéri smiled and went on up to his room.

He found it as dark and blue as a stage night. The dawn penetrated no further than the balcony, bedecked with well-trained roses and pelargoniums fastened with raffia. Edmée was asleep, her bare arms and toes peeping out from under a light blanket. She was lying on her side, her head inclined, one finger hooked through her pearls. In the half-light she seemed to be immersed in thought rather than sleep. Her wavy hair strayed over her cheek, and Chéri could hear no sound of her breathing.

"She's enjoying a peaceful sleep," thought Chéri. "She's dreaming of Doctor Arnaud, or the Legion of Honor, or Royal Dutch shares. She's pretty. How pretty she is! . . . Don't you worry, only another two or three hours, and you'll go to find your Doctor Arnaud. That's not so bad, is it? You'll meet again in the Avenue de l'Italie, in your beloved joint with its stink of carbolic. You'll answer 'Yes, Doctor; No, Doctor,' like a good little girl. You'll both of you put on really serious expressions; you'll jiggle with thermometers—ninety-nine point six, a hundred and two point four—and he'll take your small carbolicky paw in his great coal-tarry mitt. You're lucky, my girl, to have a romance in your life! Don't worry. I shan't deprive you of it. . . . I wouldn't mind, myself. . . ."

All of a sudden Edmée woke up with such a start that Chéri caught his breath, as though rudely interrupted in the middle of a sentence.

"It's you! It's you! Why, it *is* you after all."

"If you were expecting someone else, I offer my apologies," said Chéri, smiling at her.

"That's very clever. . . ." She sat up in bed and tossed back her hair. "What time is it? Are you getting up? Oh, no, I see you've not been to bed yet. . . . You've just come in. . . . Oh, Fred! What have you been up to this time?"

" 'This time' is a compliment. . . . If you only knew what I've been doing. . . ."

She was no longer at the stage where, hands over her ears, she besought him, "No, no! say nothing! Don't tell me!" But, faster than his wife, Chéri was leaving behind that childishly malicious period when, amidst floods of tears and stormy scenes which ended by her throwing herself into his arms in the early hours of the morning, he would draw her down with him into the deep sleep of reconciled antagonists. No more little games of that sort. . . . No more betrayals. . . . Nothing, now, but this enforced and unavowable chastity.

He chucked his dusty shoes to the other end of the room, and sat down on the soft lace-frilled sheets, offering his wife a pallid face accustomed to dissemble everything except his will to dissemble. "Smell me!" he said. "Come on! I've been drinking whiskey."

She brought her charming mouth to his, putting a hand on her husband's shoulder. "Whiskey . . . " she repeated wonderingly. "Whiskey . . . why?"

A less sophisticated woman would have asked "With whom?" and her cunning did not pass unnoticed. Chéri showed that two could play at that game by answering, "With an old pal. Do you want to hear the whole truth?"

She smiled, now caught in the dawning light which, with growing boldness, touched the edge of the bed, the looking glass, a picture frame, and then the golden scales of a fish swimming round and round in a crystal bowl.

"No, Fred, not the whole truth. Only a half-veiled truth, suitable for the small hours." At the same time, her thoughts were busy. She was certain—or nearly so—that Chéri had not been drawn away from her either by love or by lust. She let her acquiescent body fall helplessly into his arms, yet he felt on his shoulder a thin, hard hand, unrelaxed in its guarded prudence.

"The truth is," he went on, "that I don't know her name. But I gave her . . . wait a moment . . . I gave her eighty-three francs."

"Just like that, all at once! The first time you met her? It's princely!"

She pretended to yawn, and slipped softly back into the depths of the bed, as though not expecting an answer. He gave her a moment's pity; then a brilliant horizontal ray brought into sharper relief the almost naked body lying beside him, and his pity vanished.

"She's . . . she has kept her good looks. It's not fair."

She lay back, her lips parted, looking at him through half-closed eyes. He saw a gleam of the candid, calculating, uncharacteristically feminine expression that a woman bestows on the man who is going to pleasure her, and it shocked his unavowable chastity. From his superior position he returned this look with another—the uncommunicative, enigmatic look of the man who prefers to abstain. Not wishing to move away, he simply looked toward the golden daylight, the freshness of the watered garden, and the blackbirds, weaving liquid sequences of sound round the dry incessant chirps of the sparrows. Edmée could see signs of emaciation and prolonged fatigue on his features. His cheeks were blue with a day's growth of beard. She noticed that his fine hands were not clean, that his fingernails had not been near soap and water since the previous evening, and that the dark lines which accentuated the hollows under his eyes were now spreading, in the shape of crow's feet, toward his nose. This handsome young man—she decided—without collar or shoes, looked ravaged, as if he had had to spend a night in prison. Without losing his looks, he had shrunk in accordance with some mysterious scaling down, and this enabled her to regain the upper hand. She no longer invited him to join her, sat up in bed, and put a hand on his forehead.

"Ill?"

Slowly he let his attention wander back from the garden to his wife.

"What? . . . No, no, nothing's wrong with me, except I'm sleepy. So sleepy that I can hardly bring myself to go to bed—if you know what I mean. . . ."

He smiled, showing dry gums and lips colorless on the insides. But, above all, this smile betrayed a sadness that sought no remedy, modest as a poor man's suffering. Edmée was on the point of questioning him categorically, but then thought better of it.

"Get into bed," she ordered, making room for him.

"Bed? It's water I need. I feel so filthy, I can't tell you."

He just had the strength to lift up a water bottle, take a gulp from the neck, then throw off his coat, before he fell back like a log on the bed, and lay there without moving again, drained by sleep.

For some little time Edmée gazed at the half-stripped stranger lying like a drugged man beside her. Her watchful eye wandered from bluish lips to hollowed eyes, from outflung hand to forehead sealed upon a single secret. She summoned her self-control and composed her features, as though afraid the sleeper might take her by surprise. She got out of bed softly, and, before shutting out the dazzling sunlight, drew a silk counterpane to hide the outstretched untidy body looking like a burglar who had been knocked out. She arranged this so as to give the beautiful rigid features their full splendor, carefully pulling it down over the drooping hand with a slight qualm of pious disgust, as though hiding a weapon that perhaps had killed.

He never twitched a muscle—having retired for a few moments within an impregnable fastness. In any case, Edmée's hospital training had given her fingers a professional touch, which, if not exactly gentle, was competent to go straight to the required spot without touching or in any way affecting the surrounding area. She did not get back into bed; but, sitting half-naked, enjoyed the unexpected freshness of the hour when the sun rouses the winds. The long curtains stirred, as if breathing and, dependent on the breeze, stippled Chéri's sleep with fitful flecks of dark blue.

As she gazed at him, Edmée was not thinking of the wounded, or of the dead, whose peasant hands she had joined together upon coarse cotton sheets. No invalid in the grip of a nightmare, not one among the dead, had ever resembled Chéri: sleep, silence, and repose made him magnificently inhuman.

Extreme beauty arouses no sympathy. It is not the prerogative of any one country. Time's finger had touched Chéri only to make him more austere. The mind—whose task it is to curb the splendor of mankind while degrading it piecemeal—respected Chéri as an admirable temple dedicated to instinct. What could avail the Machiavellian deceit, the ardor and the cunning self-sacrifice imposed by love, against this inviolable standard-bearer of light and his untutored majesty?

Patient and, on occasion, subtle as she was, it never occurred to Edmée that the feminine appetite for possession tends to emasculate every living conquest, and can reduce a magnificent but inferior male to the status of a courtesan. Her lower-middle-class wisdom made her determined not to relinquish the gains—money, ease, domestic tyranny, marriage—acquired in so few years and rendered doubly attractive by the war.

She gazed at the limp, worn-out, almost empty-looking body. "That's Chéri," she said to herself; "yes, that's Chéri all right . . . That's how small a thing he is!" She shrugged a shoulder and added: "That's what he's reduced to, this wonderful Chéri of theirs . . ." doing her best to induce contempt for the man lying thus supine. She called up memories of rapturous nights, of languid early mornings bathed in sunlight and pleasure, and, as a result—since he had progressively grown to disdain her—she saw fit to pay but coldly vindictive homage to this body so sumptuously laid out under the pall of flowered silk and the refreshing wing of the curtains. She put one hand on the small, pointed breast set low on her slender body, and squeezed it like a pulpy fruit, as if calling this most tempting allurement of her young body to witness the injustice of his desertion. "What Chéri himself needs is doubtless something else. What he needs is . . ."

But vain were her attempts to put her scorn into words. Even a woman loses the desire and the ability to despise a man who suffers in silence and alone.

All of a sudden, Edmée felt satiated with the spectacle: the shadows thrown by the curtains, the pallor of the sleeper, and the white bed helped to invest it with the romantic coloring of death and the nether world. She jumped to her feet, strong and ready to face this world, but determined to avoid any emotional attack upon the traitor lying on the disordered bed, the absentee seeking refuge in sleep, silent, ailing, and repulsive. She was neither irritated nor unhappy. Her heart would beat more feverishly in her breast, the blood mount more quickly to her pearl-pale cheeks, only at the thought of the healthy red-haired man whom she called "dear master" or "chief" in tones of serious playfulness. Arnaud's thick gentle hands; his laugh; the points of light that sunshine or the lamp in the operating theater caused to twinkle on his red mustache; his very coat—the white surgery coat he wore and even took off in the hospital, just like an intimate garment that never passes beyond the bedroom door. . . . Edmée sprang up as though for a dance.

"That, oh yes, *that's* my life!" She gave a toss of the head that sent her hair flying out like a horse's mane, and went into the bathroom without turning around.

UNIMAGINATIVE in style, and in its very ordinary proportions, the dining room made no pretense to luxury except in the panels of yellow stuff starred with purple and green. The gray and white stucco of the surrounding walls deflected too much light on the guests, deprived already of all shade by the merciless glare of the top lighting.

A galaxy of crystal sequins shimmered with every movement of Edmée's dress. For the family dinner, Madame Peloux was still wearing her tailor-made with leather buttons, and Camille de La Berche her nurse's veil, under the cowl of which she bore a striking resemblance to Dante, only far hairier. Because it was so hot, the women spoke little: so did Chéri, because it was his habit. A warm bath followed by a cold shower had triumphed over his fatigue; but the powerful light, ricocheting upon his cheeks, accentuated their cavities, and he kept his eyes lowered, to allow the shadow from his eyebrows to fall directly over the lids.

"Tonight, Chéri doesn't look a day over sixteen," boomed the deep bass of the Baroness out of the blue.

No one took up her remark, and Chéri acknowledged it with a slight bow.

"Not for a long time," the Baroness continued, "have I seen the oval of his face so slender."

Edmée frowned imperceptibly. "I have. During the war, of course."

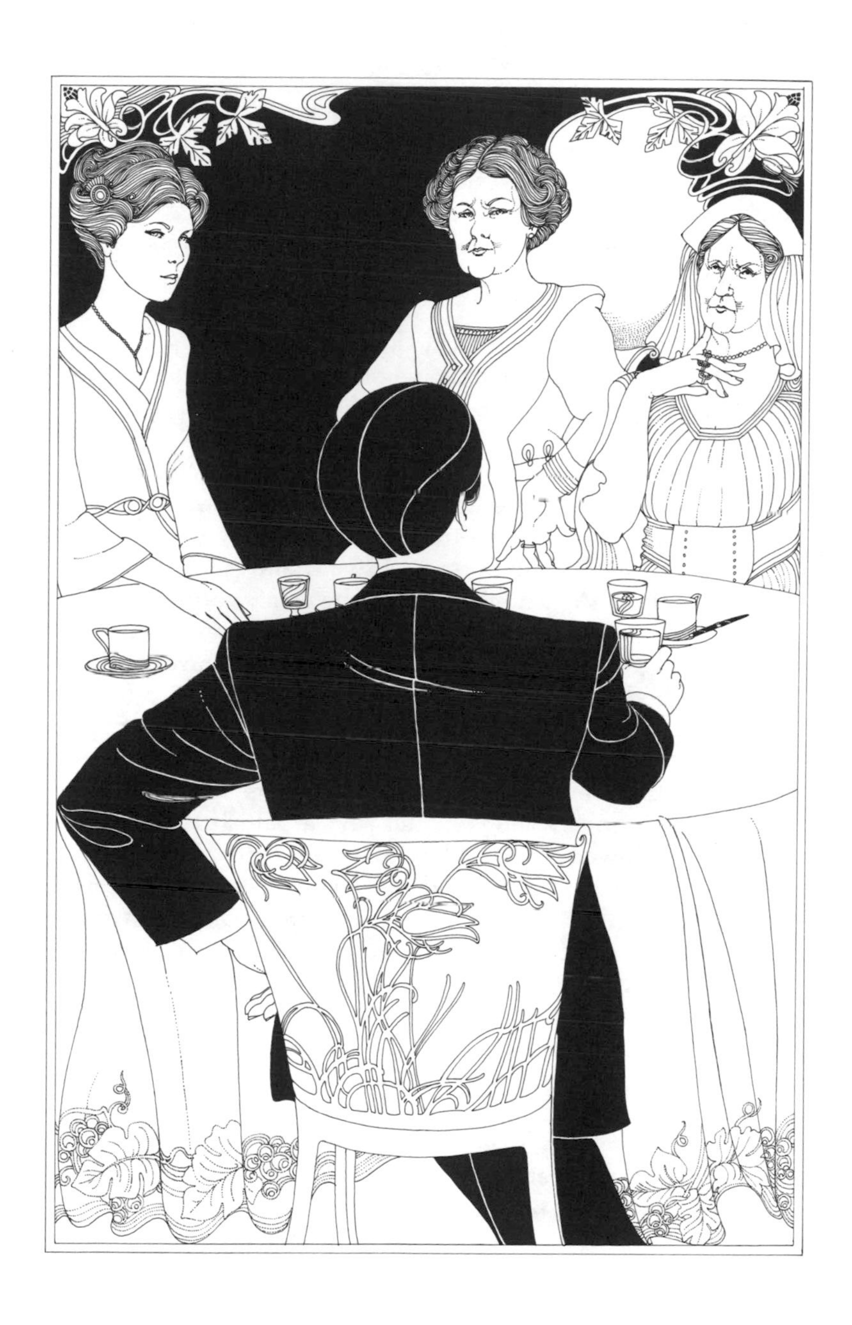

"That's true, that's true," piped Charlotte Peloux in shrill agreement. "Heavens! how worn out he looked in 1916, at Vésoul! Edmée, my dear child," she went on in the same breath, "I've seen you-know-who today, and *everything* is going along very nicely. . . . "

Edmée blushed in a docile, unbecoming manner, and Chéri raised his eyes. "You've seen who? And what's going along nicely?"

"Trousellier's pension—my little soldier who's had his right arm off. He left the hospital on June the twentieth. Your mother's taking up his case at the War Office."

She had not hesitated for words, and she let her calm golden gaze rest on Chéri, yet he knew she was lying.

"It's a question of whether he'll get his red riband. After all, poor boy, it's certainly his turn. . . ."

She was lying to him in front of two friends who knew that she was lying. "Why don't I pick up the water bottle and crash it down in the middle of them?" But he made no movement. What strength of feeling would have given him the impetus to brace his body and direct his hand?

"Abzac is leaving us in a week's time," began Madame de La Berche.

"That's not certain," Edmée took her up with an air of knowing better. "Doctor Arnaud isn't at all satisfied that he should be allowed to go off like that on his new leg. You can just see the man, liable to do any sort of silly thing, and always with the possibility of gangrene. Doctor Arnaud knows only too well that it was exactly that sort of thing, all through the war. . . ."

Chéri looked at her, and she stopped abruptly in the middle of her pointless sentence. She was fanning herself with a rose on a leafy stalk. She waved away a dish which she was offered, and put her elbows on the table. In her white dress and bare shoulders, even when sitting still, she was not exempt from a secret contentment, a self-satisfaction, which revealed her true nature. Something outrageous radiated from her soft outlines. Some tell-tale glow betrayed the woman bent on "arriving," who up till the present had met only with success.

"Edmée," Chéri concluded, "is a woman who should never grow older than twenty. How like her mother she's getting!"

The next moment the resemblance had vanished. Nothing obvious about Edmée recalled Marie-Laure: only in one respect did her daughter exhibit something of the poisonous, pink and white, impudent beauty exploited by the red-haired Marie-Laure to ensnare her victims during her palmy days—and that was in her shamelessness. Careful as she was not to shock anyone, those who still retained their native shrewdness, by instinct or from lack of education, were shocked by her all the same, as if by a second-rate racehorse, or a jewel that looked too new. The servants, as well as Chéri, were frightened of something in Edmée, whom they guessed to be more vulgar than themselves.

Authorized by Edmée, who was lighting a cigarette, the Baroness de La Berche slowly grilled the tip of her cigar before inhaling the first rapturous puff. Her white Red Cross veil fell over her manly shoulders and she looked like one of those grave-faced men who, at Christmas parties, adorn their heads with tissue-paper Phrygian caps, program-sellers' kerchiefs, or shakos. Charlotte undid the plaited leather buttons of her jacket and drew toward her a box of Abdullas; while the butler, mindful of the customs of the house, pushed within easy reach of Chéri a small conjuror's table on wheels—full of secret drawers, sliding double-bottomed compartments, and liqueurs in silver phials. Then he left the room; and there was no longer against the yellow panels the tall silhouette of an elderly Italian with a face carved out of boxwood, and crowned with white hair.

"Old Giacomo really does look an aristocrat," said the Baroness de La Berche, "and I know what I'm talking about."

Madame Peloux shrugged her shoulders, a movement that had long since ceased to lift her breasts. Her white silk blouse with a jabot sagged under the weight of her bosom, and her short, dyed, but still abundant hair glowed a livid red above large disastrous eyes and high forehead, suggesting a leader of the French Revolution.

"He's got the distinguished looks of all elderly Italians with white hair. They're all Papal Chamberlains, by the look of them, and they can write out the menu for you in Latin; but you've only to open a door and you'll find them raping a little girl of seven."

Chéri welcomed this outburst of virulence as a timely shower. His mother's malice had parted the clouds again, bringing back an atmosphere in which he could breathe. Not so long ago he had begun to enjoy discovering traces of the old Charlotte, who, from the safety of her balcony, would refer to a pretty woman passing below as "a tuppenny-ha'penny tart," and who, to Chéri's "Do you know her, then?" would reply, "No! Whatever next! Do you expect me to know that slut?" Only recently had he begun to take a confused pleasure in Charlotte's superior vitality, and, confusedly, he now preferred her to the other two creatures present; but he was unaware that this preference, this partiality, could perhaps be termed filial affection. He laughed, and applauded Madame Peloux for still being—and quite startlingly so—the woman he had known, detested, feared, and insulted. For an instant, Madame Peloux took on her authentic character in her son's eyes; that is to say, he estimated her at her proper value, a woman high-spirited, all-consuming, calculating, and at the same time rash, like a high financier; a woman capable of taking a humorist's delight in spiteful cruelty. "She's a scourge, certainly," he said to himself, "and no more. A scourge, but not a stranger." Looking at the way the points of her hair impinged upon her Jacobin forehead, he recognized a similarity to the blue-black jutting points on his own forehead, which emphasized the whiteness of his skin and the blackbird sheen of his hair.

"She's my mother all right," he thought. "No one's ever told me I'm like her, but I am." The "stranger" was sitting opposite, glimmering with the milky, veiled brilliance of a pearl. Chéri heard the name of the Duchess of Camastra thrown out by the deep voice of the Baroness, and on the stranger's face he saw a fleeting rapacity flicker and die, like the serpent of flame that suddenly flares up along a burnt vine twig before it is consumed among the embers. But she did not open her mouth, and took no part in the volley of military curses which the Baroness was firing at a hospital rival.

"They're properly in the soup, it appears, over some newfangled injection or other. Two men died within two days of being given the needle. That needs some explaining!" said Madame de La Berche with a hearty laugh.

"You've got it wrong," corrected Edmée dryly. "That's an old story of Janson-de-Sailly resuscitated."

"No smoke without fire," sighed Charlotte charitably. "Chéri, are you sleepy?"

He was dropping with fatigue, but he admired the powers of resistance of these three women: neither hard work, the Parisian summer, nor perpetual movement and jabber could put them out of action.

"The heat," he murmured laconically. He caught Edmée's eye, but she made no comment and refrained from contradicting him.

"Pooh, pooh, pooh," chanted Charlotte. "The heat! But, of course . . . Pooh, pooh, pooh."

Her eyes, which remained fixed on Chéri's, overflowed with blackmailing tenderness and complicity. As usual, she knew everything there was to be known: backstairs gossip, concierges' chatter. Perhaps Léa herself, for the pleasure of a feminine fib, of winning one last trick, had told Charlotte. The Baroness de La Berche emitted a little neigh, and the shadow of her large clerical nose covered the lower part of her face.

"God in Heaven!" swore Chéri.

His chair fell to the floor behind him, and Edmée, alert and on the watch, promptly jumped to her feet. She showed not the slightest astonishment. Charlotte Peloux and the Baroness de La Berche at once put themselves on the defensive, but in the old-fashioned way—hands clutching skirts, ready to gather them up and fly. Chéri, leaning forward with his fists on the table, was panting and turning his head to right and left, like a wild animal caught in a net.

"You, to start with, you . . ." he stammered. He pointed at Charlotte; used as she was to such scenes, she was galvanized by this filial threat in the presence of witnesses.

"What? What? What?" she barked in sharp little yelps. "You dare to insult me? a little whippersnapper like you, a wretched little whippersnapper who, were I to open my mouth . . ."

The wineglasses quivered at the sound of her piercing voice, but her words were cut short by a shriller voice: "Leave him alone!"

After three such abrupt explosions the silence seemed deafening, and Chéri, his physical dignity restored, shook himself, and a smile spread over his green face.

"I beg your pardon, Madame Peloux," he said mischievously.

She was already conferring blessings on him with eye and hand, like a champion in the ring, pacified at the end of a round.

"You're hot-blooded and no mistake!"

"He's a soldier all right," said the Baroness, as she shook hands with Edmée. "I must say good-bye, Chéri; they'll be missing me in my dugout."

She refused a lift in Charlotte's motor, and insisted on going home on foot. The tall figure, the white nurse's veil, and the glow of her cigar would strike terror at night into the heart of the fiercest footpad. Edmée accompanied the two old women as far as the front door, an exceptional act of courtesy, which allowed Chéri time to draw what conclusions he could from his wife's wary action and her diplomatic peacemaking.

He drank a glass of cold water very slowly, as he stood beneath the cataract of light, thinking the matter over and savoring his terrible loneliness.

"She defended me," he kept repeating to himself. "She defended me with no love in her heart. She protected me as she protects the garden against blackbirds, her store of sugar against thieving nurses, or her cellar against the footmen. Little doubt she knows that I went to the Rue Reynouard, and came back here, never to go there again. She's not said a word about it to me, in any case—perhaps because she doesn't care. She protected me, because it wouldn't have done for my mother to talk. She defended me with no love in her heart."

He heard Edmée's voice in the garden. She was testing his mood from afar. "You don't feel ill, Fred, do you? Would you like to go straight to bed?"

She put her head through the half-open door, and he laughed bitterly to himself: "How cautious she's being."

She saw his smile and grew bolder. "Come along, Fred. I believe I'm just as tired as you, or I wouldn't have let myself go just now. I've been apologizing to your mother."

She switched off some of the cruel light, and gathered the roses from the table cloth to put them into water. Her body, her hands, her head bending over the roses and set off by a haze of fair hair from which the heat had taken most of the crimp—everything about her might have charmed a man.

"I said *a man*—I didn't say *any man*," Léa's insidious voice kept ringing in Chéri's ears.

"I can behave as I like to her," he thought, as he followed Edmée with his eyes. "She'll never complain, she'll never divorce me; I've nothing to fear from her, not even love. I should be happy enough, if I chose."

But, at the same time, he recoiled with unspeakable repugnance from the idea of the two of them living together in a home where love no longer held sway. His childhood as a bastard, his long adolescence as a ward, had taught him that his world, though people thought of it as reckless, was governed by a code almost as narrow-minded as middle-class prejudice. In it, Chéri had learned that love is a question of money, infidelity, betrayals, and cowardly resignation. But now he was well on the way to forgetting the rules he had been taught, and to be repelled by acts of silent condescension.

He therefore ignored the gentle hand on his sleeve. And, as he walked with Edmée toward the room whence would issue no sound of endearment or reproach, he was overcome with shame, and blushed at the horror of their unspoken agreement.

HE FOUND himself out of doors, dressed for the street and hardly conscious of having put on his soft hat and light raincoat. Behind him lay the drawing room, misty with tobacco smoke; the overpowering scent of women and flowers; the cyanide smell of cherry brandy. There he had left Edmée, Doctor Arnaud, Filipesco, Atkins, and the two Kelekian girls, well-connected young women who, having done a little mild lorry driving during the war, had no use now for anything but cigars, motors, and their garage-hand friends. He had left Desmond sitting between a real estate merchant and an under secretary in the Ministry of Commerce, together with an invalided poet and Charlotte Peloux. Also a fashionable young married couple, who had obviously been put wise. Throughout dinner they had looked greedy but prudish, with a knowing expression and a simple-minded eagerness to be shocked—as though expecting Chéri to dance stark naked, or Charlotte and the under secretary to make violent love to one another in the middle of the carpet.

Chéri had made off, aware that his behavior had been stoical, with no other lapse than a sudden loss of interest in the present: an awkward thing to lose in the middle of a meal. Even so, his trance could have lasted little more than a moment, had been instantaneous, like a dream. But now he was putting a distance between himself and the strangers who thronged his house, and the sound of his footfall on the sand was as light as the soft padding of an animal. His light silver-gray coat shaded into the mist that had fallen over the Bois; and a few nocturnal loiterers must have envied a young man who was in such a hurry to go nowhere in particular.

He was haunted by the vision of his crowded house. He could still hear the sound of voices, and carried with him the memory of faces, of smiles, and especially of the shape of mouths. An elderly man had talked about the war; a woman about politics. He remembered, too, the new understanding between Desmond and Edmée, and the interest his wife had taken in some building scheme. "Desmond! . . . Just the husband for my wife!" And then, dancing . . . the strange effect of the tango on Charlotte Peloux. Chéri quickened his step.

The night was filled with the damp mist of a too early autumn and the full moon was shrouded. A great milky halo, ringed with a pallid iridescence, had replaced the planet, and was sometimes itself hidden by fitful puffs of scudding cloud. The smell of September was already in the leaves that had fallen during the dog days.

"How mild it is," Chéri thought.

He rested his weary limbs on a bench, but not for long. He was rejoined by an invisible companion, to whom he refused his seat on the bench—a woman with gray hair, wearing a long coat, who poured forth a relentless gaiety. Chéri turned his head toward the gardens of La Muette, as though he could hear, even at that distance, the cymbals of the jazz band.

The time had not yet come for him to go back to the blue room, where perhaps the two society girls were still smoking good cigars, as they sat sidesaddle on the blue velvet of the bed, keeping the real estate merchant amused with mess-hall tales.

"Oh! for a nice hotel bedroom, a jolly pink room, very ordinary and very pink . . ." But would it not lose its very ordinariness the moment the light was turned out and total darkness gave the right of entry—a ponderous, mocking entry—to a figure with vigorous gray hair, dressed in a long, nondescript coat? He smiled at the intruder, for he was past the stage of fear. "There, or in any other place, *she* will be just as faithful. But I simply can't go on living with those people."

Day by day, hour by hour, he was becoming more scornful, more exacting. Already he was severely critical of the Agony Column heroes, and young war widows who clamored for new husbands, like the parched for cold water. His uncompromising intolerance extended to the world of finance, without his realizing how grave was the change. "That company for transporting raw hides they talked about at dinner. . . . How disgusting it was! And they don't mind discussing it at the top of their voices. . . ." But nothing in the world would have induced him to protest, to reveal that he was fast becoming a man utterly out of sympathy with his surroundings. Prudently, he kept quiet about that, as about everything else. When he had taken Charlotte Peloux to task for having disposed of several tons of sugar in rather a dubious fashion, had she not reminded him—and in no uncertain terms—of the time when he had shouted, without a trace of embarrassment, "Hand over five louis, Léa, so that I can go and buy some cigarettes"?

"Ah!" he sighed, "they'll never understand anything, these women. It wasn't at all the same thing."

Thus he let his thoughts run on, as he stood, bareheaded, his hair glistening, barely distinguishable in the mist. The shadowy form of a female passed close beside him, running. The rhythm of her steps and the crunch as each foot bit into the gravel betrayed anxiety and haste. Then the shadowy woman fell into the arms of a shadowy man who came to meet her, and down they fell together, breast to breast, as though struck by the same bullet.

"Those two are trying to hide," Chéri thought. "They're deceiving someone somewhere. The whole world's busy deceiving and being deceived. But I . . ." He did not finish the sentence, but a repugnance made him jump to his feet, an action that meant, "But I am chaste." A faint ray of light, flickering uncertainly over stagnant, hitherto unfeeling regions of his inmost being, was enough to suggest that chastity and loneliness are one and the same misfortune.

As night advanced, he began to feel the cold. From his prolonged, aimless vigils, he had learned that, at night, tastes, smells, and temperatures vary according to the hour, and that midnight is warm in comparison with the hour which immediately precedes the dawn.

"The winter will soon be on us," he thought, as he lengthened his stride, "and none too soon, putting an end to this interminable summer. Next winter, I should like . . . let me see . . . next winter . . ." His attempts at anticipation collapsed almost at once; and he came to a halt, head lowered, like a horse at the prospect of a long steep climb ahead.

"Next winter, there'll still be my wife, my mother, old gammer La Berche, Thingummy, What's-his-name, and the rest of them. There'll be the same old gang. . . . And for me there'll never again be . . ."

He paused once more, to watch a procession of low clouds advancing over the Bois, clouds of an indescribable pink, set upon by a gusty wind which buried its fingers in their misty tresses, twisting and dragging them across the lawns of heaven, to carry them off to the moon. Chéri gazed with eyes well used to the translucent magic of the night, which those who sleep regard as pitch dark.

The apparition of the large, flat, half-veiled moon among the scurrying vaporous clouds, which she seemed to be pursuing and tearing asunder, did not divert him from working out an arithmetical fantasy: he was computing—in years, months, hours, and days—the amount of precious time that had been lost to him forever.

"Had I never let her go when I went to see her again that day before the war—then it would have meant three or four years to the good; hundreds and hundreds of days and nights gained and garnered for love." He did not fight shy of so big a word.

"Hundreds of days—a lifetime—life itself. Life as it was in the old days, life with my 'worst enemy,' as she used to call herself. My worst enemy! who forgave me all, and never let me off a single thing." He seized hold of his past, to squeeze out every remaining drop upon his empty, arid present; bringing back to life, and inventing where necessary, the princely days of his youth, his adolescence shaped and guided by a woman's strong capable hands—loving hands, ever ready to chastise. A prolonged, sheltered, oriental adolescence, in which the pleasures of the flesh had their passing place, like silent pauses in a song. A life of luxury, passing whims, childish cruelty, with fidelity a yet unspoken word.

He threw back his head to look up at the nacreous halo which irradiated the whole sky, and he gave a low cry, "It's all gone to hell! I'm thirty years old!"

He hurried on his way back home, heaping curses on himself to the rhythm of his quickened steps. "Fool! The tragedy is not her age, but mine. Everything may be over for her, but for me . . ."

He let himself in without making a sound, to find the house in silence at last; to be nauseated by the lingering stale smell of those who had dined, wined, and danced there. In the looking glass fitted to the door in the hall he met face to face the young man who had grown so thin, whose cheeks had hardened, whose sad, beautifully molded upper lip was unshaven and blue, whose large eyes were reticent and tragic. The young man, in effect, who had ceased, inexplicably, to be twenty-four years old.

"For me," Chéri completed his thought, "I really do believe that the last word has been said."

"WHAT I NEED is somewhere quiet, you understand. . . . Any little place would do. . . . A bachelor flat, a room, a corner. . . ."

"I wasn't born yesterday," said the Pal, reproachfully.

She raised disconsolate eyes toward the festoons on the ceiling: "A little love, of course, of course, a little kiss—something to warm a poor lonely heart. . . . You bet I understand! Any special fancy?"

Chéri frowned. "Fancy? For whom?"

"You don't understand, my pretty. . . . Fancy for any particular district?"

"Ah! . . . No, nothing special. Just a quiet corner."

The Pal nodded her large head in collusion. "I see, I see. Something after my style—like my flat. You know where I rest my bones?"

"Yes."

"No, you don't know at all. I was certain you wouldn't write it down. Two hundred and fourteen Rue de Villiers. It's not big, and it's not beautiful. But you don't want the sort of place where the whole street knows your business."

"No."

"I got mine, of course, through a little deal with my landlady. A jewel of a woman, by the way, married, or as good as. Periwinkle blue eyes, and a head like a bird; but she bears the mark of Fate on her forehead, and I already know from her cards that she can't say no to anything, and that——"

"Yes, yes. You were saying just now that you knew of a flat. . . ."

"Yes, but not good enough for you."

"You don't think so?"

"Not for you . . . not for the two of you!"

The Pal hid a suggestive smile in her whiskey, and Chéri turned from its smell—like wet harness. He put up with her quips about his imaginary conquests, for he saw, round her scraggy neck, a string of large faked pearls which he thought he recognized. Every visual reminder of his past halted him on his downward path, and, during such respites, he felt at peace.

"Ah!" sighed the Pal, "How I'd love to catch a glimpse of her! What a pair! . . . I don't know her, of course, but I can just see you two together! . . . Of course you'll provide everything yourself?"

"For whom?"

"Why, the furniture in your love-nest, of course!"

He looked at the Pal in bewilderment. Furniture . . . What furniture? He had been thinking only of one thing: a refuge of his own, with a door that opened and closed for him and no one else, safe from Edmée, Charlotte, all of them. . . .

"Will you furnish it in period or in modern style? La belle Serrano arranged her entire ground floor with nothing but Spanish shawls, but that was a bit eccentric. You're old enough, of course, to know your own mind. . . ."

He hardly heard her, far away in his dreams of a future home that would be secret, small, warm, and dark. At the same time, he was drinking red currant syrup, like any young "miss," in the red-and-gold, out-of-date, unchanging bar, just as it used to be when, a small boy, Chéri had come there to sip his first fizzy drink through a straw. . . . Even the barman himself had not changed, and if the woman sitting opposite Chéri was now a withered specimen, at least he had never known her beautiful, or young.

"They all change, the whole of that set—my mother, my

wife, all the people they see—and they live for change. My mother may change into a banker, Edmée into a town councilor. But I . . ."

In imagination, he quickly returned to that refuge, existing at some unknown point in space, but secret, small, warm, and . . .

"Mine's done up in Algerian style," the Pal persisted. "It's no longer in the fashion, but I don't mind—especially as the furniture is hired. You'll be sure to recognize many of the photos I've put up: and then there's the portrait of La Loupiote. . . . Come and have a look at it. Please do."

"I'd like to. Let's go!"

On the threshold he hailed a taxi.

"But d'you never have your motor? Why haven't you got your motor? It's really quite extraordinary how people with motors never have their motor!"

She gathered up her faded black skirts, caught the string of her lorgnette in the clasp of her bag, dropped a glove, and submitted to the stares of the passersby with the lack of embarrassment of a Negro. Chéri, standing at her side, received several insulting smiles and the admiring condolences of a young woman, who called out: "Lord, what a waste of good material!"

In the taxi, patiently and half asleep, he endured the old thing's tattle. And then some of her stories were soothing: the one about the ridiculous little dog which had held up the return from the races in 1897, and then Mère La Berche eloping with a young bride on the day of her wedding in 1893.

"That's it over there. This door's stuck, Chéri, I can't get out. I warn you, there's not much light in the passage, nor, for that matter, is there much out here. . . . It's only a ground-floor flat, when all's said and done! . . . Wait where you are a second."

He waited, standing in the semidarkness. He heard the jingle of keys, the wheezy old creature's gasps for breath and then her fussy servant's voice, "I'm lighting up. . . . Then you'll find yourself in a familiar landscape. I've got electricity, of course. . . . There, let me introduce you to my little morning room, which is also my large drawing room!"

He went in, and, from kindness—hardly bothering to glance at it—praised the room; it had a low ceiling and reddish walls, kippered by the smoke of innumerable cigars and cigarettes. Instinctively, he looked all round for the window, barricaded by shutters and curtains.

"You can't see in here? You're not an old night bird like your Pal. Wait, I'll switch on the top light."

"Don't bother. . . . I'll just come in and——" He broke off, staring at the most brightly lit wall, covered with small frames and photographs pinned through the four corners. The Pal began to laugh.

"What did I say about a familiar landscape! I was quite sure you'd enjoy looking at them. You haven't got that one, have you?"

"That one" was a very large photographic portrait-study, touched up with water colors now quite faded. Blue eyes, a laughing mouth, a chignon of fair hair, and a look of calm yet exultant triumph. . . . High-breasted—in a First Empire corselet, legs showing through gauze skirts, legs that never finished, rounded out at the thigh, slender at the knee, legs that. . . . And a fetching hat, a hat that turned up on one side only, trimmed like a single sail to the wind.

"She never gave you that one, not that one, I bet! It makes her a goddess, a fairy walking on clouds! And yet it's absolutely her, of course. This big photo is the loveliest, to my way of thinking, but I'm still every bit as fond of the others. Here, for instance, look at this little one here—much more recent, of course—isn't it a sight for sore eyes?"

A snapshot, clinging to the wall with the help of a rusty pin, showed a woman standing in the shade against a sunlit garden.

"It's the navy-blue dress and the hat with the seagulls," Chéri said to himself.

"I'm all for flattering portraits, myself," the Pal went on.

"A portrait like this one. Come now—you must confess—isn't it enough to make you join your hands and believe in God?"

A degraded and smarmy art, to lend glamor to the "portrait photograph," had lengthened the neck line and modified those around the sitter's mouth. But the nose, just sufficiently aquiline, the delicious nose with its ravishing nostrils, and the chaste little dimple, the velvety cleft that indented the upper lip under the nose—these were untouched, authentic, respected by even the photographer.

"Would you believe it? She wanted to burn the lot, pretending that nobody today is the least interested in what she used to be like. My blood boiled, I shrieked like a soul in torment, and she gave me the whole collection the very same day that she made me a present of the bag with her monogram. . . ."

"Who's this fellow with her . . . here . . . in this one underneath?"

"What were you saying? What's that? Wait till I take off my hat."

"I'm asking you who this is—this fellow—here. Get a move on, can't you?"

"Heavens, don't bustle me about so. . . . That? It's Bacciocchi, come! Naturally, you can hardly be expected to recognize him, he dates from two turns before you."

"Two what?"

"After Bacciocchi, she had Septfons—and yet no—wait . . . Septfons was earlier than that. . . . Septfons, Bacciocchi, Spéleïeff, and you. Oh! do look at those check trousers! . . . How ridiculous men's fashions used to be!"

"And that photo over there; when was that taken?"

He drew back a step, for at his elbow the Pal's head was craning forward, and its magpie's nest of felted hair smelled like a wig.

"That? That's her costume for Auteuil in . . . in 1888, or '89. Yes, the year of the Exhibition. In front of that one, dear boy, you should raise your hat. They don't turn out beauties like that anymore."

"Pooh! . . . I don't think it so stunning."

The Pal folded her hands. Hatless, she looked older, and her high forehead was a buttery yellow under hair dyed greenish black.

"Not so stunning! That waist you could encircle with your ten fingers! That lily neck! And be good enough to let your eyes rest on that dress! All in frilled sky-blue chiffon, dear boy, and looped up with little pink moss roses sewn onto the frills, and the hat to match! And the little bag to match as well—we called them alms bags at that time. Oh! the beauty she was then! There's been nothing since to compare with her first appearances: she was the dawn, the very sun of love."

"First appearances where?"

She gave Chéri a gentle dig in the ribs. "Get along with you. . . . How you make me laugh! Ah! the trials of life must melt into thin air when you're about the house!"

His rigid features passed unobserved. He was still facing the wall, seemingly riveted by several Léas—one smelling an artificial rose, another bending over a book with medieval hasps, her swan neck rising from a pleatless collar, a white and rounded neck like the bole of a birch tree.

"Well, I must be going," he said, like Valérie Cheniaguine.

"What d'you mean—you must be going? What about my dining room? And my bedroom? just glance at them, my pretty! Take a note of them for your little love nest."

"Ah! yes. . . . Listen; not today, because . . ." He glanced distrustfully toward the rampart of portraits, and lowered his voice. "I've an appointment. But I'll come back . . . tomorrow. Probably tomorrow, before dinner."

"Good. Then I can go ahead?"

"Go ahead?"

"With the flat."

"Yes, that's right. See about it. And thanks."

"I really begin to wonder what the world's coming to. . . . Young or old—it's hard to tell which are the most disgusting. . . . Two 'turns' before me! . . . and 'the first appearances,' said the old spider, 'the dazzling first appearances.' . . . And all quite openly. No, really, what a world!"

He found that he had been keeping up the pace of a professional walker in training, and that he was out of breath. And all the more because the distant storm—which would not burst over Paris—had walled off what breeze there was behind a violet bastion, now towering straight up against the sky. Alongside the fortifications of the Boulevard Berthier, under trees stripped bare by the summer drought, a sparse crowd of Parisians in rope-soled sandals and a few half-naked children in red jerseys seemed to be waiting for a tidal wave to come rolling up from Levallois-Perret. Chéri sat down on a bench, forgetting that his strength was apt to play him tricks. He was unaware that his strength was being sapped in some mysterious manner ever since he had started to fritter it away on night vigils, and had neglected to exercise or nourish his body.

" 'Two turns!' Really! Two turns before me! And after me, how many? Add the whole lot together, myself included, and how many turns d'you get?"

Beside a blue-clad, seagull-hatted Léa, he could see a tall, broad Spéleïeff, smiling expansively. He remembered a sad Léa, red-eyed with weeping, stroking his head when he was a small boy and calling him a "horrid little man in the making."

"Léa's lover" . . . "Léa's new pet" . . . Traditional and meaningless words—as common on everyone's lips as talk about the weather, the latest odds at Auteuil, or the dishonesty of servants. "Are you coming, kid?" Spéleïeff would say to Chéri. "We'll go out and have a porto at Armenonville, while we wait for Léa to join us. Nothing would drag her out of bed this morning."

"She's got a ravishing new little Bacciocchi," Madame Peloux had informed her son, aged fourteen or fifteen at the time.

But, a bundle of sophistication and innocence, brought up in the midst of love, yet blinded by its proximity, Chéri, at that tender age, had talked love, as children learn a language by ear, picking up words, pleasant or filthy, merely as sounds without meaning. No vivid or voluptuous vision arose behind the shadow of this huge Spéleïeff so recently risen from Léa's bed. And was there really very much difference between this "ravishing little Bacciocchi" and a "prize Pekingese"?

No photograph or letter, no story from the only lips that might have told him the truth, had blighted the enclosed paradise in which Léa and Chéri had dwelt for so many years. Next to nothing in Chéri existed which dated back beyond Léa: why, then, should he bother about a man who, before his day, had brought warmth or sadness or riches to his mistress?

A fair-haired little boy with fat knees came and planted his crossed arms on the bench beside Chéri. They glared at each other with identical expressions of offended reserve, for Chéri treated all children as strangers. For some time this boy let his pale blue eyes rest on Chéri, who watched some sort of indescribable smile, full of scorn, mount up from the small anemic mouth to the flax-blue pupils of the eyes. Then the child turned away, and, picking up his dirty toys from the dust, began to play at the foot of the bench, blotting Chéri out of existence. Then Chéri got up and walked away.

Half an hour later, he was lying in a warm, scented bath, clouded by some milky bath essence. He lay reveling in its luxury and comfort, in the soft lather of the soap, and in the remote faint sounds about the house, as though they were the rewards of an act of great courage, or else blessings he was tasting for the last time.

His wife came into the room humming, broke off at the sight of him, and narrowly failed to disguise her speechless astonishment at finding Chéri at home and in his bath.

"Am I in your way?" he asked, with no irony.

"Not in the least, Fred."

She began to take off her day clothes with youthful abandon, with total disregard for modesty or immodesty, and Chéri was amused by her haste to be undressed and in a bath.

"How completely I'd forgotten her," he thought, as he

looked at the odalisque back, supple but well-covered, of the woman bending down to untie her shoelaces.

She did not speak to him, but went about her business like a woman who believes she is safely by herself, and in front of his eyes rose the figure of the child who, not long since, had been playing in the dust at his feet, resolutely ignoring his presence.

"Tell me . . ."

Edmée raised a surprised forehead, a soft, half-naked body.

"What would you say to our having a child?"

"Fred! . . . What are you thinking of?"

It was almost a cry of terror, and already Edmée was clutching a wisp of lawn close to her bosom with one hand, while with the other she groped, fumbling, for the first kimono within reach. Chéri could not hold back his laughter.

"Would you like my revolver? I'm not going to assault you."

"Why are you laughing?" she asked, almost in a whisper. "You should never laugh."

"I seldom laugh. But do tell me . . . now that all is quiet and peaceful between us . . . do tell me why. Are you really so terrified at the thought that we could have had, could still have, a child?"

"Yes," she said cruelly, and her unexpected frankness shocked even herself.

She never took her eyes off her husband, lying full length in a low armchair, and she murmured distinctly enough for him to hear. "A child . . . who'd be sure to take after you. You twice over, you twice over in the single lifetime of one woman? No. . . . Oh, no."

He began a gesture which she misinterpreted.

"No, I beg of you. . . . There's nothing more to be said. I won't even discuss it. Let's leave things as they are. We've only to be a little cautious, and go on . . . I ask nothing of you . . ."

"That suits you?"

Her only answer was to put on a look, insulting in its misery and plaintive helplessness, a seraglio look that well suited her nakedness. Her freshly powdered cheeks, the touch of color on her youthful lips, the light brown halo round her hazel eyes, the care bestowed on every feature of her face, were in striking contrast to the confusion of her body, bare except for the crumpled silk shift she was clasping to her breasts.

"I can no longer make her happy," thought Chéri, "but I can still make her suffer. She is not altogether unfaithful to me. Whereas I am not untrue to her . . . I have deserted her."

Turning away from him, she began to dress. She had regained her freedom of movement and her disingenuous tolerance. The palest of pink frocks now hid from view the woman who, a moment since, had pressed her last stitch of clothing to her bosom, as though to a wound.

She had recovered, too, her buoyant determination, her desire to live and hold sway, her prodigious and feminine aptitude for happiness. Chéri despised her afresh; but a moment came when the rays of the evening sun, shining through her transparent pink dress, outlined the shape of a young woman who no longer bore any semblance to the wounded Circassian: a heaven-aspiring form, as supple and vigorous as a serpent about to strike.

"I can still hurt her, but how quickly she recovers! In this house, too, I am no longer needed, no longer expected. She has gone far beyond me, and is going further: I am, the old creature would say, her 'first turn.' It's now for me to follow her example, if only I could. But I can't. And then would I, if I could? Unlike some of us, Edmée has never come up against what one meets only once in a lifetime and is floored by completely. Spéleïeff was fond of saying that, after a really bad crash—which, however, involved no broken bones—some horses would let themselves be killed rather than take the fence again. I am just the same."

He cast about for further sporting, and rather brutal, metaphors that would make his own fall and misfortunes seem an accident. But he had started his night too early, and, dog-tired, his dreams were haunted by sweet ghosts in sky-blue flounces, and half-remembered figures from the pages of the imperishable literature which finds its way into tawdry love nests, from tales and poems dedicated to constancy and to lovers undivided in death: writings irresistible to adolescents and time-worn courtesans, who are akin in their credulity and passion for romance.

THEN she said to me: 'I know who's at the back of all this: it's Charlotte again, making mischief about me. . . .' 'It's no more than you deserve,' I told her, 'you've only to stop going to see Charlotte as much as you do, and trusting her with all your secrets.' She retorted: 'I'm a much closer friend of Charlotte's than of Spéleïeff's and I've known her far longer. I assure you Charlotte, Neuilly, bezique and the child would be a far greater loss to me than Spéleïeff—you can't change the habits of a lifetime.' 'That doesn't prevent your faith in Charlotte costing you a pretty penny,' I said. 'Oh! well,' was her answer, 'what's good is worth paying for.' That's her all over, you'll agree: big-hearted and generous but no fool. And with that she went off to dress for the races—she told me she was going to the races with a gigolo. . . ."

"With me!" Chéri exclaimed bitterly. "Am I right? It was me?"

"I don't deny it. I simply tell you things as they took place. A white dress—of white crêpe-de-chine—oriental-looking, edged with blue Chinese embroidery, the very dress you see her in here, in this snapshot, taken at the races. And nothing will get it out of my head that this man's shoulder you can see behind her is you."

"Fetch it me!" Chéri ordered.

The old woman got up, pulled out the rusty drawing pins tacking the photograph to the wall, and brought it back to

Chéri. Lolling on the Algerian divan, he raised a tousled head, and, barely running his eyes over it, flung the snapshot across the room.

"When have you seen me wearing a collar that gapes at the back, and a short coat to go to the races? Come, think again! I don't find that sort of thing at all funny."

She ventured a tut-tut of timid censure, bent her stiff knees to pick up the photograph, and went on to open the door into the passage.

"Where are you going?"

"I can hear the water for my coffee boiling. I'm going to pour it out."

"Good. But come back here again."

She disappeared in a shuffle of rustling taffeta and heelless slippers. Left to himself, Chéri settled his neck against the moquette cushion stamped with Tunisian designs. A new and startlingly bright Japanese kimono, embellished with pink wistaria on a ground of amethyst, had replaced his coat and waistcoat. The fag-end of a too-far-smoked cigarette was almost burning his lips, and his hair, falling fanwise down to the level of his eyebrows, half covered his forehead.

Wearing so feminine and flowered a garment did not make his appearance in any way ambiguous: he merely acquired an ignominious majesty that stamped every feature with its proper value. He seemed bent on death and destruction, and the photograph had flashed like a blade from his hand as he hurled it from him. Hard, delicate bones in his cheeks moved to the rhythm of his working jaws. The whites of his eyes flickered in the darkness round him like the crest of a wave, with the moonbeams interruptedly following its course.

Left alone, however, he let his head sink back against the cushion, and closed his eyes.

"Lord!" exclaimed the Pal coming back into the room, "you'll not look more handsome when laid out on your deathbed! I've brought in the coffee. Would you care for some? Such an aroma! It will waft you to the Isles of the Blessed."

"Yes. Two lumps."

His words were curt, and she obeyed with a humility that suggested, perhaps, a deep subservient pleasure.

"You didn't eat anything for dinner?"

"I had enough."

He drank his coffee, without moving, supporting himself on one elbow. An oriental curtain, draped like a canopy, hung from the ceiling directly above the divan, and in its shade lay an ivory and enamel Chéri, robed in exquisite silks, reclining upon an old worn dust-bedraggled rug.

The Pal set out, piece by piece upon a brass-topped table, the coffee set, an opium lamp capped with a glass cowl, two pipes, the pot of paste, the silver snuffbox used for cocaine, and a flask, which, tight-stoppered as it was, failed to control the cold and treacherously volatile expansion of the ether. To these she added a pack of tarot cards, a case of poker chips, and a pair of spectacles, before settling herself down with the apologetic air of a trained hospital nurse.

"I've already told you," grunted Chéri, "all that paraphernalia means nothing to me."

Once again she stretched out her sickly white hands in protestation. In her own home she adopted what she called her "Charlotte Corday style": hair flowing loose, and wide white linen fichus crossed over her dusty mourning, looking a mixture of decorum and fallen virtue—like a heroine of the Salpêtrière Prison.

"No matter, Chéri. They're just in case. And it does make me so happy to see the whole of my little armory set out in its proper order under my eyes. The arsenal of dreams! the munitions of ecstasy! the gateway to illusion!"

She nodded her long head and looked up to the ceiling, with the compassionate eyes of a grandmother who ruins herself on toys. Her guest partook of none of her potions. Some sort of physical sense of honor still survived in him, and his disdain for drugs was akin to his distaste for brothels.

For a number of days—he had kept no count of them—he had found his way to this black hole, presided over by an attendant Norn. Ungraciously, and in terms that brooked no argument, he had paid her for food, coffee, and her own liqueurs, and for his personal requirements in the way of cigarettes, fruit, ice, and soft drinks. He had commanded his slave to buy the sumptuous Japanese robe, scents, and expensive soaps. She was moved less by desire for money than by the pleasure of acting as an accomplice. She devoted herself to Chéri with enthusiasm, a revival of her old zeal as a missionary of vice who, with garrulous and culpable alacrity, would divest and bathe a virgin, cook an opium pellet, and pour out intoxicating spirits or ether. This apostolate was fruitless, for her singular guest brought back no paramour, drank soft drinks only, stretched himself on the dusty divan and delivered only one word of command: "Talk."

She did talk, following, she believed, her own fancies; but, now brutally, now subtly, he would direct the muddied meanderings of her reminiscences. She talked like a sewing woman who comes in by the day, with the continuous, stupefying monotony of creatures whose days are given over to long and sedentary tasks. But she never did any sewing, for she had the aristocratic unpracticalness of a former prostitute. While talking, she would pin a pleat over a hole or stain, and take up again the business of tarot cards and patience. She would put on gloves to grind coffee bought by the charwoman, and then handle greasy cards without turning a hair.

She talked, and Chéri listened to her soporific voice and the shuffle of her felted slippers. He reclined at ease, magnificently robed, in the ill-kempt lodging. His guardian dared ask no questions. She knew enough: he was a monomaniac, as his abstemiousness proved. The illness for which she was ministering was mysterious; but it was an illness. She took the risk of inviting, as from a sense of duty, a very pretty young woman, childish and professionally gay. Chéri paid her neither more nor less attention than he would a puppy, and said to the Pal, "Are we going to have any more of your fashionable parties?"

She did not require snubbing a second time, and he never had cause to bind her to secrecy. One day she almost hit upon the simple truth, when she proposed asking in two or three of her friends of the good old days; Léa, for instance. He never batted an eyelid.

"Not a soul. Or I'll have to hunt out some better hole."

A fortnight went by, as funereal in its routine as life in a monastery; but it did not pall on either recluse. During the daytime, the Pal set forth on her old woman's junketings; poker parties, nips of whiskey, and poisonous gossip, hole-and-corner gambling dens, lunches of "regional dishes" in the stuffy darkness of a Norman or Limousin restaurant. Chéri would arrive with the first shadow of evening, sometimes drenched to the skin. She would recognize the slam of his taxi door and no longer asked: "But why do you never come in your motor?"

He would leave after midnight, and usually before daybreak. During his prolonged sessions on the Algerian divan, the Pal sometimes saw him drop off to sleep and remain for an instant or two with his neck twisted against his shoulder, as though caught in a snare. She never slept herself till after his departure, having forgotten the need for repose. Only once, in the small hours of the morning, while he was putting back, meticulously and one by one, the contents of his pockets—key on its chain, billfold, little flat revolver, handkerchief, cigarette case of green gold—did she dare to ask: "Doesn't your wife begin to wonder, when you come in so late?"

Chéri raised long eyebrows above eyes grown larger from lack of sleep: "No. Why? She knows perfectly well I've been up to no harm."

"No child, of course, is easier to manage than you are. . . . Shall you be coming again this evening?"

"I don't know. I'll see. Carry on as if I were coming for certain."

Once more he gazed long at all the lily necks, all the blue eyes, that flowered on one wall of his sanctuary, before he went his way, only to return again, faithfully, some twelve hours later.

By roundabout ways he considered cunning, he would lead the Pal to talk of Léa, then he would clear the narrative of all bawdy asides that might retard it. "Skip it. Skip it!" Barely bothering to enunciate the words, he relied on the initial sibilants to speed up or curtail the monologue. He would listen only to stories without malice in them, and glorifications of a purely descriptive nature. He insisted upon strict respect for documentary truth and checked his chronicler peevishly. He stocked his mind with dates, colors, materials, and places, and the names of dressmakers.

"What's poplin?" he fired at her point-blank.

"Poplin's a mixture of silk and wool, a dry material . . . if you know what I mean; one that doesn't stick to the skin."

"Yes. And mohair? You said 'of white mohair.' "

"Mohair is a kind of alpaca, but it hangs better, of course. Léa was afraid to wear lawn in the summer: she maintained that it was best for underwear and handkerchiefs. Her own lingerie was fit for a queen, you'll remember, and in the days when that photograph was taken—yes, that beauty over there with the long legs—they didn't wear the plain underclothes of today. It was frill upon frill, a foam, a flurry of snow; and the drawers, dear boy! they'd have sent your head whirling. . . . White Chantilly lace at the sides and black Chantilly in between. Can't you just see the effect? But *can* you imagine it?"

"Revolting," thought Chéri, "revolting. Black Chantilly in between. A woman doesn't wear black Chantilly in between simply to please herself. In front of whose eyes did she wear them? For whom?"

He could see Léa's gesture as he entered her bathroom or boudoir—the furtive gesture as she drew her wrap across her body. He could see the chaste self-confidence of her rosy body as she lay naked in the bath, with the water turned to milk by some essence or other. . . . "But, for others, she wore drawers of Chantilly lace. . . ."

He kicked one of the hay-stuffed moquette cushions to the floor.

"Are you too warm, Chéri?"

"No. Let me have another look at that photo . . . the large framed one. Tilt the what's-its-name of your lamp up a bit . . . a bit more . . . that's it!"

Abandoning his usual circumspection, he applied a searching eye to the study of every detail that was new to him, and almost refreshing. "A high-waisted belt with cameos! . . . Never saw that about the place. And boots like buskins! Was she wearing tights? No, of course not, her toes are bare. Revolting. . . ."

"At whose house did she wear that costume?"

"I don't rightly remember. . . . A reception at the club, I believe . . . or at Molier's."

He handed back the frame at arm's length, to all appearances disdainful and bored. He left shortly afterward, under an overcast sky, toward the close of a night that smelled of wood smoke and dankness.

He was deteriorating physically and took no account of it. He was losing weight through eating and sleeping too little, walking and smoking too much, thus bartering his obvious vigor for a lightness, an apparent return to youth, which the light of day repudiated. At home, he lived as he pleased, welcoming or running away from guests and callers. All that they knew of him was his name, his almost petrified good looks fined down little by little under an accusing chisel, and the inconceivable ease with which he would ignore them.

So he eked out his peaceful and carefully regimented despair until the last days of October. Then, one afternoon, he was seized by a fit of hilarity, because he caught a glimpse of his wife's unsuspected terror. His whole face lit up with the merriment of a man impervious to all feeling. "She thinks I'm mad. What luck!"

His merriment was short-lived: for, on thinking it over, he came to the conclusion that, where the brute and the madman are concerned, the brute wins every time. She was frightened of the madman; otherwise would she not have stood her ground, biting her lips and forcing back her tears, in order to worst the brute?

"I am no longer even considered wicked," he thought bitterly. "And that's because I am no longer wicked. Oh! the harm the woman I left has done to me! Yet others left her, and she left others. . . . How, I wonder, does Bacciocchi exist at the present time? or Septfons, Spéleïeff, and all the rest of them? But what have we got in common, I and the rest of them? She called me 'little bourgeois' because I counted the bottles in the cellar. 'Little bourgeois,' 'faithful heart,' 'great lover'—those were her names for me—those were my real names: and, though she watched my departure with tears glistening in her eyes, she is still herself, Léa, who prefers old age to me, who sits in the corner by the fire counting over on her fingers: 'I've had What's-his-name, and Thingummybob, and Chéri, and So-and-so . . .' I thought she belonged to me alone, and never perceived that I was only one among her lovers. Is there anyone left, now, that I am not ashamed of?"

Hardened by now to the exercise of impassivity, he sought to endure the capricious hauntings of such thoughts with resignation, and to be worthy of the devil by which he was possessed. Proud and dry-eyed, with a lighted match held between steady fingers, he looked sideways at his mother, well aware of her watchful eye. Once his cigarette was alight, with a little encouragement he would have strutted like a peacock in front of an invisible public, and taunted his tormentors with a "Good, isn't it?" In a confused way, the strength born of his dissimulation and resistance was gathering in his inmost self. He was beginning now to enjoy his extreme state of detachment, and dimly perceived that an emotional storm could be just as valuable and refreshing as a lull, and that in it he might discover the wisdom which never came to him in calmer moods. As a child, Chéri frequently had taken advantage of a genuine fit of temper, by changing it into a peevishness that would bring him what he wanted. Today he was fast approaching the point at which, having attained to a definite state of unhappiness, he could rely on it to settle everything.

One gusty, windswept, September afternoon, with leaves sailing straight across the sky—an afternoon of blue rifts in the clouds and scattered raindrops—Chéri felt an urge to visit his dark retreat and its attendant, garbed in black, with a touch of white on the chest like a scavenging cat. He was feeling buoyant, and avid for confidences, though these would be sickly, like the fruit of the arbutus and as prickly leaved. Words and phrases of special though ill-defined significance kept running in his head: "Her monogram embroidered in hair on all her lingerie, dear boy, in golden hairs from her own head . . . fairy handicraft! And, did I tell you, her masseuse used to pluck the hairs from the calves of her leg, one by one. . . ."

He turned round and left the window. He found Charlotte on a chair looking thoughtfully up at him; and in the restless waters of her great eyes he saw the formation of a prodigious, rounded, crystalline, glistening sphere which detached itself from the bronzed pupil, and then vanished, evaporating in the heat of her flushed cheek. Chéri felt flattered and cheered. "How kind of her! She's weeping for me."

An hour later, he found his ancient accomplice at her post. But she was wearing some sort of parson's hat, bunched up with shiny black ribbon, and she held out to him a sheet of blue paper, which he waved aside.

"What's that? . . . I haven't the time. Tell me what's written on it."

The Pal lifted puzzled eyes to his: "It's my mother."

"Your mother? You're joking."

She did her best to appear offended. "I'm not joking at all. Please respect the departed! She is dead." And she added, by way of an excuse, "She was eighty-three!"

"Congratulations. Are you going out?"

"No; I'm going away."

"Where to?"

"To Tarascon, and from there I take a little branch-line train that puts me down at . . ."

"For how long?"

"Four or five days . . . at least. There's the solicitor to be seen about the will, because my younger sister . . ."

He burst out, hands to heaven: "A sister now! Why not four children into the bargain?" He was conscious of the unexpectedly high-pitched tone of his voice and controlled it. "Good, very well. What d'you expect me to do about it? Be off, be off. . . ."

"I was going to leave word for you. I'm catching the 7:30."

"Catch the 7:30."

"The time of the funeral service is not mentioned in the telegram: my sister speaks only of the laying out, the climate down there is very hot, they'll have to get through it very quickly, only the business side can keep me there, and over that one has no control."

"Of course, of course."

He was walking to and fro, from the door to the wall with the photographs and back to the door again, and in doing so he knocked against a squashed old traveling bag. The coffee-pot and cups were steaming on the table.

"I made you your coffee, come what might. . . ."

"Thanks."

They drank standing up, as at a station, and the chill of departure gripped Chéri by the throat and made his teeth chatter secretly.

"Good-bye, then, dear boy," said the Pal. "You may be sure that I'll hurry things as much as I can."

"Good-bye—pleasant journey."

They shook hands, and she did not dare to kiss him. "Won't you stay here for a little while?"

He looked all round in great agitation. "No. No."

"Take the key, then?"

"Why should I?"

"You're at home here. You've fallen into the habit of it. I've told Maria to come every day at five and light a good fire and get the coffee ready. . . . So take my key, won't you? . . ."

With a limp hand he took the key, and it struck him as enormous. Once outside, he longed to throw it away or take it back to the concierge.

The old woman took courage on her way between her own door and the street, loading him with instructions as she might a child of twelve.

"The electric-light switch is on your left as you go in. The kettle is always on the gas stove in the kitchen, and all you have to do is to put a match to it. And your Japanese robe—Maria has her instructions to leave it folded at the head of the divan and the cigarettes in their usual place."

Chéri nodded affirmation once or twice, with the look of courageous unconcern of a schoolboy on the last morning of the holidays. And, when he was alone, it did not occur to him to make fun of his old retainer with the dyed hair, who had placed the proper value both on the last prerogatives of the dead and on the little pleasures of one whom all had now deserted.

The following morning, he awoke from an indecipherable dream, in which a crush of people were all running in the same direction. Though he saw only their backs, each was known to him. As they hurried by, he identified his mother, Léa—unaccountably naked, and out of breath—Desmond, the Pal, and young Maudru . . . Edmée was the only one to turn and smile at him, with the grating little smile of a marten. "But it's the marten Ragut caught in the Vosges!" Chéri cried out in his dream, and this discovery pleased him immeasurably. Then he checked and recounted all the one-way runners, saying over to himself: "There's one missing. . . . There's one missing. . . ." Once out of his dream, on this side of awakening, it came to him that the one missing was none other than himself: "I must get back into it. . . ." But the efforts of exerting every limb, like an insect caught on flypaper, served only to widen the bar of blue between his eyelids, and he emerged into that real world in which he was frittering away his time and his strength. He stretched out his legs, and bathed them in a fresh, cool part of the sheets. "Edmée must have got up some time ago."

He was surprised to see beneath the window a new garden of marguerites and heliotrope, for in his memory there was only a summer garden of blue and pink. He rang, and the sound of the bell brought to life a maid whose face was unfamiliar.

"Where is Henriette?"

"I've taken her place, sir."

"Since when?"

"Why—for the last month, sir."

He ejaculated an "Ah!" as much as to say, "That explains everything."

"Where's your mistress?"

"Madame is just coming, sir. Madame is ready to go out."

Edmée, indeed, did appear, as large as life, but stopped just inside the door in so marked a manner that Chéri was secretly amused. He allowed himself the pleasure of upsetting his wife a little by exclaiming, "But it's Ragut's marten!" and watching her pretty eyes waver under his gaze.

"Fred, I . . ."

"Yes, you're going out. I never heard you get up."

She colored slightly. "There's nothing extraordinary in that. I've been sleeping so badly these last few nights, that I've had a bed made up on the divan in the boudoir. You're not doing anything special today, are you?"

"But I am," he replied darkly.

"Is it important?"

"Very important." He took his time, and finished on a lighter note: "I'm going to have my hair cut."

"But will you be back for luncheon?"

"No; I'll have a cutlet in Paris. I've made an appointment at Gustave's for a quarter past two. The man who usually comes to cut my hair is ill."

He was childishly courteous, the lie flowering effortlessly

on his lips. Because he was lying, his mouth took on its boyhood mold—poutingly provocative and rounded for a kiss. Edmée looked at him with an almost masculine satisfaction.

"You're looking well this morning, Fred. . . . I must fly."

"Are you catching the 7:30?"

She stared at him, struck dumb, and fled so precipitately that he was still laughing when the front door slammed behind her.

"Ah! that does me good," he sighed. "How easy it is to laugh when you no longer expect anything from anyone. . . ." Thus, while he was dressing, did he discover for himself the nature of asceticism, and the tuneless little song he hummed through pursed lips kept him company like a silly young nun.

He went down to a Paris he had forgotten. The crowd upset his dubious emotional balance, now so dependent on a crystalline vacuity and the daily routine of suffering.

In the Rue Royale he came face to face with his own full-length reflection at the moment when the brightness of noon broke through the rain clouds. Chéri wasted no thoughts on this crude new self-portrait, which stood out sharply against a background of news vendors and shopgirls, flanked by jade necklaces and silver fox furs. The fluid feeling in his stomach, which he compared to a speck of lead bobbing about inside a celluloid ball, must come, he thought, from lack of sustenance, and he took refuge in a restaurant.

With his back to a glass partition, screened from the light of day, he lunched off selected oysters, fish, and fruit. Some young women sitting not far away had no eyes for him, and this gave him a pleasant feeling, like that of a chilly bunch of violets laid on closed eyelids. But the smell of his coffee suddenly brought home the need to rise and keep the appointment of which this smell was an urgent reminder. Before obeying the summons, he went to his hairdresser's, held out his hands to be manicured, and slipped off into a few moments' inestimable repose, while expert fingers substituted their will for his.

The enormous key obstructed his pocket. "I won't go, I

won't go! . . ." To the cadence of some such insistent, meaningless refrain, he found his way without mishap to the Avenue de Villiers. His clumsy fumbling round the lock and the rasp of the key made his heart beat momentarily faster, but the cheerful warmth in the passage calmed his nerves.

He went forward cautiously, lord of this empire of a few square feet, which he now owned but did not know. The useless daily arrangement of the armory had been laid out on the table by the well-trained charwoman, and an earthenware coffeepot stood in the midst of charcoal embers already dying under the velvet of warm ashes. Methodically, Chéri emptied his pockets and set out one by one his cigarette case, the huge key, his own small key, the flat revolver, his billfold, handkerchief, and watch; but when he had put on his Japanese robe, he did not lie down on the divan. With the silent curiosity of a cat he opened doors and peered into cupboards. His peculiar prudishness shrank back before a primitive but distinctively feminine lavatory. The bedroom, all bed and little else, also was decorated in the mournful shade of red that seems to settle in on those of declining years; it smelled of old bachelors and eau de cologne. Chéri returned to the drawing room. He switched on the two wall lamps and the beribboned chandelier. He listened to faint, far away sounds and, now that he was alone for the first time in this poor lodging, began trying out on himself the influence of its previous inmates—birds of passage or else dead. He thought he heard and recognized a familiar footstep, a slipshod, shambling old animal pad-pad, then shook his head: "It can't be hers. She won't be back for a week, and when she does come back, what will there be left for me in this world? I'll have . . ."

Inwardly he listened to the Pal's voice, the worn-out voice of a tramp. "But wait till I finish the story of the famous slanging match between Léa and old Mortier at the races. Old Mortier thought that with the aid of a little publicity in *Gil Blas* he would get all he wanted out of Léa. Oh! la la, my pretties, what a donkey he made of himself! She drove out to Longchamp—a dream of blue—as statuesque as a goddess, in her victoria drawn by a pair of piebalds. . . ."

He raised his hand toward the wall in front of him, where so many blue eyes were smiling, where so many swan necks were preening themselves above imperturbable bosoms. ". . . I'll have all this. All this, and nothing more. It's true, perhaps, that this is a good deal. I've found her again, by a happy chance, found her here on this wall. But I've found her, only to lose her again forever. I am still held up, like her, by these few rusty nails, by these pins stuck in slantwise. How much longer can this go on? Not very long. And then, knowing myself as I do, I'm afraid I shall demand more than this. I may suddenly cry out: 'I want her! I must have her! Now! at this very moment!' Then what will become of me?"

He pushed the divan closer to the illustrated wall and there lay down. And as he lay there, all the Léas, with their downward-gazing eyes, seemed to be showing concern for him: "But they only *seem* to be looking down at me, I know perfectly well. When you sent me away, my Nounoune, what did you think there was left for me after you? Your noble action cost you little—you knew the worth of a Chéri—your risk was negligible. But we've been well punished, you and I: you, because you were born so long before me, and I, because I loved you above all other women. You're finished now, you have found your consolation—and what a disgrace that is!—whereas I . . . As long as people say, 'There was the War,' I can say 'There was Léa.' Léa, the War . . . I never imagined I'd dream of either of them again, yet the two together have driven me outside the times I live in. Henceforth, there is nowhere in the world where I can occupy more than half a place. . . ."

He pulled the table nearer to consult his watch. "Half-past five. The old creature won't be back here for another week. And this is the first day. Supposing she were to die on the way?"

He fidgeted on his divan, smoked, poured himself out a cup of lukewarm coffee. "A week. All the same, I mustn't ask too much of myself. In a week's time . . . which story will she be telling me? I know them off by heart—the one about the Four-in-Hand Meet, the one about the slanging match at

Longchamp, the one about the final rupture—and when I've heard every one, every twist and turn of them, what will there be left? Nothing, absolutely nothing. In a week's time, this old woman—and I'm already so impatient for her, she might be going to give me an injection—this old woman will be here, and . . . and she'll bring me nothing at all."

He lifted beseeching eyes to his favorite photograph. Already this speaking likeness filled him with less resentment, less ecstasy, less heartbreak. He turned from side to side on the hard mattress, unable to prevent his muscles from contracting, like a man who aches to jump from a height, but lacks the courage.

He worked himself up till he groaned aloud, repeating over and over again "Nounoune," to make himself believe he was frantic. But he fell silent, ashamed, for he knew very well that he did not need to be frantic to pick up the little flat revolver from the table. Without rising, he experimented in finding a convenient position. Finally he lay down with his right arm doubled up under him. Holding the weapon in his right hand, he pressed his ear against the muzzle, which was buried in the cushions. At once his arm began to grow numb, and he realized that if he did not make haste his tingling fingers would refuse to obey him. So he made haste, whimpering muffled complaints as he completed his task, because his forearm was hurting, crushed under the weight of his body. He knew nothing more, beyond the pressure of his forefinger on a little lever of tempered steel.